A GIRL LIKE YOU

To Vi, with
best wishes.

Paul Hearn

A GIRL LIKE YOU

Paul Heslop

FROSWICK

British Library Cataloguing-in-publication data
A catalogue record for this book is available from the British Library

Copyright © 2014 by Paul Heslop

Published by Froswick Press, Keswick, CA12 5TR.

ISBN 978-0-9538066-3-8

Printed and bound in the UK by TJ International, Padstow, PL28 8RW.

By the same Author

all non-fiction

This book is dedicated my grandchildren…

Conner, Laura, Shawny, Alexandra, Kevin, Jessica, Matty, Owen, Annie-Mai and Liz…

and any others that may happen along…

About the Author

Paul Heslop was born in Northumberland and served a full 30-year career in two police forces (Northumbria and Hertfordshire), retiring in 1995.

Since then he has become an established writer on such diverse topics as crime, country walking and health and safety in the workplace, writing (to date) ten non-fiction books as well as diverse articles for newspapers and magazines.

Now an established 'speaker', Paul lives in the Lake District with his wife, Kate.

She's on the bus.

He'd spotted her at her usual stop in the queue. A quick glance back and there was the unmistakeable red hair. He was sitting next to the aisle. If only she could stand near him. If only…

'Move along, please.' The conductor was doing his best. Slowly, standing passengers inched forward to make room for the newcomers. They took their places, squashed together like sardines packed in a tin. The bell dinged. The bus jolted and pulled into mainstream traffic. Passengers' hands grasped poles and dangling straps and rails on seat-backs. The conductor's voice called out pleadingly, 'Move along, *please.*'

Suddenly, she was standing barely two feet away, staring at the same boring buildings she passed twice a day on her way to and from work. His eyes fell upon her hand, now grasping the upright pole fixed to the back of the seat in front. Her hand! He wanted to touch it, so that she might invite him to speak. But he couldn't. He just couldn't.

It was usually a Friday. He'd see her on the bus. She always got on at the same stop and sat downstairs. Or, like now, stood downstairs. He fancied she was seventeen, his age. He thought about her all the time, fantasised about her. He'd even given her a name: Connie, after Connie Francis. He thought her hit record, *Stupid Cupid*, was appropriate.

The packed bus rattled along, its occupants resigned to the same space, the same air, the same body-sweat as their neighbours. Now and again he ventured a furtive glance upward at Connie's face. He loved her face. It was a young, sensual face, a face with a lovely mouth. He had never seen her smile but he imagined she would have perfect teeth. And she was always smart in her red coat and multi-coloured scarf that seemed to creep up to her nose. The red coat went with her hair, he always thought.

'Tickets please.' The conductor squeezed forward and Mark paid his fare. So did Connie, as for the first time he heard her speak. 'The Balloon, please,' she said, handing the conductor some change. She had an unexpected husky voice, a sexy voice. She always got off at the

Balloon. There was a bus stop there. *Her* bus stop.

When the conductor squeezed past behind her she stepped forward, her left thigh now pressing against his shoulder. Looking nonchalantly out through the window, he felt his pulse racing. Then she retreated slightly, but remained so close he sensed her coat brushing against his arm. When the conductor made his way to the back of the bus it all happened again, only this time her thigh continued to press against him. Finally she moved away again, but stayed close. So close yet so far, he thought.

He thought he might offer her his seat. That way there would be eye contact and a 'thank you', followed by recognition next time she saw him. But wouldn't she think it strange, a young bloke giving up his seat for a young lass? He was still deliberating when the person next to him, occupying the window seat, stood up to get off. Mark squeezed into the aisle, then hastened to the window seat as soon as it was vacated. Connie would sit next to him, surely. But then fate took a cruel hand as someone else stood up and blocked her way. She sat in their seat instead, right in front, affording him a view of the back of her head, her long red hair now draped down the back of her seat.

Approaching the Balloon, she stood up, pulled the strap of her handbag onto her shoulder and turned to leave the bus by the now-empty gangway. For a fleeting moment their eyes met and she smiled, briefly, before disappearing from sight. It was a smile of recognition, of acceptance that she knew him and maybe liked him. For a moment he considered getting off the bus with her. But he hesitated. Her smile might become a scowl if he appeared with her on the pavement. He mustn't jump the gun. He would see her again and next time he would be the one to smile. He could hardly wait.

1

The first thought that went through Mark Green's mind on Saturday morning was that he would save the dream. This was not unusual. He always awoke on the morning of his lie-in resolving to save a dream that had just slipped away into vague uncertainty. Each dream was always much the same as the last: of sex with a girl he knew or imagined, he could never remember. And, as always, he couldn't remember what the dream was exactly, except that it was good. Damn good.

As he opened his eyes he heard Mam's voice below his bedroom window. She was in the backyard, talking to Ada next door. About the weather. It was always the weather. Cold wind, Ada. Aye, Nancy. Looks like a drop of rain. Oh aye. She'd be leaning over the gate now, he imagined, looking up and down the Terrace, eager to pass her predictions on the weather to anyone who happened to be passing. Then he heard her returning to the house and the sound of the back door closing.

Raising his head, he looked at his brother's bed at the far end of the long bedroom, beyond the window through which sunlight now streamed, dappled with floating dust. Bob's blankets were turned back, the pillows strewn haphazard. Just as he expected. Bob would be scoffing his breakfast by now. He lay back and turned his attention to the ceiling, and thought about the dream. There was never a face. Just a blurred image. Everything else was clear, though. She was slim, she was shapely, she wore a short nightie and sweet perfume. Was she fact or fiction? Maybe it was Connie, which wouldn't have surprised him.

A lone cobweb clung to the ceiling in the corner above Mark's head. It was quite big, and had been there for weeks. Never once had he seen any victims trapped in it. Sometimes he fancied he could make out a face in the gossamer-like threads. He was still staring at it when Bob opened the bedroom door and stuck his head in.

'If you want some breakfast you'd better be getting' up. Mam's goin' out shortly.'

'Where to?' Mark asked, as though it was the strangest thing ever.

'They're going into town. So… gerrup!'

'They' were Mam and Dad. Dad getting the bus to Newcastle. It must be important.

Reading Mark's face, Bob shrugged. 'It's nothin'. Just a new cage for Billy or something. Anyway, I'm starting on the new bathroom in a minute.'

Bob backed away and closed the door.

Mark lay back, his gaze returning to the cobweb. He thought about Connie and wondered what she did at weekends. Probably had a boyfriend, he mused. Not that that would stop him. If only knew how to contact her. As it was he'd have to wait until next week for a chance sighting on the bus. She'd smiled yesterday, so she knew he existed. Might even be lying in her own bed thinking about him, who could say? Meanwhile there was Kev at the Spanish City tomorrow evening. Burn-up on the bike, lots of lasses wandering around. Great music. Last minute visit to the chippie when they got back.

A muted knocking started. Mam tapping the kitchen ceiling below with the end of the broom handle.

'Comin', Ma.'

As he swung his legs from his bed he realised he was wet about the groin. Again. Fred at work said it was time he did something about it. He often did, but maybe not quite in the way Fred meant.

Downstairs, after breakfast, he sat in silence, his brain cells busily taking in the contents of the novel he was reading, sneaked out of the sideboard drawer where Dad had hidden it. *Lady Chatterley*, after a dull start, was turning out to be quite a surprise.

The sound of *Saturday Club* filtered from the radiogram. Mark didn't much care for the programme. He preferred *Pick of the Pops*; but that was for tonight. Right now Billy the budgie was arguing with his image in his grubby little mirror, and fluttering back and forth in the restricted environs of his cage. Oh well, a new one soon, and bigger presumably. The mantel clock ticked steadily, revitalised by its Saturday morning wind-up by Dad. And, this morning, banging and clattering filtered through the connecting door between the living room, where Mark sat, and the kitchen, from what had been the pantry but was going to be the new bathroom. None of these noises distracted Mark in the slightest as he eagerly read about Lady C and her amorous gamekeeper.

Then came the curse. It was loud, it was graphic, and it was followed by its author who entered the living room in obvious pain. Mark looked up to see blood seeping through Bob's fingers as he cradled his injured thumb in the palm of his right hand. Bob rifled through the sideboard drawers. 'Where's them sticking plasters?' he was asking himself. 'Gimme a hand, Mark,' he pleaded, sitting down at the dining table, holding his thumb. 'I'm bleeding to death, man.'

Mark went to the drawer and pulled out the contents: Mam's pills, Phensics, Dad's drops for his ears, packets of this and that which had been there for years, all Mark's life in some cases. The last packet was the sticking plasters. He opened it, selected one and wrapped it around Bob's injured thumb.

'I knew that hammer couldn't be trusted,' said Mark, as his brother sat nursing his thumb.

'It's all very well you taking the piss,' said Bob,' but I don't see you getting off your arse to help out. Someone had to get to grips.'

'I'm an electrician, not a plumber,' Mark replied, without taking his eyes from his book. 'I did say I would give you a hand if you wanted. Anyway, it was you who suggested installing a bath. "No need to get a plumber in Dad. I can do it Dad".'

Bob wiggled his thumb, checked the plaster was secure. 'I'm sick of having to take a bath in front of the fire. Mrs Stephens almost walked in on me last week.'

'She used to watch me in the bath when I was a kid,' said Mark. 'Mam said she was used to seeing lads' todgers.'

'Aye, well I don't want her seeing mine. I'm twenty-five, for God's sake. Christ, this thumb doesn't half throb.'

Mark turned a page. 'It's not all that throbs round here.'

'Meanin'?'

'Saturday nights. When Mam and Dad at the club. You and Joyce. Me and Kev saw you the other week through a crack in the curtains.'

'Bloody peeping toms,' Bob retorted, leaning over his brother's shoulder to see the book. Mark flipped it over, showed him the cover.

'Lady Chatterley! It's time you were doing it, not reading about it.'

'Who with round here?'

Bob shrugged. 'What about her down the street? Wotsername.'

'Joan Hepple? She's barely sixteen, if that. Anyway, she looks like Tommo's horse. Pullin' his ragman's cart would suit her if you ask me.'

Bob shook his head and ran a finger along the bars of Billy's cage. Billy flapped in panic. 'How old are you when you're at home, anyway?' he asked. 'Seventeen at the last count. Anyway, if they're big enough they're old enough. Isn't that right Billy?'

Billy cocked his head, pinged the mirror. 'He's lovely for his mother y'know,' he chirped.

'He's lovely for his mother!' echoed Bob. 'That's what Mam tells you. Why don't you say something else for a change?' Billy cocked his head. 'Up yer bum, Mum. Say that, Billy.'

Billy head-butted his mirror and jumped to another perch. 'He's lovely for his mother y'know,' he repeated. 'Up yer bum, Mum,' said Bob. Billy fell silent.

Bob went to the window. 'You want a woman that can cook, a woman that can sew and a woman that can keep her trap shut'

'That's three women,' said Mark.

'Smart arse.'

'Is that why you go out with Joyce? Because she keeps her trap shut?'

'She meets the criteria,' said Bob philosophically.

'This gamekeeper bloke didn't care if Lady Chatterley could cook.'

'That book's just about sex. It's not about love. It's not about caring for somebody.'

'Have you read it like?'

'Course I have. Look, like I said, one man, one woman. You'll find a mate, don't worry.'

'A mate? Like Tarzan and Jane? I don't want one mate. I want lots of girls. As many as I can. Anyway, like *I* said, who with round here?'

'It needn't be round here,' said Bob. 'The world doesn't end at the bottom of our street. You should venture out into the world.'

Mark looked up. 'You mean Partners Dance Studio? Victor Sylvester and all that.'

'It isn't just Victor Sylvester. They play the Top Twenty an' all. Anyway, dancing's a means to an end. Christ, will you put that bloody book down when I'm talking to you.'

'It's the bit about John Thomas.'

'Who's he when he's at home?'

'I thought you said you'd read it.'

Bob turned away and watched Billy again, as Mark resumed interest in Lady Chatterley. 'Is that how you met Joyce, then? By asking her to dance?'

'Sort of.'

'What – "May I have the pleasure?" or something?'

'No, you don't say that. You just say, "Would you like to dance?".' They usually stand up and walk out onto the floor. Takes guts sometimes. Some say no on purpose, just to show you up.'

Mark shrugged. 'Nobody to go with.'

'What about Julian?'

'If his mam'll let him out.'

'Kev?'

Mark laughed. 'They'll have to let him wear his crash helmet.'

Suddenly Dad walked into the room, carrying a gleaming new budgerigar cage. He was closely followed by Mam, whose eyes fell directly on Lady Chatterley.

'Eeh, Charlie, I told you that book should never have come into this house.' She snatched the book from Mark's hand and thrust it behind her back. She looked at her husband, waiting for him to deal firmly with their younger son. Charlie stood as though trapped in time, looking at Mark, then Nancy, then at Mark again. Bob slipped discreetly from the room. Still Charlie hesitated, before finally spluttering into life. 'Do 'im good,' he declared, plonking the cage onto the living room table. 'I'll put the kettle on, eh.'

Nancy sighed and slipped the book into the sideboard drawer. 'We've bought you a new cage, Billy,' she declared, picking it up for Billy to see. 'Y'can spread your wings a bit more in this one.' She clicked her tongue. 'He's lovely for his mother, y'know,' she said, as Billy chirped and pinged his mirror. 'Mark, do something useful and put Billy into his new cage.'

Mark stood up and opened the door of Billy's cage, just as Bob re-entered the living room and Charlie simultaneously opened the back door on his way to the lav. Billy, seeing the way clear, flew from his cage and through the two open doorways to freedom. Nancy shrieked and ran after him, closely followed by Mark and Bob, almost knocking Charlie over in pursuit. They all ran to the back gate and watched as Billy flew upward and landed on the roof of the house opposite. 'Billy! *Billee!*' screamed Nancy.

'Up yer bum, Mum,' chirped Billy. But he was too far away for them to hear.

Pulling on his black leather jacket, Kevin Marsh stepped outside the back door of the house and carefully removed the tarpaulin from his newly-polished Norton 350. Taking great care in the narrow confines of the alleyway, he eased the motorcycle from its stand and pushed it towards the front gate where the morning sunshine now reflected off its white faring. His pride and joy. His baby. His mean machine. He hoisted it on to its stand and took a rag from his pocket. The silver wheel rims were gleaming, but merited the once-over anyway.

First, though, he glanced up and down the street. Theirs was a council semi, one of dozens, all with small front gardens of lawns in varying condition: some closely-cropped and smart, others, like the

Marsh's, ragged and infested with dandelions and nondescript weeds. Some had hedges, like theirs, needing a haircut but serving as a boundary between the garden and the public footpath beyond.

Next door's moggy appeared, sniffed at the front tyre of the motorcycle and moved on to more interesting things. Away somewhere a dog yapped remorselessly. Kev often thought of shooting it with his air rifle, if only because he didn't like its owner. Sometimes he even thought about shooting the owner, a surly-faced individual who spoke to no-one. After a few minutes came the sound of his mam's voice, calling loudly in a way that suggested she knew he was outside. 'There's a cuppa here if you want it.' 'Right, Mam,' he called back. He kept polishing the wheels. She'd bring it out in the end.

Crouching, he rubbed Autosol paste onto the silver wheel-rims, taking care not to miss the places round the spokes. Scarcely had he began when a shadow fell over him. He knew who it was before he looked up.

'Wotcha, Kidda.' He stood up to see Mark, looking downcast, hands in pockets, lean and casual in his corduroy jerkin.

'What's put your face out of joint, then?'

'Nothin'.'

Kev wiped his hands on the rag. 'Time of the month, or what?'

Kev's mam appeared, carrying the tea. She plonked it on to the garden path next to the motorbike.

'How's you ma, Marky?'

'Champion, thanks.'

She nodded and retreated to the house. Kev waited until she was indoors before he spoke again. 'Still getting hard over what's 'er name then? Carrie.'

'Connie.' said Mark. 'Saw her on the bus yesterday.'

'And?'

Mark shrugged. Kev shook his head, in a 'when are you going to do something about it?' gesture. 'So, what's up with your face?'

'Billy's escaped.'

Kev lit a cigarette. Flicked the match over the hedge.

'What happened? Did he tunnel his way out?'

'It's not funny,' said Mark. He explained events. And it was all his fault.

Kev shrugged. 'Pigeons'll get him.' He sipped his tea. 'You're okay for tonight though, Kidda? The Stoll. Right?' *Brigeet Bardo. Haw-haw-haw.*' He grinned, cupping imaginary breasts, then frowned on sight of his friend's face. 'Aw, c'mon. Show some enthusiasm. Or have you got any better ideas?'

'I was wonderin'. D'you fancy going to a dance?'

'Only if you wear a dress.' He saw Mark was serious. 'What you on about? Not that place Bob goes to.'

'That's where he met Joyce.'

'It's for puffs and softys, Kidda. "Take your partners for the cha-cha".'

Without further ado Kev pushed the bike off its stand and manoeuvred it through the gate. It was Saturday. It was bike time. 'Let's go to the Stoll,' he said dismissively, kick starting engine. 'Then there's the Spanish City tomorrow.' He revved the engine. 'See you at six. Don't forget to wear a tie for the Stoll, mind.' With that he roared off, like a cowboy on a horse at a rodeo. His dad appeared, placed two empty milk bottles on the front doorstep, nodded at Mark and closed the door. The moggy reappeared, took a disinterested glance at Mark before slipping underneath the hedge. Which reminded him: Billy was still on the loose. Maybe he would bump into him on the way home.

That afternoon, after a further search for the family's feathered friend having proved futile, and his failure to persuade his human friend to go dancing, it was hardly surprising that Mark turned up at the football field, his usual haunt on Saturday afternoons when Weston Old Boys were at home. He was alone, which wasn't surprising either. He never sought out the company of others save his immediate pals: Kev, Julian Popham and Robbie Nash. Julian, he knew, would be at his granny's, and Robbie would be at work at the Co-op. Kev would sooner polish his motorbike than watch football.

Slipping a Mars Bar into his saddlebag, he cycled the mile to the footy field. His bike was second-hand, presented to him by his parents. It sported a black saddlebag complete with side pockets, and had been the onetime pride and joy of a youngster. But cycling was old hat to a lad of seventeen who wanted a motor bike, even though, as an apprentice electrician on three quid a week he had neither the means to pay for one, nor the consent of his parents to borrow the money.

Weston were playing a team from a posh Newcastle school. Weston were in faded dark blue, save for the right half who wore red. The snooties wore red and black striped shirts with numbers on the back, and black shorts. He recognised their centre forward, a local lad called Donaldson, a gangling youth of six-foot-odd who reminded Mark of a gazelle as he ran at the Old Boys' defence, such as it was.

Mark disliked Donaldson, as did everyone else who resented, or maybe envied, his privileged education, and aloof manner when encountered in the village. He had always been known as Donaldson, never by his first name which no-one knew. Once, Donaldson had dropped an expensive fountain pen which Mark, some yards behind, picked up and after chasing after him had returned without receiving any acknowledgement.

It was a cold, autumnal afternoon. Mark sat astride his bike on the footpath that ran alongside the pitch, one forearm resting on the rail of the fence for balance. A crowd of twenty or so stood shivering along one touchline, the far one at the bottom of the sloping pitch being permanently waterlogged. He had arrived about ten minutes after kick-off, just in time to see Donaldson run gazelle-like from the half-way line and drive the ball into the Old Boys goal. One-nil already, Mark thought, until 'three-nil already' wafted across from the huddled group on the touchline. As he reached subconsciously into his saddlebag for the Mars the gazelle was at it again, bearing down on goal only to be felled by the fellow in the red shirt. Penalty! The snooty team's full back stepped up and blazed the ball so far over the crossbar it ended up in the back garden of a house on the nearby council estate. Spectators watched as the Weston goalie trotted off to retrieve it. Then Mark saw Beryl.

She was younger than Mark. Their paths hadn't crossed much in school. Contact between them had always been minimal, but lately, along with all the young lads in the village, he had begun to notice her as she openly flirted and made the most of her increasingly attractive appearance. She was walking straight towards him, held firmly by the outstretched arm of Tom Clark. Tom was a hard case. When they were kids he'd meted out occasional thick ears to his peers, including Mark, who kept his distance.

They passed Mark by, Tom casting Mark an unwarranted glare. After a few seconds Mark twisted around on his bicycle seat and was treated to a view of Beryl's shapely backside – and Beryl's face, since she had simultaneously glanced back to see if he was looking. Blushing, he turned his attention to the football, just in time to hear the ref blow for half time, and watched as the muddied players trudged from the pitch to drinks of Bovril. Mark could smell it wafting across from the small hut-cum-changing room they shared.

Slowly unwrapping his Mars, he surveyed the line of spectators, now rubbing palms together in vain efforts to keep warm. Most were men in their thirties or older. Some were there with their wives who were now huddled together in a separate group. A pair of tots kicked a ball around the edge of the now-deserted pitch. Inevitably, Mark glanced behind to see Beryl and Tom pressed up against the fence a few yards away, his hand now conveniently cupped around her bum. He watched as Tom kissed her cheek, then her lips, and he heard them laughing quietly. Then, as they embraced, Beryl looked directly at him and smiled. Blushing again, Mark turned his gaze away.

What had it meant, that smile? Was it a come-on? Surely not. She was making fun of him. She knew Tom was a hard case, knew Mark would be scared if Tom threatened him. Yet, although brief, it had been a warm smile, a friendly smile. He waited a few moments before returning his gaze, only to find Beryl and Tom were now chatting, his forearms resting on her shoulders.

He sat there for what seemed ages, shivering and blowing warm air into his cupped hands and wiggling his toes. Cold air and boredom were taking control and as the players trooped back on to the pitch he thought about leaving. But his route home would lead him past Beryl and Tom, so he hesitated, slowly chewing his Mars and looking on in boredom as Weston's Old Boys struggled to cope with their opponents.

A few minutes later one of the Weston defenders booted the ball hard and low into touch. Mark didn't follow its flight, but his attention was immediately attracted to a loud thud behind him. He turned to see Tom lying flat on his back, with Beryl standing over him, her hand to her mouth in shock. Mark leapt from his saddle, his legs becoming entangled in the bike's frame before he ran to the stricken Tom. Players and spectators grouped around the casualty, all eyes peering down at the unconscious figure lying on the path. A large, muddy mark on Tom's left temple marked the point of contact with the ball.

Everyone was standing there: players and spectators alike, looking at Tom's prostrate form. Mark had learned about artificial respiration at St John's Ambulance Brigade meetings. He stepped forward and slapped Tom's face. 'Wake up. Wake up,' he cried. But Tom didn't respond. He glanced at Beryl, standing within the circle, watching his efforts to revive him. He was in a state of panic. Practising at St John's Ambulance was one thing, and that had been two years or so ago; now, in a real emergency situation, he struggled to remember what to do exactly. He cupped his hands under Tom's knees and bent his legs, shook his shoulders, undid his belt. When he slapped his face again Tom responded, his face twitching, saliva dribbling from the corner of his mouth. His fingers clawed at thin air as he spluttered back into consciousness. Mark slid a hand behind his head, and others reached out to help him sit up. As Tom opened his eyes he recognised him, and seemed bewildered and angry at the same time. Mark stood up and stepped back, then glanced at Beryl again. To his surprise she was looking at *him*.

It was a strange look. A look he could not quite understand. It was a look that expressed *interest*, he thought. As their eyes met, she kept on looking. She didn't seem to be concerned about Tom at all. He tried to hold her gaze but felt himself blushing again, so he watched as willing hands lifted Tom to his feet.

'Sorry old chap.' The words came from the Snooties player whose clearance had knocked Tom cold. Tom didn't appear to hear. The players moved away then, and made their way back onto the pitch. Some spectators lingered, including two women who showed much concern for Tom. Mark looked at Beryl again, but her attention was now on Tom as she led him slowly away. Mark picked his bike up and looked again at the slowly departing couple. He didn't want to ride past them, so he rode off in the opposite direction and then home, all the way thinking about the sly smile Beryl had given him, then that strange look.

He was met at the door by Bob.

'Kev called. Says he can't make tonight. He'll meet you tomorrow as arranged for the Spanish City.'

'What should I do tonight then?' Mark enquired.

'You can always look for Billy' was all his brother could think of. He didn't add, 'Don't forget Joyce comes Saturdays,' although his face carried the same message. Mark decided to call on Robbie. A night at the flicks would be OK.

Robbie lived down the Terrace, Mark pushed the back gate open to find his mother hanging up washing in the yard. 'He's got diarrhoea,' she said. 'He's lying on the settee.'

Mark went inside to find his friend reading *Scouting for Boys*. Hearing the door, Robbie looked up but remained where he was.

'Got the shits,' he announced.

'So your ma said.'

'What? That I had the shits?'

'Aye. "Robbie has the shits." That's what she said. I heard her distinctly.'

Robbie laughed, looked back at *Scouting*.

'I was wondering if you fancied the flicks tonight.' Mark asked.

Robbie shook his head. 'Can't. I keep wanting the bog.'

'There's a bog at the flicks.'

Robbie shook his head. 'It's every five minutes, man.'

Mark nodded, and stood up. 'See ya when your guts are sorted,' he said, before walking off and going to Julian's, only to find, as expected, he was still at his granny's. So he went home, where, passing through the back gate, he glanced up to see Billy perched on the toilet roof. Billy was looking at him, casual-like, as though a budgie standing on a toilet roof was the norm. Mark made a few clicking noises, and at the same time climbed onto the wall that ran from the corner of the toilet, where he poked his head up to find himself less than three feet from the family pet. 'Billy,' he whispered, slowly extended a hand. Billy often perched on his finger. He looked interested now, but then the back door opened and Bob appeared. Billy flew off and disappeared over the eaves of the house.

For Carol Kemp, it was just another Saturday.

Dad, as usual, was feeling sorry for himself. Three days' stubble, open-necked shirt with the detachable collar missing, striped braces dangling, cigarette smouldering between nicotine-stained fingers, eyes staring into the abyss. And it was all his wife's fault.

It was three months now. Three months since she had disappeared, leaving Carol only a brief message on the back of a Weetabix packet: 'Can't take any more. Look after yourself and your dad. Mam'. A former sergeant major, Lennie Kemp had left the army and brought his parade ground doctrine into the family home. Barking out orders had come naturally to him. This had led to verbal then physical abuse when he came home from the pub. He always regretted it, saying it would never happen again. But it did. It always did.

They'd gone to the police station to report her missing, but the policeman said she wasn't a missing person. 'She's an adult. She can do what she likes,' the constable had said, adding, 'And she did leave a message, so she's not missing, is she?' Enquiries of relatives and friends had been fruitless. Freda Kemp, aged 39 years, of Jesmond, had gone. The report, a couple of weeks back, of a woman being found in the Tyne at Walker had been scary. She still hadn't been identified; but whoever it was, it wasn't Carol's mam. The police had asked for dental records and said they could tell by her teeth.

Carol shook the chip-pan and turned down the heat on the baked beans. 'Sausages are ready,' she declared. Lennie Kemp's face bore no expression, no acknowledgement to the announcement that his daughter was about to serve up his tea.

'Look after your dad', Mam had written. Well, she was looking after him. At least he was still going to work, or had been until last

Tuesday when he'd called in sick. He was depressed, she knew. He'd been beastly to Mam, she knew that too. She'd got out of bed once and come downstairs, just in time to see her father strike Mam across the face. The morning after he'd said sorry. It was Newcastle Brown Ale's fault, he said. It wouldn't happen again, he said. But three months ago Mam had fled.

She spooned the baked beans onto the plate alongside the chips and sausages, and served her dad his tea. He accepted it without comment, lavished the food with H.P. sauce, picked up his knife and fork and tucked in. Carol stood by the cooker, watching him. It was the one time he always looked happy, she thought: when he was feeding his face.

Glancing up, he suddenly spoke. 'That a new dress you're wearin'?'
She nodded.
'Smart lassie. Goin' somewhere special?'
'I'm going dancing, with Emma.'
'Oh aye.'
'Well, dancing classes, more like. There's a place in town called Partners Dance Studios. They do lessons on Saturday evenings.'

He stopped chewing and held his fork prongs-upright, as though frozen in time. 'How y'goin' to afford dancin' lessons? I can't give you the money.'

'It's not private tuition. It's lots of people in a group. Emma's been. She says it's great.'

The fork moved again, stabbing another chip. He looked uncomfortable. She knew he would be and she knew why.

'I'll catch the last trolley home. Don't worry, Dad. I'll be fine.'
He was looking at the kettle. She filled it and lit the gas ring.
'Back here no later than eleven mind.'
'Oh I expect it'll be before that. D'you want some pud?'

He nodded. She reached into the kitchen cabinet for a tin of creamed rice and took a saucepan from the shelf. 'You're a good lass...' he muttered as she emptied the contents of tin into the pan. She placed it onto the hob and turned the gas up low. He would see to it now.

She moved into the passage for a final check in front of the mirror. She applied lipstick and pressed her lips together before turning her head left, then right, and gently patted her hair at the back before reaching for her coat. She pushed the door open a few inches to bid her father goodnight, but her words stuck in her throat at the sight of him still seated at the table, his face cupped in his hands, sobbing uncontrollably. She lingered but a moment before slipping away, closing the front door quietly behind her.

2

Until Joyce Shippen appeared on the scene salad had never featured in Mark Green's life. Julian's family, he knew, ate it, always at weekends for some reason. But lettuce, radishes, something Mam called scallions and other associated rabbit food had never been dished up by Mam or appeared on dinner plates at school. Bob had always scorned the notion of eating leaves and things, arguing that humans were carnivorous and should therefore eat meat. But the arrival of Joyce had changed all that. Joyce ate salad. Salad was healthy. Salad was nutritious. Salad was *in*. So there was Bob unscrewing the lid on a new jar of salad cream as the family patiently waited for it to be passed round the table – after Joyce had first shake, of course. How appropriate, thought Mark, that his family were the Greens.

Joyce was tall and skinny. Joyce wore glasses. They had round lenses and perched delicately on the end of her pointed nose. Mark thought she looked like Swanky Lanky Liz. She was a receptionist or something at an office block somewhere. She had Bob under the thumb anyway.

Today it was tuna salad. Mark ate the tuna and tomato but left the lettuce, radishes and oniony things. 'You'll never get hairs on your chest,' said Dad, even though hairs on Mark's chest were already well established. Bob tucked in as though he was enjoying it. Mark watched as he chewed eagerly away. Joyce ate daintily, as always not quite finishing the meal, before placing her knife and fork onto her plate, dabbing her mouth with a paper napkin – another new feature in the house since her arrival – and staring straight ahead whilst allowing her hands to rest gracefully on her lap. Dad and Mam ate in silence. For them, later tonight, it would be pig's trotters. Mark had seen them in the pantry.

It was a typical Saturday evening. After tea, Mam and Dad would be off to the Club, Bob and Joyce would have a night in, ostensibly sharing meaningful thoughts about the books they were reading, but which Mark knew, as his parents must have known, would really be a night of sofa-sex. He, Mark, could either stay in and play wallflower, or get the hell out and otherwise occupy himself. He always chose the latter option, but now that the promised visit to the Stoll with Kev was off and Robbie was indisposed, what exactly was he to do?

He slipped his coat on and headed for Julian's. He'd be back from his granny's now, but whether his parents would let him out was another matter. His mam, that is. His dad wouldn't care. Julian's dad always reminded Mark of a ghost: he drifted about aimlessly, sometimes seeming to pass through walls. Mark couldn't remember ever hearing him speak. The Pophams had TV so maybe he would be invited in. On the way he passed the Club. Early arrivals were making their way through its hallowed portal. Mark knew the form: it would be 'Eyes down for a full house' followed by the Go-as-you-please. His Uncle Ernie, known as the Tommy Steele of Weston, was a regular winner.

Going to the Stoll had been Kev's idea. Kev had been several times, and had told Mark about the X-films. Now he'd disappeared. With some lass, presumably. Probably pulled on his motorbike. Turning into Julian's street, Mark saw the Pophams' Austin 7 at the front gate. He glanced briefly inside. He loved looking into cars, at the shining dashboards, the neat control knobs. Like their house, the Pophams' car was always immaculate. He could almost smell the leather upholstery from outside the vehicle. Julian's mam was the driver. His dad just went to work and played classical music at home.

He walked up the short garden path, pressed the illuminated bell-push and waited. Through the glass of the porch door he saw the inner door opening, and Mrs Popham emerged to open the front door. As usual she was smiling. As usual she looked as immaculate as the house and car. Her hair was dyed blonde, her clothes were in fashion and there was always a strong smell of perfume about her. 'Hello Mark, we've just got in,' she trilled.

Before Mark could speak, she stepped back and closed the inner door in a manner suggesting she didn't want anyone inside to hear what she was going to say. Then, lowering her voice conspiratorially, and even glancing at the front gate to see if anyone might be approaching, she came to the point.

'I'm afraid you can't see Julian.' She glanced towards her own bay window. Mark followed her gaze to see Julian's pasty face through the glass. 'He's not at all well. He has an upset tummy. Must've been something he ate, but not in this house, mind. I'm always strict with what he eats.' Julian was looking wistfully at Mark. Like 'if only I could get out of here', Mark thought.

'I'll tell him you called,' said Mrs Popham, stepping back into the porch. Then she saw Julian looking. 'You see?' she declared. 'He doesn't look well at all, does he?' She gave Mark a moment to consider her son's appearance, before addressing him again. 'And how are you, Mark? You always seem so healthy.'

'I'm fine,' Mark replied, removing his gaze from Julian and looking directly at his mam.

'Such a nice lad.' She lingered at the door, before slowly pushing it to. ''Bye then', she said at last, before slowly closing the door, keeping eye contact until the last moment.

At the front gate, when Mark looked again, Julian had disappeared. He glanced into the car again before wandering up the street, and presently found himself in the recreation ground, or rec as everyone called it. In gathering dusk, the scene of so much of his childhood was deserted. Nothing had changed over the years. The rusting goal posts, leaning at an angle over the muddy goalmouth; the circular sandpit containing a few wisps of sand, some empty sweet-packets and the inevitable dog-poo; the teapot lid, where he'd been sick from the spinning platform; the elongated rocking horse that sat eight in a row.

He sat on the rocking horse now, in the middle and sideways on.

The air was dank, the grass long and wet. Behind him, over the fence, the bowling green was deserted, the familiar 'clunk' of the woods having ended for the day. His wandering thoughts reflected on some of his fellow-apprentices at work, and Tommy and Fred, his workmates, then strayed to Connie, and he wondered if he might see her on the bus next week. He should have got off yesterday when she smiled. He wished he had. Never mind, he would say something next time, even offer to walk home with her. He thought of Beryl. She'd smiled too. Then there had been that look.

A dog appeared and sniffed in the long grass before wandering up to one of the goal posts to cock a leg. It roamed here and there, sniffing, peeing, moving on. Finally it passed out of sight along the path. Then a long, moaning sound permeated the still air. A ship's foghorn. The Tyne wasn't so far away.

Mark felt his stomach rumble. A meagre portion of tinned tuna having failed to satisfy his appetite he slid from the rocking horse, pushing its back end to send it rocking before setting off down the Avenue for food. If the street was empty, the chippy wasn't. A small, orderly queue extended through the door and halfway down the steps. He waited patiently, savouring the smell, as one by one people emerged, suppers wrapped in newspapers. Slowly, people moved forward until he was in the shop, where the queue ran along one wall to the far end before doubling back to the counter where Eddie and his plump missus, Freda, were frying tonight.

Freda was serving a small boy. 'Fish and chips twice, fishcake and chips, sausage and chips and an extra portion of chips, please,' said the youngster, his elbows and forearms resting on the counter which was so high he could barely see over it.

'Fish and chips twice, fishcake and chips and... what was it again?'

'Sausage and chips and an extra portion of chips.'

Freda picked up a pair of tongs and reached for a fish, then hesitated.

'Haddock or cod?' she asked.

'Dunno,' said the boy. 'Me ma just said fish and chips.' He handed her a piece of paper bearing the order. Customers smiled patiently.

Freddie reached for two pieces of cod, conveniently fried and ready on the hotplate. He wrapped individual parcels in greaseproof paper, then wrapped the lot in a few pages of the *News of the World*. The little lad paid, the queue moved forward and there was Beryl.

Mark hadn't noticed her, standing to one side. But she had moved around with the queue and was barely six feet away. By her look of surprise, seen clearly in the mirror on the wall behind the counter, he realised she had only just noticed him too. She wore a long coat that was open at the front. For a moment their eyes met in the mirror's reflection, before she looked away; but then, a moment later, looked again to see if Mark was still looking. He was.

'Yes love?'

'Bottle of Pepsi, please,' said Beryl. Mark's gaze remained transfixed on her reflection, which showed a pale blue, unbuttoned cardigan, and ample breasts pushed firmly against the cotton material of her blouse. She paid her for her Pepsi before walking directly out of the shop without so much as a glance at Mark. He thought he might follow her. He had hesitated over Connie on the bus; maybe this time he should be more positive. As the queue inched forward he kept glancing at the door.

'Yes?' Freda was addressing him as though she'd never seen him before.

'Portion of chips, ta.' He waited as she scooped them up and slid them into a packet.

'Open or wrapped?'

'Open,' said Mark, taking hold of the packet before applying salt and vinegar and leaving the shop where, to his surprise, he found Beryl gurgling sown the last drops of her Pepsi. 'Thought you'd died in there,' she said, before glancing down at the packet of chips. 'Give us a chip, then.' She took a long one from the packet and tentatively bit the end off, sucking cold air into her mouth.

'Saw you looking in the mirror,' she said at last. She was about five foot nothing, but looked straight up into his eyes. 'Fancy me, don't you? – Ow!' Mark saw her finger was stuck in the neck of the now-

empty Pepsi bottle. 'Look what you made me do,' she declared, holding the bottle in one hand as she tried to extricate her finger. Mark
stepped forward, held her wrist and slowly prised her finger free. Close-
up, he caught the strong whiff of her perfume. 'My knight in shining
armour,' she laughed. Mark realised she'd done it on purpose. 'Come
on, Sir Lancelot, You can walk me home if you like.' She walked off,
leaving the Pepsi bottle standing on the wall outside the chippy. Mark
followed and fell in alongside.

'Is Tom your boyfriend, then?' he asked. It was all he could think of.

She laughed. 'I'm too young for boyfriends, including you.' She
took another chip. 'I live along here,' she said. Of course, he remembered: her dad was a G.P. He knew the house. The street was dark,
with only two street lights, one of them flickering weakly. They walked
in silence before she stopped abruptly at the dark gateway. She turned
to face him. The flickering streetlight illuminated her face and white
blouse. The effect on the latter made her breasts look huge.

'Well?' she whispered.

Her face was inches away from his. He could smell her chippy-
breath. Finally she spoke. 'Fancy seeing me tomorrow night?' His surprise was matched only be his sexual arousal. She thrust two fingers
into the now-soggy chips packet. She took the last chip, made an 'O'
with her mouth and slid it slowly inside. 'We could meet after I've been
to my gran's. Say nine o'clock? That's if you'd like to.'

'Where?' he replied weakly.

She thought for a moment. 'Behind the Club? You know, next to all
those empty crates. Okay?' She stood on tiptoe and kissed his cheek,
smiled and stood back apace. 'Don't be late.' She turned, opened the
gate and disappeared in the darkness. Mark peered through the gloom,
finding himself in the company of an empty chip packet and a stirring
erection. The smell of chips and her perfume lingered as he walked
off slowly, and wondered how to fill in the rest of the evening before
venturing home.

He walked to the road end and stopped. Where to go? For some
reason he took the footpath by the side of the main road leading
through the village. His shoulders were hunched, his eyes looking at

the footpath immediately in front. He wasn't walking anywhere in particular, he was just walking. And thinking. Of Beryl and what just happened. He found himself opposite the flicks and wandered over. There was wasn't a soul about. He could hear voices, and instinctively went to the side of the building and looked up to the open hatchway of the projection room. Old Frank, the projectionist, was out of sight but he knew he would be busy with reels of film, keeping an eye on things as the night's main movie rolled. He'd often stood here with Robbie, eating chips, listening to Hollywood's best without seeing the film. The voices were loud, almost always American.

He checked his watch. Too soon to go home yet. He stood at the corner of the building, and thought of Bob and Joyce. They'd be starkers now, he mused. Probably banging away on the sofa. He imagined her skinny frame. Bob grunting, saying 'I love you.' Or maybe he would be at the radiogram, putting on a romantic, meaningful record. *Stranger in Paradise*, probably. Joyce always said she liked Bing Crosby. So did Dad. 'All their daddies' he called him. No matter who was singing, Elvis, Cliff, the Everleys. According to Dad, Bing was all their daddies.

It started to rain. Lightly at first, then heavier. He pulled up his coat collar, stood back against the wall. But water ran down his forehead, then his nose and into his mouth. He licked his lips, wiped his face. When it started seeping through his shirt he'd had enough. He walked away decisively, head down, and hurried up the Terrace. Joyce or no Joyce, he was going home. It was nearly time for *Pick of the Pops* anyway, which he could happily listen to whilst his parents, having tanked up at the Club, slobbered over their pig's trotters.

***

Carol hated Sundays. As though regular washing and cooking for her dad wasn't enough, Sunday was the day she had to do the housework, top to bottom, as well as cooking the Sunday dinner and ironing afterwards. It was a routine into which she had been thrust since Mam had disappeared. This Sunday was no different. Dad was still a-bed, sleeping off the inevitable effects of the previous night's booze. She glanced at the clock. In ten minutes she would make him a cup of tea. Then she would boil his morning egg, which he would eat over the *News of the World* she had already been out for.

Mam had gone but the bitter memories of her cries on Saturday nights, and the bruising and black eyes on Sunday morning had not. Such punishment had not been meted out to Carol. She was a good girl, Dad said. He seemed to mean her mother had not been good, because she had left them. Carol was confused. She sympathised with Mam, yet resented her for leaving her to cope with Dad. She resented Dad for his drunken behaviour, yet felt sorry for him. He was her dad, after all, and it was her duty to look after him. That's what she believed. Yet she felt it wasn't fair. She was young, attractive and enjoyed her job at the electricity company. She felt she should be free to live her young life without suffering through her parents' domestic upheaval.

She carefully removed ornaments from the mantelpiece, along with three photographs of Mam, and applied the duster. Spic and span, everything just so. House clean and tidy, just as Mam always insisted. Dad kept saying he loved his wife, and his insistence that the photographs were on the mantelpiece seemed to say so too. There was a large photograph of her on top of the radiogram. She lifted it up, swept the duster over the polished lid and held the photograph in her hand before replacing it. It showed Mam smiling, at the coast somewhere. Tynemouth, probably.

'That's one of my favourites.' She turned to see Dad standing in the doorway. What a mess he was. Unshaven, clad in a ragged dressing gown. Bare feet. Hair tousled. 'I'll have my egg at the table, pet.' He picked up the newspaper and shuffled across to the kitchen table. 'Put the kettle on, eh. You're a good lass, our Carol. I always said so. So did your ma.'

She brewed up, reached for a small saucepan and took an egg from the box. 'Your ma,' he was saying. 'Where the devil'd she go, eh? If only she'd talked about it before flitting off like that.' She knew what was next. It was Brown Ale's fault; then it was Mam's fault. Never his fault. He was full of self-pity and she had to bear the brunt of his remorse, his anger, every day; but somehow Sundays seemed the worst.

It had been a great night at Partners. Emma had met a good looking boy. He'd asked to walk her home and she'd said yes. She wondered how she'd got on. She wondered what Dad would think if she turned up at the door with a boy. It was almost as though he was reading her thoughts.

'What time did you get home last night, then?'

'Just after eleven, Dad. Got the last trolley. No problem.'

'Aye. It's just I saw Emma walking down the street after midnight.'

'Oh, someone took her home.'

'Aye. She was with a young bloke. Didn't recognise him.' He folded his newspaper. 'Just make sure you get yourself in of a night, lass. None of this after midnight stuff. You're too young to go courtin', just remember.'

She plonked his egg on the table. Then the bread. Then the salt. She left him to it and went with her duster into the hall.

Carol hated Sundays.

Mark liked Sundays.

Morning fryup. Sunday lunch. Spin on the bike with Kev, ending up at the Spanish City. Only this Sunday was different. Kev had disappeared off the radar, and even if he turned up there was the rendezvous with Beryl tonight. There was one more thing: Dad had ordered him to find Billy.

For an hour he walked the streets, peering at the rooftops of houses, coalhouses, outside lavs, before calling it a day and heading off to Kev's. His knock was not answered, and he slunk off home with the news of his failure to find Billy. Never mind, said Bob, take a bath. So he did.

For the first time in his life Mark Green reclined in a bath filled with hot water in his own home. Hot water from taps attached to the bath, that is. He'd had baths – proper baths – before: on holiday at the relations, and twice at Kev's when the Greens had had company. After allowing as much water as possible into the bath, he leaned forward and turned off the taps, and lay back, the water lapping right up to his chin, with only his knees protruding slightly. And bathing, he discovered, was a time to reflect, especially now that no-one would unexpectedly walk into the room

His quest for girls was made at the whim of his friend, Kev, or at least whenever he deigned it expedient to go looking, the Spanish City being virtually the sole venue. A promenade between the Waltzer and dodgems, wearing plastic jackets and savouring the deafening sounds of the latest hit records. They'd linger here, saunter there, inevitably end up at a chippy. There were girls, but none seemed interested in a couple of young studs who shared a motorbike. Bob's alternative appealed to Mark. Go dancing. Not for the dancing itself, but for the girls. But Kev was giving it the cold shoulder. Julian shared his desire but did not have the freedom. Robbie had the freedom but not the desire.

His thoughts strayed to Connie. It seemed an age since her smile on the bus on Friday. He'd probably have to wait a whole week before he saw here again, and only then it would be by chance. He could always hang about at the stop she got on, but she might think him some sort of weirdo. Well, anyway, he was bound to see her, sooner or later. In the meantime there was Beryl. He thought of her face, her figure, her perfume. Even her breath when she'd pecked his cheek, and never mind it smelled of chips and vinegar. And her eyes, looking right into him. That look when Tom was flattened at the footie. She had asked to see him tonight. To see *him*. He wanted to be with Beryl tonight, not Kev.

But if he wasn't going to the Spanish City tonight, how could he tell Kev? He couldn't say he was seeing Beryl behind the Club. He wouldn't put it past him to turn up for a piece of the action. He'd have to tell him something. Kev would want to know. Bob's voice interrupted his thoughts. 'Have you died in there?' He spoke again before Mark could reply. 'Kev's here. Stop playing with yourself and make him a cup of tea.'

He dried and dressed quickly, emerging from the bathroom with hair wet and bedraggled. Kev was sprawled in an easy chair, dressed in black, legs outstretched, feet apart and resting on their heels. From where Mark was standing his black boots looked enormous. 'Posh now, eh?' said Kev.

'Better than the old tin can anyway.'

'Saw it in the yard,' said Kev. 'Tommo'll have it.' He laughed. 'He'll probably use it.' Mark gestured a tilting motion with his hand. 'No thanks, Kidda. Just had a cup.'

Mark sat on the other chair. He knew Dad would be in the garden seeing to his pigeons. Mam would be at the shop. Bob seemed to have disappeared.

'You're wonderin' where I got to last night, right?' said Kev. Mark shrugged.

'Good news, kidda. I went for a spin to Tynemouth? Parked up at the Plaza. There were two birds. Anyway, to cut a long story sideways...' He drew in his legs, leaned forward. 'We're fixed up for tonight, and yours is called Rita.' He sat back again, beaming. 'Better than the Stoll, eh?'

'Tonight?'

'Aye, tonight. Why, is that a problem?'

'Well...there is, actually.'

'Eh? What like? Don't say you've met some bird.'

Just then Bob appeared carrying the kettle. Mark and Kev shook their heads. Bob lingered, looking at Kev. 'How's the machine?'

'Aye, grand. Goin' like a train. Over a ton yesterday on the Coast Road.'

'I'm thinkin' of getting a car,' said Bob. 'Ford Pop for sale up the road.'

'Oh aye,' said Kev, the brevity of his response making his lack of interest clear. Bob cottoned on and went into the kitchen, closing the door behind him.

'Go on then Kidda. Who?'

'Just some lass.'

Kev's smile disappeared, giving way to a look of astonishment, or possibly disbelief. 'Dark horse, you, Kidda.' He waited, like a schoolteacher waiting for an answer from a recalcitrant pupil.

'Name's Beryl' said Mark finally.

'Beryl who?' Mark was silent. 'Christ, it's like pulling teeth. Look, those two I met at the Plaza. Mine's Betty, yours is Rita. Now that wasn't hard to do, was it?' He waited. 'So?'

'Mark shrugged. 'Don't know her surname. But...'

Kev turned his head slightly to the right whilst keeping his eyes on his friend.

'You don't mean Beryl Spry, do you.' He cupped his hands under his chest, lifted them up and down a couple of times. Mark's face said it all. 'Bloody hell,' said Kev. 'Beryl the bloody Peril. How'd you manage to pull her?'

'We met in the chippy.'

Kev sat back. 'Well, you're a real Clark Gable you. And talking of Clark, she's been knocking about with Tom Clark, mind.'

Bob came in carrying a mug of tea, and sat on the sofa.

'Hope I'm not interrupting anything.'

'Nope. Just goin'.' Kev stood up, wandered out through the kitchen. Mark followed.

'So where are you taking her?'

Mark shrugged again. 'Might go to the flicks in town.'

Kev nodded. 'I told those lasses we'd see then outside the Plaza tonight.' When Mark didn't say anything he said, 'Well, I'm going with or without you.'

Mark's silence seemed final. 'Aye, well, see you,' said Kev, and with that he hurried through the gate, kicked the motorcycle into life and roared off, his black hair rippling in the wind. Bob, emerging from the house, saw him go. 'He should wear a crash helmet,' he declared. 'Aye,' said Mark, his thoughts already turning back to the prospects the evening might bring.

But they weren't his only thoughts. Like Kev, he wanted a motorbike. He'd already spoken to Dad about it, but his only reply had been 'We'll see'. Lots of other lads had a motorbike; why not him? He could pay for it on hire purchase. He imagined what he could be doing tonight if he had a motorbike. He could take Beryl out on it. Better than the back of the Club.

Charlie Green's thoughts were far-removed from motorbikes. He was at his pigeon cree at the top of the garden. Roger, next door, ambling up his garden path found him shaking a tin of corn as his life depended on it.

'Look at him,' said Charlie.' Roger looked up and saw a lone pigeon gracing the rooftop, next to the chimney, his head cocked to one side, and looking about as though taking in the view. 'He's come all the way from France and he's sitting there looking at me.'

Charlie shook the tin. 'C'mon. Come to Charlie. There's a good lad.' The pigeon cooed, shuffled along the roof.

'The little tinker,' said Roger.'

'The stupid bastard,' said Charlie, *sotto voce*, as though afraid the pigeon might hear.

'He must be one of the first back,' observed Roger.

'It's no use if he sits there looking at me,' said Tommy, adding quietly, 'I'll ring his bloody neck if he doesn't get his arse down here.'

'How will you manage that exactly?' Roger enquired.

'C'mon, there's a good lad,' Charlie called out, shaking the tin. The pigeon took off, flew in a circle and landed on the cowling of next door's chimney pot.

'Come down, you stupid git,' called Charlie, face reddening in annoyance. Finally he put the tin down and wiped some saliva from the corner of his mouth. 'Fuck it,' he said at last.

The pigeon took flight then, and flapped around in a circle before landing on the guttering just above the living room window. Encouraged, Charlie shook the tin.

'He's definitely interested,' said Roger. But just then the back door slammed, and the pigeon flew off again and landed on top of the chimney. Charlie looked to see Mark approaching. 'What is it about you and birds?' he asked. 'There's serious money going on here.'

'Sorry Dad.'

The pigeon was in flight again. 'He's flying round in circles,' said Roger.

'He'll disappear up his own arse in a minute,' retorted Charlie, as once more the pigeon settled on the roof.

'Look,' said Roger.

'I am looking,' said Charlie.

'No, *look*.'

'It's Billy!' exclaimed Mark on sight of the family escapee, now plainly in view and not more than a few feet from the pigeon.

'By lad, you're right,' declared Charlie, his eyes darting between the pigeon and the family pet. They all stepped forward, Mark calling out Billy's name and making clicking noises with his mouth. Both birds then took off, Billy flapping out of sight on the other side of the house, the pigeon landing on the cree. Charlie moved close, speaking softly and encouragingly, and the bird landed on his outstretched hand. He adeptly removed the ring from its leg and stamped it in the clock. Mission accomplished, Charlie looked at Mark as one might look at a stranger who had wandered into his living room. 'What are you after anyway? Last time you were in this garden you were in your pram.'

'It's about a motorbike.'

Charlie sighed. 'That again. You know what your mam'll say. She thinks they're death traps.'

'Lots of my mates have got 'em now, Dad.'

'Aye, and lots of your mates have dads with money. Either that or they've saved up for one. I'm not signing hire purchase papers. There'll be no debt in this house.'

Roger was still peering upwards. 'Can't see him now,' he called out.

'Can't see who, Roger?' Nancy appeared with a mug of tea for Charlie.

'Billy,' said Charlie and Mark in unison. Nancy checked in her stride and looked skywards. 'He was on the roof,' said Charlie, 'but he flew off when he heard Mark closing the door.'

Nancy glared at Mark who set off apace, passing through the house to the back yard to see if Billy might have landed on the lav or the coal-house. He hadn't; he was perched instead on Mrs Swinburne's washing line in next door's yard. Mark had had trouble with the Swinburnes, over balls landing in their yard, and they didn't care much for the sound of Kev's motorbike either. Jimmy Swinburne was a big man, with strong arms and perpetually-clenched fists. He had a bald head that earned him the nickname the Eggshell Blond, or simply Eggshell, among the young lads who lived on the Terrace.

Gingerly, Mark opened the Swinburnes' back gate and moved up close to Billy. But Billy took off and flew off across the houses on the opposite side of the street. Swinburne – Eggshell – saw Mark through the kitchen window and emerged on the back doorstep, arms folded and wearing a frown.

'What's goin' on?' he demanded.

'Our Billy. He was on the washing line.'

'Aye, well he's not there now so clear off. And close he gate after you.' Eggshell's dog, a Jack Russell known as Scamp but to Mark and a few others as Jane, appeared, yapping away. Mark hurried off, scanning rooftops. But there was no sign of Billy. Indoors he sat and read the *News of the World*, and cast his eyes over a few shapely pinups. They reminded him of his forthcoming rendezvous with Beryl.

Not that he needed reminding.

He left the house at seven, having decided any later would have attracted curious questioning from Mam and Dad. Bob certainly. It wasn't that it was late; it was unusual. So it was he found himself wandering the streets for a second consecutive night. Heading to nowhere in particular, he began to have misgivings. Would Beryl turn up? What if she'd gone out instead with Tom Clark? What if she'd told Tom about their cosy little arrangement and he turned up? What if she'd been leading him on, or simply changed her mind? But then he remembered the look she'd given him at the footie. And how she'd waited for him coming out of the chippy. He'd go to the Club. The thought of her being there in the darkness excited him. It was like a new adventure.

He was wearing dark clothing. This was a secret tryst, after all. He wandered down the Avenue before meandering aimlessly around the streets of the private semis near the rec. At least it wasn't raining or cold. After an hour, perhaps less, walking through the village, he saw her on the opposite side of the road, heading towards her gran's presumably. She didn't see him and he didn't call out. Instead he slunk into the darkened grounds of the chapel until she was out of sight, hiding among the shrubbery in the shadow of the clock tower. It occurred to him that this was a better venue than the back of the Club. Too late to change things now.

At a quarter to nine he headed towards the Club. There wasn't a soul about as he walked approached the back of the building, negotiating the empty beer crates and barrels. He stood against the wall in the darkness not far from a small, dimly-lit window. Anyone passing wouldn't see him, their vision blurred further by the light from the window, and from here he would able to see Beryl as she approached. The window was slightly open, and from it he could hear the muted sound of women's voices. Belatedly he realised he was outside the ladies toilets. He was unable to move further away as he may have been visible to anyone walking to the rear of the building, however unlikely.

The longer he stood there the more uncomfortable he became. If, perchance, anyone discovered him lurking in the shadows outside the ladies, what would they think? He shuddered at the thought of word getting round the village. For some reason he wondered what Julian's mam would think if she found out. But he wouldn't be discovered, surely, standing in total darkness and total silence, save for the sound of banging doors emanating from within the ladies toilets, and now and again the muffled voices of women in brief, passing conversation. He checked his watch. 9.15. Still no Beryl.

He realised Beryl mightn't be expecting him to be concealed in the shadows at all. Maybe she had suggested meeting at the back of the Club because she couldn't think of anywhere else on the spur of the moment, and it was just a convenient rendezvous from where they could go for a walk, or even just chat. What would she think of him, lurking in the darkness? 'What kind of a girl do you take me for?' she would say. He was excited at the thought of being with her, but wasn't sure of the ground rules. He was on the verge of leaving his hiding place when she appeared, illuminated by the glare of the streetlamp on the corner. She was standing right in front of him, barely ten yards away, looking about. For a moment he froze. But when she lingered he became bolder.

'Psst!' he hissed. She heard and looked about with uncertainty.

'Beryl,' he called out softly, waving his hands in front of his face. She saw the movement, and approached between the crates and barrels, her dark outline silhouetted against the light behind. Her coat was undone. He could see it flapping as she approached.

'Couldn't see you,' she whispered as she stood facing him in the darkness. A toilet flushed and there were women's voices. 'The ladies lav,' she laughed. 'How romantic.'

She was close to him, almost pressing him back against the wall. He could smell her breath, her perfume. He felt the warmth of her soft body, her breasts brushing gently against his chest. He could barely see her face, just the vague outline of her head. She slid her arms around his waist and pulled herself even closer.

'How's your gran?' he asked. It was all he could think of.

She laughed softly. 'Is that why you wanted to meet me? To ask about my gran? Would you rather be with her than me?'

Looking down, he could see her face more clearly as his eyes became more accustomed to the darkness. Her eyes shone brightly, like two small lights. He lowered his head slightly and kissed her briefly on the mouth.

'Sorry,' he said, awkwardly.

'What for?' she enquired.

'It's just you're so lovely,' was the best he could do.

'I bet you say that to all the girls,' she whispered, looking up into his face. 'Kiss me, then. Properly'

He wrapped his arms around her and kissed her, raising his hand to stroke her hair. It was wonderful, a moment he would never forget. He made to pull away but she held his mouth to hers, then licked his lips with her tongue before sliding it into his mouth. He had never knew anyone would do such a thing. He slid his tongue into her mouth in response as he felt a tightness in his jeans. She felt it too, and slid her hand down to his thigh, then slowly felt the bulge in in his groin. She was breathing heavily. 'Touch me,' she pleaded.

He lowered a hand to her hip. '*Touch me*,' she hissed.

Suddenly the voices from the ladies toilet window became louder. They belonged to two women who had moved close to the window.

'Well, he turned up, just like he said,' said one. Mark recognised the voice immediately. It belonged to Ada from next door.

'What, at your house?' her companion was saying.

'Aye, at midnight. He was waiting in the lav. Saucy bugger. Roger was out for the count, as usual.'

'He's got some front, mind. Was it dark?'

'Gloomy. I opened the door and he was just standing there, waiting.'

'And?'

'Well, you know...'

'Just as well Roger didn't want a pee.'

They both laughed, and their voices faded as they moved away from the window. A door banged and all fell silent.

Beryl giggled. 'What was all that about?'

'Sounds like somebody's bonking Ada in her lav.'

'Really?' Beryl whispered, reaching for his groin again, and pushing herself against him. He slipped his hand under her coat and over her jeans, grasping her bottom, subconsciously thinking that was exactly what Tom Clark had done only the day before. They were locked together, joined by mouths and hands. He moved his hand inside the front of her jumper until his fingers were touching the underside of her bra. He felt the weight of a large breast on his knuckles, then opened his palm and closed his fingers gently over it. She sighed deeply, and moved her hand to the top of his jeans and took hold of the zip with the tips of her fingers. She tugged. It wouldn't come.

She stood back slightly and reached forward with both hands, undoing his belt and, pulling his jeans and pants down to his upper thighs. It was merciful release for his erection. She kissed him again. She was sighing deeply, her arms wrapped around his waist under his jacket, fingers clutching his shirt. He held her close as she worked herself against him, breathing hard into his ear, gasping, moaning.

A sudden, loud crash made them jump. They looked sideways to see a door flapping open, and light spilling out across the crates and empty barrels. The dark silhouette of a man appeared, as though illuminated by a spotlight.

'It's Walter.' Mark exclaimed.

But Beryl was already fleeing between the crates and barrels. She knocked noisily into a few before running off across the car park.

'Who's there?' Walter, the Club steward, stepped further outside.

Mark took off, his pants and jeans still sagging around his thighs.

'Who is it?' Walter called, as Mark fled across the car park. Walter was too fat to catch him, but he didn't want to be recognised. 'I know your game mister,' Walter called out after him. Mark ran to the footpath leading to the Terrace, where a streetlight illuminated the corner. As he approached he saw Mrs Armitage from the shop on the Avenue approaching, her unmistakable bulky shape illuminated in the pinky glow of the light. He scurried past her without glancing back and disappeared into the darkness. As he ran he could hear Walter screaming after him: 'Bloody pervert! Bloody peeping tom!'

At a safe distance Mark stopped running, pushed his limp manhood back into his pants and pulled his jeans up. He walked quickly, but with fast-beating heart, towards the Terrace, his mind in turmoil: still sexually aroused but mightily relieved at his escape. Even so, he knew there may be trouble ahead. If Walter had recognised him he'd tell the men at the Club and the word would get back to Dad; if Mrs Armitage had recognised him she'd tell the customers at her shop and the word would get back to Mam. He could feel butterflies fluttering deep in his belly at the thought. Hell, it didn't bear thinking about at all.

On the beach at Whitley Bay, Kevin Marsh was fastening his trousers too. A moment later Betty got to her feet, stepped into her knickers and pulled on her jeans. She popped a cigarette into her mouth, fumbled for her lighter and lit up. Twenty yards away, her friend Rita, sitting alone on the grass at the edge of the sand, puffed at a cigarette of her own.

3

Closing the gate behind him, Mark pulled up the collar of his donkey jacket and set off purposefully down the Terrace. The rain swept directly into his face as he walked, one elbow held rigid against his haversack strung over his right shoulder. The tools inside made it heavy, but he was used to it.

It always took him thirteen minutes to walk from home to the bus stop. It was Monday morning, twenty to seven and still dark. He was in a private world of his own. His thoughts, not surprisingly, were of Beryl; her touch and smell, their sexual encounter so rudely interrupted by Walter. He wondered what she would be thinking this morning. As far as he knew she had just left school, but he didn't know if she was working yet. He felt very close to her, *cared* about her. He wanted to see her again, yet it was only now dawning on him he didn't know how to get in touch with her. Other than knocking on her door, of course. But what if her mam or dad answered? Would she have told them about him? He doubted it. Even now, thinking of her at the back of the club, he felt himself stirring. If it hadn't been for Walter...

He crossed the main road to the bus stop, where the usual faces were waiting. No-one ever spoke. They were just strangers who happened to gather every morning for the seven o'clock bus to town. Like him, they were going to work. Like him, they were there because they had to be. The bus rolled up, on time as always. Dad said you could set your watch by it. A dozen silent souls climbed aboard, smokers upstairs, the rest occupying the mainly empty seats below. Mark sat on the nearside, by the window. Beryl was first and foremost in his mind, but he had not forgotten Connie. He always looked out for her when the bus approached the Balloon. She never appeared in the mornings, probably, thought Mark, because she worked in an office somewhere and didn't start work till nine.

The bus stopped at every stop in the village. Soon it was standing room only. Full, it swept past the Balloon without stopping. For quarter of an hour its occupants sat in stony silence, the only sound the conductor's 'Tickets, please,' and each passenger's declared journey: 'Single to town,' or 'Ninepenny one please.' Nearing town the driver let rip, making up for the lost time caused by so many stops earlier. What if we crashed? Mark wondered. Would anyone say anything then?

He alighted at Gallowgate, the rain sweeping spitefully into his face. Passing traffic splashed through roadside puddles, throwing water against his legs as he hurried towards the Haymarket. He looked enviously at bus drivers occupying their cabs. He always thought it must be great sitting in a private cab on mornings such as this; instead he was out in the rain, getting wet. Wet hair, wet legs. He was otherwise dry when he pushed open the door to the workshop where he found his bedraggled workmates standing in their own private puddles. No-one said anything, other than 'Close that bloody door.'

It was an apprentices' gathering, young lads like himself sent to collect electrical items from old Bert in the Stores. Bert appeared now, at the wide hatch. His floor was lower than the workshop's, causing him to look tiny. The electric lighting reflected off his bald head as he placed boxes and lengths of cable on the wooden counter, constantly checking order slips. 'Good weekend?' The enquirer was Jimmy, a tall, gangling lad who usually had a civil word for Mark. 'Aye. You?' Jimmy answered in the affirmative. His enquiry paved the way for general conversation among those present, about weekend activities, girls, football and the inevitable lewd remarks about Miss Raine, the boss's secretary.

The door at the top of the steps opened and Mr Smith – Smudger – appeared. Diminutive, with a pointy nose, a chain smoker, Smudger was foreman. Wearing his battered trilby, he scanned the small gathering before descending the steps to the shop floor in a cloud of smoke.

'All present this fine Monday morn, are we?' He removed his cigarette with nicotine-stained fingers just as the back door opened and Bobby Hall – Horlicks – appeared, wet through by the rain. He stood just inside the door, shaking water from his coat. Smudger allowed him a moment before addressing him directly.

'Sleep in, then, did we?'

Horlicks, who hadn't seen him through sodden eyelashes, looked up sharply.

'Better late than never.' Smudger let it go at that, before turning to Mark.

'Nothin' for you, lad. Off you go. I've sent Fred so you've two masters.'

Old Fred. He was near retirement and past climbing ladders. The lads wondered how he was still on the books. Probably because he'd been with the firm from the off, years ago. That was the chat.

Mark nodded, picked up his haversack, headed off along the lane. The rain was lighter now. He was bound for an office in Northumberland Street. In truth he was usually anxious about going on to a new job for the first time. Shyness was the reason. He always felt he would be the focus of the attention of strangers. This time it was worse, an office staffed by women. He walked apace on damp pavements. It was just after eight-fifteen when he arrived at a doorway just past C&As. He read the business plates on the wall, and climbed to the first floor to a glass door bearing the name, in large letters: Murchison & Co. He pushed it open and pressed the bell push on the Enquiries counter.

For a few minutes nothing happened. Then an inner door opened and a tall woman in her 40s appeared. She had peroxide blonde hair and smelled strongly of perfume. For some reason Mark suddenly thought of Horlicks, dripping on the floor back in the workshop. Horlicks always described women of over forty as mutton done up as lamb. He would have here, but Mark would have disagreed. The woman didn't speak, just gave him a 'Can I help you?' smile.

'I'm from Robson's.'

She kept the smile, otherwise her expression was blank.

'The electricians.'

'Oh!' She crackled into life, as though switched on like a table lamp. Still smiling, she lifted the hinged counter and beckoned him through. 'Paul, isn't it? Your friends said you would be here.'

'Mark.'

'Oh. Sorry. I knew you were a saint.' She laughed out loud and led him into a huge office, with lots of desks occupied by lots of typewriters. The chairs were unoccupied.

'I'm Maggie. You're through there.' She pointed at a door in the corner. 'Small kitchen. That's your base.' She was positively beaming. 'I'll just tell your friends you're here. You looked soaked through. You can hang your coat up here if you like.'

She indicated a row of hooks in the entrance lobby. He nodded, pulled off his jacket. She took it from him without invitation and hung it up. 'There's a kettle in there. Everything you need.' Still smiling, she walked off apace through the empty office, her high heels clattering on the polished floor.

Mark went directly to the kitchen, where he found two haversacks belonging to Tommy and Fred, along with a pile of new five-foot fluorescent fittings and miscellaneous electrical fittings still in their boxes. There was a small table and four chairs. He dumped his sack and was filling the kettle when the door opened and Fred appeared.

'Hah! Tea! He's got you well trained, I can see that.' Without further ado he plonked himself on a chair, took a packet of cigarettes from his overalls pocket and lit up. 'He'll be here in a mo'. That's if he can keep his mitts off wotsername's arse.'

'Maggie?'

'Whatever.'

Fred, overweight and usually wheezing, was past it. Past working, past everything. As Tommy said, though, the one thing he did still possess was a shrewd brain. 'Where others rush in, Fred ponders.' Not that there'd be much to ponder here, thought Mark. They were simply replacing old lamps for new. It would mean taking the old ones down, drilling the ceilings for new fixings and hanging the fluorescent fittings. He doubted Fred could manage the steps.

'Good weekend?' Fred leaned forward, handed Mark his jar of coffee and broke wind simultaneously.

'Aye.'

'Sorry, lad. It's the missus. Brussels sprouts Sundays.'

Mark carefully spooned coffee into two cups and poured in water. The door opened. Tommy walked in and stepped back apace.

'Jesus. You could cut through that with a knife.' He glared at Mark.

Maggie appeared, stepping briefly into the kitchen to collect a tea-towel from the worktop. She smiled and left without comment.

Tommy shook his head. 'That woman is tact personified. Either that or she has no sense of smell. Either way, I'd like to rattle her cage.' He sat down. 'Tea for me, Mark, ta.' Mark reached for a cup. 'No more of those, eh. Y'never know who's gonna walk in here.'

'Hands up, I'm guilty.' Fred delved into his bag and pulled out his sarnies. He opened them, the unmistakable smell of eggs permeated the air.

'Hens' farts again,' he declared.

'You could always do your own sandwiches, Fred,' said Tommy, taking the *Daily Mirror* from his sack.

'What? Keep a dog and bark meself?'

They settled down with their drinks and snacks, the only sound the clunk of the electric wall clock's pointer clicking every minute. Inevitably, Mark's thoughts turned to Beryl: her open coat and the warmth of her body when she pushed herself against him against the wall at the back of the Club. Fred's voice broke the spell.

'Get yer leg over at the weekend, did yer?'

'Might've.'

Fred laughed. 'Oh aye. That means you didn't. He still thinks it's for pissin' over high walls,' he added, apparently for Tommy's benefit.

'If the Lord made anything better than sex he kept it for himself,' said Tommy, without taking his eyes from his *Mirror*.

'What did you do at the weekend, Mark lad?' asked Fred. 'Anything you'd be ashamed to tell your ma about?'

'Look at this,' said Tommy, interrupting. 'Says here, fifteen thousand Ban the Bomb protesters were in Trafalgar Square. How can they ban the bomb when the Ruskies have just let another one off?' They're even building a bloody wall across Berlin.'

'Nothin' exciting,' Mark reported, for Fred's benefit.

'They should stick with sending them astronauts into space, if you ask me,' said Tommy. 'Then they can all go and live on the bloody moon.'

'Cosmonauts,' said Mark.

Tommy lowered his newspaper. 'What?'

'Cosmonauts. The Americans are the ones with the astronauts.'

'They're all the bloody same.'

The door opened suddenly. Mark was smitten instantly by the young woman who appeared. She was nineteen-ish, with dark brown hair and brown eyes. She glanced confidently around the kitchen, her eyes resting on all three occupants in turn before she stated her business. 'Sorry to interrupt. It's just Mrs Dellow wants to know how long the electricity will be off upstairs.'

'Not long, darlin',' Fred told her. 'I'll be up soon as I've had me coffee.'

'Okay,' she purred, making to close the door.

'Want a cuppa?' asked Fred.

She smiled. 'No thanks. Just had one.' She was looking at Mark.

'His name's Mark,' Fred told her. 'He's shy, but he's available.'

She laughed. 'I'm Marie,' she said, directing the information at Mark.

'And what did you do at the weekend, Marie?' asked Fred.

She shrugged her shoulders, before adding matter-of-factly, 'Went dancing with my friend. To the Oxford.' She looked at Mark. 'Do you ever go there?'

'No, but I'm planning to go to Partners. Do you know it?'

'Yes. We had dancing lessons there. Proper ones you have to pay for.'

There was the sound of someone calling.

'Oh-oh. Her ladyship. Must go.' She disappeared, pulling the door to.

'There y'are,' said Fred. 'She's keen on you, I can tell. That right, Tommy?'

'It says here,' said Tommy without looking up from his newspaper, 'the youngest Tory MP is a woman called Thatcher. A *woman*.' He stood up, folded his paper and shook his head. 'What's the point of havin' a woman MP? I'd never vote for a woman, that's for certain.'

'She could make prime minister,' Fred ventured.

Tommy laughed. 'Pigs'll fly.'

The stepladders were extraordinarily high. But they were sound and rigid. Mark had no fear of falling off. He was not afraid of heights.

He looked about apprehensively. Not at the prospect of perching on top of the ladders, dismantling electric light fittings. It's just that when he opened the door to the main office, where before there had been empty chairs, now there was a sea of heads and the clattering of type-writers. The heads would all be turned his way the minute he climbed the ladders; Women and girls, all eyeing him up. He felt his face going red just at the prospect of it.

Tommy had told him to place the stepladders as best he could among the heads and shimmy up to each light fitting; they wouldn't be stopping work on his behalf. 'Make haste,' he told him; he and Fred couldn't put the new fittings up until he had started to take the old ones down. So they allowed Mark a half-hour to get cracking, whilst they unwrapped and inspected the new fittings. 'It smells like a Fili-pino brothel in there,' said Fred encouragingly. 'The smell of all that makeup will float right up to the ceiling. Y'lucky bugger.'

Before venturing into the main office Mark removed his overalls. It would be warm work on top of the steps. Then he collected the steplad-ders and entered the main office. He paused, expecting to be the focus of curious attention. Instead, other than one or two casual glances, there appeared to be no interest in him at all. He manoeuvred the steps carefully, opened them under the first light fitting and placed them next to one of the desks. Its occupant was a woman in her mid-twenties who ignored him completely and continued to type, her eyes focused on documents set to one side on her desk. Mark watched her fingers on the keyboard. They seemed more mechanical than human. She never once looked up from her work. All around him was the same.

He checked his pockets: screwdriver, insulated pliers. A final glance around the room showed no-one was taking the slightest notice of him. He climbed the steps, almost to the top, until his head was almost touching the ceiling. Scanning the room from his vantage point to see if anyone was watching, to his astonishment every face was now raised in his direction. Typewriters were silent; the junior office clerk had stopped on the way to somewhere; a deafening silence pervaded the room. Work at Murchison and Co had ceased.

He was surprised to find the experience quite pleasing, his embarrassment slipping away like water down a drain. The faces bore the looks of interest. There were no snide remarks, which he might have endured had they belonged to, say, a group of welders or fitters in a factory. He felt calm as he started to unscrew the ceiling rose. He imagined he was a sex object, a male Brigitte Bardot, the typists' Stoll experience. But then, after a few minutes he glanced down to find only one or two still casually looking his way; otherwise the typists of Murchison and Co had returned to their work.

Tommy appeared. 'How y'doing?' he asked, peering up to the now vacant space above. Mark said he was fine, that the ceiling rose had offered no resistance. 'If they do don't worry about it,' said Tommy. 'Just break them. They're scrap anyway.' As Mark went to move the steps, Tommy lingered. 'You're probably wondering why Fred's here,' he said. 'He's ill, lad. That's why. He's got cancer. Smudger said to keep an eye on him.' He said it so matter-of-fact it sounded uncaring. 'Keep it to yourself though. OK?' Mark, perplexed, nodded. 'Lung cancer,' Tommy explained. 'Smoked all his life.' He raised his nicotine-stained fingers and looked at them reflectively. 'Must give it up myself. Bloody cancer sticks.'

Fred appeared. 'C'mon,' said Tommy, walking off. Fred followed. Mark moved the steps. It was time to dismantle the next light fitting.

Now he was part of the scenery interest in him had faded. His thoughts wandered from Beryl to Connie, then to Marie, whom he had not seen for an hour or so. She didn't appear to be anywhere in the main office. Moving forward, following the line of light fittings, Mark noticed a desk he'd not seen before. It was tucked into a corner of the office, hidden from view until now. And there, concentrating on her work, sat Marie.

He looked at her for a while, expecting her to look up and see him at any moment. Instead, her eyes remained focused on her desktop. He wanted her to see him, and to know her reaction if she did. After waiting in vain he picked up the stepladders and, bypassing the next two fittings in line for dismantling, he placed them purposefully alongside her desk. Even then she did not look up. He coughed quietly, and spoke to her directly.

'Sorry to interrupt.'

She raised her head, showing him a look of surprise, before smiling and waiting for him to speak again.

'Got to take this fitting down.' He looked up to the light fitting above. It was obvious that he wouldn't be able to reach it unless her desk was moved out of the way.

'Oh, of course.' She stood up. She was, he decided, exquisitely lovely. 'We can move it together, yes?' She slid her fingers under the desktop. He did the same, and they carefully moved the desk a yard or so to one side.

'Well...' She surveyed the scene for a moment, noting that it was now impossible for her to continue working until the desk was replaced. 'Sorry,' was all he could say. In truth, he was lost for words. 'Might as well have my break, then,' she declared, stepping aside as if to go. 'Would you like a coffee?' He said he would: milk, no sugar. 'Sweet enough already,' she purred, before strutting off in the direction of the kitchen.

Mark climbed the stepladders, finding the ceiling rose was painted over so he was unable to unscrew the cover. He tapped it with his pliers before deliberately breaking it, only to find he couldn't undo either of the two screws that held it in place. To get more leverage he clambered to the platform on top of the steps, now having no hold against falling. When the screw gave suddenly the steps wobbled dramatically as he struggled to maintain balance. Then, unexpectedly, they steadied, and he was able to stand down a couple of steps and grip the sides in relief. Looking down, he saw the anxious face of Marie looking up, her hands gripping the steps. She smiled and nodded encouragement as he reached up and managed to undo the remaining screw.

'Thanks for that,' he said, after climbing down to floor level again. She handed him a mug of coffee. 'That's alright,' she declared, lingering as though waiting for him to speak. He wanted to speak but he couldn't think of what to say. After taking sips they made prolonged eye contact until, at last, she laughed out loud at his obvious shyness.

'D'you still go to Partners?' he asked weakly.

'Yes, sometimes, but not for lessons. That all ended last year. We go to the Oxford now, nice and early on Saturday nights. You have to go early to dance, before the drunks start arriving.'

'You go with your boyfriend?'

'Oh no. With a friend. We have the same dancing partners we learnt with. But they aren't our boyfriends or anything. You should learn to dance too,' she added, 'then we could dance together. You could learn at Partners on Saturday nights. Quickstep, foxtrot and tango.' She was just two feet away, looking right into his face. She never took her eyes away, just kept looking right at him. He had never seen anyone so lovely. He wondered where he could go from here. She could dance; he couldn't. She was brimming with self-confidence; he wasn't.

She plonked her coffee on to the desk. 'Oh-oh, her ladyship. And she's looking my way. Sorry.' With that she headed off across the floor, and spoke to a stout, authoritative-looking woman before hurrying from the office. The stout woman looked up at the ceiling, at the places where the light fittings had been, then towards Tommy, who was up another stepladder being held by Fred. Then she turned and followed Marie from the room.

Mark did not see Marie again that day, nor the rest of the week. He was told that she had been sent temporarily elsewhere, which was normal practice. Fred went sick on the Tuesday, and remained so the rest of the week which passed uneventfully, except that on Wednesday evening Mark had an unexpected surprise.

He had caught the usual bus home after work. When it stopped at the Balloon he was looking out the window, thinking about Connie, when, lo and behold, there she was, on the pavement, chatting to someone. She'd not got off the same bus, he was certain. As he looked, she glanced in his direction and their eyes met simultaneously. He thought he saw the semblance of recognition, a smile even. Then she raised her right forearm slightly, and lifted her hand palm-forward in greeting. It was a momentary gesture, but it was unmistakable. She continued looking at him even as she was speaking to her companion. Finally, as the bus moved off, she looked away. She had recognised him; she had acknowledged him, Mark had no doubt. It was only afterwards that he realised he had not returned her greeting; but he didn't care. It was only a matter of time before she was talking to him. Friday evening, maybe, when he hoped to see her on the bus. This time he wouldn't hesitate; this time he would smile, speak to her if he could, get off the bus if he had to.

All of which reminded him of his encounter with Beryl. Three days had passed since he had smelled her, touched her, felt her hands on him. The chance sighting of Connie had turned him on, made him feel optimistic. And so, when the bus reached Weston, he got off one stop early, at the end of Beryl's street. It was impulsive, silly even. But it seemed the right thing to do. He thought that maybe if he hung around he might see her. He sat on a low wall at the end of her street and waited for twenty minutes before deciding it was futile. She could be anywhere: at home, unaware of his waiting presence; at college or work. Anywhere.

And then, just as he stood up to go, he saw her. She was crossing the road, heading towards him, accompanied by a man and woman whom he thought must be her parents. As she approached he saw her look of recognition; but she hurried past, eyes front, as though he wasn't there, her father and mother casting puzzled looks in his direction. After they passed by he saw her father glance back and speak to her, something like 'Who was that?' perhaps. Calling for her now was out of the question. He turned and headed for home, his thoughts ranging from the greeting offered by Connie to the frustration he felt at having seen Beryl.

Beryl. Marie. Connie. They vied for position in his thoughts as he turned up the Terrace. When he opened the front door Bob had news: Billy had flown home, and, sure enough, there he was, resplendent in his new cage. The bad news was, he was swearing, but Mark didn't care. Things were on the up.

4

Although Mark was disappointed at not seeing Marie again that week, he felt confident he would encounter her at Partners or the Oxford. By now he was on familiar terms with most of the women in the office, as was Tommy, who, although attracted to just about every one nevertheless told Mark to 'Keep your eyes at home, lad' if he stole a glance at someone in high-heels crossing the office floor. On one occasion Tommy raised his hand, pointed to the gold ring on his finger and declared, 'If it wasn't for this…'. His nicotine-stained fingers would have turned most women off anyway, Mark thought.

At tea-break on Friday Tommy looked up from his *Mirror* and declared, 'We'll be finished by mid-day.' He took a sip of his tea without taking his eyes from his newspaper. 'We'll have a flier, Mark me boy. An' right an' all. We're at the gasworks on Monday. That'll be fun, I can tell you. Straight home mind. No hangin' about town.'

'A flier?'

'Look.' Tommy lowered the *Mirror*. 'There's no point going back to the workshop.' He shrugged. 'So we'll have a flier. Don't worry. You won't get the sack. You should be pleased to be working with such a considerate mate.' With that he returned to his newspaper, at the same time taking a bite from his sandwich. Clearly there was nothing else to be said. Having half a day off was all very well, but what about Connie and the hoped-for encounter on the bus? Tommy looked none too pleased at his apparent disappointment. 'Christ. Why are you looking so pissed off? Anybody else would be chuffed to have some time off.' He went back to his *Mirror*. It was fait accompli.

Once again girls vied for position in Mark's thoughts as he strode up the Terrace. But if their combined presence in his sexually-active mind left him frustrated, his heart sank on nearing home at the sight of the car pulled up at the back gate. He recognised the black Ford Popular from two-hundred yards. Aunt Ettie was here. And so would be Avril, her darling daughter, he had no doubt. Beryl, Marie and Connie kept disappearing over the horizon, but fag-ash Avril and her ghastly mother were waiting on a day when he would normally still be at work.

He considered walking past his house but Ada appeared for a lean over her gate with a 'Hi Mark', and that was that. Crossing the yard, he recalled what he had heard her say as he stood waiting for Beryl outside the Club. 'He was waiting in the lav', she'd said. He was wondering who 'he' was as he opened the living room door to find, as expected, Mam, Ettie and Avril sitting in a fog of cigarette smoke. They fell silent on his arrival, and looked at him as one, surprised at his unexpected appearance.

'Aunt Ettie and Avril are here,' Mam declared, unnecessarily.

Ettie wasn't really his aunt, but an old friend of Mam's. He'd known her as Aunt Ettie since he was a child. Bob called her Aunt Enema: 'She gives me the runs. I run here, there, anywhere to get away from her.'

Ettie drew on her cigarette. 'And how are we today, young Mark?' she enquired. He felt like telling her about his tryst with Beryl, how he'd ran off with his pants round his knees, but he held his tongue.

'Say hello to Avril, then,' said Mam.

Mark nodded curtly in Avril's direction, and noticed Mam's face had turned into a scowl. 'I was wanting a word with you about our Billy,' she declared, before addressing her next remark to Ettie. 'Billy's been learnt to swear, y'know.'

Three pairs of eyes focused eagerly on Mark; three pairs of ears awaited his response to what amounted to an accusation. His first thought was to deny teaching Billy to swear, but he considered it would not be believed; his second was to truthfully lay the blame with his brother, but he was no snitch – although he may have done had Bob been present. 'Maybe someone taught him after he escaped,' he ventured. Mam frowned but said nothing. Instead she changed the subject.

'Our Mark is going to go to ballroom dancing lessons.'

Ettie beamed. 'Ee, that's just what you were on about. Isn't it, our Av?'

Avril nodded imperceptibly, her ciggy smouldering in her right hand, smoke curling up her sleeve.

'Why don't you take Avril with you?' Mam asked.

'I'm goin' with me mates,' he replied.

'Kevin Marsh?'

'No, Julian. He's gonna ask his mam.'

Just then Avril leant forward and threw her stumpy fag-end into the fire. Mark took the opportunity to flee upstairs.

In his room he lay on his bed and looked up at the cobweb. A minute creature was caught in the gossamer. It struggled weakly to escape. No sign of Mr Spider. He lay there, still in his work clothes, thinking about girls. Especially the three girls who were constantly at the forefront of his mind. As he drifted into slumber there was a gentle tap at the door. Surprised, he sprung up sharply and opened it to find Avril on the landing.

'Your mam says do you want a cup of tea?' She spoke in hushed tones, as though what she had to say was a secret.

'No,' Mark replied simply, stepping back to close the door.

'Are you really going to dancing lessons?' she asked, standing her ground. 'It's just I want to learn as well.'

She was standing in semi-darkness, her huge bosom just visible, as though held by an invisible strap draped about her neck. He lifted his gaze to her face, and focused on her eyelids. They seemed to be too big, mechanical even, as though they were on hinges. In truth he found her repulsive. He closed the door abruptly in her face, returned to his bed and closed his eyes. He had been enjoying dropping off until the unexpected interruption, but in a moment he was interrupted again.

He opened the door sharply to find Avril was still on the landing.

'Are you sure you don't want a cup of tea?'

'No, I said' he replied, closing the door again. As he lay on his bed again, he looked at the hapless creature in the cobweb and thought about tactics.

Going to Partners with his mates had been a throwaway remark for Avril's benefit, but the reality was that Kev wouldn't be interested, and Robbie wasn't into lasses. Julian *might* be keen if he could overcome shyness and get the OK from his mam. Mark knew he liked girls. He'd noticed *Health and Efficiency* magazines in his school satchel. He knew he had a crush on someone called Monica, whoever she was. He – Mark – would have to sell the idea of dancing to his mother. She seemed to like him, so maybe he could.

Positive vibes he had about asking Julian to go to Partners with him now muted into positive thoughts about Connie. It was a mile and a half to the Balloon. He could walk there and wait in the bus shelter across the road and keep an eye out for her. Never mind what she might think if she found him loitering near her stop. He'd dithered enough. He checked his watch. Just a couple of hours to kill. He'd stay in his room, put on some other gear and wait until Aunt Ettie and Avril buggered off then wander down to the Balloon.

It was just before four when he heard the back door and the sound of voices, Aunt Ettie's shrill 'Ta-ra Nancy' announcing imminent departure. He heard the car doors slam, then the engine turn over a few times without starting. Avril will be at my door again, he thought, asking me to give them a push. He was relieved when the motor dragged itself into life. After a few more 'Ta-ras' the car spluttered off.

A few minutes later he slipped downstairs, grabbed his jerkin and headed for the Balloon. Half an hour would do it. He took the public footpath between the gardens, the one that led to the Club – along which he had fled from Walter. As he approached the Club he glanced over to the area at the back, where the empty crates and barrels were. There was no sign of him. He breathed a sigh of relief and headed towards the main road. It was best, he thought, for him not to see Walter for a while, until the embarrassing incident with Beryl had faded from his mind. Even if he hadn't recognised him he would still be wondering who the peeping tom was.

And then, straight ahead, he saw Walter heading towards him. He was still a fair way off, but he knew it was him by the old blue boiler suit and his flat cap. He considered turning round and retracing his steps, but knew that might lead Walter to the accurate conclusion about the identity of the person who had run off with his strides down last Sunday evening. Walter, fat and out of condition, was wheezing from the effort of carrying a heavy shopping bag. He could hear him gasping as they approached each other, his face redder than usual. As they met Walter nodded imperceptibly and continued on his way. Mark breathed a sigh of relief, resolving never to rendezvous with anyone at the back of the Club again. Not even for Beryl's sexual charms.

The bus shelter outside the Balloon had a glass front, convenient to stand behind and look through at buses that stopped opposite. The glass was scratched and smeared, so he wouldn't be easily seen from across the road. A huge poster was stuck on the glass. It had a picture of a litter bin and a message about using it to deposit litter into or be fined. It was wasted on the locals, as old crisp-packets, empty pop bottles and other debris, along with the grubby pages of a newspaper, lay scattered on the ground below. He detected a hint of urine. Blokes coming out the Balloon after last orders, probably. Or maybe it was dogs'. Both probably.

He checked his watch. She should be here about five, he thought. Now ten to. Then he started to have misgivings again. What would she think of him appearing unexpectedly with a silly smile on his face? It was one thing to acknowledge him when he was passing, another to find him on the pavement, like an animal stalking his prey. But now a bus was coming, a double-decker from town. It rolled up and stopped. It looked chocker. Half a dozen people got off, but not Connie. A single decker rolled up a few minutes later. One man got off. After a while he checked his watch again. Quarter past five. Time yet. A few minutes later another double-decker stopped. Two or three passengers alighted. Then his heart skipped a beat as he caught sight of the unmistakable red hair. She was on the pavement opposite, looking out for approaching traffic before crossing the road. They would be face to face in just a moment.

Just then a double-decker travelling to town rolled up and stopped at the shelter, blocking his view. Two passengers alighted and hurried off, as at the same time an old lady appeared from nowhere.

'Is this the bus for Gateshead?' she enquired.

Mark nodded, even though he hadn't a clue where it was going. She didn't look convinced.

She hastened to the back of the bus laid a foot on the platform.

'Is this the bus for Gateshead?' she asked the conductor. He nodded and she climbed aboard. Mark heard the bell ring and the bus pulled away, leaving him with a clear view across the road again. But there was no sign of Connie. He rubbed the glass with his sleeve, but he couldn't see her. He hadn't a clue which way she'd gone. He stepped out of the shelter and crossed the road, looking in every direction but to no avail. He re-crossed and looked along the road that ran alongside the Balloon, but could see no sign of her. He crossed the road again, and even paused in the carriageway in his endeavours to catch sight of her. He had good vision in all directions, yet she had disappeared. He lingered, hoping that somehow she might reappear, but she'd gone, vanished. Or so it seemed.

He didn't know whether to feel disappointment or relief, and slowly headed back to Weston, telling himself that he'd see her on the bus again and next time it would be more natural to approach her than appearing from across the road at her stop. Thus cheered, he quickened his pace as he headed for Julian's. The worst that could happen when asked if he wanted to go to Partners was that Julian or his mother would say no.

From the bedroom window of her parents' flat above the Balloon, she watched in amazement as the young chap she saw on the bus from time to time crossed and re-crossed the road outside. He appeared to be looking for someone. She wondered if it might be her, and smiled at the thought. She hoped so. She quite fancied him actually.

***

Returning home from work, Carol spotted the letter the moment she opened the door. It lay in the centre of the doormat. Picking it up, she saw it bore her name and address in typed lettering. She thought Dad would've picked it up by now. He was still off work and she wondered why he hadn't. She soon had her answer.

'That you, pet?'

His voice came from upstairs. Nearly five o'clock and he was just getting out of bed.

'Yes, dad.'

She wandered through to the kitchen, filled the kettle and checked the name and address again; yes, it was addressed to her. She tore the envelope open. The letter was in Mam's handwriting and it was brief: 'Hello pet. Just a line to let you know I am well and thinking about you. I am missing you. I hope you are looking after your father. Don't show him this letter. I need time to sort things out. Mam.'

***

'Do they served alcohol?'

Mrs Popham was sitting on a posh-looking settee, looking intently at Mark. He and Julian occupied the two easy chairs in the well-furnished room. In the hall, just audible, came the soft chimes of the wall clock marking the hour: six o'clock. This was followed by the sound of the front door closing, Arthur Popham arriving home from work late from the bank where he worked in Newcastle or somewhere. He stuck his head round the open door. 'Hello love. Hello son. Hello Mark.' Then he disappeared. Almost immediately the sound of classical music could be heard, emanating from somewhere in the house.

'It's just that you boys are too young to be drinking. And maybe too young to be where others are drinking too.'

Whether or not Partners sold booze had never occurred to Mark. Maybe they did, maybe they didn't. He wanted to learn to dance; he wanted to learn to dance to meet girls. He didn't care about alcohol. He assured her drinking was not on his agenda. Partners in Newcastle gave dancing lessons for an hour on Saturday evenings, followed by dancing itself until eleven o'clock. It was ballroom dancing. Not that rock and roll stuff, teddy-boys in drainpipe trousers, crepe-soled shoes and things.

'Eleven o'clock? I expect our Julian to be home by eleven o'clock.'

Mark held his tongue. Julian looked too scared to say anything even if he had wanted to.

She sipped her tea. 'Well,' she said at last, 'you are a good boy Mark and if you and Julian want to learn to dance I suppose that should be alright.' It was hardly convincing, but it was encouraging. 'When are you going?' she asked, as if hoping Mark would say it wouldn't be for weeks yet.

'Tomorrow.' Tomorrow was Saturday. 'That's if Julian can make it.' Julian nodded. His mam had given consent. Game over.

'Well, I have to cook tea, and I expect you'll be wanting yours.' Doris Popham stood up, placed her teacup and saucer on a small table and waited for Mark to do the same.

'What time tomorrow?' Julian enquired. Mark said he would call at six. Lessons started at seven. That would give them plenty of time. They'd have to wear a suit, and collar and tie of course.

Mrs Popham stepped from the room and opened the door into the porch. Mark followed. 'You boys are growing up so fast,' she said. She gave him a lingering look with close eye contact. 'Well, see you tomorrow.' She held the door, leaving a space so narrow Mark had to squeeze past. He smiled and left. Homeward bound, he felt pleased with himself. Bob was right. Dancing was a great idea. Meeting girls was better than looking at them at the Stoll. His stomach rumbled. Mrs Popham was right about it being time for tea, too.

Saturday morning. The smell of bacon and egg brought him downstairs. Not even sexy thoughts about girls could compete with that, not this Saturday morning anyway. Mam asked him if he wanted black pud. As though she needed to. He sludged his bread around the runny egg yolks, sliced the rind from the bacon then ate it anyway and washed it all down with tea from his half-pint pot. Then he sat down to take stock.

He'd knock on Kev. Ask him if he fancied Partners, but Julian was coming like it or not. He, Kev, would probably be seeing Betty or whatever her name was anyway. Her mate, Rita, could look like Tommo's horse for all he knew; Mark wasn't interested. Kev would've picked the good looking one for sure. He'd noticed that about lasses in twos: one always a good-looker, the other an also-ran. Well, he'd find his own at the dance, and there was always Beryl, Marie and Connie in the pipeline.

'I'm just popping to the shop,' Mam called out. She had her coat on and was carrying her shopping bag. That meant she was going to Mrs Armitage's. Butterflies fluttered in Mark's belly at the thought of what Mrs Armitage might be telling his mother in five minutes' time: 'Hello Nancy. Saw your Mark the other night. Running from the club with his strides round his knees and a hard on fit for a horse.' He tried to apply his brother's philosophy; 'Never worry about something if you can't do owt about it.' Well, he couldn't do owt about it, but he was still worried. As Mam took her purse from the sideboard drawer, he fancied she hesitated, probably at the sight of *Lady* Chatterley. Then she hurried out, leaving him to the happy sounds of Billy, chuntering in his new cage. Squawk, tweet, ping mirror, flap, shit, up-yer-bum-mum.

A minute or so later the knock at the door was barely audible. He opened it to see Beryl, radiant in tight sweater under her open coat. She was smiling. 'Surprise, surprise.' She almost sang the words. Mark couldn't find a reply. Instead, he just looked at her.

'You look like you've seen a ghost,' she ventured.

Mark didn't know about ghosts, only what Mam would have to say in front of the cause of his embarrassment if Mrs Armitage blabbed.

'Sorry about the other day, not speaking to you. That was my mam and dad I was with.'

'My mam'll be here in a minute,' he said, looking anxiously at the back gate.

'So? Does she bite?' She was looking up at him, her eyes instruments that demanded attention. It was a defiant look, an I'm-not-afraid-of-anything look. When he hesitated she asked, 'What's wrong? Are you ashamed of me or something?'

He shook his head, looking at her, then the back gate then her again.

She shrugged and stepped back half a pace, her smile changing to a look of contempt. 'I came round to say sorry, actually. I mean, at the Club. Leaving you like that. With your trousers down.' She giggled then, and briefly put her fingertips to her mouth as though to stifle further comment.

'It's okay. I managed to get away.' He was looking at the gate again. Still she lingered.

'So did you intend seeing me again?'

He nodded. 'I didn't know how to contact you. I didn't know if it was okay to call at your house.'

Suddenly Mam's grey hair appeared at the back gate. Turning, Beryl smiled. He was mortified at the thought that Mrs Armitage might have said something, thinking it would be amazing if she had and the girl he'd been with on the night happened to be standing right here, right now, in their backyard. Mam said 'Hello pet,' to Beryl and brushed past Mark and into the kitchen. He stepped outside then, and pulled the door to.

'I wondered if you fancied the pictures,' she ventured.

'The pictures? What about Tom Clark?'

'He won't know. If I don't tell him.' She added the last part slowly, as though it was an afterthought. 'Tuesday would be nice,' she was saying. 'I was thinking of the Odeon.'

He nodded. 'Okay. Tuesday. See you there?'

She nodded. 'At seven. Don't you dare stand me up.' With that she turned and walked briskly to the gate, where she turned and flashed him a smile.

'What's on anyway?' he called, almost as an afterthought.

'Does it matter?' she called back before disappearing from sight.

With mixed feelings he stepped into the kitchen. Mam was sorting groceries. 'Who was that?' she asked, casually yet firmly enough to require an answer. 'Just some lass,' he ventured, grabbing his jacket from behind the door. Beryl looked young, that's what Mam would be thinking. And he should be past getting involved with schoolgirls. Without further ado he scarpered, wondering, as he headed for Kev's, why it was that his life when it came to girls was so bloody complicated.

Kev opened his toolbox lid and took out a feeler gauge. He measured the gap in the plug. 'Bit delicate this. Just like touching up Betty.'

Mark had wondered if Kev might be interested in going to Partners. But as he was working on his motorcycle...

'You're seeing her tonight I take it.'

Kev nodded, threw the plug contemptuously on to the lawn and picked up a new one. 'What about you?'

'Partners. With Julian.'

'Get on. Is his ma comin'?'

'I'd wondered if you wanted to come.' Kev's face gave suitable reply.

Kev crouched low, started inserting the new plug. 'I don't know why you're going in for this dancing crap. You could've had your leg over with Rita if you'd wanted. Save getting dressed up and going through that "May I have the pleasure?" stuff. Too late now though. Rita's got the right hump with you, according to Betty.' He tightened the plug and stood up. 'Mind, that Beryl's bonny. Wouldn't mind a taste myself.'

'Tea, Kevin!' Mrs Marsh carefully placed a mug of tea on the front doorstep. She saw Mark. 'How's your ma, Marky?' she enquired. She was fine, Mark told her, as she retreated into the house. Kev started packing his tools away. The moggy appeared, sniffed the discarded spark plug and moved on.

5

As *Wheels Cha-Cha* played, Mark and Julian waited for the one hour's 'free tuition', lost souls in a jungle of bodies. Everyone present, Mark thought, seemed to be in familiar, to them, surroundings; others were strangers in the night. Most were late teens or early twenties, a few were older. A couple of blokes looked past it. Late forties at least.

Most importantly, as far as Mark was concerned, there were girls. Happy, smiling, sexy girls. Some queued at the downstairs cloakroom, patiently waiting to hand in their coats. Others, emerging, wore smart dresses, some carrying dancing shoes, clasped tightly to show the world they were here to dance and they were serious about it. The most tangible thing, he thought, was the smell of perfume and makeup. When Mam applied makeup, not that she did much but a visit to the Club would merit a once-over, he never cared for the smell. But here the smell was of sex. As he and Julian made for the stairs, Mark noticed a few guys standing by the door, eyeing up the field before they even got to the dance floor. A crafty tactic, he thought.

They went upstairs, surrounded by girls on the narrow staircase. A long dance floor of hard, polished wood led off from the top. Two giggling young lasses were cha-cha-ing to *Wheels*, having their own little fling before the action started. Most of the girls, Mark noted, were in pairs. Only a few were with boyfriends. He thought there were around thirty in the room, a few less lads. Fine by him.

Julian said something but his words were drowned by the music. Mark stooped slightly, and cocked an ear, inviting Julian to repeat what he had said. Just then *Wheels* terminated abruptly, the needle scraping noisily across the record. Silence reigned for a moment, and those who knew the form moved over to the perimeter of the room. A quiet hubbub of voices lasted for two or three minutes, before a short, dapper man, fifty-ish appeared, walking with purpose to the centre of the room. He was wearing a light-grey suit and smart, shiny black shoes with steel-tipped heels that clicked sharply on the wooden floor. He was smiling, he looked confident. He stopped sharply and pirouetted, clasping his hands as he looked to all four points of the compass and then spoke in a loud, clear voice.

'All-righteeee!' He pirouetted again. 'Lads along *that* wall, lasses along *that* wall.' Bodies moved. Mark and Julian, being at the correct wall, remained where they stood. Opposite was a long line of females. Then the man broke into song. 'You may see a stranger...across a crowded room...'. He broke off abruptly, leaving the room in total silence, and pausing before addressing his eager audience.

'My name is Ken, and this...' he paused dramatically, and gestured to a woman who stepped forward at the far end of the room. She was wearing a long dress and had long, light brown hair. 'And I'm Val,' she trilled, her voice upbeat, like Ken's. She was smiling and looked rapturously happy.

'The *beautiful* Val,' Ken declared, pausing during the muted laughter that followed. 'Val and I have been married, oh, fifty years. That right, my love?'

'Not quite.' She forced a laugh.

'Feels like Fifty,' said Ken, directing his remark to the male side of the room to muted response. His remark earned him a few smiles. He got back to the point. 'This is a *beginner's* course. That's a course for beginners.' He waited in vain for laughter. 'Anyone not a beginner?' As he spoke he spun on his heels, hands clasped tightly together. 'We were beginners once. Right, Val?'

'We certainly were,' replied Val, beaming.

'Right,' said Ken. So don't worry about tripping over your feet or falling on your head.' He paused again to faint laughter. 'Val and I met doing a waltz. That's what ballroom dancing can do for *you*. But I can see some shy faces, so just to break the ice…would anyone care to shout out a name?'

Silence reigned.

'Come on. Any takers?' He looked to one side of the room, then the other, inviting someone – anyone – to speak up. 'Ah! Gent with his hand up.'

'Roger.' The voice came from an unseen male further along the wall. Ken looked for its owner in what to him would be a sea of faces. 'Thanks, *Roger*,' he replied before spinning dramatically to face the girls. 'Ladies?'

Val cackled into life. 'Anyone?' From somewhere came the faintest of replies.

'Rose.'

'Didn't catch that luvvie.' Ken cupped a hand to his ear.

'Rose.' It came again, scarcely louder. Ken was in song again. 'Just a rose in a garden of weeds…'

'What a tosser,' Mark whispered to Julian.

'I'd rather be at the flicks than here,' Julian muttered into Mark's ear. But Ken was engaging gear.

'Right. Gents, I will be looking after *you*.' He lowered his voice conspiratorially. 'Not as desirable as the lovely Val, but…' He raised his voice again. 'Val?' Val stepped towards the ladies. Ken stepped towards the men, still clasping his hands. 'Gentlemen. If you'll kindly line up in single file.'

Feet shuffled as the male contingent stretched out along the wall. 'It's like a bloody identification parade,' whispered Mark to Julian, but loud enough for Ken to turn his head and bark out sergeant major fashion: 'Silence that man. I'm in charge.' Faint laughter rolled along the line. Ken returned to the business in hand.

'Right, gents. I want you to stand with your backs to the wall. And, it's difficult I know, but I want you to ignore the ladies opposite.' Feet shuffled. 'We're going to start you off with a quickstep.' He paused, looked left and right, and continued. 'Now, everyone, say after me:

slow, slow, quick-quick, slow. Let's hear it. Not too loud or you'll put the ladies off. And...' He joined in with the muted response. 'Slow, slow, quick-quick, slow.'

'Good-o. And again, just a little louder this time.' 'Slow, slow, quick-quick, slow.' And again...

They went through it several times, on each occasion being followed by the muted voices of the ladies opposite, going through the same process.

'You'll notice the rhythm. Two slow-slows followed by two quick-quicks, then a final slow. That's the pace, you see. Slow, slow, quick-quick, slow. Let's run through it again, just once more. And...' They were in concert now: slow, slow, quick-quick, slow.

'Now watch me...' Ken turned his back, raised his arms and bent his elbows, his hands holding an imaginary female partner. Then he moved forward, left leg first, his steel-tipped heels clicking on the floor. 'Slow, slow, quick-quick, slow,' he said as he moved. 'Notice I'm on my heels for the slow-slows, on my toes for the quick-quicks.' He demonstrated, crossing the floor gracefully with practised ease. He stopped and looked along the line. 'Now you try it. Say "slow, slow, quick-quick, slow" as you move forward. And remember, heels for the slows, toes for the quick-quicks.' A mass of male bodies slowly, reluctantly, moved forward. The entire process descended into farce as bodies collided and everyone started laughing.

'That's great,' Ken was saying. He shuffled them back into line. 'Come on now, try it again.' He moved forward, demonstrating.

'I feel a right ponce,' said Julian, 'especially with me elbows sticking out.'

'Concentrate that man,' barked Ken, looking in Julian's direction. And so it went on, lasses on one side of the room, lads on the other, slow-slowing and quick-quicking, heels and toes and uplifted arms. Finally Ken called a halt.

'Very good! Now, music, Sidney, per-lease!'

A Victor Sylvester number started up, ran a few minutes and was abruptly terminated. 'Y'hear that?' Ken looked about. Mute faces stared back. 'And again, Sid. Victor Sylvester played again, this time a little longer. 'Now let's do the steps again,' said Ken, 'this time to the music. And remember, this is the quickstep.'

As Victor Sylvester cackled into life again, Ken called out to the entire room. 'Come on, everyone, off you go.' Bodies moved forward, practising recently-learnt steps to the music. The lads moved forward, elbows out, the lasses backward, their arms raised as though held by invisible hands. Mark found it surprisingly easy, as he moved across the floor. After a few minutes, when the music was cut again, Ken addressed the entire room.

'And now, ladies and gents, to see how it's *really* done…May I introduce…Simon and Leanne.' As he spoke a couple swept on to the dance floor, taking huge strides as they launched into the quickstep. 'Simon and Leanne are *professionals*. Watch and learn. Watch and learn.' Ken folded his arms, and looked on with deliberation as the music started up again and Simon and Leanne glided effortlessly across the floor, his right hand around her waist, his left holding her right high in the air. They moved quickly, in perfect time, even dancing lightly on the spot in places before he swept her off again. At times she was leaning so far back it seemed she might fall over. Their faces were expressionless as they held centre stage.

'Good, aren't they?' whispered Julian into Mark's ear.

'I came here to meet lasses,' said Mark. 'Not ponce about like that.'

Everyone watched until, finally, the music ended. There was muted applause as Simon held Leanne's hand, bowing low, she curtsying, each mouthing a silent 'thank you' to one and all. *Wheels* started again as they strode gracefully from the floor, still holding hands.

'Right,' said Ken, clasping his hands together. 'Coffee time. And afterwards we'll practise with *each other.*' There was murmuring as everyone followed Ken into an annexe just off the dance floor. A huge woman was behind a counter, pouring tea. A tall, thin woman was next to her, pouring coffee. Mark and Julian stood centre-floor, surrounded by bodies.

'I've seen mine,' Mark said.

'Her with the glasses?'

'No. She's yours.'

Bodies crushed together. Mark felt the warm flesh of a girl's arm against his hand, whilst another brushed tantalisingly against his arm. Finally they reached the counter. Julian did the honours as Mark stepped back. Turning, he bumped into the person behind. She was holding her cup and saucer gingerly. He could see that coffee had spilled into the saucer.

'Sorry.'

'No harm done!'

'Mark. D'you take sugar?' Julian called from the counter.

'Two, thanks.'

'Sweet tooth – Mark' The girl was smiling. She was short, just over five feet he thought, with mid-brown hair and green eyes that were looking directly into his. *Wheels* ended, leaving only the mangled hubbub of conversation. They stood facing each other for a moment in an awkward silence. She might have turned away. Instead, she held out her right hand.

'I'm Carol.'

She held her hand in place until he nervously clasped it before letting go. She laughed. 'And you're Mark.'

Another girl appeared. 'This is Emma' said Carol. 'Emma this is Mark.' This time a nod sufficed. Julian appeared, carrying two coffees. He handed one to Mark before noticing they had company.

'Hi. I'm Emma.' Julian looked at her as though she was an alien.

'You must have a name Sweetie.' Emma waited for him to answer.

'He's called Julian,' said Mark when none came.

They stood together, sipping their coffees. Mark and Carol with the eye contact, Julian and Emma on different planets. Finally, Mark spluttered into life.

'Do you come here...'

'...often?' said Carol, and they both laughed. An invisible force switched them into relax-mode. 'We're learning to dance,' she said. 'Haven't seen *you* before.' It was their first time, said Mark. She sipped her coffee. 'I suppose you go to the Oxford?' she ventured. Aye, said Mark, instantly regretting the lie. Why did he say it? He didn't know.

'They play good records here, don't they?' said Emma, to no-one in particular.

'I like the Bradford Barn,' said Carol. 'Then you get to meet everyone as you move around the room.' They watched as a few couples moved on to the floor, dancing to Bobby Vee. 'Can you do the Twist?' asked Carol. 'It's all the rage in America. They say it might catch on here.'

Mark was trying to figure out an answer when the music was cut abruptly, and Ken walked briskly on to the dancefloor. He turned to face the crowd. 'Right,' he called out loudly. 'Time for the real thing. A tinkly piano number started up. 'Gentlemen,' take your partners for the quickstep.' No-one moved. 'C'mon now. Don't be shy. They won't bite. Not till you're in the divorce courts anyway.'

A few couples moved on to the floor. Carol placed her now-empty cup on to a table and addressed Mark directly. 'Would you like to dance?' When he hesitated she laughed. 'Come on.'

An invisible hand seemed to be clawing him back. 'I'm not sure how to do it.'

She took his cup, put it down beside hers, and led him by the hand on to the floor and stood facing him. 'I suppose you're used to jiving at the Oxford,' she said. Mark nodded. 'Well, this is just the same really, only with contact.' Her eyes were twinkling, her mouth was smiling. 'You don't mind contact with me, do you?'

As she waited for an answer, their stationary position was causing an obstruction. He felt a surge of panic, anticipating Ken or his wife, whatever her name was, to tell them to get off the floor. Carol just stood there, smiling, waiting. When he didn't speak she almost stood on tiptoe to calmly pass instructions into his ear, her face so close their cheeks almost touched.

'Put your right arm around my waist, just like you were shown.' He laid his hand meekly on her hip. 'Further round my waist,' she repeated, and when he did she took his left hand in her right, and looked up at his face. 'Now push forward with your left foot.' He did as he was bid and they stumbled, across the floor. At one point he trod on her foot, his 'sorry' being dismissed with a smile.

If he looked nervous, it was because he was. But inside he was aroused by the girl whose body was so close, her smell so alluring. They struggled on until the music stopped. 'C'mon,' she said, 'we'll watch the next one.'

They stood at the side of the floor together, in silence, but holding hands. Slowly he felt confident, assured, on equal terms with her. He wanted to speak to her, but couldn't think of what to say. Of Julian there was no sign, but he didn't care. And then, speak of the devil, he appeared, Emma in tow. They all stood together in silence until, at last, the tempo changed to pop. Cliff Richard's voice resonated across the room.

'D'you like Cliff?' Carol bellowed into Mark's ear. He was okay, he called out loudly. 'Elvis?' 'He's my favourite.' 'He's supposed to be coming to England,' she said. 'Would you take me to see him?' 'You bet,' said Mark, who, turning, to face her, all confidence now, shouted, 'Let's dance!'

He led her on to the floor. They jived, looking into each other's faces, before Mark found himself singing along…

'Here I am, there you are,
Together baby we should go far.
Girl like you, boy like me,
Two hearts together like they ought-a-be,
Can't believe I've got a girl like you…'

When the record ended they left the floor. 'You were great,' she said, still with the eye contact. He, holding the contact, replied simply, 'Cos I'm with a girl like you.' It sounded so corny he bit his lip after saying it, but her laugh was the laughter of someone who was enjoying herself.

They sat the Bradford Barn out. Emma was up there, but there was no sign of Julian, until, that is, Mark saw him sitting alone on a line of chairs by the side of the dancefloor. Until just over an hour ago Mark would have loved to be taking part in the Bradford Barn, meeting a new girl every minute, moving round to the music, two steps in, turn, two steps out, move on. A quick chat to every partner, setting down roots for the next dance. But now, with Carol, he was content to watch others, smiling faces all as they moved to the gentle rhythm. When it was over Emma and Julian appeared. Julian looked worried.

'Mark. The last bus. Mam said not to miss it.'

'I'm not going for the bus yet. Have a dance with Emma.'

'Let him go home to his ma,' said Emma. Julian looked away, staring at some non-existent object.

A tango started up. Carol was on her feet. 'C'mon Mark. You'll love this.' She pulled him on to the floor. He said he couldn't do it. She said it didn't matter.

'Put your arm round me. Not like before, *right* round. Now pull me close.' He felt her pelvis hard up against him. 'Now...' As she led off, their bodies could not have been closer; they were almost joined at the hips. He could smell her breath, feel her thighs against his. They moved across the floor, clumsily but happily, blissfully unaware of those who passed by. They were nose to nose, eye to eye, together as one, moving forwards, backwards, anywhere. He longed to kiss her mouth, it was so close, so inviting. Then, face to face, their noses almost touching so he could smell her breath, they bumped into another couple.

'Sorry!' Mark glanced to his left apologetically. He found himself looking at the glaring faces of Simon and Leanne.

'Why don't you watch where you're going?' Simon said crossly.

'Really!' Leanne exclaimed haughtily. 'The only people who should be on the floor are those who can dance.' Mark felt his face redden with embarrassment.

'If you can't dance then you should sit down,' said Simon.

'And leave the floor to those who can,' Leanne added, glowering at Carol.

'Oh, sod off, you tart,' snapped Carol.

Leanne stood, mouth agape. 'Well, *really*...'.

They moved on...

When the music finished Carol and Emma went off to the ladies. Julian appeared, looking as though he might be facing a firing squad when he got home. 'Mark, I have to be going.'

'We're both going,' said Mark. 'That's if you want to take Emma home. Don't worry,' he added, seeing the look on his friend's face. 'I think they live in Jesmond so there'll be a late trolley. We've scored, man. Make the most of it. Better than lookin' at your ma's catalogues, eh?'

It was cold for September. But the night was dry, and the foursome had an uneventful journey to Jesmond. It was made in almost total silence: walking to the bus stop, sitting patiently on the trolley and walking down the road where Carol and Emma lived. Yet for the two couples the experience was totally different: for Mark and Carol, the unspoken words did not detract from the bond that had developed between them; for Julian and Emma, unspoken words merely highlighted the difference, or indifference, between them. As Emma guided Julian across the street towards her house, Mark walked on with Carol until she stopped suddenly at a small gate in the hedge that bordered the tiny garden in front of a terraced house.

'We're here,' she said simply.

The sparse streetlighting meant her face was little more than a shadow to Mark. It didn't matter. He could still feel her sexual presence. She was looking directly at him, her eyes small pools of light in the gloom. She shuddered slightly, pulling her coat collar up.

Mark thought briefly of Beryl, and their tryst outside the Club. The situation now, he thought, was similar. Darkness. A pretty girl. Instant sexual arousal. But the similarity ended there. Beryl was sexy, yes. But this was something different. Where Beryl had launched herself into uninhibited sex, Carol was reserved yet still sexy. He was, quite simply, turned on.

He followed her along the little path that ran up to the front door, just half a dozen paces. Here it was even darker than before, so that now he could barely make out the outline of her head. Yet he could still her eyes were shining. Suddenly she stood on tip-toe and kissed him briefly on the mouth. He went to respond but she drew her head back and laughed quietly. He gently slid his arms about her waist, but not tightly. She was leaning back slightly, her pelvis thrust forward. He was certain she could feel his growing erection.

'Did you like it, then?' she asked. 'Partners that is.'

'Aye. I did.'

'You haven't really been to the Oxford. Have you?'

Mark laughed quietly.

'Will you be there next Saturday? At Partners?'

'If Julian can come.'

'Is that necessary? I mean, can't you come on your own?' She fell silent for a moment. 'Or couldn't you bring another friend?'

'Kev *might* come.'

'Might see you next week then,' she said, standing on tip-toe and kissing him briefly again. He hesitated for a moment, then bent forward and kissed her, a long, lingering kiss that lasted until they finally came up for air. 'Wow,' was all she could say before she stepped back, fumbled in her handbag and produced her key.

'Night-night, then,' she whispered, before opening the door and stepping inside the passage beyond. She was lost in the darkness as she closed the door, leaving him alone and in silence, save for the Westminster chimes of a distant church clock, and sensing a strange yet familiar smell that drifted from inside the house, a smell he could not quite identify. He went to the little gate, closed it behind him, and nearly jumped out of his skin at the sudden sound of Julian's voice. He was waiting in the darkness, the faint glow from the streetlight reflecting off his Brylcreemed hair. They walked together towards the main road for a hoped-for trolley back to town.

'Are you seeing Emma again?' Mark enquired. 'Like next week?'

'D'you think me mam'll let me out next week?' Julian replied. 'And how are we getting home exactly. The last bus will have gone.'

Mark was too happy care. He ran ahead, sprinting, turning and whooping 'Yee-hah', his voice loud enough to wake the neighbours. At the road end he stopped and waited for Julian to play catch-up. 'C'mon,' he cried. 'Here's the last trolley.' And, as they waited, he realised what the familiar smell had been.

It was the smell of booze.

6

Mark stood in the workshop with his bleary-eyed workmates. They all had jobs to go to, but Bert had put them on hold. 'Boss has left a message saying nobody's to go anywhere till he's had a word.' Which boss? Bert didn't know. At 7.30 in the morning, Smudger probably. But eight o'clock had chimed and still they waited. Maybe it was old Robson himself, wanting to speak to a gaggle of apprentices. Either way it was probably a bollocking for some reason or another.

They stood in their donkey jackets and jeans, all carrying weighty haversacks. In the dimly-lit workshop, the sea of heads reminded Mark of a group of parachutists waiting to jump from a bomber taking them over enemy territory, just like in the old war movies. Silent. Pensive. Ready to go. Waiting for the signal. At ten past eight a noise on the other side of the door leading to the offices, out of bounds territory for lads who got their hands dirty, heralded the imminent arrival of someone. The door was located at the top of three steps. Every face looked up to the door. Who would open it? Robson? Smudger?

The handle rattled and the door swung open to reveal the unmistakable profile of Miss Raine, her face in shadow caused by the bright light shining in the corridor behind. She wore a light-coloured top and tight black skirt, and paused, celebrity-like, milking the sexual aura emanating from fifteen or so silent young men who were staring at her.

'There's a telephone call for Mark Green.'

Every head in the room turned at once, every pair of eyes were directed at Mark. He stood still, frozen in time, rapidly feeling his face going beetroot. He uttered not a word as Miss Raine stepped back half a pace, turned and walked away, her hourglass figure silhouetted in the narrow corridor.

'Aye-aye. What's this about then?'

'Look at his face.'

'It has to be crumpet.'

'Dark horse, you, y'bugger.'

They watched, smiles slowly replacing looks of astonishment. One or two lifted their forearms, clenching fists suggestively. Mark clicked into life and followed Miss Raine to her office. She was already seated at her typewriter. When he appeared in the doorway she indicated the posh-looking red telephone receiver, lying on the desk close by where she sat.

'Who is it?' asked Mark.

She shrugged. 'She didn't say.' She? Mark picked up the receiver.

'Hello?' he said uncertainly.

'Hi Mark!' It was the voice of a young woman. When he didn't reply she spoke again. 'Mark. Can you hear me? It's Marie.'

'Marie! Oh. Hi.'

'Sorry I've not seen you. They sent me to our Morpeth branch, and someone told me you'd finished at our Newcastle office. So…'

'Oh.'

Miss Raine temporarily abandoned her typing and tactfully occupied herself with some paperwork.

'Ah, you can't talk. It's just you mentioned going to the pictures. I was thinking the Odeon, Wednesday. If that's OK.'

He hesitated. 'Yes. OK.'

'Great. It's West Side Story. See you at seven outside. 'Bye then.'

''Bye.' Just like that, Mark thought.

He hung up and looked at Miss Raine. 'She sounds nice,' she remarked with a smile. Mark, blushing again, nodded. She was looking directly at him, her wrists resting on the edge of the desk, fingers poised above the typewriter keyboard. They were two people caught up in a moment of time, her eyes twinkling at his embarrassment. Finally, saying 'thank you,' he hurried from the office and back to the workshop, but before the inevitable comments a hush fell with the appearance of Smudger. Mark went down the steps, but Smudger remained at the top, a suitable spot from which to address his audience.

Wearing his battered trilby, he took his time, taking a few drags on his cigarette before speaking in the gravest of tones through a cloud of smoke. They knew it must be serious, as he had discarded his natural Geordie dialect for his foreman's voice.

'Now you lot listen. It's come to my notice, and don't any single one of you deny it, that on some mornings, if not every morning, after you leave here, instead of going diligently about your work, some of you are going to the café in the Haymarket and sitting there drinking tea.' He paused, allowing a moment for the gravity of his message to sink in. 'Well, I'm telling you this. You can drink tea during your tea breaks. But not otherwise in the firm's time. And I'm telling you something else. If Mr Robson or me finds out that you're skiving again you'll be sacked. I hope that's clear.'

An awkward silence followed, after which they all turned to go – but Smudger wasn't finished.

'Just a minute.' They paused as one, some remaining in a half-turned position. 'Bert, pass me the list.' Bert, standing at his counter, reached up and unpinned a sheet of paper from the wooden hatch-frame. He leaned forward and handed it to Horlicks. Horlicks passed it to Smudger.

'As you know, this is a list of your names. It's there so Bert can write down where you are every day, so I know where you are and so I can tell your mammies where you were if ever you have an accident or mysteriously disappear.' He waved it about briefly. Mark thought he looked like Chamberlain waving his piece of paper in the old newsreels. 'The problem is, Bert can't write down where you are on this sheet because some bugger else has written something.' He handed it back to Horlicks, who looked at it for a moment before passing it on. Smudger calmly allowed time for everyone to have a look. When Mark had his turn, he saw that something had been written alongside each name, such as: 'The Dickhead', 'Donkey Davidson', 'Harry the Homo'. His own name had been prefixed by 'Skid'. Alongside Alan Perkins's name was written 'The Greatest'.

Smudger kicked into life again. 'I suppose it's too much to ask who wrote the cryptic comments…' He paused, waiting in vain for someone to admit to the crime. 'Well, enough is enough. I don't want to see any more of this nonsense. That's another reason for the sack, mark my words.' With that he turned, closed the door and disappeared.

No-one said anything, at least until they emerged into the lane, when a few mutterings of complaint were exchanged and someone gave Alan Perkins a kick up the backside. There had been rumours of lay-offs and even sackings through work drying up, so no-one was in any doubt about the sincerity of Smudger's words. They dispersed, and Mark headed off to catch a bus to Walker. The gasworks awaited. As he walked he reflected on his two forthcoming visits to the Odeon to see the same picture twice in two days, on each occasion at the behest of his female acquaintances.

He thought about the three young women who had crept into his life: Beryl, Marie and Connie. They occupied his thoughts from first thing in the morning until last thing at night. In his imagination he had taken them to bed with him, explored their bodies and smelt their skins even as he drifted off into sexual slumber. Yet now, at a stroke, they had been shunted to the sidings by someone else. He could not stop thinking about Carol, of how natural it had seemed to be with her, even though they had just met. She'd smiled, and held his hand, and they'd kissed. She'd be at Partners again next Saturday. He'd be there too. With Julian, Kev, alone. Whatever.

He alighted from the bus and made his way to the gasworks where he found Tommy and Fred in subdued mood. There was none of the usual piss-taking banter, no enquiries of his weekend activities; there wasn't even a tea-break. The reason was soon apparent. Mark found himself in a world of huge steel tanks containing a bubbling mass of strange gaseous liquids. Outside were slag heaps of chemical waste. He thought the site looked like a scene from a science fiction picture, a grim landscape of ash following the destruction of the world. It stank, and Mark realised he would too by the time they'd finished for the day. 'Fart away,' Fred said reassuringly. 'No-one will notice.'

'We're only here two days, thank Christ,' said Tommy, handing Mark a hammer and chisel even though he had his own. 'Use these. You have to use non-ferrous metals to avoid sparks. It's the atmosphere in here. Don't want to be blown to kingdom come, do we.' They were there to install new lighting. 'We'll take our breaks outside, Mark lad. But first you can start by taking the old fittings down.' A series of old glass-covered lights adorned the walls. Removing light fittings was becoming a habit, Mark thought, only this time instead of being surrounded by attractive girls he was standing up a ladder close by the tanks of bubbling gases. Too close for comfort, in fact. Tommy saw him looking. 'Don't fall in,' was his unnecessary advice.

It was a hateful place, devoid of anyone save for Mark and his workmates. He climbed the ladder, removed an old light fitting, then used the non-ferrous hammer and chisel to drill new holes for Rawlplugs. A few sparks shot through the air alarmingly. By the end of the day he felt sick through working inside such a place. Never had he been so relieved to stop work for the day and make his way home, honking so bad he hoped they wouldn't throw him off the bus. When at last he alighted at Weston he gave silent thanks to his brother for installing the new bath. But there was bad news: the bath was out of order, Bob said. Something to do with a blockage in the drain. He washed as best he could and put on clean clothes for his visit to the Odeon.

Beryl awaited, but Mark couldn't stop thinking about Carol.

Carol couldn't stop thinking about Mark.

He was the sole focus – almost – of her every thought. She loved his sparkling blue eyes, his winning smile. He seemed uncertain of himself, yet bore an air of confidence. He'd even sang for her! He, like herself, was a virgin, she was certain. She imagined he would be understanding of any problems, supportive and reassuring. Just the sort of person she'd hoped to meet. Yet even as his image penetrated her mind, so did Mam's. Her letter meant she was well, but where was she, and why didn't she come home? Dad, that's why. Part of her wanted to leave the house, to get on with her life, perhaps with Mark. Part of her wanted to stay, to see her parents reunited, their problems solved.

'Excuse me.'

She looked up to see Joan from accounts standing in front of her desk, clutching a bundle of important-looking documents.

'Miss Carr wants to see you in her office.'

Joan shrugged at Carol's enquiring look and walked off.

Carol went directly to Miss Carr's office, and knocked gently on the open door. Her supervisor, seated at her desk, looked up and gestured 'come in'. When she did Miss Carr walked behind her and closed the door. 'Sit down,' she said. Carol sat and Miss Carr returned to her seat, where she sat looking at some documents without saying anything.

Miss Carr had been with the company for years. She was regarded as a disciplinarian who ran a tight ship. She was in her mid-thirties, tall and thin and possessed boundless energy. Some said she lived to work rather than the other way round. As she waited, Carol's eyes surveyed the office. She'd been in it before, but never with the opportunity to really see it. The office was sparsely furnished, with a bookcase behind Miss Carr's desk. It was packed with paperbacks mainly, with some hardback volumes on the top shelf. A solitary chair stood against the otherwise bare wall on the right hand side of the room. On the left a huge black and white poster-size picture of a glamorous woman adorned the otherwise bare wall. The woman had short, light brown hair and wore a small black hat with a gossamer veil draped over her face, and black gloves. In one hand she held a smoking cigarette. Her piercing eyes stared straight out from the picture. She was undeniably beautiful. A film star of times past, Carol thought.

She began to feel apprehensive, although she could think of no reason to be. Suddenly Miss Carr looked up and spoke. Her accent was 'posh', Carol thought, wondering subconsciously where she was from.

'So! What's the problem then?' said Miss Carr. She obviously meant Carol's problem. Carol couldn't think of what to say.

'Staring vaguely into space may seem fine with you,' Miss Carr was saying, 'but it is of no use whatsoever to me. Or, more to the point, Northern Electricity.'

She was staring straight at Carol, her piercing eyes unwavering as she waited for her subordinate to speak. 'Monday mornings don't suite everyone, I know. But you were the same all last week. Sitting at your desk in a dream. What's the matter? Tell me. I have to know.'

Still Carol was silent.

'Is it boyfriend trouble?' Carol thought the question was put in such a way there would be no sympathy if it was.

Miss Carr sat back resignedly. 'You aren't the first and you won't be the last. But I have to tell you I won't tolerate you bringing problems in your love-life into this office.' She picked up a ballpoint pen and twirled it between her fingers, peering at Carol, waiting for an answer that didn't come.

'Well?'

Carol put her face in her hands and burst into tears. She sobbed for a few moments, until her nose started running. Miss Carr stood up and offered a handkerchief. Carol took it and blew her nose. Miss Carr wasn't letting up. Instead she sat on the edge of the desk next to Carol and waited.

And then, between sobbing and sniffing and with the proffered handkerchief held to her nose, Carol told her about her mam: how she'd left home because of her dad's drunkenness and abuse, and her dad not going to work and turning to drink, and how she had to look after him, and the short note from her mam, saying she was OK and would be in touch shortly. Surprisingly Miss Carr responded by putting a matronly arm around Carol's shoulder, and allowed her all the time she needed to get it all off her chest. Finally, composing herself, Carol lowered her hands to her lap, still clasping the handkerchief, and looked straight ahead, resigned to Miss Carr's response, whatever it was.

It was, simply, that she understood how she must feel and she, Carol, was not to worry, that she was not in trouble. She told her she could go home if she wished. But going home was the last thing Carol wanted: home to either an empty house, or to her dad, who might or might not have decided to get out of bed yet. She would stay at work, she said, and with that thanked Miss Carr for her kindness and walked back to her desk in the main office, where, tolerance of her conduct now being officially accepted, she allowed her thoughts to drift from Mam to Mark. He was something worth thinking about.

Mark stood back from the rain, seeking shelter under the Odeon's wide canopy of bright lights, and checked his watch. A quarter to seven. He was early, but only because the bus had got him into town early. He had not been in a rush to keep his appointment with Beryl.

An early finish at the wretched gasworks had afforded him ample time to think of Carol. Not Beryl. Not of tonight's encounter which, before his visit to Partners on Saturday, would have been his only thought. Not Marie, either, whom he'd agreed, on being taken by surprise, to take to the pictures tomorrow. And not Connie, even though her alluring image still infiltrated his mind. Carol, somehow, was different. He still saw her looking up at him in the dark doorway of her house. He remembered her kisses. And her perfume…

But even Carol couldn't block out the lingering thought of what might have happened at the gasworks that morning. He'd been up the ladders, directly above one of those huge tanks of frothy chemicals, when the ladders had slipped on the floor. Only by a few inches, but the movement was sudden and unexpected and had caught him by surprise. His electrician's pliers had fallen with a dull 'ploop' into the gassy, stinking liquid in the tank below, from which, he knew, there would have been no escape if it had been him. He'd have died of asphyxiation, not drowning. That's what Tommy had told him, and he quite believed it. Or, as Fred had put it, 'If you fall in there Marky, lad, don't expect me to come in after you.'

Well, he'd lived to tell the tale, if he cared to tell it, and he'd gone into town to enjoy the charms of Beryl. He didn't want to go, he told Bob, whose considered opinion was that he should. 'You only met Carol on Saturday night. She mightn't be at the dance next Saturday. In fact you might never see her again. So go and enjoy yourself. West Side Story isn't bad either.'

The Goldsmith's clock chimed seven. No sign of Beryl. He wondered if she was coming. Would he mind if she didn't? Yes, he would, he decided, thinking of her voluptuous breasts and hot kisses. Bob was right. For all he knew he might never see Carol again. For all he knew she knew other blokes. She might even turn up the Odeon tonight. But he was kidding himself; he wished it was Carol he was taking to the pictures. He checked his watch. 7.03. He'd give Beryl until 7.15, then he was going home.

He watched as other couples hurried through the rain, dashing across the street to the sanctuary of the Odeon, where males sought out their wallets and their partners shook water from their coats and umbrellas before going inside on to the thick-piled carpet of the foyer. Maybe the rain's put Beryl off, Mark thought. Or maybe she's thick as thieves with Tom Clark again. Or maybe Kev's been there sniffing. Surely not. The watch again. 7.10. He was cold and he was fed up. He didn't even fancy the picture. He didn't like musicals. He was tempted to go, but resolutely stood his ground. He had resolved to wait until 7.15. Wait he would.

The soft chimes of the Goldsmith's clock finally brought the hour of judgement. He was going. Yet he lingered. He wanted the intimacy with Beryl, just tonight. After tonight there'd be Carol. He was confused. Then, finally, as he was about to walk off into the rain, she appeared in front of him, all smiling and sexy.

'Sorry I'm late.' She shook her umbrella before stepping into a corner under the canopy. She looked lovely, twenty at least. Even in the damp corner by the ticket kiosk he could smell her perfume. 'Bus was late,' she explained. 'It's OK,' she added. 'Doesn't start till half past.' She stepped on to tip-toe, kissed him on the cheek and giggled. He put his hands on to her waist and stooped to kiss her on the mouth. She laughed and turned her head. 'Go on, then, get the tickets. Can we go upstairs in the Circle please?'

He paid, and turned to take her hand. But she'd moved inside, where she'd taken off her coat, revealing a bright red blouse and beige skirt. He saw two young men giving her their undivided attention as they passed with their girlfriends. Another, standing further into the foyer, was staring at her. She smiled and took Mark's hand, leading him up the stairs. In the Circle the usherette showed them to Row 'J' and they squeezed past others couples to their seats.

Mark surveyed the heads around where they sat, young men and women patiently waiting for the lights to go out. Marie had asked for seats in the Circle. She must have been here before, he thought. With Tom Clark, he supposed. As they sat, more couples arrived, obliging those already seated to stand and allow them to pass along the row. Finally everyone was in place, like athletes on starting blocks waiting for the starter's pistol.

Some of the males, Mark noticed, were sitting with their arms around their partner's shoulders. Others, like him and Beryl, sat apart. When, at last, the lights dimmed and the bright Technicolor images on the screen illuminated the auditorium, it was time for Pearl and Dean and the inevitable ads for cosmetics and local restaurants. There was movement all around, some couples embracing, others sitting apart, until a forthcoming film was trailed. It occurred to Mark that every single person present would not have the slightest interest in any of what they were obliged to see and hear before the main feature, which would either entertain them or at least give valid cause for physical contact. When, after a brief period of total darkness, West Side Story began to roll it was as though a straitjacket had been removed and everyone could relax.

He glanced to his left to see Beryl staring directly ahead at the screen. It occurred to him she might not want to engage in petting. Maybe she wanted to enjoy the picture. But even as the credits rolled couples were embracing, so he cautiously slid his arm around her shoulders. She moved slightly towards him, and he to her as far as he could until he felt the hard arm of the seat touching his side. But still she faced the screen, not turning her face to him for the hoped-for kiss. This was the eager girl who had met him behind the Club, who had so excited him by taking the lead. His early endeavours thwarted, he faced forward himself. He would need to take his time and not rush things.

But the smell of her, the softness of her hair against his nose when he turned his head, the knowledge that she was sexually aware, the urge to explore was too great to resist. So, even as she continued to shun him – and by this time everyone seemed to be kissing – he turned slightly and allowed his free hand to stray towards the top of her blouse. There it lingered a short time before the tips of his fingers slowly sought out the buttons, which he deftly flicked open, so that now he could slide his hand underneath the silky fabric. At any moment he expected his hand to be blocked, but she sat impassively, offering no resistance. When his fingers touched the top of her bra, he carefully slid them inside until, at last, his hand covered her breast. It was big and firm. He could feel the nipple in the centre of his palm. They sat awhile, his hand cupped around her breast until, resigned to her apparent indifference, he withdrew his hand and turned his face to the screen again.

Looking down at the heads in front, Mark could see couples in various states of contact. Everyone, it seemed, was having a feel. He wondered if he might slide his hand up Beryl's skirt, and moved it into position just above her knee. But he felt her stiffen and push her knees together in a gesture of obvious reluctance and moved it back to her lap. Finally, exasperated, he withdrew it altogether and watched the film. He was slightly wet in his pants through his early grope, which didn't help his mood, and more than a little relieved when, at last, the film ended and National Anthem heralded the end of the night's entertainment, with every person present standing up respectfully as Her Majesty, dressed in scarlet, rode her white horse in front of Buckingham Palace or somewhere.

They filed out slowly, two people in the throng, many of whom were adjusting clothing and putting on raincoats in anticipation of the weather. When they emerged the rain had stopped, leaving damp pavements and puddles in the road. They caught the bus to Weston, with not a word spoken between them. He was seeing her home when she stopped a few yards short of her front gate and stood in the shadows, facing him. He stooped to kiss her but she turned away.

'What's wrong?' he enquired. 'Didn't you enjoy the pictures?'

She nodded imperceptibly, then stood on tiptoe and kissed his cheek. She stood back a few moments, looking at him. 'I thought tonight was going to be great,' she said, 'but you spoilt it.' She turned, and hurried off, then, reaching her front gate, turned again and called out loudly to him.

'Mark Green, you *stink!*'

The morning after. The usual crew at the bus stop. No-one communicating. That suited Mark, who was lost in his own thoughts. Last night he had told Bob what had happened about Beryl, and once Bob had stopped laughing he had offered the advice which Mark knew was right: that an end to seeing Beryl was for the best. She was too young, probably promiscuous – according to Bob anyway – and just imagine if she got pregnant. It was for the best, said Bob, that she'd effectively terminated their liaison, rather than the other way around. 'Hell hath no fury like a woman scorned,' said Bob, in such a way that led Mark to conclude such a meaningful statement was some sort of catchphrase rather than Bob's own words. But he took the point. It was Beryl who'd walked away. The gasworks had been a two-day nightmare, but had at least provided the Final Solution: no more Beryl.

Then, even as he'd finished talking to Bob, the sound of a motorcycle engine cutting out he knew heralded the unexpected arrival of Kev. He went out to meet him at the gate.

'Hey, Kidda.' Kev closed the gate behind him and came straight to the point. 'Guess what,' he said, and before Mark could he told him what the 'what' was. 'Betty's chucked me,' he declared with a couldn't-care-less shrug. 'Rita was peed off playing gooseberry.' Before Mark could say anything he slapped him on the shoulder. 'Never mind, Kidda. Plenty of fish in the sea, eh. But I haven't come round here just to tell you that. What I was wondering, was, if you're going to that dance place Saturday I wouldn't mind tagging along. Not for that quick-quick-slow stuff, mind. For the lasses. Even if Julian's going.'

'You won't get in wearing your motorbike gear, mind.'

'No prob, Kidda' said Kev. And with that he nodded to Bob and opened the gate. 'Six o'clock to town Saturday then. Best bib and tucker and a packet of three.' He straddled his bike, kicked-started the engine and roared off, his greasy black hair ruffling in the slipstream. As Mark watched him go he reflected on his next problem: another rendezvous at the Odeon; another dose of West Side Story.

He could always stand Marie up, but that wasn't his way and any-way he thought she would probably seek him out for retribution. She knew where he worked. She was utterly lovely, and he told himself he should be flattered she had telephoned him and asked him out.

At work Smudger pulled him to one side, told him Fred was off sick again and that he'd dispatched Tommy to a workingmen's club in Durham somewhere, a big job that Tommy and Mark would be on soon. Today, said Smudger, Mark would be out 'jobbing' – doing repairs locally on his own. He waited for over an hour until Smudger handed him a few slips of paper with customers' details and the work involved, and told him to 'make a good job of them'. Mark checked out the addresses. They were all in walking distance, the first, and closest, in Jesmond. He was half way there before he realised he could go there by a short diversion along Carol's street.

The problem of Marie niggled as he walked. What if Carol found out he'd been to the flicks with her? It was Carol he wanted, after all. He decided to call Marie and call off their meeting tonight, and headed directly to a telephone kiosk and opened the thick directory. Murchison and Co was listed in bold letters. He hesitated, knowing he'd get a right bollocking from Smudger if he found out he'd been making contact with a girl in the firm's time. But then he picked up the receiver and dialled.

'Murchison's,' a female voice almost sang into his ear.

'Could I speak to Marie, please,' he enquired, trying to make it sound as though the call was of a professional nature.

'Just a moment.'

After a half a minute or so a woman's voice cackled into his ear. 'Hello?'

He swallowed nervously. 'Hi Marie. Mark. Look, I can't make it tonight. I can't make it at all. The fact is, I'm seeing someone else and it just wouldn't be right. You know. So, if it's OK with you, I'd rather leave it.'

There was a brief silence before the voice spoke again.

'I'm afraid I haven't faintest idea what you are talking about. If this is a personal call you've got the wrong Marie. You probably mean Marie Titterington.'

'Can I speak to her then?' he replied weakly.

'I'm afraid not. She isn't here, and as her supervisor I should tell you even if she was she shouldn't be taking personal calls at work.'

Mark remembered the stout woman who had spoken to Marie, 'her ladyship', as she had called her. 'Sorry, it was a bit of an emergency,' was the best he could do before replacing the receiver. He fled the kiosk as though her ladyship might appear and chastise him, and hoped she wouldn't guess it was him who had called.

A few minutes later he was in Carol's street. He crossed to her side, and walked alongside the low garden walls and hedges. The terraced houses all looked the same, and he wasn't sure which one was hers. But there was the little gate and the short path leading up to her front door. Just by the gate he stopped and looked directly at the front doorstep, the very spot where, only a few nights ago they had kissed. It was a special place, he thought, shrine-like even. All thoughts of Marie and her supervisor evaporated as he stood there, alone on the pavement. Then, suddenly, the front door opened, and a man appeared. He looked about fifty. He was unshaven and scruffy. The man stood glaring, and seemed about to speak. But Mark wasn't waiting. Instead he hurried off. It was then he remembered the smell of booze when Carol had opened the door and gone inside her house. Was that her dad? he wondered. If so, he didn't care for the look of him at all.

7

Approaching the Odeon, Mark felt hesitant about keeping his appointment with Marie. OK, what young buck wouldn't appreciate sitting in the Upper Circle with her, and never mind the film? Yet still his thoughts were of Carol. One night at a dance, one walking her home, one goodnight kiss had cemented her image in his mind. There was no room for anyone else. But he was here, where he didn't want to be, because he said he would be. So he crossed the road, resolved to wait and when Marie turned up he'd tell her he'd met someone else and he was sorry but at least he hadn't stood her up.

But he wouldn't have to wait for her, as it happened, because she was waiting for him. She stepped forward, smiling, on his approach, her coat falling open to reveal her lovely figure. Kev would have described her as 'serious meat'. He couldn't have argued.

'Hello you!' She stood on tip-toe and pecked his cheek.

'Hi' he said weakly, amazed that she seemed to like him so much. She looked so lovely.

'Quite a rush, after work.' She paused, and he was silent. 'But here we are!'

He relaxed. He wanted to say it was too wonderful an evening to spend at the pictures, that maybe they should be walking by a river, or standing by the sea. But they were here, as she said, and West Side Story was waiting. He fumbled for his wallet, but she touched his arm as he stepped forward to the kiosk. 'Wait' she said. 'I fancy the pictures, but not here.'

'D'you want to go to the Haymarket instead?'

'Actually, I fancy the Stoll.'

The Stoll! Kev's image flashed through his mind. Kev holding imaginary breasts and going 'Haw-haw-haw'. The Stoll, where you went to see X-films. 'What's on?' he asked weakly.

'Does it matter?'

She waited, allowing him time to take in what she had suggested and to respond. 'The Stoll,' she repeated. 'Sexy-exy.' She was smiling again, only this time it was a mischievous, let's-do-something-naughty smile. Then she stood on tiptoe and whispered into his ear. 'Sexy scenes and actors with foreign accents *turn me on.*'

'Okay,' he said, as nonchalantly as possible, and turned to go. When he did she slipped her arm through his, clearly delighted to have got her way. He, equally delighted at the prospect of seeing a sexy film and not to having to endure West Side Story again, came to terms with what was happening: Carol remained in his thoughts, but he reasoned he could manage to get through the next three hours or so without feeling too guilty. As Kev had said on many occasions, 'You only live once Kidda.'

They headed through the city streets in silence before she spoke again.

'Did you call me today?'

The question came unexpectedly as they waited to cross the road. He'd wondered if she might ask, but as she hadn't he thought it likely she wasn't aware of his telephone call. His face gave her the answer.

'I should have told you. Her ladyship doesn't like staff taking personal calls at the office.' She waited a moment, but he was silent. 'Was it to tell me you didn't want to meet up tonight?'

'I'm not sure,' he lied.

She looked at him a moment longer, then smiled. 'Oh, well, we're here now. So…C'mon.'

With that she tugged his arm and nudged him on to the road. A few minutes later they were outside the Stoll. She stood back, waiting for him to buy the tickets. He bought two for the Upper Circle and they stepped into the foyer. 'You are eighteen, I take it?' she said, laughing as they approached the woman inside, who tore their tickets in half and allowed them to proceed. They sat near the back, patiently awaiting the lights to dim and the inevitable Pearl and Dean, and the trailer for a forthcoming French film, The Green Mare's Nest.

Tonight's main feature was also French, with English sub-titles. As the credits rolled he wondered about strategy. In front of them others were already coming to grips, males with arms around their partner's shoulders, a few early kisses. Tentatively he reached out with his left arm. She responded by leaning close to him, expectantly. He felt her relax, and placed his free hand on hers as they lay on her lap. He stole a glance sideways to find her looking at him, the whites of her eyes highlighted in the flickering light. He lifted his hand to her cheek and kissed her mouth. It was a wonderful kiss, soft and warm. She opened her mouth, just as Beryl had done, and there was her tongue. Away somewhere he could hear voices talking in French. He didn't understand what they were saying and didn't care about subtitles. He just wanted the kiss to last forever. He had never known anything so wonderful. Finally they disengaged and came up for air, and turned their faces to the screen.

And then, even as they watched events on-screen, he felt her hand on his crotch, squeezing and rubbing gently. In just a moment he could feel an approaching orgasm, and lay his hand on hers to prevent further movement. As he reached for the buttons on her blouse, she sighed as once again their lips met and their eyes closed, while exotic French voices accompanied their sexual embrace.

Lying in bed in the darkness, the only sound Mark could hear was Bob's heavy breathing and the clank of bottles on Dixon's milk lorry outside. Must be around 4 a.m., he thought, wondering if Mr Spider was active in the top corner. Did spiders hunt in darkness, he wondered? And if they did, did they sometimes lose their grip and fall? Subconsciously he closed his mouth He didn't want an eight-legged creature wriggling around in it.

What a night it had been. He had enjoyed every intimate part of Marie's perfect body, his exploratory fingers even finding their way past the tops of her stockings and beyond as she succumbed to his touch. She'd had no inhibitions, none at all, her final orgasm loud enough to be heard in the gods. No-one seemed to notice, since everyone else seemed to be doing the same thing. Or so it seemed. Outside, he'd offered to take her home. But she had declined, saying they both had work tomorrow and must catch their respective buses home. They embraced in silence in a dark doorway, and parted with no more than his 'I'll give you a call' when she handed him a slip of paper with her telephone number.

That was last night. Now, once again, his thoughts were with Carol. Marie knew what she was doing; she had done it before, it was obvious. It would be just as likely she would be doing it with someone else tonight. That's what he thought. But Carol was different. Carol wanted what he wanted; a loyal and loving relationship. He felt that theirs was a bond that would never be broken, even though, as Bob said, he might never see her again. He knew, too, that he may have made a mistake about seeing Marie. It's just that she sometimes went to Partners; what if she turned up Saturday and he was with Carol? It didn't bear thinking about. As he fell asleep again, his thoughts inevitably drifted back to the haunting memory of Marie's warm, soft thighs.

***

Saturday evening – at last.

Mark hadn't been on a bus with Kev since they were 14-year old newspaper delivery boys. And he'd *never* seen him wearing a suit. It made a change from the silver-studded black leather jacket, oily jeans and the crash helmet, the latter a seemingly permanent feature wherever he went. With his black, Brylcreemed hair and broad shoulders Kev could pass for twenty.

When would Mark be getting a motorbike? Kev enquired. Then they could take Betty and Rita to the Lake District, or stay in his Aunt Hilda's caravan at Warkworth. Soon as I'm eighteen, Mark replied, which was when he would get a pay rise, although there still remained the question of his parents' consent. But motorbikes and lasses were not on Mark's agenda tonight. He could hardly wait to see Carol, although the thrill of his hopefully imminent meeting with her was laced with the worry of Marie turning up at the dance studio. 'Don't worry about it,' was Kev's advice. 'Any probs and I'll step in. If this Marie's as hot as you make out it'll be a pleasure.'

The bus stopped at the Balloon. No sign of Connie. When they alighted at Gallowgate Mark headed towards Partners, but Kev had other ideas. 'C'mon Kidda. Got to get a pint in, eh?' He led Mark directly to the King's Head. Loud music blared from the jukebox as Kev opened the door. The place was packed. Aside from working in licensed premises, it was the first time Mark had ever been in a pub. They pushed their way to the bar. Kev was holding a crisp ten shilling note to attract the barman's attention.

'What's your poison?' He had to shout.

Mark looked at the row of pump-handles on the bar counter. 'Half of shandy, please.'

'Bottle of Broon and a pint of Exhibition, ta,' said Kev to the barman, who was looking at Mark. Or Mark thought he was. If he'd asked his age he'd have confessed to being seventeen. But after plonking the Newcastle Brown Ale on the counter, along with a straight glass, and pouring a pint of Exhibition, he happily accepted Kev's money.

They threaded their way to an unoccupied table in the corner. Kev poured his brown ale into the glass and downed a mouthful. A dollop of froth clung to his nose when he removed the glass. Mark took a sip of the Exhibition. *Runaway* blared. 'Music's great, eh,' Kev shouted above Del Shannon's high-pitched voice. Mark looked around at the crowd of men packed into the large bar, some dressed in jeans and old shirts, others suited up with stiff collars and wearing ties. 'Scruffos are the regular pissheads, Smarties are for the Oxford,' Kev explained. Or Partners, Mark thought. Kev clunked his already empty glass against the equally empty brown ale bottle. 'Your round Kidda. Don't worry about the under-eighteen thing. They'd serve a babby here.' Mark, not yet halfway through his pint, gulped it down under his friend's watchful gaze, then pushed his way to the bar counter. He'd order a half shandy this time, but the same barman, seeing him place the empty glasses on the counter served up the same. He returned to the corner to find the table unoccupied, and no sign of Kev. He sat at the table listening abstractedly to the Geordie voices buzzing around his ears, audible now that the music had stopped, temporarily at least. They'd drink up and head for Partners. He couldn't wait to see Carol.

Kev appeared. 'Just stuck Runaway on again,' he declared, pouring the brown ale slowly into the glass, tilting it to avoid too much head. 'We could just go the Oxford if you like,' he said after taking a mouthful. 'There'll be a lot more women there and none of this mamby-pamby dancing lessons crap.' One glance at Mark's face and he dropped the subject with a resigned shrug.

The music came on again, Shirley Bassey's *Reach for the Stars*. With not a woman in the place Mark wondered who put such a dreamy number on, and why. As they sat in silence, Kev's brown ale disappeared rapidly. 'Off to the Gents,' he announced, standing up and disappearing into the throng. Mark was feeling giddy. He sipped the remains of his second pint slowly, waiting for Kev's reappearance. Reappear he did, carrying more booze, *Runaway* blaring again.

'We've to be going,' Mark protested. But he picked the glass up and took a mouthful. It was good. The beer was making him relax. They'd be late at Partners, but it didn't matter, he told himself. They'd miss Ken and Val's free tuition at the start, that's all. He and Carol didn't need that. She wouldn't mind him smelling a little of drink. She'd understand. She'd be fine. And pleased that he'd brought someone for her friend, what was her name again? He couldn't remember. His bladder bursting, he stood up to go to the gents, and when he did his legs almost buckled under him. He steadied himself, brushing against the table. He saw Kev grab his glass, then headed for the toilet, pushing his way through men who stood chatting, pints gripped firmly. He was just in time, and he sighed on relieving himself. Back at the table Kev was waiting, his glass empty. Mark picked his up and swallowed the remainder of his third pint. Kev gestured another, but Mark shook his head and headed for the door. Stepping into the street he felt the fresh air on his face. As he breathed in deeply, everything was spinning around and he momentarily placed a hand on to the wall to steady himself.

The fresh air seemed to combine with the alcohol, making him feel more drunk. He took deep breaths as he walked alongside Kev, and the next thing he knew he was going downstairs somewhere else. Another bar, another group of men. This lot looked spruced up and were in company with smart, attractive women. Kev handed Mark an empty glass and poured something into it from a small bottle. 'Bit more class in here,' he was saying as he poured his own. 'None of your pints. Foreign booze only. Dead exotic.' Mark sipped his drink. It tasted bitter and seemed strong. 'Get it into you,' said Kev. 'Bloody costs plenty.' Mark drank half, finding he couldn't take any more. Kev shrugged, took the glass and downed the remaining contents in one. 'C'mon then,' he declared, 'let's go and meet these lasses of yours.'

Outside, Mark's legs could scarcely carry him as his staggered along the pavement behind his friend. When they entered Partners he could hear the music booming from upstairs. Kev stood aside to allow Mark to lead the way, and made a beeline for the gents whilst Mark went off in search of Carol. He walked alongside the wall where the ladies stood waiting to be asked to dance, then to the tea room where they'd first met, then stood at the side of the dancefloor, scanning the bodies moving to the quickstep. Kev appeared with an expectant look on his face. 'I can't see them,' Mark declared, before shooting off to stand outside the door to the ladies, where he waited in vain for the emergence of Carol. 'She's not here,' he declared finally, and even as he did he felt the room spinning as Victor Sylvester's music played relentlessly. He leaned back against the wall, breathing heavily, then staggered off again.

'Sit down a mo,' said Kev, pulling up a chair.

Mark sat, and saw they were in the tearoom again. 'She's not here,' he repeated, his drunken brain unable to cope with the disappointment. Kev went to the counter and bought two coffees. Mark gulped some down, and tried to gather his thoughts.

'Never mind Kidda,' Kev was saying. 'Plenty of other lasses to choose from. Just take a minute, eh.' Mark's head sank between his knees as he struggled in vain to come to his senses. 'Just take a minute,' Kev repeated, standing by his friend. They sat awhile, Mark with his head hanging low, Kev sipping coffee. Finally Mark lifted his head, and after drinking his coffee quickly, he stood up, took a deep breath and, without a moment to lose, darted to the gents where he knelt on the floor in the toilet and was violently sick.

It was a ghastly experience, retching and heaving, holding on to a ceramic bowl used by others in their ablutions. It took a while, but finally he stood up, wiped his mouth with paper from the dispenser and, feeling better if still wobbly on his feet, he returned to the tea room. Kev wasn't there, so he wandered to the edge of the dancefloor where he scanned the room as best he could through the myriad of bodies moving slowly to a waltz. The lights were dimmed, but through a gap, facing his way on the opposite side of the room, there stood a girl who took his eye: a girl who stood alone in the glare of a solitary spotlight, looking stunning in a long red dress that matched her long, red hair; a girl waiting patiently to be asked to dance; a girl who looked so beautiful, he thought, that only a brave man would have the courage to approach her.

The girl was Connie.

He stood and stared. As far as she could see she was alone, but there might be someone, a boyfriend maybe. He needed to be calm and collected, but he was feeling fuzzy, and everything was spinning again. He decided to get out of her line of vision, to go somewhere, anywhere, to think about what he should do.

Back in the tearoom, he sat at the table he had just vacated. The serving hatch was now closed. He sat there alone, his feelings ranging from excitement to anger to sheer frustration. Excitement because, at long last, he was, or might be, in a situation where he could approach Connie; anger because when the situation had presented itself he was drunk, and felt ill; and frustration over the non-appearance of Carol, who had promised to be here tonight. A sudden movement caught his eye. Kev was standing right in front of him.

'You'll never guess what,' said Kev, clearly excited. 'Betty's here. So's Rita.' Mark looked up at the grinning face of his friend.

Just then the sound of Bobby Darin replaced Victor Sylvester. 'C'mon. They're jivin' now.' Kev shot off towards the dancefloor.

Mark stood up, and shook his head. Connie's here, he told himself. Connie, who gets off the bus at the Balloon. Connie, who smiled and waved to me. She's here. He walked unsteadily and cautiously to the place where, moments before, he had seen her on the other side of the room. She was no longer there. But nearly all the girls were along *this* side of the room, waiting to be asked to dance. He threaded his way through the densely-packed bodies, *Multiplication* booming out from the speakers. He bumped into some guy, spilled his drink. 'Sorry,' said Mark, checking to see if the guy was alright about it. He was. He moved on to where the crowd thinned out, and there she was, standing by the wall. She was looking at him with a smile of recognition.

'Hi!' she said simply.

Before he could reply Kev appeared, holding a young woman's hand. 'There y'are!' he bellowed at Mark.

They formed a small group then, occupying its own space. Mark looked at Kev, then at Connie. There was an awkward silence before he was able to speak again. He raised his hands in a gesture of introduction. 'This is Connie,' he said for Kev's benefit. He looked at Connie. 'This is my mate, Kev. Kev the Rev.'

Kev and his young lady laughed, but Connie didn't. Instead, her smile having disappeared, she said, simply, 'Eh?'

'Kev the Rev. Just a joke.'

'Mark,' said Kev calmly, 'this,' he gestured to the girl he was with, 'is Betty. And this,' he gestured to Connie, 'is Rita.'

'Pleased to meet you,' said Betty to Mark.

Mark's head was fuzzy. The ceiling was spinning.

'Who's Connie?' asked Rita.

'Connie Francis,' Mark explained. 'Stupid Cupid.'

'Who's stupid?' She was looking angry now.

'Excuse me…' Mark tried to explain, but his addled brain would not engage.

'There's no excuse for you,' said Rita, before addressing her friend. 'And this is the guy who stood me up. You can keep him.' With that she walked off, followed by Beryl. Mark and Kev watched them heading in the direction of the Ladies.

'What the fuck are you on about, you dipstick?' said Kev, shaking his head. 'I told you Rita was here.'

'She's the lass I was calling Connie,' Mark explained weakly.

To Mark, at that moment, the entire room was spinning around. He staggered off. 'Where y'goin'?' Kev called after him. Ignoring him Mark found himself at the top of the stairs. He felt sick again and needed fresh air. Desperate not to throw up on the carpet he hurried to the door, opened it, fell to his hands and knees and was sick on the pavement. He got to his feet, and shook his head. Everything was spinning around: shop windows, streetlights, the pavement, the road. He was confused, disappointed, angry. Carol. Where was she? As he stood on the pavement, muffled by the closed door of Partners, came the sound of *A Girl Like You*. Carol's song. Their song. Where was she? Where was the girl he loved? And Connie. Or Rita. Whatever her name was. Why did he have to meet her when he was pissed? He remembered Marie. Marie who gets turned on by erotic films. She'll be at the Oxford.

He moved away, and headed in the direction of the Oxford, his reluctant legs barely able to take him. He staggered forward, but somehow kept to his feet. Outside the dancehall there was no queue. He paid, went inside, visited the gents and went in search of Marie.

As he entered the main ballroom area he was astonished at its size. It was vast, with a high ceiling and balconies, and even had private, dimly-lit seating areas where couples chatted and held hands. Some sat together, kissing. One bloke had his hand away in some girl's blouse. A live band on a low stage played the waltz. He stood at the side of the dancefloor and watched as men of all ages approached groups of women, and emerged with new partners for a dance or two, or maybe the start of a lifelong relationship. He mingled with the ladies-in-waiting in a vain search for Marie before emerging to find there was a bar in the corner. He approached the counter, and stood behind customers already there, waiting to be served. Then a space opened, and the barmaid was looking.

'A packet of cheese and onion crisps, please,' he said, reaching for coins in his pocket.

'Sorry, pet. We don't do crisps.'

She looked so smart, so attractive, he was taken aback by her broad Geordie accent.

'Packet of salted peanuts, then,' he ventured.

She shook her head. 'D'you wanna drink or what?'

He was too embarrassed to retreat. 'Pint of...' he looked at the pump handles on the bar counter. 'Newcastle Exhibition, ta.' She pulled the pint, plonked it on the counter. A fellow behind bumped into him as he walked off, spilling beer over the rim of the glass and over his fingers. He took a sip, meandered over to a pillar, leaned against it. Strangely, he didn't feel too downbeat about the unfortunate tryst with Connie – or Rita, as she was. He'd see her on the bus, get off at the Balloon, talk to her, apologise and say can we start again. He felt she liked him really. So he relaxed and watched the action. It was a fox-trot, but there were so many bodies couples were hardly dancing, just holding each other and moving to the music as best they could. He remembered Marie had said she came early, when there was space and you could dance properly. Maybe she'd been and gone this very night. As for Carol, there must be a good reason why she hadn't turned up at Partners. He'd find out in the end. They'd meet again, he felt certain. Everything was fine. He was here now and there seemed to be plenty of girls to choose from.

He pushed himself away from the pillar, sipping his pint as he moved forward unsteadily. Against the next one a man and woman were kissing, he pressing hard against her, she with her back to the pillar. One of his hands was cupped around her bum, a cigarette protruded from the fingers of the other. Two young blokes stood close by, watching them, glasses of beer in their hands. He walked on to the far end of the ballroom, finding it virtually deserted, with no customers at the bar counter there. He supped the last of his pint off and ordered another from the bored barman.

He walked unsteadily down the other side of the floor, passing the stage. A woman singer, fifty-ish, was in full flow, her strapless dress hanging low over her large breasts, showing lots of cleavage. The speakers here were huge and so close her voice was deafening. Beyond, he mingled with the throng of girls by the side of the floor, sipping his pint, eyeing up possible liaisons. He felt confident. Finally he placed his glass onto a small table and stepped up boldly to a girl wearing a cream-coloured dress and pink cardy.

'D'you wanna dance?' He was conscious of his speech being slurred but did his best to provide a winning smile, and held out a hand expectantly.

She looked at him for a moment, and shook her head. He hesitated, taken aback at her apparent refusal and not sure about what to do next. 'No thank you,' she said at last, looking away. Fair enough, he thought. Bob said some women take pleasure in turning you down. He moved on a few paces and asked another. She was tall with glasses and long hair that flowed down her back. She didn't speak, just gave him a quick glance and shook her head. He asked the girl standing next to her. She was unattractive and overweight, not his type but he didn't care. Anybody would do. She ignored him completely and walked away when he lingered in front of her.

He returned to the small table to find his pint gone. A woman clearing tables had taken it. He thought he'd try and get it back, but she was pushing a trolley festooned with glasses, many of them still half-full. The band struck up an excuse me quickstep. Bob had told him about them. You just went up to a couple on the floor, said 'excuse me' and the man was obliged to walk off. He surveyed the couples as they shuffled past, and saw a fellow his own age walk directly on to the floor and tap a man gently on the shoulder. The man stopped, and after the young fellow said something – 'excuse me', presumably – he walked off and the lady had a new partner.

A moment later it happened again, when a fellow approached a couple and before he even reached them the man courteously thanked his partner and walked away, leaving his replacement to take her in his arms. The whole scene before him, Mark thought, was crazy. So many people on the dancefloor, but no-one was dancing, not properly. Everyone was just muddling through, their un-rhythmic movements an excuse to chat or hope that in some way it might lead to something. Like sex, judging by some of the blokes. They looked like wolves on the prowl.

His thoughts ranged from clear and confident to fuzzy, drunken bewilderment. He felt sick again, and found a pillar to lean against. He felt better, then the music stopped only to start up again. A waltz. He scanned bodies and spied a pretty girl on the dancefloor. She was slim and wore a long dress and was chatting to her male partner. Pushing himself from the pillar he moved in for the kill. In just three or four paces he was standing immediately behind the man. He tapped him on the shoulder.

'Excuse me,' said Mark, and waited for the compliant response. When it didn't come he tugged the fellow's coat-sleeve. 'Excuse me,' he bellowed. The man turned, and Mark found himself looking at his angry face. He made to step forward, to take his partner's hand. But the man raised an arm and blocked his way.

'Excuse me.' Mark repeated, and tried to step forward. The man was about forty and well-built, and over six feet tall. He didn't move.

'This is an excuse me,' Mark bellowed.

'No it isn't,' the man replied. 'The excuse me is over, so push off.' Mark stood in drunken bewilderment, glancing first at the man, then his partner.

'Go away,' the man snarled. He turned his back, leaving Mark staring at his broad shoulders. Mark walked around him, and saw the couple were holding hands, ready to resume dancing. He reached forward and tried to pull them apart. The man turned and pushed him violently. He staggered back and fell over, finding himself among a sea of legs. People stepped aside, leaving him sitting on the polished floor. He rolled onto his knees and looked up at the angry face of his assailant. He tried to get up, but the spinning started again. He blinked, and shook his head. Faces all around stared down at him. Then he was assisted to his feet by two pairs of strong arms as he was seized under the armpits.

He found himself looking at two men, each now with a firm grip on his upper arms. They wore dark suits and white shirts, and bow ties. 'C'mon bonny lad,' one said. 'Time to go home, eh.'

He felt himself being propelled forward, his toes barely touching the floor. There were images of people's faces, the lights of the bar, tables with half-filled glasses. With a supreme effort he broke free and faced the two bouncers. He took a swing at one of them, but could only stagger forward as he failed to make contact. He fell forward, and was pulled up again, and dragged backwards across the floor, his heels trailing along the thick carpet of the foyer. His last sighting of the dancehall was of people's faces turned towards him, receding into the distance, then there were doors crashing and two uniformed bobbies, both smiling as he passed by at speed. A moment later he was outside, alone on the pavement, swaying and barely able to keep his feet.

He wanted to walk away but didn't know which way to go. He looked about, but there wasn't a soul in sight, save for a man and woman across the street. She was screaming at her companion, swinging her handbag repeatedly at his head. The man stepped back, grabbed the handbag strap and pulled her towards him. They staggered drunkenly, he dropping to one knee as she snatched her bag free. As he watched, transfixed, he heard a voice, close by.

'You alright, pet?'

He turned to see a woman. She had long dark hair that fell over her shoulders and down the front of her coat. She looked thirty, forty. He didn't know. She pulled long and hard on a cigarette before speaking again.

'You're in a state, mind.' He could see her face, but it kept going out of focus. 'C'mon,' she said in a kindly voice, 'I'll look after you.'

She crooked her arm, inviting him to thread his arm through. He did, and they walked. His head was spinning and he was still unsteady on his feet, but she was strong enough to keep them walking in a straight line. He didn't know where they walked to, although it wasn't far. There were unfamiliar dingy streets, then some glass doors that led into a tower block, then they were in an elevator. It seemed to go up a long way before the doors clattered open. She led him out and fumbled for keys. They were on a landing where there was a strong smell of cats' pee. She opened a door and he found himself in an apartment, the pall of cigarette smoke hanging strongly in the atmosphere. He was swaying, and had to grab the back of the settee to steady himself. The woman took her coat off and draped it over a chair and moved close to him at the back of the settee.

'Been havin' a good time with yer mates, 'ave yer?' She was smiling, her face just inches from his. 'Tried to find a lass and couldn't, eh?'

She was kissing his cheeks, lightly-touching kisses as she brushed her lips briefly against his. He was aware of her long hair, and ran his fingers through it. Then she was kissing his mouth, so forcefully he was bending backwards over the back of the settee. She stopped, allowing him to stand up straight again, teasing him by gently brushing his face with her mouth. Then he felt her fingers passing over his crotch, coaxing an erection that wasn't forthcoming. After a few moments she stopped and spoke calmly to him. 'Just go through there, why don't you. I'll make you a nice cup of tea.' She opened a door for him and ushered him into a dark room. She clicked the light switch and left, closing the door behind her.

He was in a bedroom. An unmade double bed stood against the far wall. A dressing table stood to one side. It was covered in bric-a-brac. Women's things: make-up, hairbrush, comb, lipsticks. There were pictures of pop stars: on the walls, on the dresser. A tattered picture of Elvis was stuck to the mirror of the dresser, its corners curling inwards. A fly-paper dangled from the lampshade, with lots of hapless flies sticking forlornly to it.

He began to feel safe. A Good Samaritan was looking after him. He could relax. He could sleep. He tossed his jacket onto a chair, then his tie, then kicked off his shoes. He walked over to the bed and flopped down on his back, his head resting on a lovely soft pillow. Dark, billowing images spun around in his brain, but he was content. His thoughts drifted to Carol: her smile, her kiss outside her front door that time. Even now he could feel her warm breath on his face, her lips on his. She was unbuttoning his shirt, fumbling with his belt, undoing his trousers, pulling them down. Then she was kissing him again, on his mouth then on his exposed chest and even down on his belly. He could feel the tip of her nose in his belly-button. It tickled. Her face grew larger in his thoughts, then receded again, then came back and smiled for him. Carol's face. Smiling. For him.

8

For Carol, these days, Sundays were pretty rotten. But this particular Sunday was the worst. As she sat at the kitchen table eating her corn-flakes, the table cluttered by Dad's empty beer bottles and his overfilled ashtray, she reflected on the events of the past few days. On Friday afternoon, at work, she was told there was a telephone call for her – a *personal* call, as Marjorie on the switchboard had described it. It must be Mark, she thought. Mark, who'd occupied her thoughts so much since they met at Partners. At work, at home, even through the night, Mark's face and his sparkling eyes were just about all she'd thought about. Except, when she got home after work, there was Dad, sullen and boozy. Dad, waiting for his dinner. Dad, fretting after Mam.

She'd picked up the receiver, scarcely able to contain her excitement at the thought that Mark couldn't wait to see her, that maybe he was going to ask her out. To the pictures, most likely. She'd love to see West Side Story. She'd say yes if he asked her.

'Hello?' She spoke nervously into the receiver.

'Hello pet.'

The sound of her mother's voice took her completely by surprise. And, she would have to admit, left her disappointed.

'Sorry to call you at work, but needs must. You know.'

And her need, as it turned out, was to arrange a meeting with Carol on Saturday evening, at Front Street, Tynemouth, 'at the Priory, where the big red mine is.' It had to be Saturday, she said, because since leaving home she'd found a job on weekday evenings, and Saturday was the only option. She couldn't make Saturday morning or afternoon, and if it was Sunday Dad would be suspicious if Carol went out. And this Saturday, well, it was important she saw Carol. It was about Dad but she couldn't discuss it on the phone, obviously. 'Seven o'clock, then. You can get the Number Eleven. Drops you right at the Priory.' The telephone clicked. Typical Mam, thought Carol. Decision made, and never mind she had a life of her own and had hoped to see Mark on Saturday evening.

She was so disappointed she considered not going to Tynemouth at all. Why should she? Mam and Dad were old enough and mature enough to sort their problems out without her, surely. But then if there was a chance that Mam might be persuaded to come home, her parents would be reunited and Dad would hopefully make an effort to stop drinking and get back to work. She'd go, and hoped Mark would be at Partners the following week.

And gone she had, stepping from the bus at the naval mine, now a giant red moneybox that Carol had dropped pennies into when she was little. Dad had held her up so she could reach the slot. The mine was still there. And so was Mam.

Carol thought her mother looked pale and thin, although she didn't say so. She checked her watch; about now Mark would be arriving at Partners, and he would be looking out for her only to find she wasn't there. She had tried to persuade Emma to go, and pass on an appropriate message; but Emma wouldn't go on her own.

'Shall we have a walk along the pier?' Mam turned and gestured. It would be dark soon, but they walked down the hill towards the Spanish Battery, pier-bound. 'Such a lovely evening. Seems a shame to spend it inside a pub or somewhere.' She asked about Dad, naturally. Carol told her that her father wasn't coping. The truth, she thought, might be enough to persuade Mam to come home.

In front of them now were the heaving waters of the Tyne. Her parents had brought her here often as a child. Carol had always been in awe of the river. It looked so strong, so menacing, especially when big waves crashed against pier, throwing spray everywhere. The pier had been washed away once, Dad had said, which was hardly reassuring. They used to stay with Aunt Gladys in North Shields, before she died. They'd take the bus to Tynemouth, just as she had done today. Now she was here with Mam. They walked in silence, unspoken words cementing the bond between mother and daughter, both affected by the man in their lives: Lennie Kemp.

Halfway along the pier Mam spoke again.

'He's still drinking, I suppose.'

'More than ever,' said Carol. 'He might stop if you would only come home.'

'I was considering coming home, but only *after* he stops.'

They walked further until they were at the lighthouse at its lonely outpost at the end of the pier. They placed their hands on the railings together and looked out to the wide expanse of sea, disappearing now in the gathering gloom. In the middle distance all was darkness, save for a solitary light: a homeward-bound trawler probably, bound for the fish quay. Across the river the lights of South Shields twinkled and reflected in the water.

'So,' said Mam at last, without looking at her daughter, 'tell me what's what at home.'

Carol, too, kept her gaze fixed on the empty ocean. 'He's gone sick from work and lies in bed until the afternoon. I have to cook his dinner when I get in from work. I wash his clothes and do all the housework. And I go dancing now with Emma.'

Freda Kemp turned and faced her daughter.

'A sob story for my benefit, eh?' She regretted her words and spoke again before Carol could protest. 'I appreciate the situation you are in, and you will think it's unfair, which it is. But let's have one thing clear. I may be the one who deserted the ship, but it's your father's fault, not mine. He's the one who took to the booze. He's the one who started thumping me. And he's the one who should be out of the house, not your mother.'

The trawler was nearer now, aiming for the wide gap between the piers. 'We had lovely times here when you were little,' Mam was saying. 'Remember? Fish and chips from Front Street, a walk along the pier, then along the front. As far as Whitley Bay sometimes. Then tea at your Aunt Glad's before hometime.'

'We got as far as St Mary's Island once,' said Carol. 'You wore me out. I was only about ten.

'Your dad never drank then, did he? Just a pint, maybe two. He never came home drunk. He never missed work either.' Freda turned to face her daughter again. 'Look at me,' she said quietly. Carol turned to face her. 'I wanted to see you because I have something important to say to you.'

Carol's face was expressionless as she waited for her mother to explain.

'Your dad, my husband, is – or was – a good man. I was happy with him. I want him back. I want to come back. But I don't want the man he is now. I want him as he was. Do you follow?' Carol nodded, saying nothing. Freda opened her handbag, fumbled in it and pulled out a crumbled photograph. She handed it to her daughter. Carol recognised it; it was a photo of Mam, Dad and her, taken on Tynemouth sands years before. Everyone was smiling and she, Carol, held a candyfloss. 'That was my family then. That's the family I want back.' Carol handed her mother the photograph, and she slipped it back into her bag. 'I will come back home,' said Freda, 'but there is a condition and I want you to tell your Dad from me what that condition is. I want you to tell him to stop drinking altogether, completely and absolutely. I'm sure if he does everything will be fine again.'

'And you'll come home?'

'It's not quite as simple as that. I want him to stop drinking for a period of one month. At the end of that time you and I will speak again, and I want you to report to me truthfully whether he has stopped the drinking or not. If he has...'

'*Then* you'll come home!'

'I will arrange to meet him to discuss the *possibility* of my coming home. And before I do come home, if I do, I want to make it clear to him that having stopped drinking he mustn't go back to it again. D'you understand what I'm saying?'

Carol nodded.

'I'll call you again in a month,' said Freda. 'I expect you to be truthful, mind. If he stops drinking he might get his wife back. If he doesn't...' She shrugged. 'Y'know, I may be pushing forty but though I say it myself I'm not a bad catch. I'm slim, in good health and I've stopped smoking. I can turn the eye of a good man. I want our life back, that's your dad, you and me. But I could always get a life with someone else if I had to. So you pass on my message. And let me know what's what in a month. Okay?' Carol nodded. 'By the way,' she said finally, 'tell him not to try and find out where I'm living. It's somewhere in Shields, but I don't want him knowing.'

As they turned away from the rail and began to make their way back along the pier, Carol realised that for another month at least life would go on as before, with her looking after Dad.

'When do you go dancing, anyway?' asked Freda.

'Saturdays,' her daughter replied. 'I was going dancing tonight.'

Her mother laughed. 'Sorry, pet. Better luck next week.'

***

As he opened his eyes to the new day, Mark sought out the cobweb. Up in the corner, where the ceiling met the walls. He couldn't see it. Mam must have swept it away with that feather duster thing. But now he noticed, instead of magnolia, the wallpaper was a deep-red colour, embossed with grotesque flower patterns and multi-coloured, giant leaves. And the top of his head seemed to be touching the bars of an iron bedstead. It took a few seconds for his befuddled brain to react. When it did he sat up sharply, which was when his head told him to lie down again. Then he remembered: Kev and Partners and, oh yes, the Oxford. And all that booze. And all that spewing up.

Other thoughts slithered through his mind. He'd seen Connie or whatever he name was and made her cross. Carol hadn't turned up so he'd gone looking for Marie. Then there were more images: women waiting at the side of a huge dancefloor; that bloke in the excuse me; men wearing bow ties dragging him across the floor; smiling polises.

There was another thought, too: Mam would be worried sick because he hadn't come home last night. And that woman he'd met outside. Who the hell was she?

Just then the door opened and an old lady entered the room. She had long hair that fell over one shoulder and down the front of the drab dressing gown she wore. She was carrying a mug of tea or coffee. A cigarette poked from the fingers of the same hand.

'Ah, you're awake,' she said in a croaky voice, before shuffling over to the window where she swished the curtains open. Daylight penetrated the net curtain and streamed across the room. She turned to face him, her face now in shadow. 'Well, you might as well get your arse outta here for what use you were.' She headed slowly for the door again. 'Your clobber is there, on that chair.' Then she disappeared, leaving behind the smell of cigarette smoke.

He sat up again, and only then realised he was naked. Yet he couldn't remember undressing. In fact, he couldn't remember much at all after the encounter with the woman outside the Oxford, except a vague recollection of walking the streets with her and being in a lift. And the place stinking of fags, he remembered that. Oh, God, that old woman: he was kissing her last night. Feeling nauseated, he turned onto his side and slid his legs out of bed, wincing with the pain in his head. He sat awhile before getting gingerly to his feet and picking up his underpants. He put them on with difficulty, then reached for his shirt. As he slid his arms through the sleeves the old woman reappeared, still carrying her mug of tea, coffee, whatever.

'Y'needn't check your wallet. Haven't touched it. Haven't charged you for services not rendered. Christ, you weren't even good company.' She took a long drag on her cigarette, and blew smoke forcefully off to one side. 'Good Samaritan, that's me, eh. Well, get a move on. And if you'll take my advice, which is also on the house, you should keep off the drink till you're man enough to take it.'

She left the room again and he buttoned his shirt with all haste before reaching for his trousers. He dressed as quickly as he could, except for his shoes which he couldn't find, but a search located them just inside the door to the flat. He put them on and left, closing the door quietly behind him. He didn't want to see her again; he didn't want anything but to get out of the place. On the landing the strong smell of cats' urine was another reminder of last night. He stumbled down several flights of stairs before emerging to a sunny morning and fresh air. He paused and took a few deep breaths before checking the time, and only then realised he was missing his wristwatch. He turned to go and get it but changed his mind. As he walked quickly, his head started to clear, enabling him to gather his thoughts. He seemed to be the only person in Newcastle, and was certainly the only person on the bus as it turned up Gallowgate. He was hungry but at least he was going home.

Home to Mam and Dad. What were they going to say when he walked through the door? What was *he* going to say about being out all night? As the bus headed for Weston he tried to think of a plausible story. It wasn't easy. The best he could come up with was to say he'd met a girl at Partners and walked her home – nothing wrong with that. She lived in Jesmond and he'd missed the last bus, so her folks had said he could stay over and sleep on the settee. That was better than taking the all-night bus, Mam would agree; the bus that was always full of drunks. He'd lost his watch, hadn't a clue what happened to it. And now he realised he was missing his tie. Must've left it at the girl's house in Jesmond. 'The girl'. He couldn't say that. She'd have to have a name. He'd tell the truth, that he'd met a girl called Carol, and never mind it was the week before. He'd bat away any further questions, play the shy-guy. Mam would understand. Dad wouldn't care as long as his wife was content. Bob would ask questions later.

Nearing the Balloon he looked out the bus window for Connie – or Rita, as he now remembered her. There was no sign of her. Working girl, probably still abed on a Sunday morning. He alighted from the bus, and walked boldly up the Terrace, head down, ready for engagement: 'Where've *you* been all night, then?' That would be the question. Then he spotted Tom Clark on the other side of the street. He was heading in his direction. He hurried on, but Tom was crossing the road towards him, calling. 'Hey, Greeny! Just a mo!' Tom stood in the middle of the foot-path, facing him, barring his way. 'Got something to say to you Greeny.'

As ever, he looked threatening: fists clenched, strong arms emanating from broad shoulders, a menacing look on his face.

'Seems I owe you one, said Tom.' He waited for Mark's response. When there wasn't any he went on. 'Beryl told me what you done at the footy the other Saturday. Slapped my face an' that when I was out cold. You might've saved my life, Greeny.'

'It's just what I learned in first aid,' Mark replied, making to walk on. But Tom stepped to the side to bar his progress.

'Yeah, well, there's somethin' else. I wanted a word about Beryl.' Tom's face looked grave, the way he had looked in past times when he'd seen fit to give Mark a thump. 'Been to the flicks with her, eh?'

Mark stayed silent.

'She's *my* girlfriend,' said Tom. 'I don't like anybody else messing around with her. Right?'

Mark nodded.

'Right? Say it.'

'Right.'

'Yeah. Right. Y'might've saved my life, so I'll not biff you this time. But you keep well away from her, or else.'

They were face to face, Tom maintaining his threatening manner, Mark waiting to be told he could go now. But Tom wasn't quite finished. 'Never could fight, could you Greeny? But you've got some bottle, I'll give you that. Taking her out when you knew she was my bird and I might find out.' He was staring at Mark, who wasn't sure what Tom would say or do next. 'Well, I did find out cos she told me. So like I say, keep your distance.' With that he jabbed Mark in the chest with a forefinger and walked off, leaving him to continue home to face his parents' inquisition.

He opened the back door to find Mam standing in the kitchen, a tea-towel draped over her arm.

'Ee, you're home, you little monkey,' she declared, a look of relief on her face. A look that quickly turned to annoyance. 'Where've *you* been all night, then?' she enquired, but before he could reply she opened the door to the living room and called for her husband. A moment later Dad appeared.

'Where've *you* been all night, then?' he asked. 'Your Mam's been worried sick about you, lad.'

Mark gave his planned explanation. 'Sorry Mam,' he concluded, 'but I know you wouldn't have wanted me on that all-night bus.'

'You should have been on the last bus,' said Mam, but with less severity in her voice.

Dad nodded. 'Well, if you missed it you did right, lad. But don't let it happen again.' With that he went to the front door and collected a bunch of keys from a hook. It was time to see to his pigeons.

'Our Bob's had his breakfast,' Mam was saying. 'But I'll put yours on. You must be starving.'

Mark said his thanks, relieved there were no comments about his missing tie. Breakfast coming up, what he wanted most was a hot bath, to clean away all traces of the ghastly flat and the ghastly old woman. Without further ado he went to the bathroom and ran the hot water. Bob appeared, winked and gave him a thumb's up, before disappearing again. He was finding bath-times good times for reflection. Lying in hot water, full stretch, was still novel to him. He was relieved that he was home safe and well after being so blind drunk he hadn't been in control. Right now a full fryup awaited. So, where was he in the great scheme of things?

Why Carol had failed to appear at Partners was a mystery; but, as Bob had said, she might never have intended to see him again. That didn't mean he wouldn't try to see *her* again. It was amazing that he had met Connie, and that she had turned out to be Rita, Betty's friend. He had annoyed her, but he could put that right. He'd see her on the bus, get off with her and talk to her. His thoughts drifted to Marie, of their sexual encounter with more to come if he wanted it. He could still feel the warmth of her, and sense the smell of her breath, her kisses, her face, her self-confidence. It took loud banging by Mam to awaken him from slumber, summoning him for his breakfast. He dressed hastily and sat down to his fryup. Life was good. It would be even better, he thought, if he could see Carol again.

As Mark was drifting into sexual slumber in the bath, Carol was sitting at the kitchen table at home, looking at her fingernails with mixed feelings of hope and melancholy. Mam could be home in a month, if only Dad would agree to keep off the drink. But a month was a long time in a house with her father. Off work through some contrived sickness, he continued to languish in bed nearly all day, only emerging for food and to put his coat on to go to the pub. She was fed up cooking for him, clearing away after him, washing the dishes after him, cleaning the house and having to listen to his pitiable moaning. Yet she couldn't abandon him, not least because she was too young to be able to afford to live elsewhere and he was, after all, her dad. She was wondering how to tell him of Mam's pre-condition for her return when the door opened and he walked into the room. He was unshaven, and wore a dirty vest and worn-out trousers held up on one side by braces.

'Aye, lass.'

He sat down and reached for the *News of the World*. It lay where she'd put it, on the table, neatly folded. She watched him unfold it and flick idly through the pages. He looked up, and tilted a hand, his 'cup of tea' gesture. She filled the kettle, clicked the automatic gas-ring lighter and after a moment's pause turned to face him.

'I saw Mam last night.'

He looked up sharply without lowering the newspaper. 'What did you just say?'

At that moment Carol, for the first time, felt a pang of fear. Fear of her father. Fear of what he might do, to her, if he became angry. She thought it would be the same fear her mother had had to endure: fear of assault.

'I saw Mam last night. She called me at work and asked to see me. So I went.'

'You went? What do you mean, you went?'

'She wanted me to pass on a message to you.'

Lennie Kemp lowered his newspaper. 'What the hell is this, secret squirrels?' Carol looked down at the floor before his penetrating gaze. 'Why didn't she ask to see me if she had a bloody message?' When she didn't reply her father spoke again, this time more gently.

'Where did you see her anyway?'

'At Tynemouth.'

'Tynemouth? Is that where she's living?'

'She's living in North Shields. She said you wouldn't know where and she didn't tell me. She wanted me to give you a message. That's all I can say.'

'And the message?'

'She wants you to stop drinking for a month.'

'And then she'll deign to come home?'

'And then she'll agree to meet you. And if you promise never to touch alcohol again she'll consider coming home.'

'Oh really? Well, it's a bad job when a working man can't have a bloody pint, that's all I can say.' He stood up then. At six-feet tall, his bulky frame towered above her. 'And how will she know if I've stopped drinking for a month?'

Her back pressing against the cooker, her father standing in front of her, she looked him in the eye. 'She's calling again in a month. I'm to tell her whether you've stopped drinking or not.'

The kettle was singing. Carol slid away, picked up the empty teapot and carefully spooned in fresh tea leaves, her hand trembling as she scooped them from the jar. Her father stood in silence, waiting for her to finish. 'Don't blame me if you're upset, Dad,' she said without looking up. 'I'm just passing on Mam's message.'

'Aye. Well, when I want a pint I'll have a pint. You can tell her that.' He sat down then, and picked up his newspaper. But although he was looking at it, she knew he wasn't reading it. He was angry, hurt, shocked. She poured his tea and set it down on the table before him.

'Bacon and eggs?' she asked, trying to sound cheerful. He looked at her, his eyes moist, his face tormented.

'Aye, lass. Bacon and eggs for your da.'

That evening, Walter Smith, Weston Workingmen's Club steward, stepped out of the back door of the club and surveyed the empty crates and aluminium beer barrels that had for months littered the ground by the back door. They stood haphazardly over a wide area, reaching as far as the public right of way. He'd meant to have them removed, or at least sorted them out, but kept putting off the day. The decision to deal with them had been made for him by two members of the Club committee who had told him to have them collected. 'There'll be rats living there, Walter. So let's have the place tidied up, eh.'

It was a chore, but he started to move them, clearing a space where he could apply the broom. With much banging and clanging and lifting and stacking he swept the ground, restacking as he went. The last part to be cleared and swept was just under the window of the ladies toilets, where, perchance, he noticed a small, coloured piece of folded card lying where it had fallen. He picked it up. It bore the heading, 'Electrical Trades Union' with a space for the Member's Name below. He looked at the name, written in biro. It was very interesting. Very interesting indeed.

9

The moggie eyed Mark curiously, but only for a moment before slinking away through the hedge into next-door's garden. Not the friendly cat their Maxi had been when he was a kid, Mark thought. Rubbing his head against people's legs, lying on his back, twisting around on the dirty ground before getting to his feet again, fur covered in muck.

Kev's motorbike was hoisted onto its stand on the garden path. It gleamed in the sunshine, might've passed for new. Mark knocked and waited. A few moments later the door swung open. Two o'clock on a Sunday afternoon, Kev was eating stotty cake.

'Ah, the wanderer returns,' said Kev, notwithstanding the gobful of food. He stepped back, holding the door open. 'Enter ye within and tell me what the hell happened to you last night, O drunken cavalier of the west – or should I say Weston.' Mark did as he was bid, being met by the smell of Sunday lunch being cooked by Kev's mam. He sat on the settee as his friend flopped into one of the armchairs by the fireplace, and took a swig of tea from an enormous mug before shoving the last of his stotty into his mouth. 'So? What happened? You didn't end up in a black maria, did you?'

'Went to the Oxford,' said Mark with a shrug.

'And?'

'And that's it. I went to the Oxford.'

'You don't seem very keen to tell me how you got on. Like who did you meet, and did you cha-cha and did you take her home afterwards? C'mon, tell uncle Kev.'

Mark's response was to look vaguely at the blank screen on the TV.

'Did you meet someone in the Oxford, or were you too pissed to remember? Ah! I can tell by your face you encountered a member of the fair sex. A bit of advice, Kidda. Don't ever play Poker for money.'

Kev's mam appeared, wearing her pinny. She looked hassled. 'Oh hello Marky,' she said. 'How's your ma?' Before Mark could answer she turned to Kev. 'Dinner'll be half an hour. Tell your dad. He's out the back.' With that she disappeared into the kitchen.

'You just buggered off without so much as a by-your-leave,' said Kev.

'Cos you got me pissed.'

Kev sat forward in his chair, and shook his head. 'Uh-huh, Kidda. Let's get one thing clear. I didn't get you pissed. You got yourself pissed. I wasn't exactly holding you down and pouring it down your throat, was I?' He paused, and drank the remaining contents of his mug. They held their tongues for a moment before Kev plonked his now-empty mug on to the hearth and changed the subject.

'Me and Betty are back together,' he announced. 'I'm seeing her tonight at Blyth. Sex on the beach at Seaton Sluice. Yee-hah!'

'She's good looking,' said Mark, weakly.

'Aye, an' if you had wheels you could be there with Rita. Or Connie as you call her. She's good looking an' all, right?'

'I doubt if she'll want anything to do with me even if I had a bike. Not after last night.'

Kev glanced at the door to the kitchen, as though about to divulge a great confidence that he didn't want his mam to hear. 'That's where you're wrong, Kidda. Me and Betty had a word with her after you'd gone. Levelled the plain.'

'Levelled the plain?'

'Paved the way, then. Christ, you know what I mean. Once Betty and me were an item again we all went into the tearoom and had a chat. I told Rita you were a good guy, really, that you weren't usually pissed and that you'd been spouting on about seeing her on the bus for weeks. She likes you. I can tell you that. And I can tell you something else. You know Betty lives at Blyth? Well, Rita lives with her folks in a flat above the Balloon. The bloody Balloon! She stays with Betty at weekends, with her folks at Blyth. Rita and her folks lived at Blyth too, but her dad had to do a moonlight flit for some reason. Anyway, she'll be wallflower tonight, cos I'm picking Betty up at seven. Burn-up the coast somewhere then midnight serenade on the dunes.'

'Moonlight Serenade.'

'Aye, right. We take a big towel. Sand gets everywhere. Must be shit having your leg over in the Sahara.'

'So how've you paved the way, as you say?'

Kev shrugged. 'You can knock on Rita's door now you know where she lives, and ask her out. Say sorry for being pissed last night and Bob's your auntie. Not *your* Bob, of course.' He laughed out loud at his own humour.

Kev's mam reappeared, with a 'dinner's nearly ready' look. Mark went to the door. 'Call for Rita one night after work, Kidda,' Kev called after him. Mark waved in acknowledgement and headed for Robbie's. As he walked he thought it strange that, after weeks of being haunted by the girl on the bus, now that he'd been told where she lived he didn't seem to give a toss about her. It was Carol he cared about. At work, in bed, right now. Then the image of Marie crept into his mind. Marie and sexy movies. He quickened his pace. Robbie would be over the shits by now, surely.

'The Stoll? Tonight? Mam wouldn't like that.' Robbie looked gobsmacked.

'I'm not asking your mam.'

'What's on anyway?'

'Dunno,' Mark admitted. 'Does it matter? It'll be an 'X'. Better than your mam's catalogues.'

Robbie was usually easily persuaded to do something, but it seemed this was a step too far. Not because he didn't want to go, but because his parents wouldn't approve and he wasn't one for lying to them. When he remarked, 'We're not even eighteen' Mark knew it was a hopeless cause.

'What about the Regal?' Robbie enquired. 'It's Marlon Brando in One-Eyed Jacks.'

Mark liked Marlon Brando. He liked westerns. He liked the Regal. He'd call at six, after tea.

Monday morning. On the way to work, on the bus: Carol was smiling. Smiling because of unexpected events.

Dad hadn't gone to the pub last night. Dad had stayed home, and listened to the wireless. Dad had said he was going to work this morning, and the dirty teacup and cereal bowl on the breakfast table this morning were proof that he had. She thought of his 'Goodnight girl' at bedtime, the way he used to say it when she was little, and when he and Mam were the happy couple. Mam had said it would be a month before she would call. It seemed a long time. But it would be worth it if Dad was his own self again, and she could tell Mam.

She walked sprightly to the electricity company offices, arriving at the same moment as Miss Carr.

'How are we today, then?' Miss Carr enquired. She was smart; she was smiling. She clutched a wad of papers under her arm, clearly work she'd taken home for the weekend.

'I'm fine, thank you.' Carol almost began to tell her of the meeting with her mam and Dad not drinking last night but she was too shy.

'You look a lot better, I must say.'

They walked across the foyer together. Miss Carr pressed for the lift. 'Has your mother come home?' she enquired, a kindly smile on her face. She hadn't, said Carol, but she had seen her and was hoping things would improve. 'That's good news,' said Miss Carr as they waited for the lift. Carol glanced at the indicator panel. The lift was on Floor 5. Miss Carr looked at the lift indicator panel. 'Always miles away when you want it,' she said. The red indicator light changed to '4'. 'Ah, it's coming.' They stood together in an awkward silence until the doors suddenly clattered open.

'After you.' Miss Carr gestured. Carol entered the empty lift. Miss Carr followed and pressed for Floor 3. The doors closed and with a shudder the lift rose upwards. 'I'm sure someone will get stuck in this old thing one of these days,' Miss Carr remarked, looking up as though that might help the lift along its upward journey. They reached the third floor, the doors juddering open. Carol was about to walk off but Miss Carr put her hand gently on her arm.

'You know, my door is always open for you. If ever you need to chat. OK?'

'Thank you, Miss Carr.'

'Look.' Miss Carr glanced left and right, before resting her fingers on Carol's forearm. 'You can call me Judith. When there's just you and me. OK?' Carol nodded.

Her boss smiled. 'Miss Carr when it's formal, mind. Otherwise Judith.' With that she walked off, taking long strides across the floor in the direction of her office. Carol watched her go before heading to her own workplace. Miss Carr was really, really nice she thought, although it made her feel a little uneasy, she had to admit, being asked to call her Judith. She never knew her first name was Judith, and doubted if any other of her colleagues did either. But as Monday mornings went, this one was proving to be fine.

Pulling his coat collar tightly around his neck, Mark made a dash for it. The rain was tipping down and his hair was soaked by the time he reached Tommy's car. He opened the rear nearside door, threw his haversack in and dived in after it. At the same time Horlicks entered by the offside door, and the pair sat laughing and shaking water off their hands.

Tommy and Fred were already on board. Tommy gave the two apprentices a moment to sort themselves out before turning on the ignition. When he did there was a splutter and the engine gave a sickly croak.

'Bloody battery's flat,' Tommy declared, stating the obvious, half-turning his head to speak to the lads in the back. 'One of you, then. Starting handle's in the boot.'

'You're Tommy's mate,' said Horlicks. 'And it's his car.'

Mark got out and opened the boot. It contained their haversacks, numerous tools and an empty cardboard box. He had to take them all out before, at last, he located the starting handle which lay on the spare wheel. Stuffing everything back, he went to the front, inserted the handle and gave Tommy the nod before cranking the engine. It took half a dozen turns before the motor spluttered into life, by which time he was soaked through.

They were off to the new job in County Durham. A workingmen's club was being refurbished. Tommy had said where it was but Mark couldn't remember the name. 'It's over twenty-five miles away,' Tommy said, 'so there'll be lots of travelling.' Horlicks would only be with them a couple of days, after which Tommy and Mark, assisted by the ailing Fred, would have the electrical installation work to themselves.

'No tea in the Haymarket. That's what Smudger said.' Tommy turned for Northumberland Street and the A1.

'Nowhere to park anyway,' said Fred.

'And the bloody thing won't start again,' said Mark. Tommy, not listening, was rifling his pockets for his cigarettes, holding on to the steering wheel with one hand. Nothing more was said until they were crossing the Tyne Bridge, when Fred asked Mark if he had his passport. 'You need a bloody visa for where we're going,' said Tommy.

The rain eased as they passed through villages with obscure place-names. By the time they got to 'the job' the sun was shining. They went inside the club to have a look, finding it occupied by busy workmen. Some walls had already been demolished; dust hung heavy in the air and floated through the sunbeams that penetrated the windows. 'Christ almighty,' was all Tommy had to say, before telling the foreman who they were and dropping his haversack in a dusty corner. Fred gestured 'tea' to Mark, who joined other apprentices at a huge dixie containing hot water, fuelled by a Calor-gas ring. It looked as though it might take the rest of the day to boil.

As he waited Mark fumbled in his sack for tools. 'You won't be needing your tools today, son,' said Tommy. 'It'll take a few days to reccy this place before we start doing anything.' With that he stuck his hands in his pockets and started wandering about. Mark knew the score: Tommy would spend all the time he thought was necessary to acquire a good understanding of the building and the work that would be necessary before getting started.

Tea up, Tommy picked up his *Daily Mirror* and sat with Fred on two bar stools in the corner. Mark and Horlicks sat on the floorboards a few feet away.

'Do much at the weekend?' Horlicks was bound to ask.

'Went to Partners with a mate.'

'And?'

'Then the Oxford. You?'

'Nowt much,' said Horlicks. 'Me and a mate went to the Spanish City Sunday.'

Mark wasn't surprised to discover one of Mam's rock cakes in his bait, made especially for Joyce but any not used being leftovers convenient for baitboxes. Horlicks cackled into life again. 'Good, the Oxford, isn't it. Y'can't fail to score there, that's for sure.' Mark's silence invited a 'Well, did you?' It was the first time he'd been, Mark explained, expressing surprise at the number of women who stood around the dancefloor saying 'no' when someone asked them to dance. 'Was that a problem for you?' Horlicks enquired. 'Lasses saying 'no'?'

'Don't know why they bother going if they say 'no',' said Mark.

'You probably made the same mistake as me when I first went. Charging round like a bull elephant, asking this one, then that one, then another one. They see you coming, Marky. Probably think you're pissed, you just want your leg over and anybody'll do. You need to be more subtle.'

'How, like?'

'First, you get yourself a pint. Then you drift casually to a pillar or other vantage point. Then, all nonchalant, you survey the field. You'll see the pissheads charging about. The women see them too, and politely decline their invitations. Then, when you've had a good look and you've identified one or two likely targets, you sup off your pint and politely ask them if they would like to dance. Come up on their blind side, so to speak. Works every time. Most times anyway. Some of 'em still say no. Could be cos they don't fancy you, which is fair enough.'

Mark hadn't worked with Horlicks before, but now that he was getting to know him he was beginning to think he might be better company than Kev. And certainly more worldly than Robbie or Julian.

'Actually,' Horlicks was saying, 'I always make a note of the ones who say 'no', and them's the ones I go for. Just for the hell of it. They say 'no' to a few saddoes, then the next thing they know they're looking at me – suave, polite, a man-of-the-world. "Excuse me," I say, "would you care to dance?" Then I make a half turn towards the floor, and raise a hand invitingly. Bowls 'em over, Marky. Just one golden rule. Never, *never* ask a lass up to dance if she's seen you get a refusal from somebody else. She'll say 'no' if she does. Too proud, y'see.'

Fred, now standing close by, was smiling and shaking his head. 'Man-of-the-world? You? You've never been south of Gateshead.'

Horlicks shrugged and got to his feet. 'I'm south of Gateshead now, aren't I?' he declared, before walking off to the gents.

That evening, on the way home, Mark thought of calling for Rita, but changed his mind at the last moment. It was just that with his hoped-for tryst with Carol on Saturday, he didn't want to chat Rita up only to find Saturday was the one night she would go out with him. Carol on Saturday: it seemed a long time to wait. At home his thoughts were interrupted when he stepped from the kitchen into the living room. Dad, seeing him enter, stood up from his easy chair with an 'I've got something to say' look.

'Aye-aye lad.' He waited for Mark to close the door. Mark did so, and turned to face his father. 'Your mam and me's had a bit of a chat. Y'know how she worries about you, but, well, it's your eighteenth birthday soon and so, providing you pay for it, you can have your motorbike.'

Mark beamed. 'Thanks Dad, that's great. I get a pay rise when I'm eighteen so there'll be no problem buying it on hire purchase.'

Charlie Green smiled and picked up his *Evening Chronicle*. 'Aye well...steady as you go. And just make sure you keep up with the payments.'

Bob, now in the doorway, gave the thumbs up. 'We're both gonna be mobile,' he said. 'I'm buying a Ford Consul from a bloke at work.'

Shortly afterwards Mark was reclining in the bath. He'd come home filthy today. All that dust and grime. But soon he'd have wheels. Carol

Saturday. Rita on the dunes sometime. Marie waiting in the wings. He was still enjoying positive thoughts when Mam came knocking at the door, calling him for his tea. Monday was corned beef and chips, and loadsa baked beans. His favourite.

**

Lennie Kemp was still off the booze. Carol was thrilled: hopeful, too, that things would stay that way. By the weekend it would be three more weeks till Mam made her promised contact and she could tell her the news. Meanwhile she hoped she would see Mark on Saturday evening at Partners. She had already arranged to go with Emma. Maybe Mark would have a new friend too and they could make up a foursome.

Arriving at work she was singing as she passed through the revolving doors to the lobby. Forsaking the lift, she bounded up the stairs to the third floor. Later, she was just about to go for coffee when someone thrust a bundle of papers into her arms and asked her to hand them to Miss Carr on the way to the canteen. No problem, said Carol, before heading off in the direction of her boss's office.

Miss Carr's door was open. Carol place a foot inside and knocked, only to find the office unoccupied. She walked boldly to Miss Carr's desk, placed the bundle on it, and as she turned to go she caught sight of the picture that occupied the otherwise blank wall opposite. She paused to look at it. The picture was huge. The woman in the picture had beautiful eyes, Carol thought. They stared from behind her veil, as though they carried a message – of sadness, maybe. The veil reminded her of the one her mother wore many years ago when she was little. In fact the entire image reminded her of her mother: there was no colour in the picture, just as there was no colour in her memory of her childhood.

'Do you like it?'

Miss Carr was standing in the doorway, one arm raised and resting against the doorpost. Carol turned to go, but Miss Carr blocked her way. 'Do look at it as long as you wish,' she said. 'You'll notice it's right opposite my desk, so I see it every time I look up from my work.'

She stepped into the room and joined Carol in a joint appraisal of the picture. They stood in silence awhile, and when Carol looked at Miss Carr she found Miss Carr was looking intently at her.

'Do you know who it is?' she asked. 'The woman in the picture?'

Carol shook her head. 'A film star, I would say.'

'Quite right. But she was more than that. That woman is Marlene Dietrich. Have you heard of her?' As Carol shook her head her boss pushed the door so that it was almost closed. 'A bit before your time. Before my time too, come to that. Have you heard of the song, "Falling in Love Again"?'

Carol nodded. 'I think so.'

To her surprise and embarrassment Miss Carr started singing. She sang slowly, in a low voice: *'Falling in love again, never wanted to. What am I to do? Can't help it.* Lovely words, don't you think?' She went on, *sotto voce*, maintaining eye contact: *Love's always been my game, Play it how I may; I was made that way. Can't help it.'*

She paused, then looked back at the picture. 'Marlene Dietrich was a legend,' she declared, before walking to her desk. She picked up the bundle of papers Carol had left before turning around and addressing her again. 'She was a German national. Yet she hated the Nazis. Not many people in this country understood that, but it's true.'

Carol could think of nothing to say.

Miss Carr moved closer, until they were standing face to face. She was tall and slim with a commanding presence. Carol had to look up to maintain eye contact. 'She was bisexual, you know,' Miss Carr was saying. 'Do you know that that means, Carol? Bisexual? It means she was attracted to women as well as men. Some people are like that. Made that way, like in the song. It's the way of the world.'

The door opened. A woman member of staff came in and stood at Miss Carr's desk. 'Thank you, Carol,' said Miss Carr, dismissively. Feeling strange, yet happy, Carol left the office and went for coffee. She never knew Miss Carr could be so friendly. Or so approachable.

Striding up the Terrace Mark was upbeat. He would start looking for a motorbike at the weekend. With Kev, if he'd come. He was sure he would. They could visit the motorbike shops in Westgate Road. He'd need a crash helmet too. And goggles. And a leather jacket. And some new tools.

Crossing the backyard he didn't notice the black pedal cycle leaning against the wall. Indoors he found Mam in the kitchen, cooking dinner. To his surprise she wore a frown, the look she had when there was a problem and Mark was in the mire. 'There's someone here to see you,' she said.' Nonplussed, he went into the living room where he found Dad sitting in his usual seat by the fire; and opposite the unmistakable form of Police Constable Moon, the village bobby. PC Moon held a small plate, covered with crumbs, in one hand, a mug of tea in the other. His helmet lay on the floor at his side. PC Moon always reminded Mark of Mr Portly, the Policeman in one of the picture books he had as a kid.

'Now then Mark,' said PC Moon, with an official air.

Mark had never been in any kind of trouble, but he and his mates had always been greeted with a stern 'Now then' whenever PC Moon passed on his bicycle. And now the policeman was sitting in their living room drinking tea, and had polished off one of Mam's rock buns by the look of it.

PC Moon pushed his bulky frame from the back of the chair, set down the now-empty mug into the hearth and handed the empty plate to Mark's mam. She took it, but remained present to hear whatever was about to follow. Charlie addressed his son. 'Mr Moon has something to ask you, Mark lad.'

PC Moon took something from his tunic pocket, leaned forward and handed it to Mark. It was a small, folded card. He identified it at once as his Electrical Trades Union membership pass. He hadn't seen it for ages, not that he had cared particularly since he'd not the slightest interest in union matters. He had attended one meeting, something about being sworn and seconded, but had not returned. The card has his name on it, and even his signature.

'Recognise it, do you?' PC Moon's voice was cold and formal.

'It's my union card. I wondered where it was.'

'I'll tell you where it was,' said Moon. 'It was lying on the ground at the back of the Club. Just below the window of the ladies toilets.'

Mark said nothing, but felt his face redden as he stared vacantly at his card.

'It was found by Mr Walter Smith, the club steward,' said Moon. 'Any idea how it might have got there?'

Mark's shake of the head was barely discernible.

'The thing is,' Moon went on, 'a week past Sunday evening Mr Smith happened to step outside the club by the back door, for a breath of air like, when he saw somebody lurking in the darkness below that window. A peeping tom, as they say.'

'What made him think it was a peeping tom?' asked Charlie.

'Well…' PC Moon, glancing at Nancy, gave a cough, 'when whoever this fellow was saw Walter – Mr Smith – he upped and legged it.'

'Might've been somebody after stealing the empties,' ventured Charlie. 'Wouldn't be the first time somebody stole empty bottles from the back of the club and handed them in at the front for the threepence you get for their return.'

PC Moon shook his head. 'I take your point, only Walter says when the prowler ran off his strides – his trousers, Mrs Green – were round his knees. If you see what I mean.'

A short silence followed. 'Is Walter sure about that?' asked Nancy.

'He says he is. He even shouted "Peeping tom" after the blighter. Anyway, when this fellow ran off, Walter saw a woman crossing the car park.' He fumbled in his tunic pocket and pulled out his notebook, and flipped the pages. 'This woman, Mrs Armitage, saw the prowler too. She could hardly miss him as he ran right past her. He made off along the Club Path. In this direction.'

'Well, I see Mrs Armitage every day in the shop and she's never said anything to me,' said Nancy.

'Well, that would be because although the prowler ran right past her she didn't see his face because it was in shadow from the light on the corner.' He paused, before adding, 'And she says he had his trousers round his knees as well.'

'She saw his todger then,' said Charlie. 'That should make an interesting identity parade.'

'Charles Green!' said Nancy. 'This is no laughing matter.'

There was a brief pause before Charlie spoke again. 'When did Walter find Mark's union card anyway?' he enquired.

'Sunday evening last,' PC Moon replied.

'That's a week after he saw the prowler.' Moon could only shrug.

Charlie addressed his son. 'Well, Mark. Were you peeping into the ladies' lavs at the club?'

'No Dad.'

'And have you any idea how your union card was found there?'

Mark shook his head.

PC Moon stood up. 'Best we draw a line there, I think,' he said. 'There's no harm done and you've got your union card back.' He tapped his nose with his forefinger. 'Mind how you go though, Mark lad.' With that he picked up his helmet and left the room, chaperoned by Nancy. When the back door was heard to close she returned at once.

'Mark Green,' said Nancy. 'Your face. The polis might be satisfied but I'm not. Come on, out with it.' Mark stood in silence, gazing at his union card.

'Come on lad,' said Charlie. 'You were brought up to tell the truth. Were you peeping into the ladies toilets that night?'

'No Dad, I wasn't.'

'You were hanging round the back of the club though, weren't you? That's how Walter found your card.' Mark nodded. The silence that followed demanded more. When more wasn't forthcoming Charlie spoke again, this time sympathetically. 'What were you doing at the back of the club, then? Speak up!'

'I was with a lass.'

'I knew it!' Nancy glared at Charlie, and sat down in the chair vacated by PC Moon. 'It's that book, Lady whatever-her-name is. It's put ideas into his head.'

'The lad's coming up eighteen, pet,' said Charlie softly. 'I would be surprised if he didn't have a few ideas in his head at his age.' Nancy's silence was the key for Charlie to address Mark again.

'Just one question. Did anything happen with this lass, as you call her?'

'It wasn't her what called for you that day, was it,' Nancy interjected. 'She hardly looks old enough to be canoodling with a boy at the back of the club.'

'Did anything happen?' Charlie repeated. 'She's not gonna be pregnant, is she?'

Mark shook his head.

'Right then.' Charlie stood up. 'Go and get yourself cleaned up for you tea, and we'll hear no more about this. Except I'm not sure about this motorbike business now. We'll have to think about that. And that goes for going out on Saturday night into town as well.'

Mark went upstairs and flopped on his bed. Above him, the spider had resumed its work, a new web now adorning the corner, just waiting to trap an unsuspecting fly.

10

The next two days Mark spend in abject misery. At work, with Fred off sick again and Horlicks now off the job, he counselled Tommy, explaining that from being told he could go and buy a motorbike, now he'd been told he couldn't; and, on top of that, he wasn't allowed to go the dance in town on Saturday. He knew lads his own age who'd been dancing in town for ages; some even had girlfriends who were pregnant. One was even getting married and only just eighteen. When Tommy had enquired of the reason Mark was in the mire, Mark told him about his sexual tryst with Beryl at the back of the club, how she'd undone his strides and Walter had seen them, how he'd ran off and unwittingly dropped his union card so the police had been round.

If Mark expected a sympathetic ear he was disappointed. In fact, Tommy could hardly contain his laughter, which increased at every stage of the story, culminating with PC Moon's visit to Mark's house. 'Well,' said Tommy at last, 'if it's advice you want I can hardly give it, except in one respect.' He took a swig of tea and wiped a tear from his eye as Mark waited for his workmate to proffer the advice of an older man. 'Listen,' said Tommy, 'if you're shagging someone in secret, *never* carry any identification. Otherwise, you're only doing what all blokes have done since Adam met Eve in the apple orchard.'

On Friday evening, having been away in County Durham all week, they'd returned to the workshop to check for any messages. Nothing for you, Bert had declared. But as they were about to leave Miss Raine appeared at the top of the stairs to catch Mark's eye. He climbed the steps and joined her in the gloomy corridor.

Miss Raine always smelt lovely, whatever perfume she used. 'That young lady who called you,' she whispered. 'She called again this week – three times. She said you'd know who it was, but the last time she called, this morning, she said her name was Marie.'

'Did she leave a message?' Mark enquired nervously.

'Not on the first two occasions, but this morning she said to ring her. She says you have her telephone number. I must say she was quite persistent.'

Mark, in close proximity to Miss Raine, found himself lingering in the confines of the corridor. She didn't seem in any hurry to return to her office. 'Thank you,' he said at last, and turned away reluctantly. He felt flushed. Miss Raine was about twenty-five, too old to be interested in him. But she lingered in his thoughts anyway as he hurried to catch his bus. He felt good knowing Marie had called, but he resolved not to call her, just yet. It was Carol who was foremost in his mind.

He sat on the crowded bus on the way home in a state of melancholy. The weekend loomed, and he was grounded. Approaching the Balloon, his thoughts strayed to Rita. Dad had barred him from going into town. Maybe he could knock on Rita's door and invite her for a walk in Weston rec Saturday evening. They could sit on the rocking horse. He smiled at the thought. And then, before his eyes, she appeared in front of him, her red hair a beacon among the heads and bodies crowding the gangway. All the way from town she must have been sitting there, hidden by standing passengers. And now there she was. She was bound to see him, no matter where he looked. So he looked at her.

She looked lovely, he thought. No wonder he'd been so captivated by her for so long; no wonder he'd dreamed about her, looked out for her on the bus. To think, all the time she'd lived above the Balloon with her folks.

And then they had eye contact.

If he thought she would ignore him he was in for a surprise. Instead, she was smiling a smile of recognition, of being pleased to see him. As she squeezed past him with a 'Hi,' her thigh brushed his shoulder. Was it deliberate? His mind was in turmoil: should he follow her, chat her up on the pavement? If he didn't, would she think he wasn't interested and that would be that? He could ask her to the local flicks tomorrow night. Would she like that? But no, it was Carol he wanted to see. But he couldn't see her because he wasn't allowed into town. Caught in two minds he remained seated, frozen in time whilst Rita was now on the platform at the back of the bus. The bus stopped, and he saw her on the pavement, walking briskly. The bus moved off and she was gone. Gone till another time, perhaps. But gone.

He walked quickly up the Terrace, resigned to the barren weekend ahead. Dad was standing at the back gate. He nodded to his son, and followed him indoors. In the kitchen he had something to say. 'I've been speaking with your mam,' he said. 'She was upset, mind, about your antics with that lass at the back of the Club. But...' he shrugged and nodded his head slowly, as though trying to reassure himself, 'you're nearly eighteen now, so...'

Mark stood in silence, looking at a man who clearly felt uncomfortable, yet was determined to say his piece. Dad looked him in the eye and smiled. 'We hope you've learned your lesson, that's all. So, you're okay for the dance in town tomorrow. And to buy your motorbike.'

Mark felt a mixture of relief and happiness. So much so he was close to tears. But he needn't have worried on that score; there were tears in his dad's eyes too.

Friday evening, Carol knew, was crunch time. Dad had been off the booze all week, but Fridays had always been his night in the pub for a pint after he finished work.

Everything had been great. Dad back at work, coming home to read his *Chronicle* and have his tea, then watching TV, or fiddling with friends' pocket watches he was repairing, or trying to repair. He'd spread a newspaper on the kitchen table and sit for an hour or more, tinkering with tiny mechanisms, a small torch strapped around his head. Carol always thought he looked funny then. Like a nutty professor she said once to him. This week Dad had been in bed by ten every night without touching a drop of alcohol. A bottle of Newcastle Brown Ale had stood, untouched, in a kitchen cupboard all week. That wouldn't have been the case before she'd passed on Mam's message. But Friday was pub night. A pint or two was fine, but could he walk away and come home for the dinner she would be cooking him?

She opened the front door, picked up the mail from the doormat and hung her coat up. She walked through the living room to the kitchen and put the kettle on. Everything looked shipshape. Clean and tidy, just like Mam kept it. She could walk in here now and not have to lift a finger to do any housework.

She was troubled, slightly, at her encounter with Miss Carr. Judith, as she had been told to call her. Miss Carr had a well-earned reputation as a strict disciplinarian, someone a young woman like her should respect and even fear. Yet today she had been friendly; she'd even sang for her. And bisexual. That was a new word to her. The woman in the picture, Marlene somebody, was bisexual, Miss Carr had said. Thinking about it, she'd have thought she was the type who'd have a picture of Rock Hudson or Cary Grant. But no, her boss had the picture of a woman on the wall in her office. A *bisexual* woman. Seemed strange, she thought.

Preparing dinner, her thoughts drifted inevitably to Mark. Tomorrow, she hoped to see him at Partners. She wasn't optimistic. It's just that her failure to appear last week might have put him off. She had resolved to put her mother off if, perchance, she telephoned again seeking a meeting tomorrow night. She had a life too. But her life was so uncertain! Would Dad come home sober? Would Mark turn up, and if he did would he still be interested in her?

Then, the sound of a key in the lock. 'I'm home, pet,' Dad called, closing the door behind him. He appeared in the kitchen doorway. He was smiling. He was sober.

'Half an hour, Dad,' she said. 'It's the usual for Friday.'

He picked up his *Chronicle* and repaired to the living room. Carol started humming, softly. What were the words to Miss Carr's song again? She couldn't remember. She didn't care.

***

Saturday morning. Mark's breakfast fry-up. Mam barely spoke. Even Bob was taciturn. Mark went to his the bedroom and took a small piece of paper from where he'd hidden it, in the drawer containing his underwear. He sat on his bed and looked at Marie's telephone number.

He was seeing Carol tonight – he hoped. He'd not forgotten that night in the Stoll with Marie, and she hadn't forgotten either, judging by the numerous calls she'd made to work. She said she sometimes went to Partners. She could be there tonight. She'd not expect to be fobbed off if she was. Rita could be there too, although it was unlikely, he reasoned, if Betty was out with Kev. What a show that would be: dancing with Carol, Marie and Rita at the edge of the dancefloor looking on, waiting for the music to stop before they all stood around him, seeking his affections. Kev would give anything for the attentions of three girls. But, right now, Mark wanted only to see Carol.

He knocked for Kev to tell him the news: he could have a motorbike and how about looking at some in town? But his friend was out. His mam didn't know when he'd be back. 'I think he's seeing some lass,' was the best she could offer. And so, as usual, Mark called on his first reserve: Robbie. Did he fancy going dancing at Partners this evening? He might be able to introduce him to Carol's friend, if they were there. Robbie had never expressed any interest in dancing, or even girls, so Mark was surprised at his 'yes', which came after reassurances that you didn't have to be able to dance, that being taught was actually fun and in the Bradford Barn you met lots of girls but you didn't have to enter into meaningful conversations with any because you keep moving on to another one. And the music's always great. 'They play Del Shannon,' Mark lied.

And now they were on the bus, wearing suits and ties. Mam called Robbie 'a nice, quiet lad'. He was quiet now, probably nervous about going to a dance, Mark thought. But this suited Mark, whose brain was planning what tack to take with Carol. 'Be cool,' would have been Kev's advice. Bob's would have been different. Be polite. Be kind. Be courteous. Be a gentleman. Above all, be yourself.

If Carol wasn't there tonight, he'd be disappointed, but he knew where she lived. He'd knock on her door another time. He wouldn't give up on her. Somehow, the nearer they got to town, the more certain he felt that she wouldn't be there. She wasn't there last week, after all. She could be at the Oxford, although he wasn't sure he could show his face there yet.

At Gallowgate Mark led Robbie directly to the door of King's Head. Mark made to enter, but his friend held back.

'What are you doing?' asked Robbie, standing forlornly on the pavement.

'Just going for a swift one.'

'We're not eighteen.'

'C'mon. We're big boys now.' Mark started to push the door again. Music blared from inside. 'Just one,' Mark pleaded before entering the bar, hoping Robbie would follow. He did, looking ill at ease. 'Just get me a glass of lemonade, thanks,' he said, looking around as though a police raid might be imminent.

'Pint of Exhibition and a glass of lemonade,' said Mark to the same barman who had served him and Kev last time. They drifted to a corner, Mark sipping his beer as he went. He offered his glass for Robbie to have a taste. His friend shook his head, his face tripping him up. Mark drank quickly. The beer made him relax. He handed his empty glass to Robbie.

'You gonna get me one in, then?'

Robbie shook his head. 'I'll give you the money but you'll have to get it.' He handed Mark a ten shilling note. Mark bought another pint and joined his friend in the corner. They stood in silence as the music blared, Robbie continually eyeing the door. Feeling awkward, Mark drank quickly. When he'd finished Robbie walked off. Mark followed him into the street, where the fresh air hit him like a fist and his legs almost buckled. He had to put a hand on the wall to steady himself.

'Brilliant.' Robbie was standing there, looking at him. 'I put a bloody suit and tie on, polish my shoes and you're pissed.'

Mark took a few deep breaths before sighing deeply and, for some reason, checking the knot in his tie. 'I'll be okay,' he said at last. 'Just needed some air, that's all. C'mon.' With that he started walking, determined to shake off the effects of the rapidly-drunk booze, but angry with himself for drinking it. Tonight of all nights, when he hoped to meet up with Carol. He gulped air as he walked, and tried to think clearly. He thought a couple of pints would have set him up, made him feel confident and happy. 'I feel like shit,' he said at last. Robbie nodded, too concerned about his own nervousness at going to a dance for the first time, and knowing that in just minutes he would be embracing a girl and learning to do the quickstep or the waltz.

Mark stopped abruptly under the Goldsmith's clock. 'Tell you what,' he said, 'I need some fresh air and exercise. Can we have a walk down to the Quayside and back?' Robbie nodded and they headed towards the Tyne, walking in silence. Apart from feeling rotten, Mark didn't want Carol to know he'd been drinking. Half an hour's respite was all he needed. They reached the Quayside, which was deserted.

'It always stinks down here,' Robbie said. 'Makes me want to puke.'

At his words Mark turned away, crossed the road, knelt on the pavement and threw up into the gutter. Robbie stood back and waited. Mark turned to face him, wiping his mouth with the back of his hand. 'You probably did me a favour. Kev says you feel better after you spew.' Sure enough, Mark felt a lot better as they headed for the city centre again.

'I hope my breath doesn't smell of alcohol,' he remarked.

'Probably smells of sick,' was his friend's unsympathetic reply.

Fifteen minutes later they were at Partners, too late, Mark new, for the dancing instruction. They checked in their coats and stood in front of the full-length mirror at the foot of the stairs. Robbie combed his hair. Mark checked the knot in his tie. 'C'mon then,' he said at last. He led the way up the stairs, the music of Victor Sylvester getting louder with every step. At the top they found themselves looking at a sea of bodies, moving slowly around the dancefloor.

'This is a waltz,' said Mark. He led the way along the wall where women waited to be asked to dance. They reached the tearoom. He looked inside. It was deserted, although a woman waited patiently at the serving hatch.

'Could do with a coffee,' said Mark. Robbie sat down and Mark brought two cups to the table. 'We'll have these and go looking,' he announced. 'There's lots of lasses just waiting to be asked up.' So there were, but he wanted to find Carol – if she was there. He drank the hot coffee gratefully. It was just what he needed. They sat in silence, whilst just feet away, around the corner, dozens of people danced and talked or simply lingered in expectation. Robbie stood up and looked before returning to the table. 'You'll never find anyone in there,' he remarked.

Just then the music stopped and the lights came on, illuminating the entrance to the tearoom. Mark tipped the last drops of his coffee down his throat. Robbie lingered with his as a few couples wandered in, chatting. 'C'mon then,' Mark urged his friend, but even as he spoke Carol appeared in company with a young man. They were laughing heartily, and after pausing for a moment, clearly asking her what she would like to drink, the young man went to the serving hatch.

Robbie finished his coffee. 'Ready when you are then.'

Mark didn't move. 'That's her,' he said. 'That's Carol. She's with that bloke.'

Emma appeared, and sat beside Carol. Then the fellow who'd gone for drinks returned to the table, carrying two cups. Emma went to the serving hatch.

Jiving music started up. 'There's lots of lasses here, not just them,' said Robbie, getting to his feet. 'I can't do the ballroom stuff but I can jive.' With that he walked off and disappeared into the throng on the dancefloor. Mark stayed put. Carol had her back him and Emma, who had returned to the table with her drink, didn't seem to be taking any notice. Ten minutes passed before Carol, Emma and the young man left the tearoom and returned to the dancefloor. Mark waited a minute or so longer before doing the same, by which time the lights were low as Victor Sylvester played a foxtrot.

He stood by the side of the floor, in shadow, trying to catch a glimpse of Robbie. Before him, young men and women danced to the music, either following the proper steps or simply muddling through. He was still feeling the effects of the alcohol, and now had the makings of a headache. He wanted to go. He moved away from the shadows, scanning the floor for Robbie.

'Mark!'

Her voice came from nowhere. He turned to find himself looking at Carol's smiling face – and those eyes again! He caught the smell of her perfume. And now, even as he stood momentarily speechless, Carol stood on tiptoe and kissed his cheek. She stood back again, laughing.

'Well...Hi!' She waited for a response.

'Hi,' he said simply, feeling numb, yet happier by the minute. 'I didn't see you...'

'Obviously.' She looked so happy to see him. But even as they stood looking at one another, a puzzled look fell over her face. 'Is something wrong,' she said at last, her smile changing to a look of concern.

'Aren't you with someone?' he enquired.

She laughed. 'Of course. A young lady doesn't go dancing alone.' She waited, puzzled at his non-response. 'I'm with Emma. Remember?' He nodded. 'And you are with your friend, what's his name again...'.

'Julian? No, not this week.' There was an awkward pause before he spoke again. 'I saw you just now,' he said. 'In the tearoom. You were with someone.'

'I was. Emma and Mike. Mike is Emma's brother. He's here with some mates.' She gave him a moment to take it in. 'So, who are you with this week?'

On cue, Robbie appeared. 'Him,' said Mark. 'Robbie, Carol. Carol, Robbie.'

Carol and Robbie exchanged smiles. 'Emma's around somewhere,' said Carol. 'I'll go fetch her. Don't move.' She disappeared into the throng of bodies.

'That bloke we saw with Carol is Emma's brother,' said Mark to Robbie, before Carol reappeared with Emma. Robbie and Emma exchanged 'hi's'. Smalltalk followed as jiving started up again. Robbie and Emma took to the floor. It was *A Girl Like You*. 'Our song,' said Carol.

'Let's dance,' said Mark.

'Let's sit down,' said Carol. They went to the tearoom and sat down at a table.

'I'm sorry I couldn't make last week,' she said. 'I wanted to come to see you but I couldn't. A family problem. Nothing serious, but...'

'I wanted to see you too. But it's okay, we're here now, aren't we?'

She laughed softly. 'We are.' They both fell into relax mode. 'Did you come last week?' she asked. 'And did you meet anyone?'

The image of the old woman flashed through his mind as he replied yes and no. She smiled. He could tell she was pleased.

'I love your smile,' he said.

'I love *your* smile,' she replied. They laughed and leant towards one another for a kiss, but she sat back sharply.

'You've been drinking.'

'Only a quick pint. That's all.'

She saw his concern over her reaction. 'Well, a quick one... that's okay. I suppose.' Her hands were resting on the table. He reached forward and held them gently in his. 'I've thought about you every day ever since we met,' he said softly. 'I'm so pleased we've met again tonight.'

'So am I,' she replied. 'So am I.'

The little gate creaked slightly as she pushed it open. He followed her to the dark shadow by her front door. The sound of Emma's clicking heels receded into the distance as she headed for her own house, accompanied by Robbie.

'Well,' she whispered, looking up into his face and sliding her arms loosely around his neck. 'Here we are – again.' He slid his hands inside her open coat, pulled her gently towards him and held her tight, feeling the warmth of her against him.

They kissed, softly at first, then more firmly until, at last, she broke off laughing. 'I can't breathe,' she declared, her eyes as ever looking directly into his. They kissed again, more passionately now, her hands caressing the back of his neck.

The effects of the alcohol and his emerging headache had gone, driven off by her presence and the happiness he felt being with her. They stood in silence but in close physical contact until, at last, she withdrew slightly, twirling his tie between her fingers. 'Would you like to come in for a coffee?' she whispered. 'We'll have to be quiet, mind.

My dad's in bed and he might be cross to find an unknown stranger in the house.' Mark hadn't liked the look of the man he thought was her dad saw that time when he saw him outside the house, but if it was OK with Carol...

She didn't wait for a reply anyway. Instead she fumbled in her handbag for her key, then slipped it into the lock and quietly turned it, pushing the door open slowly and silently. He followed her into the dark hallway, then into the living room. She switched on the light and gestured for him to remove his coat, which she tossed over the back of a chair with her own. She kicked off her shoes, whispered 'won't be long' and disappeared into the kitchen.

Mark removed his shoes, and stood where she had left him. The room was small, with a three-piece suite, sideboard and a large cabinet all crammed in. It was clean and neat. Mam would like it, he thought. A television set occupied a corner. The Radio Times lay on a coffee table in front of the settee. He could hear Carol in the kitchen and thought he would join her but thought better of it. Instead he wandered over to the fireplace, where his gaze fell on several photographs of the same woman. She looked about forty, Mark thought, and had Carol's features. He thought one picture was of Carol, but it had obviously been taken some years before. In the background he recognised Tynemouth Long Sands. He looked at the others, picked one or two up for closer examination.

'That's Mam.' Carol appeared, carrying two mugs of coffee. She plonked them on the coffee table.

Mark was still holding one of the pictures. 'Is she...?'

'Dead?' Carol laughed. 'No. She's just...away at the moment. Do you take sugar?'

He shook his head. They sat on the settee and she picked up her coffee. 'Dad wouldn't want me bringing anyone into the house,' she said. 'I never have before now,' she added, taking a sip.

Mention of her father reminded Mark of the strong smell of alcohol when Carol entered the house last time he was here. He couldn't smell alcohol now. But he did feel apprehensive about the possibility that her dad might appear, although Carol didn't seem to think he would wake up.

'Emma likes Robbie,' Carol was saying. 'I can tell, and anyway she said so.'

'He's usually quiet,' said Mark. 'I was surprised when he said he would come to the dance.'

'Would you have come without him?'

'Yes. Because I wanted to meet you again.'

She reached out and took his hand, and sidled closer to him. He kissed her as they sank back against the back of the settee, his hand caressing her face. Her eyes were closed and he slid his hand to her shoulder then down her upper arm. She was motionless, totally relaxed, her chin raised, their mouths locked together.

Mark had never felt so happy. After their meeting at Partners they had talked and laughed together. The time had flown. He had enjoyed his trysts with Beryl and Marie, and been haunted for weeks over Connie – Rita, he reminded himself. But Carol was different. The others were all lovely, and sexy. But Carol had that something he couldn't define. Was this love? Was this what love meant? He couldn't stop kissing her. Even her breath was wonderful. As they kissed, he wanted her, to explore her. He pulled his hand back slightly, cupped it over her breast. It felt wonderful, but the moment was shattered when she sat forward violently and pushed him away.

She was on her feet. 'What on earth are you doing?' she hissed. She glared at him, her lips pursed in anger.

'Sorry,' he gasped.

She was livid and looked it. She stood there, looking at him before she stepped back half a pace. 'You'd better go,' she said.

He stood up, but remained silent. All the waiting to meet her again. The physical contact tonight, the way he felt. He'd thrown it all away. He hadn't meant to offend her, to hurt her. But now she was leading him into the hall. He followed meekly. Somehow he knew protest would serve no purpose. He pulled on his shoes, tied the laces quickly and reached for his coat, all the time hoping she would say she didn't mean it, that she didn't want him to go, that she understood. Instead she kept her silence. He opened the front door, and turned to face her.

'I'm so sorry,' he said. 'I thought...'

'You thought I was easy, that's what you thought. Drinking beer then thinking you could come here for sex. I'm not like that. I didn't think you were.'

She held the door, ready to close it the moment he stepped out-side. 'Will I see you again?' he asked. 'I want to. I want to put things right.'

She looked up at his face, and almost seemed to melt before his pleading gaze. 'I don't know,' she said at last, before closing the door, leaving him alone in the darkness.

As he set off to walk into town for the all-night bus, he gathered his thoughts. He'd come on too strong, been too familiar. Thinking about it, he could never imagine Joyce being 'familiar', but she and Bob were together now. He should have taken his time with Carol. She had enjoyed their kissing, had even welcomed him into her house. He wouldn't give up on someone as special as her. Maybe he could write. He checked his stride at the thought, then turned and went back to her house. He could see no number on the gate, and her front door was in darkness. Next door was number 41, and beyond that 39. So hers was 43. He'd write.

Drunken men sat at the back of the bus, singing and swearing. Mark sat alone at the front and ignored them. He was relieved to get to Weston without incident. Some of the revellers looked nasty and one had even threatened the conductor who cleared off without taking the fare. He walked quickly up the Terrace, pushed the backyard gate open and was crossing the yard when he heard a penetrating screech. It sounded like a tom cat. He hesitated in the darkness. Silence prevailed, until he heard the sound of a sort of smothered cry. It seemed to come from next door, from Roger and Ada's backyard. When it happened again he stepped up to the dividing wall and looked over it. All was in darkness as he stood and listened. Then he heard the sound of a wom-an sighing, followed by banging noises and a male voice grunting.

Suddenly, next door's toilet door opened. In the darkness he could discern two figures. One moved swiftly to the back door, the other to the back gate. When the back door opened he saw the unmistakable silhouette of Ada entering her kitchen. Then he heard the click of a back gate, and in the glare of the streetlight he saw shiny top of a bald head. Moments later there was another click as the gate on the other side of the Greens' yard was opened. Turning, he watched the dark shadow of a burly figure crossing to the back door. When the door opened a dog yapped. It was just the sort of noise a Jack Russell would make.

11

On Monday Mark celebrated his eighteenth birthday. Not that 'celebrate' was featuring in his mind when he came downstairs in answer to Mam's ceiling-knocking at six o'clock that morning. There'd be no fuss, and he didn't want any. Birthday parties and presents were for kids anyway.

Still, a present did await him. A soft, square-shaped package, carefully wrapped in coloured paper, lay forlornly on the table next to the cornflakes. Written on it, in biro, 'Happy birthday, Mark', in Mam's scrawly handwriting. Next to it were two large white envelopes, which he knew without opening them were birthday cards from his parents, and Bob and Joyce. He opened Mam's parcel. It contained three white handkerchiefs, each with a blue embroidered 'M' in the corner. The envelopes he decided to leave until he got home from work at tea-time.

Sunday he'd spent fretting about Carol; but a walk to the rec and ten minutes on the rocking horse helped to clear his thoughts. He could have done with company, but Kev was nowhere to be found, Julian was out and Robbie, as usual, was lying in bed until whatever time he would deign to get up, if at all. He could talk to Bob, but only when Mam and Dad were out, which they weren't on Sundays. His sighting of Eggshell and Ada, emerging from next-door's lav, was amazing but he couldn't think who, if anyone, to tell. Who would believe him?

He had resolved not to give up on Carol. He couldn't explain it, but he knew, for him, she was special. He loved being with her; loved *her*, in fact. The rift between them was his fault; it was something he would put right. But he wasn't going to sit on the fence in the meantime. He would telephone Marie and knock on Rita's door. Even so, this Monday morning, as he lingered in the workshop waiting for Tommy to sort out electrical fittings with Bert, it was Miss Raine he was looking out for, his gaze constantly directed to the door at the top of the steps that led to her office. As he waited it opened once, but it was only Pam the cleaner, ciggy dangling from her mouth, struggling with her bucket and mop as she negotiated the steps into the workshop. Of Miss Raine there was no sign.

The back door opened and Fred came in. Mark was shocked at his appearance. He looked pale and gaunt, as though he'd had a rough night on the booze the night before. But Fred was teetotal, as Mark knew. Smudger appeared at Bert's hatch, wearing his battered trilby. Mark noted the look of concern his face as he caught sight of Fred. Anyone who was late for work could be assured of a few dry remarks from Smudger, if not a bollocking, but Fred was spared the experience.

'Aye Fred,' said Smudger, trying to sound upbeat. Fred simply grunted. 'Make Fred a cuppa son,' said Smudger to Mark. 'No need, no need,' said Fred. He always wore a cap, and he reminded Mark of a late uncle who had died a few years ago. Then Tommy appeared with his haversack, ready to go. When Fred went to the lavatory Smudger spoke to Tommy and Mark.

'Look after him, lads,' said Smudger. 'He looks ill to me. I mean, really ill. Shouldn't be at work really.'

'Might as well be at work as sitting on my arse at home.' Fred, appearing quickly from the toilet, was in ill-health, but there was nothing wrong with his ears. He, Tommy and Mark left the workshop together. 'Another day, another dollar,' said Tommy, leading the way to his car. It was parked close by, not, as usual, on the waste land half a mile away. That meant he'd put money into 'one of them new-fangled parking meters'. 'Let's have a cuppa in the Haymarket,' said Tommy. 'Smudger wouldn't begrudge you a cuppa, would he Fred?' Judging by Fred's appearance, Mark wondered if a visit to a hospital would be more appropriate.

Tommy and Mark worked hard all that day, while Fred mooched about and took over Mark's tea-making duties. At lunch, with Tommy perusing his *Daily Mirror*, Fred managed a few of the usual half-hearted remarks about Mark's weekend activities. Did he go to the dance? Did he see that girl he mentioned? Did he have sex? 'I'd have had her drawers off by now when I was your age.' But even though his questions went largely unanswered, he didn't seem to care. His listlessness left Mark feeling awkward, but Tommy kept him so busy it hardly mattered. Even so he was relieved when it was time to pack up and go back to town, not least because he had resolved to call Marie when Tommy dropped him off.

Sitting in the back of Tommy's car Mark closed his eyes and allowed his mind to wander. He'd have to apologise to Marie for not calling earlier. He'd say he'd been busy, working in Durham somewhere, not getting home till late every night. He didn't foresee any problem. After all, she'd called him three times last week, even left her name. He closed his eyes and thought of that night in the Stoll. It would be like that again, maybe better. He wondered if she might want to go all the way, and where could they go if she did? Opening his eyes again, he looked idly at the back of Fred's head, his old cap covering his baldness, wisps of grey hair sticking out and running straight down the back of his head. He must be worried about his health, Mark thought. Fancy having cancer. Tommy, chain smoking at the wheel: he's the one who should have it. He closed his eyes again as his mind drifted back to Marie. Her face. Her perfume. Even now the thought of her was turning him on.

At that moment the familiar sound of the motor stopped. When he looked of the window he saw they were in the middle of nowhere as the car drifted to a standstill, traffic overtaking noisily.

'We've conked out,' declared Tommy, his hands still holding the steering wheel.

'Fucking Fords, they're all the same,' was Fred's contribution to the situation.

They all got out.

There was a gap in the verge about twenty yards away. 'Let's push it,' said Tommy. Mark and Fred pushed from the back, Tommy at the driver's door, one hand through the window holding the steering wheel. When they reached the gap Fred sank to his knees out of breath, his face ashen. Tommy stood behind him and lifted him up by the armpits. 'Sit in the car,' Tommy told him. Fred did as he was bid.

Tommy lifted the bonnet, and he and Mark perused the engine. Mark didn't know much about engines, except for points and spark plugs. Tommy reached forward, checked the leads to the battery, the leads to the spark-plugs and generally touched this and that. 'There's petrol in the bloody tank I take it,' called Fred, as traffic roared past, too close for comfort Mark thought.

Tommy went to the boot and returned with his tools. 'I'll check the plugs,' he said. 'You go and sit with Fred.'

Mark did as he was bid. He and Fred sat in silence, with Tommy's torso just visible through the windscreen between the dashboard and the bottom of the upturned bonnet. After a few minutes Mark noticed Fred's head lolling forward onto his chest, before he sat upright with a start.

'I want a piss,' said Fred, reaching for the door handle.

'You can't here,' said Mark, 'not on this busy road.'

Fred remained where he was, looking straight ahead. 'I feel like shit,' he murmured. Mark could think of nothing to say, but inside he felt a deep pity for the man who was so highly regarded by his workmates and who was now so ill.

Ten minutes later Tommy appeared on the offside and plonked himself in the driver's seat. 'Cross your fingers,' he muttered as he inserted the ignition key. He pressed the starter. The engine turned but failed to start. After three or four attempts he gave up and returned to the front. Mark got out and joined him. As he did the bus to Newcastle sped by. He checked his wristwatch. It was after six o'clock. He could be too late to call Marie, even if they got going now.

Tommy reached forward and undid the distributor cap. Next thing he was rubbing a small piece of emery paper on the points. He put it all together again. 'Tell you what, there's a bit of a slope up yonder. Think we can push her that far? Then I'll jump in and we'll give her a go.'

Tommy and Mark pushed the car slowly forward. When they reached the top of the slope the car picked up momentum and Tommy jumped in. 'Keep pushing Mark lad,' he called, grasping the steering wheel. He slipped the car into gear as it gathered speed. Almost reluctantly the engine kicked into life. He stopped long enough only for Mark to get aboard and they were on their way. 'See what crossing your fingers does?' said Tommy in triumph.

'It's my bloody legs I'm crossing,' barked Fred.

Mark made a beeline for the telephone kiosk opposite the Odeon. Carefully unfolding the now-crumpled piece of paper bearing Marie's number he made the call. It rang for so long he almost hung up, but at the last moment he was answered by a female voice saying, simply, 'Hello?' He knew it wasn't Marie.

'Is Marie at home?' he asked, trying to sound matter-of-fact.

'I'm afraid you've just missed her,' said the voice. It seemed to be the voice of an older woman. 'Who's speaking?'

'It's Mark,' he replied, hoping that perhaps she might have mentioned his name.

'Oh, well Mark, she isn't here right now. I'm Marie's mam. Can I take a message?'

'If you could just say I called.'

He replaced the telephone handset, pushed the kiosk door open and headed for his bus stop. Even as he walked he realised that at that moment he might not be so far from Marie. I bet she's off to the Stoll, he told himself. And if she was she wouldn't be on her own. For a moment he thought of going there to see if she turned up, and who with; but his stomach was rumbling and in any case, he decided, he'd put things off long enough: he'd call on Rita.

Nearing the Balloon he felt nervous. He was still in his work clothes; what would Rita think of him, standing at her door all mucky? But, as he would explain, he was asking her out on another time, tomorrow perhaps. He didn't have her telephone number after all. He checked his watch. It was nearly eight o'clock. She'd have had her tea, might be watching telly.

Would she be pleased at his unexpected appearance, he wondered.

'Balloon!' The conductor's voice boomed out from the back of the bus. Mark felt like a parachutist about to make the drop into enemy territory, like in the war films. The awful moment they had to jump. He was jumping now. Getting off the bus anyway. On the pavement he hesitated and stood there awhile, looking at the pub on the opposite side of the road. The windows above must be where she lived, he thought. She could even be looking at him now. What would she think if he bottled it and walked off? He thought of her and the times he'd looked out for her on the bus, how he'd not been able to get her out of his mind for weeks. Now he was just yards away from her door. He crossed the road and walked to the side of the pub to a blank door.

High on the wall, at the side of the door, was a plastic bell-push. He stood on the step and looked at the name, written in biro, on a small piece of paper behind a plastic cover. 'Bell', it said. Was that her name or was it stating the obvious? He pressed the button, not hearing any response from within, but as the flat was upstairs he hardly expected to. He waited awhile without response, and tried again. Nothing. He knocked firmly on the door. There was no reply. He stood back and looked at the door for a moment and turned away. In a way he felt relieved.

He crossed the main road and headed for home. It started to rain, a few spots at first, then heavier. He pulled his collar up and thrust his hands deep into the pockets of his donkey jacket, and quickened his pace. The wind had got up and it looked as though he was in for a battering. Eyes down, collar up, he didn't notice the black Austin 7 gliding silently alongside the kerb. The sudden, sharp sound of the horn made him jump. He looked to see the blurred image of the driver through the rain-lashed window, waving to catch his attention.

He went to the nearside door and opened it to see the smiling face of Julian's mam at the wheel. 'Hop in!' she called, her voice almost lost in a gust of wind that blew spray into Mark's face. He did as he was bid, dumping his sodden haversack on his lap.

'I thought it was you,' she was saying, checking her mirror and slowly driving off. 'Looks like I've saved you from a soaking.' Mark nodded, at the same time wiping water away from his eyes. 'Have you just finished work?' she asked, looking ahead through the rain-lashed windscreen. He told her all about breaking down on the way back to town. Her silence merited a glance in her direction. He knew what she was thinking. 'I got off the bus at the Balloon to see a friend,' he explained. Well, she said, she would run him home.

'How's Julian?' he asked, for the want of something to say.

'Julian's fine. He did enjoy the dance that night. I think he wants to go again, but you know I do worry about the town and the drunks. One hears such terrible stories.'

They were approaching the Terrace.

'I live up here,' he said, laying a hand on the door handle.

'I can drop you near your house,' she replied. 'You'll get soaked if you walk.'

She turned up the Terrace and stopped where he indicated, just a few yards short of the back gate. He wondered what she made of terraced houses, compared to her private semi.

'There we are,' she said, applying the handbrake. She looked directly at him. 'I always think you're a good boy, Mark,' she said. 'I often tell Julian to do things like you. You know, like making sure he gets a haircut and keeps himself smart.' She smiled now, her hand resting on top of the gearstick. 'Isn't it your birthday about now?' she asked, maintaining eye contact.

'I'm eighteen today actually,' he replied.

She laughed. 'I know. Julian mentioned it. Well, many happy returns.' She put a hand on the dashboard, leaned over to him and planted a kiss on his cheek, lingering slightly, her face so close to his he could smell her perfume and feel her warm breath. Then she sat back, her face changing to a look of concern. 'Won't you be late for your tea or party, or whatever…?'

'We never bother.'

'Mark,' she said, looking serious now. 'Could I ask you a personal question?'

He looked at her without reply.

'Do you think I'm attractive? I mean, be honest. Tell me.'

She was looking right at him, *into* him almost, as she waited for his answer. He felt his face redden.

She laughed softly. 'Too embarrassed to say anything,' she said. But she was still waiting. 'Well?' she said at last. 'Do you?'

He nodded, his eyes meeting her gaze. 'You smell nice,' he said.

She looked serious again. 'You know, Mark, I have a very good marriage, a good husband and a lovely son. But Arthur – that's my husband – Arthur, well, he's only really ever been interested in his work and his classical music. He's never really been interested in *me*.' She paused. 'It's as if I'm only there to cook his meals and keep the house clean, you know…' She looked away, almost theatrically – like Hollywood actresses did, Mark thought – before continuing. 'A woman has many needs. Physical needs, Mark.' She turned to face him again. 'If you do find me attractive, Mark, I would like you to know I have those physical needs, as I'm sure you do too.'

Nonplussed, he could only return her gaze.

She smiled and adjusted her position in the driving seat. 'Well, I expect you'll be wanting your tea. So, off you go…' She reached across and squeezed his hand before slipping the car into first gear. He opened the door and got out to find the rain had stopped. She drove off, leaving him perplexed but looking forward to his tea.

At the back gate, Charlie stood and watched his youngest son emerge from the mysterious black car parked just down the road. It was driven off by a woman who looked in her forties, as far as he could tell. He went indoors to report the arrival of his son to his wife.

One glance at his mother and Mark knew he was in bother: hands on her hips, elbows out, stern-faced and ready for war.

'And where have you been till this time of night, pray?' She wiped her hands on her pinny, waited for his explanation.

'Sorry Mam. We conked out.'

'Your dinner's been ready three hours. *Three hours*.'

Charlie appeared in the doorway. 'Whose was that car I just saw you get out of?' he enquired.

'Julian's mam's. She gave me a lift from the Balloon.'

'From the Balloon? What were you doing at the Balloon?'

'I know a lass there.'

'A lass?' Nancy Green turned to her husband. 'He's seeing a lass and here's me cooking his dinner. And on his birthday too.'

Charlie looked at his wife. 'Nancy, the lad's eighteen. He's entitled to be seeing a lass.'

'He's too young to be seeing lasses.'

'Oh aye. And how old were you when we got to know each other?'

She didn't reply, but instead picked up a tea towel and took Mark's dinner from the oven and plonked it on to the worktop. 'Aunt Ettie and Avril came to see you, because it's your birthday. Avril even made you a lovely cake. And you weren't even here to say thank you.'

Charlie laid a hand gently on Mark's arm. His place was laid at the table in the living room. Still being in his work clothes, he hesitated before sitting down. 'Just wash your hands, son. You can have a bath later,' said Charlie, who remained in the kitchen to help his wife. Mark did as he was bid and went into the living room to find Bob sitting by the fire.

'Looks like you don't need to go dancing to find lasses, then.' Bob spoke in a low voice, not wanting his words to stray into the kitchen. 'The lassie's found you.'

'What lassie?'

'Avril, of course. She was here. Even baked you a cake.'

They both laughed, as Mark scrutinised the five envelopes containing his birthday cards, and a second small parcel. The first two cards, as he had anticipated, were from his parents, and Bob and Joyce. The third was from 'Aunt Maggie' in Doncaster, Mam's sister whom he'd never met but who had sent him birthday cards since he was a baby. She and Mam rarely communicated for some reason, but she never forgot her nephew's birthday. The card had a picture of the Flying Scotsman on the front. The next one, bearing no stamp, had a picture of a footballer on the front and was from 'Aunt Ettie and Avril'. The printed message inside read, 'With best wishes on your birthday'. Underneath, in scribbly handwriting, was the message, 'With best wishes on your birthday'.

Just then Mam plonked his dinner on to the table and left the room without a word. He was ravenous, and tucked in. Bob sat reading the *Chronicle*. When he'd finished he pushed his plate aside and picked up the fifth envelope, by far the largest. He didn't recognise the handwriting on the envelope, and couldn't guess who it might be from. Sliding his fingers under the flap he pulled out the card. It bore a picture of a distinguished-looking man wearing a smart trilby, collar and tie, sports jacket and grey flannels and smoking a pipe. A spaniel sat obediently at his side, and in the background were fields and trees, and distant birds in an azure sky. The message inside, in neat handwriting, read, 'To Mark, wishing you many happy returns on your birthday. Mr and Mrs Popham and family'.

Mam brought his pudding, this time with a friendly 'Five cards this year, then.' She lingered at the table, looking them over, before picking up the Pophams' card and checking the message without comment. She pulled Avril's cake closer to Mark. 'We can all have a nice slice of your cake later, after you've had your bath.' She kissed him on top of the head and left the room again. Before starting on his pudding he picked up the second parcel. The writing on the small tag dangling from it read, 'To Mark, Happy birthday. Avril'. Bob, smiling, was looking on curiously. Mark carefully tore the wrapping paper aside to reveal a small box containing three white handkerchiefs, each with a blue embroidered 'M' in the corner.

***

That Wednesday Fred failed to appear at work. Tommy and Mark hung about, then Smudger told them to go. 'Have a cuppa in the Haymarket,' he said. 'Just this once, mind. If Fred turns up I'll send him along.'

'It's all very well saying that,' Tommy complained to Mark as soon as they left the workshop. 'But that means me putting more dosh into the bloody parking meter.' He fed the meter anyway and they wandered along to the café where four of their colleagues were ensconced in the corner. One of them was Horlicks. 'He can't sack six of us, surely,' he said, pulling two extra chairs up to the table. 'Just you four,'

Tommy replied. 'We're here officially, waiting for Fred – if he shows up.' He handed Mark some change. 'Tea for two, Mark.'

Horlicks and the others left, leaving Tommy to read his *Mirror* and Mark to twiddle his thumbs. His gaze fell upon the girl behind the counter. She was plump and jolly. She was always there, and always with a smile for customers. She was nibbling a piece of cake, waiting for the door to open to serve someone else. Mark looked at the door. Would Fred enter, he wondered? But Fred never appeared. They went to the job without him. Tommy spent part of the day tinkering with his car, so not much was achieved. They returned to the workshop that evening, to find Bert shaking his head: nothing heard of Fred. As they were about to leave Miss Raine appeared at the top of the steps. She was looking at Mark, her right hand raised to her head, holding an imaginary telephone.

She led the way to her office. 'I think it's that girl again,' she said, sitting down at her typewriter. Mark picked up the phone, and the same time looked nervously at Miss Raine whose attention was on some documents but whom he knew couldn't help overhear.

'Hi Mark.' Marie sounded as upbeat as ever. 'You called. I'm so pleased.'

'You called me.'

'Yes. I fancied the pictures. Blue Hawaii. It's on at the Haymarket. It's Elvis. If you fancy it on Saturday.'

He hesitated. He still didn't know what to do about Carol, and Saturday would be the next opportunity to see her.

'Mark?'

'Yeah, yeah. Okay. Saturday's fine.'

'Oh great!' She was bubbly, as always. 'See you outside at seven?'

'Seven,' he replied, feeling uncertain. Then she hung up. That was that, then.

Miss Raine was looking. 'That sounded like a date for Saturday,' she said. Mark nodded, wondering at the same time what it would be like having a date with her – at the Stoll, accompanied by Brigitte Bardot's sexual moaning. She was still looking, as though defying him to leave the office. The sudden appearance of Smudger commanded her attention, and

Smudger's 'what are you doing in here?' look ensured his swift departure.

That evening being Bingo at the Club, Mark had the opportunity to speak to his elder brother in private. The minute his parents left the house he went into the sitting room where he found Bob sitting by the fire reading *Lady Chatterley*. He sat in the armchair opposite, and poked at the coals awhile, wondering how to broach the subject of Carol. Bob, lowering his book, gave him the opening.

'Lost your virginity yet, then?'

Mark gave him the lowdown: the way he felt about Carol, the way he thought she felt about him – and the way he had messed up by making the pass in her living room. He couldn't understand her reaction, he said, not after his experiences with Beryl at the back of the Club and Marie at the Stoll.

'Women.' said Bob. 'They're not all the same. Take me and Joyce.' Mark saw his brother's face had taken on a sage-like countenance. Like the old-timers in those Randolph Scott Westerns. He'd seen Julian's Mam acting Hollywood; now his brother. 'When I first met Joyce, I would never have tried my hand with her, not the way you did. I realised it would take time. So I'd just kiss her goodnight at first, and give her a cuddle when we were alone. Believe me, it must've been best part of three months before anything happened.'

Mark believed him.

'Don't worry, you haven't blown it,' said Bob. 'Not if she likes you, as you say. You offended her, that's all. A decent lass has self-respect. Standards, like. She won't want to be taken for granted. But I'm sure you can put it right.' He leaned forward, holding *Lady Chatterley* between his knees. 'She'll be at the dance again. When you see her just say sorry. And take it from there.'

'If she goes to the dance again.'

'Well, you know where she lives. Knock on her door and say sorry. Or send her some flowers.'

'Flowers?'

'Of course. You know her address. It'll knock her for six. Guaranteed.'

'How do you send flowers?' Mark had a vision of wrapping a bunch of flowers and taking them to the Post Office.

'Go to a bloody florists and they'll deliver them. Make it a Saturday when she's likely to be at home.' Bob looked down at the cover of *Lady Chatterley*. 'Interesting what this gardener bloke gets up to in this book, mind.'

Not as interesting as what goes on in next door's lav, Mark thought, wondering if he should say anything about it to his brother. He doubted if he would believe him and he was back into his book anyway so he left it. He thought of writing a meaningful letter to Carol. But the flowers idea seemed better. As long as he didn't have to actually carry them in public himself.

That night Septimus – his resident spider – appeared. He – or she – came crawling along the ceiling, right above his head as he lay in bed. The web was empty. No supper for you, Mark thought. He wondered if he should kill it. Mam lived in terror of spiders, so he'd be doing her a favour. Instead, he lay there, watching – and thinking. Flowers, was it? If Bob was right all would be well and he'd be back on board with Carol. Except, of course, he'd arranged to see Marie on Saturday. Sex in the stalls. Might as well enjoy it when I can, he mused. What the hell.

***

The tinkling bell was enough to cause the woman to look up. She held a large pair of scissors in one hand, a flower with a long stalk in the other. Mark saw her cut the stem, place the flower carefully on to the counter and pick up another. He went to the counter and waited, watching as she picked up flowers, one at a time, and snip the stems. He had never been inside a florist's shop before. The smell was almost overpowering. He waited, but the woman ignored him. It was as though he wasn't there. At last, she cackled into life. 'She'll be with you in a minute,' she muttered, without looking up.

As if on cue, 'she' appeared, emerging through coloured beads that dangled across a doorway. Mark's spirits lifted on sight of her. She was about his age, he thought, perhaps slightly older, with a sharp-featured face and short, dark brown hair. She wore a pink-coloured overall over a trim figure. What she didn't wear was a smile. She stood on the opposite side of the counter and looked at him for a moment before she spoke.

'Can I help you?'

'I want to buy some flowers.' He smiled, hoping in vain for a similar response.

'What sort of flowers?' she raised her hand in a gesture that meant 'there's plenty to choose from'.

'I'm not sure,' he replied. 'I'm not used to buying flowers, like.'

'Well, what we have is what you see.'

Without looking up, the woman spoke to her young colleague in the same muttering tone as before. 'He wants them for his girlfriend. Either to tell her he loves her or they've fallen out and he's trying to make up.'

The young woman remained silent. Mark noticed a small badge with the name Carol on it pinned to her overall. Somehow he maintained his smile. 'She's right. A girlfriend with your name as it happens.'

She sighed and waited.

He turned away and meandered among the flowers that adorned the floor of the shop. They were stacked in vases, strewn on the floor, lying in opened cardboard boxes. He recognised roses, nothing else. Glancing up, he saw the girl – Unsmiling Carol, as he'd already dubbed her – was still standing at the counter. The more he looked, the more difficult he found making a choice. Some he liked, but they had no price. Others had price tags on cellophane labels, but for how many flowers was unclear. A bunch of six, maybe. He didn't know. When he looked up again Unsmiling Carol had disappeared. Her colleague was still at the counter, snipping away impassively.

He wandered about, finally selecting a bunch of flowers with large pink blooms, lifting them carefully from a huge pot that contained lots of others. There was no price tag. He stepped up to the counter, holding them away from his body as water dripped from the stems. He wondered if the woman would serve him, but she remained where she was, indifferent to his presence.

Unsmiling Carol re-appeared. She took the flowers, placed then onto the counter and reached for a roll of wrapping paper, deftly tearing a sheet off. As she did Mark impulsively turned, lifted a second bunch from the same pot and plonked it on the counter. 'I'll take two bunches,' he declared. She put the two together without comment and started to wrap them.

'Oh, I forgot. Could I have them delivered?'

She nodded. 'As long as it's in the area.' She looked up, awaiting his response.

'Jesmond.'

She wrapped them up, placed them to one side.

'When and where?' she enquired, sliding a writing pad across the counter. 'If you could write down the address.'

He didn't have a pen. Nor did she. After checking among papers on the counter and opening and closing a couple of drawers, she disappeared through the beads and emerged with a biro. He wrote 'Carol', then realised he didn't know her surname. He said so. It didn't matter said Unsmiling Carol. When he'd finished she pressed the keys on the till. 'There's a delivery charge, of course.' She looked up, awaiting his sanction to proceed, without saying what it was. He nodded, glad what was turning out to be a bit of an ordeal was nearly over.

He passed her a pound note, and she gave him his change along with a small folded card. 'You can write a message if you like.'

He looked at the card. It had a red rose on the front and was blank inside.

He picked up the pen but hesitated, wondering about what to write. She was tapping the counter with the tips of her fingers and looking up at the ceiling. Feeling flustered he wrote, simply, 'Thinking of you. Love, Mark.'

She took the card, looked at it briefly and slipped it into the wrapping. 'Thank you,' he said, relieved it was over. She turned and placed the flowers on top of a table, then passed through the beads again without a word. He left the shop, irritated, and annoyed with himself for writing 'Love' in his message. Maybe she'd think he was too forward. Maybe he shouldn't have sent flowers at all. The situation was so delicate it was walking through a minefield. That's how it seemed. Then he wondered if he'd put the right address. He wasn't sure. He'd find out sooner or later. Possibly.

12

For Carol, Friday meant another week completed of her dad's teetotalism; another week closer to Mam's phone call when she, Carol, would be the bearer of glad tidings. If only she could call Mam, to tell her. The bottle of Newcastle Brown Ale still stood unopened in the cupboard. Dad hadn't been to the pub all week. He was back at work, happy to tinker with his clocks of an evening when he got home. Now, with the weekend looming, her thoughts were of Mark. Last Saturday had ended disastrously. Since then, with time to reflect, perhaps her reaction to his sexual pass had been too extreme. After all, like her, he was still developing as a person – and boys were almost always less mature that girls. He probably thought he was expected to try his luck; and it did show that he wanted her, that he found her attractive. They could easily put things right. A cup of coffee, a chat, a 'sorry' or two, a kiss. A few kisses. She was looking forward to Saturday night. She hoped Mark would be at the dance. Emma had told her she'd hit it off with his friend – Carol couldn't remember his name – and said they had agreed to meet again the following week. They'd stood on the doorstep until after four o'clock in the morning, chatting.

The late September sunshine greeted her as she alighted from the trolley and entered the main door of Northern Electricity. She felt happy, optimistic. There had been no sign of Miss Carr all week. On leave, she presumed. It mattered not. She sat at her desk, at friends with the world.

On the stroke of ten someone called her name. Phone call in Miss Dyer's office. She went there directly. Miss Dyer was away, but someone had taken the call and the telephone receiver lay on the desk waiting for her to pick it up. Mark, she hoped, picking up the handset.

'Hello pet.' Mam's familiar voice seemed close. Carol was disappointed – at first. But then pleased. Hadn't she just been wishing she could phone Mam that very morning? And here she was, on the phone now.

'How are you, love?' Love. Mam was calling her love. She'd never called her love before. To Carol it meant she was treating her as an adult, that they were on equal terms rather than mother and daughter. Carol said she was fine.

'And how's your father?'

Dad was fine, said Carol. Dad was off the drink. Dad hadn't gone to the pub last Friday. Dad hadn't even touched a bottle of Newcastle Brown that had been in the cupboard for ages. She had taken it out and left it on the worktop and he still never touched it. He was back at work. 'You needn't wait the month,' she told her mother. 'You can come home now – or at least come and see Dad.'

'Well...' Mam sounded hesitant. 'The thing is, I've got a bit of a problem.'

'A problem?'

'Well, it's not a problem, love. It's just I've met someone. A chap called Ted. He's ever so nice. Lives in North Shields.' She paused, as though allowing time for Carol to take it in. 'He took me out last week for a meal. To Tynemouth. That place by the old priory. He's a bit older than me. Well, nearly fifty. His wife died of cancer a couple of years ago. He's been on his own since, trying to get over it. He says he feels ready to start a new relationship. I know it's early days, but...' She paused, as though inviting Carol to speak. But her daughter was silent. 'Well, anyway, he's taking me to the pictures tomorrow night. So...'

Carol was close to tears. 'What about Dad?'

'Well, I don't know yet, do I? I mean... You surely wouldn't mind your mam trying to do the right thing for herself, would you?'

'But you promised to meet him if he stayed off the drink.'

'I know. And I'm not saying I won't. And I did say a month. I only called today to see how you were and to be honest about myself. So please don't be upset.' There was an awkward silence before Mam spoke again. 'Well, better let you get back to work. I'll call again. And don't worry about anything.' She hung up with a click, leaving the receiver buzzing in Carol's ear. She took a moment to compose herself before returning to her desk. No use jumping to conclusions, she told herself. This Ted chap could be a ship in the night. Mam had said she'd give it a month, after all. Meanwhile, she thought, there was tomorrow night at Partners.

That cheered her up, but she crossed her fingers just the same.

Fred had turned up for work that morning, having missed the previous two days. Mark thought he looked awful: pale, gaunt, a shadow of the man he was only a week or so back. 'He looks like death warmed up,' he muttered to Horlicks. 'He looks like death, nowt else to it,' was his friend's reply. He was coming on the job anyway said Tommy. Smudger, puffing at his ciggy, looked on anxiously as they left the workshop.

Fred was on the job, but not doing it. When Mark brewed up morning tea Fred sat in an old armchair he'd earlier taken from the club lounge where he'd fallen fast asleep, his head lolling forward onto his chest. Tommy said to leave him. At one o'clock he was still there. Tommy even checked his wrist for a pulse. As Mark looked on anxiously Tommy looked up and shook his head. 'He's gone,' he muttered, finally letting go. Mark put his St John's Ambulance training into practice, placing the tips of two fingers onto Fred's wrist. He held them there for what seemed ages. 'There's a weak pulse,' he said at last. Tommy looked relieved.

'This can't go on, Mark lad,' said Tommy, shaking his head. 'He'll be dying on us one of these days.' They left Fred sitting where he was until he finally awoke at 3 o'clock. 'Let's go now he's awake and can walk,' said Tommy. They packed their tools and headed for Newcastle, Fred following them from the building like a zombie.

They drove in silence, Tommy pulling the car over on to some waste ground near the workshop. 'We're a bit early,' he said, pulling on the handbrake and cutting the motor. He took out his now-crumpled *Mirror* and laid it against the steering wheel.

Fred had perked up. 'There can't be much more in that rag left to read,' he declared.

'It's a working man's newspaper,' Tommy replied, lighting a cigarette.

'Ach, it's all socialist crap.'

They sat in silence until Fred, clearly bored, half turned to Mark, seated in the back. 'What 'y' doin' the weekend, then?' he asked.

'Pictures tomorrow night,' Mark replied.

'Oh aye. Where?'

'The Haymarket, to see Blue Hawaii. It's Elvis Presley.'

Tommy cut in. 'Elvis Presley! He can't act.'

'He can't sing either,' said Fred, glancing over to Tommy's *Mirror*. Tommy had it sprawled open, over the steering wheel. 'What's that about VD?' Fred asked, leaning over a little for a better view.

'They're having a big campaign about venereal disease,' Tommy replied.

'Syph and Gon we called it in the army. Most of us copped it. Had a dose of the clap myself once.'

'What's clap?' asked Mark.

'Gonorrhoea. But don't ask me to spell it,' said Fred.

'Says here,' said Tommy, 'that VD is rife in the UK. ''Specially in big cities and naval ports.'

'There's a surprise,' said Fred.

'They're urging people with the symptoms to go to their local hospitals for check-ups. In confidence, of course.'

'I don't know what the fuss is all about,' said Fred with a snort. 'Half the British army have it. Not bloody surprising either, some of those tarts the blokes pick up on foreign postings.'

'It's pretty explicit, mind, what it says. The symptoms for syphilis. A hard, roundish wart-like lump on the penis.'

'Henry VIII had syph and he was king of Britain,' said Fred.

'England,' said Mark.

'Clever dick. You haven't got a lump on *your* dick, have you, lad?'

Under Fred's gaze Mark felt his face glowing red with embarrassment. 'Cor, look at his face,' Fred declared. 'Struck a bulls-eye, have we?'

Tommy skewed his head round to face Mark. 'Got a lump on yer willy, lad?'

Mark nodded.

'Don't know about dancing,' said Fred. 'I reckon he spends his weekends along Elswick Road.' The two men looked at him for a few moments, both twisting around in their seats. Then they twisted back again, facing forward.

'Dark horse, you,' said Fred. 'Mind you,' he added philosophically, 'they do say you can catch it off toilet seats.'

At the back door of the workshop Tommy held Mark back as Fred went inside. 'Get yourself checked out, lad,' he said. 'No need for anyone to know. Not even your GP. Go to the General. They've a special ward there. All confidential. Best to be on the safe side, eh?' Mark nodded, grateful for his advice, but worried nonetheless as he remembered the night he was drunk and the wretched old woman.

But not as worried as he was at the thought of his mam finding out.

***

Saturday lie-in. The flowers would be delivered today, probably this morning, Mark thought. And having sent them to Carol he was seeing Marie tonight. But maybe it was the best strategy. If Carol was delighted with the flowers, as he hoped, she would probably go to Partners hoping to see him and he wouldn't be there – *but*, as he would explain when he next saw her, he didn't want to push things, to take her for granted. All in all he reckoned it a smart move. It would make her want to see him all the more. Meanwhile, tonight he could resume his exploration of Marie's anatomy. She'd said the Haymarket. He wondered if she'd opt for the Stoll again.

No sign of Septimus. What do spiders do anyway, when they're not mating and devouring one another? That's what Mr Griffiths had said when he was in Junior school. The female eats her partner after coitus, as Mr Griffiths called it. He was dropping off to sleep again, wondering what a female spider might be called, when the bedroom door opened and Bob's head appeared.

'You've a visitor,' he announced. 'Gerrup.'

A visitor. Not Carol surely.

'Who?'

He just caught Bob's reply. 'Robbie.'

Robbie. So early. He was never out of bed before noon at weekends. He dressed quickly and went downstairs to find him sitting in a chair by the fire.

'What's up?' Mark enquired.

'Just wondered what time tonight?'

'Tonight?'

Robbie nodded. 'Aye, we're going to the dance, aren't we?'

'Can't,' Mark replied. 'Going to the pictures.' Robbie looked shell-shocked. 'Sorry, mate,' said Mark. 'I've got a date.'

'But last Saturday,' Robbie replied. 'I told Emma I'd be there.'

'You can to go on your own. You don't have to have me with you.' But even as Mark spoke he felt like someone stabbing a friend in the ribs, knowing Robbie wouldn't want to go to a dance by himself. 'Just pay to get in and find her. You don't have to worry about asking other girls up to dance.'

Robbie turned his gaze to the fire. Mam was cooking breakfast. She appeared in the doorway and asked Robbie if he wanted any, but he shook his head. Mark couldn't think of anything else to say. If he couldn't, Robbie could. 'D'you know, that night we took them home Emma and me were on her step till four o'clock in the morning.'

Mark smiled. 'You lasted longer than me and Carol, then. She invited me in but then threw me out.' Rob waited for an explanation. 'Tried my hand. You know.'

Robbie's face beamed. 'Emma and me got on like a house on fire. Couldn't stop talking. She's fantastic. We said we'd go to the pictures, maybe meet up at Whitley Bay.' He looked at Mark wistfully. 'Can't you come tonight? It'll be great. We could get together for nights out.'

Mark thought about it for a moment. He could call Marie, cancel the Haymarket. Emma was bound to have told Carol about how well she got on with Robbie. She'd be expecting him to be at Partners, especially after receiving the flowers. But he thought it best left as it was, until next week maybe. And he was really up for Marie tonight. 'Next week,' he told Robbie. 'We'll go then. Honest. But don't worry about going on your own tonight. If you do Emma will be really chuffed, I bet.'

Mam came in with his breakfast. Robbie stood up, his face crestfallen. He left with a 'See you' as Mark sat down for his fryup. He was just finishing when a familiar voice hailed him from the kitchen.

'Kidda!' Kev breezed in and plonked himself on the chair by the fire, the one vacated by Robbie. 'So, where's this motorbike you're getting?'

'Haven't looked yet,' Mark replied. 'You said you were coming with me but you're never in to ask.'

'I've been staying over at Betty's Saturday nights. It's getting serious. Her folks think I'm the bee's knees with knobs on.' He watched as Mark cleaned his plate with the last of his bread. 'I wish to hell you'd get a bike and take Rita out on it. She tags along like Lady Wallflower. We all have to walk to the bloody beach from Betty's, then walk all the way back again. She sits there when Betty and me...' He glanced at the door to the kitchen. 'Y'know. When we're at it.'

'Can't take Rita anywhere on a motorbike till I've passed my test.'

'Ach! Who cares about that? Any tea on the go?'

Mark went into the kitchen to find Mam already filling two mugs.

'You know,' Kev was saying, 'Rita's a smart bird. If I wasn't in with Betty I'd fancy her myself. Best you ask her out before somebody else does.'

'I called at her flat. There was no answer.'

'That's it for six months, is it? Try again. Today. Now. After you've slurped your tea.'

Mam brought the tea in.

'Anyway,' said Kev, 'tomorrow night. Betty and Rita. Spanish City and the beach after. How about it? We can go on the bike.'

Mark thought about it. As Kev said, they could go to the beach – although there was the little matter of the wart. Could still be fun though. Okay, he said. Spanish City tomorrow. Kev said he'd call at six. Then he was off, leaving his tea on the hearth and Mark musing about the delights of the evening to come. And the thought that Carol would be getting her flowers. He checked the time. Could've been delivered by now.

***

She answered the knock at eleven precisely. Emma, she thought. Instead it was a young woman wearing a green overall and carrying two bunches of chrysanthemums. From Mam for Dad? Surely not.

'Miss…' The young woman tailed off, unable to find a surname.

'Kemp,' said Carol, bemused.

'Are you Carol?' She nodded and accepted the flowers. She closed the door, and took them into the living room.

'What have you got there?' Lennie Kemp looked up from the clock he was repairing, his eye-glass looking like a growth on his forehead. An answer wasn't necessary. She placed the flowers carefully on to the table and withdrew the small message card.

'Who are they from?' Lennie held a small screwdriver in one hand, the guts of the clock in the other. Time had stood still, in more than one sense.

'Mark,' she said simply. She looked up to see his enquiring face. 'Just a boy I met at the dance.'

'What does the card say?'

'"Thinking of you. Love, Mark",' she said.

'So…who is this…Mark?'

'I met him at partners.'

'How does he know where you live?'

'Oh Dad he took me home the other night. That's all. There isn't a problem. He's really nice, actually.'

'Aye, well, he must be, if he takes you home. You know how I worry about you on the streets at night. And he must be a nice bloke if he's sending you flowers. They must have cost a bit.'

'It's the not the cost,' she said, smiling. 'It's the thought that counts.' But she could hardly contain her delight at the thought that he'd spent so much on her.

'You should've invited him in for a coffee,' said Lennie, turning his attention to his clock. 'Maybe I'll get to meet him next time.'

The irony of the remark was not lost on her, but she remained upbeat. 'I'll make *us* coffee in a minute,' she almost sang, picking up the flowers and taking them into the kitchen. Mam kept several vases in the cupboard. She took two down from the shelf, picked up the scissors and started cutting the stalks.

She felt so happy. Mark sending flowers. Two bunches! He didn't seem the sort who would do such a thing; hardly any young men did. But he had, and there could only be one reason. That he was sorry for what happened and wanted to see her again. Tonight! They could meet tonight at the dance. That's what the flowers were for. To say so.

She picked up one of the vases and gave it a quick rinse. The vases reminded her of Mam, and what she had said about meeting another man. Ted, she'd said his name was. How she wished she could see Dad, now he was off the drink. Off the drink he was the man he used to be: kind, tolerant, loving. A good husband and dad. The bottle of Newcastle Brown Ale still stood unopened in the cupboard. But mam seeing another man was a black cloud in an otherwise sunny sky. Or maybe a grey cloud, she told herself. A grey cloud that would blow over, if only she would come home.

There were too many flowers for the vases. She picked some up and hurried into the hall for her coat. 'I'm just off to see Emma,' she called out. With that she dashed off to see her friend, to present her with some of Mark's flowers.

Mark, meanwhile, had put thoughts of the flowers behind him – for now. Carol was for the future; the present, or this evening at least, was Marie. He sprawled in one of the armchairs by the fire, idly thinking of good things to come in the darkness of the Haymarket, or Stoll, if that was what she wanted. He imagined he was touching her even now. He closed his eyes and thought of the warm skin above her stocking tops. His growing erection made him feel uncomfortable because of the wart. Then sleep crept up on him, caused by a combination of the fire and Mam's breakfast. His mind drifted to Fred with his cancer, looking grey and old and ill; then to the man he saw at Carol's that time, her dad, he imagined; and the old woman. Oh God, the old woman!

He opened his eyes to see Bob was smiling, and looking pleased with himself. 'C'mon and see what I've got,' he was saying. He waited for Mark to stir himself before walking out the back door, glancing over his shoulder to see if his younger sibling was following. Mark struggled to his feet, half asleep and went into the yard after him.

'C'mon,' Bob repeated, opening the back gate and stepping onto the footpath. He waited till Mark caught him up.

'Da-da!' Bob turned his beaming face to the object of his attention. Mark found himself looking at a black Riley car. It was parked next to the kerb, all alone in a street not usually occupied by motor vehicles of any kind. The paintwork looked immaculate, all shining and clean. He looked at it for half a minute, then wandered up to the driver's window and peered inside.

'It's real leather upholstery.' Bob opened the door. 'Smell that.' Mark looked in awe at the panelled dashboard and leather seats, and touched the steering wheel almost reverently. 'Y'can keep your motorbikes, Mark. This is luxury.' Bob brushed him aside and climbed inside, resting his hands on the wheel. 'She's a beaut, eh?'

Mark stepped back, admiring the sleek, shiny bodywork. He walked around it, touched it here and there. There was a scratch or two. Otherwise it was immaculate.

'A bloke at work told me about it, Bob purred. 'Lives in Wallsend. He's emigrating to Australia. He wanted a quick sale, so...'

Mark ran the tips of his fingers along the black, shiny paintwork of the front wing, stood back to admire its sleek beauty. 'It's a two-point-five,' said Bob. 'Beats your motorbikes, eh?'

Aye, it did beat motorbikes, Mark thought. He'd love a car like this. He'd love it now. Imagine picking Carol up in it and taking her for a drive. 'You'll have to save up, brother,' said Bob. 'And you won't be able to do that if you buy a motorbike on H.P.'

'Take me for a spin, then,' Mark pleaded, wandering around to the front passenger door.

'Er, can't just yet,' said Bob. 'There's a problem with starting her up. I'm gonna work on it this afternoon.' He climbed out of the driver's seat and Mark got in. This was for him, he decided. A car like this. Soon as possible. Reluctantly he got out and went back into the house. He went into the living room and looked out of the window, and saw Dad in the garden, sitting by his pigeon cree having a cigarette. Roger was at the fence, talking to him. In his own garden Eggshell stood alone, not part of the conversation. If only Roj knew what Eggshell was up to with Ada, Mark thought.

On impulse he got his bike out and headed for the school field. Maybe the Old Boys would be playing. Maybe he'd see Beryl. He wondered if she was still with Tom Clark.

He was early for the pictures, but even so Marie was there before him. She was wearing a smart red coat and a gorgeous smile. She kissed his cheek. He could smell her breath, her perfume. He wished Kev could see her with him, just to show her off.

'You're a difficult person to get hold of,' she was saying, her voice exuding happiness. 'Whoever answered the phone to me sounds nice. Dishy is she?'

'Who, Miss Raine?' he replied, offering no comment.

Marie smiled. 'Bet she is. Dishy, I mean.'

'Not as dishy as you.' His reply earned him another kiss.

He wondered what tack to take: to ask her if she really wanted to go to the Stoll, or see Elvis. She turned towards the kiosk, and waited for him to step up to the cashier. 'Can we go upstairs, please?' she said. 'In the Upper Circle.' He bought two tickets and followed her inside.

'I love Elvis,' she was saying as they crossed the carpeted foyer. 'He's so sexy. Such a turn-on.' He could hardly keep up with her as she headed for the stairs, even though they were early. When they reached the Upper Circle and she made a beeline for Row J, he sensed the reason she hurried was to claim a seat in a favourite spot. The lights were still on, and they found seats just a couple in from the aisle.

She leaned forward and removed her coat, and carefully folded it before placing it onto her lap. Underneath she was wearing a silky blouse and short skirt. Mark felt relaxed in her company. Mantovani played. People drifted in. They had to stand up a few times to allow some of them to squeeze past. He thought of Carol and wondered if she'd gone to the dance. He felt guilty to think she may have. His thoughts were interrupted when Marie started chatting: about work, about Elvis.

The lights dimmed and Pearl and Dean's adverts came on, followed by two trailers for forthcoming shows. Then, finally, in a blaze of Technicolor and fanfare, Hal Wallis's *Blue Hawaii*. Soft Hawaiian music permeated the cinema. Mark stole a glance at Marie. She was looking intensely at the screen in anticipation. It was as though he wasn't there, he thought. Then he glanced around the auditorium. It looked full. He relaxed, and slipped his arm around her shoulder. She moved her upper torso slightly closer, and rested her elbow on the armrest between them.

They sat awhile, watching the movie. After about fifteen minutes he moved his free hand from her hands, where they rested on her lap, upwards, and gently cupped her breast. She offered neither encouragement nor rejection. He squeezed slightly, before slowly undoing one of the buttons of her blouse. She remained impassive, even as he slipped his hand inside; but then she brought her elbow back in an obvious gesture meaning 'stop'. So he placed his roaming hand back onto her lap, where her hands rested on top of her folded coat.

After a while he looked at her again. She was still facing forward, apparently intent on watching the movie. A few minutes later the same. Then again, this time as Elvis was singing – and now her face was turned towards his. She was looking into his eyes, her upturned face appearing pure white in the flickering glow of the projector light. She looked beautiful, he thought, as he kissed her gently on the mouth. He lifted his free hand and caressed her cheek until, after what seemed an age they turned to look again at the events on screen. And now, he sensed, knew in fact, that she was ready for him. It was Elvis he had to thank; Elvis was her turn-on.

He waited until the next song, and slowly slid his hand inside her blouse. She responded by sliding forward in her seat. They kissed passionately, licking each other's tongues. He slid his hand under her folded coat and then up her skirt, seeking out warm thighs. She sighed. He was in control as Elvis sang, as though especially for them, her writhing body sliding forward in her seat. Then, just moments before she would have surely climaxed, Mark felt a sharp tap on his shoulder and heard a woman's voice.

'Will you behave? We've come here to see the picture, not listen to your shenanigans.'

Marie responded at once, sitting sharply back in her seat, eyes forward, as though she'd been sitting like that all the way through the film. Mark turned to see a woman in the row behind staring at him, her face illuminated by the flickering glow of the projector lights. She looked angry, menacing even. All around her, other faces were turned towards him. He looked away, only to find a sea of heads turned, countless eyes looking in his direction.

He left his arm in place around Marie's shoulders, and faced forward, trying to look nonchalant, determined to sit out an embarrassing moment. But almost at once an usherette appeared in the aisle that ran across the auditorium a couple of rows in front. Her head and shoulders were silhouetted against the screen. Then a flashlight beam was shining in his face. He hoped she would move away, that the moment would pass, but she was joined at once by another. He could see them muttering, and looking towards him. 'God...,' hissed Marie. 'It's OK,' he whispered, but even as he tried to reassure her a third figure appeared, this time in the portly shape of a male, who joined in the whispered dialogue taking place in the aisle.

The group of three moved to one side, and one of the usherettes stepped up to the end of Row 'J' and leaned over the person seated there. She was looking directly at Mark.

'Will you come this way, please,' she said quietly. 'Both of you.'

Mark and Marie stood up and threaded their way past people sitting nearby, who turned their legs aside to let them pass. 'Come this way,' said the usherette. They followed her down the steps and through the door marked 'Exit' into the brightly lit corridor outside the auditorium. The man Mark had seen was waiting.

'We've been watching you two for about ten minutes,' he said. 'Where on earth do you think you are? Your behaviour is totally unacceptable.'

Just then the door to the auditorium opened and a woman appeared. Mark heard Elvis's singing briefly before the door closed again. The woman was looking sternly at him. He realised it was the same one who had tapped him on the shoulder. Her face was wracked with anger.

The man spoke again. 'I'm the manager, for your information. And I have to say your conduct is intolerable.'

Before anyone else could say anything the door opened yet again and another man appeared. He stood next to the woman who had tapped Mark on the shoulder. Then the woman spoke directly to Mark. 'We've come here tonight to watch the picture, and all we get is you two canoodling and groping and behaving like savages. Who the *hell* do you think you are?'

'Just a moment, madam.' The manager addressed the woman, clearly wanting to have control.

'Never mind just a moment. I don't know what things are coming to, I really don't. You should get their names and addresses and tell their parents what they get up to when they go to the pictures. They were almost *doing* it!'

'Madam, my attention was drawn to them and I saw for myself what they were doing. It's not acceptable, but they weren't almost *doing* it, as you say.'

'Look at her,' said the woman, directing a contemptuous gaze at Marie. 'She's nothing more than a trollop. Her skirt's so short she might as well not be wearing it.'

'Is that so?' Marie retorted. 'Well, it might interest you know I'm not wearing any knickers either.'

'That will do,' said the manager.

'I'm not having her talk to me like that.' Marie was almost shouting. She turned to the woman again. 'What's the matter with you anyway? We were just having fun.'

'That will do.' The manager raised a hand slightly, gesturing mark and Marie to walk down the corridor. He walked between them, chaperoning them towards the exit. Marie turned suddenly. 'You fucking Aberdeen Angus!' she screamed at the woman. Then she looked at her male companion. 'You must be mad, going out with a frigid cow like her!'

The manager opened more doors and calmly accompanied Mark and Marie to the exit, leaving them without further comment as they stepped into the street. It was raining steadily. They stepped on the wet pavement. Mark turned his collar up.

Marie turned to face him, clearly upset. 'Walk me to my bus stop, please,' she said. 'I just want to go home now.' They crossed the road and walked to her stop in silence. It wasn't far. They sheltered in a shallow shop doorway, waiting for the bus. 'Sorry it ended up like this,' she said, smiling faintly. A few raindrops trickled down her cheeks as she spoke. Mark felt numb. Ten minutes ago they were in a sexual embrace, in a world of their own despite the presence of so many people; now here they were, waiting for her bus.

The bus came and she got on board the platform at the rear. 'Ring me,' she called out, before disappearing inside. The conductor rang the bell, and he watched the bus pull away, leaving him alone on the pavement. He checked his watch. It was only ten past eight. For a moment he thought about going to Partners, but he rejected the idea: he was wearing a jacket and flannels, not a suit, and had no tie. And anyway, like Marie, he just wanted to go home.

Although the evening had ended in disaster with Marie, walking up the Terrace his thoughts were of Carol. He felt certain she'd have gone to the dance, and if, as he hoped, she was knocked out by the flowers, she would have been looking out for him. He wished he'd gone to the dance now. And then, nearing his back gate, he realised he had a problem: Bob and Joyce. They were probably at it right now, on the settee, not expecting his imminent appearance. He stopped short on the pavement, and wondered where he could go to avoid an embarrassing interruption. Nowhere was his conclusion, and he was in no mood to linger by the projector room door at the flicks. He walked boldly up to the back door, knocking loudly and allowing a reasonable time before entering. As he pushed it open he was met by a fully-clothed Bob. Glancing into the living room he saw no sign of Joyce.

'She's chucked me,' Bob explained, trying to smile about it. But Mark could see he wasn't really smiling. 'She saw the car and went ballistic. Good thing Mam and Dad had just gone out.'

'Just a minute,' said Mark, hurrying upstairs to his bedroom. Despite the upsetting scene at the pictures, and Bob's news, something else was troubling him more. His penis was feeling really sore. He dropped his trousers and checked out the wart. It seemed bigger and all around was red and inflamed. And now, for the first time, he could see a clear liquid seeping out. He wiped it with his handkerchief and pulled his trousers up, then went downstairs to find his brother waiting, as though anxious to impart the details of his bad news. They sat in the armchairs by the fire, facing one another.

'She just walked out,' said Bob. 'When I told her about the car she said she wanted me to use the money I've saved towards the cost of getting married and a deposit on a house. She went mad. Stormed off big time.' He ended with a shrug. 'Bugger it. I'd rather have the Riley.'

Mark was so worried about the wart Bob's angst passed over his head. Instead of offering a word of sympathy he felt impelled to impart some news of his own.

'I think I've got syphilis.'

Bob looked at him, his face showing a distinctive sign of incredulity.

'Whaaaat?'

'I've got the symptoms. Wart on my willy and now it's oozing stuff out.'

'How would you have syphilis? Have you been up the West End?'

Mark shook his head.

'You've been with a lass though. Right?'

'I'm not sure.'

'How can you not be sure? Either you've bonked somebody or you haven't. You're bound to know.'

'There was this old woman.'

'You've bonked an old woman?'

'I don't know. I was pissed. I might have. I think she was on the game.'

Bob was silent for a moment.

'This wart. What's it like?'

'It seems to be getting bigger,' said Mark. 'It's really sore.'

'Let's have a look at it then.'

'Bugger that!'

'Well, you'd better go to the doctor's. See Dr Evans unless you want a woman doctor looking at your tool.'

'There's a special ward at the General. Tommy at work says I can go there in confidence.'

'You mean you've told somebody at work about it? Christ.' Bob looked thoughtful for a moment. 'They say you can catch it off toilet seats. Syph, that is.'

'That's what Fred said.'

'Fred? Who the hell's Fred?'

'Just old Fred at work. He was there when Tommy read about VD in the paper.'

'*You'll* be in the paper if you're not careful.'

They sat in silence for a few minutes before Mark spoke again.

'Eggshell's bonking Ada in her lav.'

Bob was speechless. Mark spoke again.

'Eggshell's bonking Ada…'

'Yeah yeah, I heard you the first time. Who told you that, for Christ's sake?'

So Mark told him how he'd come home late and heard strange noises coming from next door's lav, followed by Ada emerging and going indoors; then seeing Eggshell crossing the yard, the sound of the back gates and then entering his own house. He didn't say anything about overhearing Ada at the Club that time.

'You couldn't make it up,' said Bob. 'Have you told anyone else?'

'No. Not a soul.'

'Eggshell must be desperate.'

'So must Ada.'

They sat awhile in silence, two brothers each with their own thoughts.

'Anyway,' said Bob finally, staring into the fire. 'That's that with Joyce. We've been together all this time, and just cos I buy a car... I mean, it was for her an' all.'

'She'll come back,' said Mark. 'She's narked just because she hasn't had things her way.'

But Mark could hardly believe it. Bob, who had counselled him about girls. Bob, the man-of-the-world. He'd blown it just by buying a bloody car. Billy, flapping in his cage, started tweeting. 'He's lovely for his mother y'know,' he trilled, pecking at his mirror.

'Will you ring that fucking bird's neck, or should I?' asked Bob.

13

Carol stood at the kitchen sink, the soft, soapy dishwater caressing her hands. She was miles away, her eyes almost sightless as she gazed forlornly out of the window. She picked up a plate, absent-mindedly wiped it, placed it on the drainer and reached for another.

She felt hurt, bewildered, helpless. Why, she kept asking herself, would a young apprentice boy spend so much money on flowers, have them delivered to her home address, then fail to appear at the dance when he must have known, or at least hoped, that she would be there? Surely his kindly, romantic gesture had paved the way for her forgiveness, for them to be together, to smile again.

She rebuked herself for being so harsh the night she had told him to get out. She had over-reacted. She should have simply said 'stop', and left it at that. Everything would have been fine if she had. He'd have understood, backed off, kissed her and asked to see her again. If only she could contact him to tell him everything was OK. But she didn't know where he lived, or where he worked; she knew practically nothing about him. If he wasn't going to make contact with her that was that, they'd not meet again, unless, by chance, they turned up at the dance on the same evening sometime. But he'd probably have met someone else by then. Someone who wouldn't foolishly reject his advances, someone who would encourage physical contact. He was a boy, after all. And wasn't that what all boys expected?

Emma had been disappointed last night too. She and Robbie had so much in common. Last week, they'd lingered on the doorstep for most of the night. He'd been reserved, shy, yet hadn't tried anything. But Robbie hadn't turned up at the dance last night either, probably, she thought, because Mark had chosen not to. So Emma had been left in the lurch as well.

She knew Dad sensed something was wrong. He knew someone had sent her flowers. He knew she got home last night early. Even so, at breakfast, he'd not said anything. He was upstairs now, stripping wallpaper in the main bedroom 'for when Mam comes home,' he said. The thought that Mam was interested in another man repelled her. What it would so to Dad if he found out she could hardly imagine. She couldn't contact her either. She thought she might wander around North Shields looking for her, but she might be anywhere. She'd have to wait till she called her again, that's all.

Dad appeared. 'Making a brew love?' he enquired, as he passed through the kitchen into the outhouse. He was wearing his overalls, clearly determined to work long and hard on the bedroom. She put the kettle on, then took the Pledge from the cupboard under the sink. At least housework kept her occupied. And there was work tomorrow; that was something else to take her mind off things.

Around two o'clock that day Mark headed for the park to sit on the rocking horse. Head down, he crossed the grass only to find his seat of contemplation occupied by a couple of toddlers, their mothers in close attendance. One pushed the back of the horse up and down gently with one hand, whist holding a smouldering cigarette in the other. Her friend wheeled a pushchair back and forth, its discontented occupant whimpering, fighting sleep. The two women were talking about shopping or visiting the doctors or something. Kids on the rocking horse. He'd never seen that before. He went and sat on the rickety wooden bench by the sandpit instead.

He sat in solitude, looking about at nothing in particular, ill at ease with himself. His thoughts drifted to Ada and Roger, and his sighting of his arch-enemy Eggshell, and what, if anything, to do about it. Then there was the damned wart. He'd have to sort it out, this week some-how. He was worried about word getting round at work. Tommy would keep mum, he was certain. But Fred, he wasn't sure. If Horlicks found out – well, it just didn't bear thinking about. What would Smudger say if he thought he had VD? He might even sack him.

Two small boys appeared. One carried a football, an old laced-up caser. They wore football shirts and shorts and football boots, and pro-ceeded to kick the ball about by the old iron goalposts that stood amid a sea of dried mud in the middle of the rec. It reminded him of the time he would do the same thing in the same place, wearing his black and white Newcastle United strip, imagining himself as Jackie Mil-burn as he appeared in a picture in his football book. If it was wet he'd come home covered in mud. Mam didn't seem to mind. She would just throw his kit into the wash with a smile. He knew a lot about football: he read his football books and knew the laws of the game. But he was never good enough for the school team.

He felt irritable, unsettled, and looked over to the rocking horse which was now free. The toddlers were on the swings now, their mams still yakking. He left the rec and wandered off to Julian's. His friend answered the doorbell and invited him into the living room.

Julian's mam was sitting in an easy chair, his dad on the settee. Mrs Popham smiled on sight of Mark and indicated the other chair. Her husband smiled and nodded. Julian sat next to his dad, the leather cushion emitting a rude report under his bodyweight. He blushed with embarrassment, but no-one said anything. The four of them sat awhile in silence, Mr Popham finally getting up and excusing himself. A few minutes later the sound of classical music drifted from the depths of the house somewhere.

'Do you like music, Mark?' Mrs Popham enquired. Mark nodded, saying he preferred Cliff or Elvis, but liked classic stuff too. Her con-tinued stare seemed to invite 'such as?' Mantovani was the best he could do.

'Our Bob's bought a car,' he declared.

'What's he bought?' asked Julian.

'A Riley. Black colour. Two point five.' He wasn't sure what the two point five meant exactly, but he said it anyway. 'I was going to save up for a motorbike,' said Mark. 'But now I'd rather have a car.'

'They're much safer,' said Mrs P. 'Motor cycles are death traps. I'd never let Julian have one.' Mark saw she was looking at him more intently than before. 'You'd have to pass your test before you could drive,' she was saying. 'That would mean driving lessons. Do you have a provisional licence yet?'

'Oh yes,' he lied. At least he had the application form that Mam had brought for him to fill in, from the Post Office.

'Well then. I could teach you and it wouldn't cost you a penny. Our car is quite small, ideal to learn in. I expect I'll be teaching Julian once he's eighteen.' Her remarks were directed at Mark, as though Julian wasn't in the room. 'Would you like me to teach you, Mark?' He felt he should say yes, whether he did or not, and did so. 'That's settled then,' she said. 'Now, Julian, go and make Mark a nice cup of tea.' Julian dutifully left the room. Mark followed him into the kitchen and accepted a ginger snap. There was something about Julian's mam, he thought. She wasn't like his mam, or Kev's, or Robbie's. The thought of being out and about in her car with her was appealing, and had anyone asked he would have had to admit it wasn't only because she was teaching him to drive.

***

The Coast Road might have been custom-built for Kevin Marsh and his sleek machine: straight and true, ideal for the ton-up. Mark thought a crash helmet would have provided precious little protection if, for any reason, they were to take a spill, as Kev called it.

Not for the first time Mark found himself with his arms around his friend's waist, hands clasped firmly together, his face pressed against his leather jacket and his eyes closed. He hated driving at high speed. He was scared, he would readily admit. He thought it all so unnecessary – so much to live for, so easy to die. Why do it? he'd asked Kev. The thrill, Kev said. 'You only live once, Kidda.'

Kev had called at six o'clock exactly, plonking his old crash helmet onto the table with a 'There y'are, that'll keep your ma happy.' When Mark looked he saw his friend sporting a new helmet. It was black and shiny, with a black and white motif of some kind on the front, and matched his motorcycle leathers. The motif turned out to be a skull and crossbones. He tried Kev's old helmet on and looked in the mirror. 'It's to stop your head from being caved in, not for appearances,' said Kev. 'I'm sure Rita will like it when she sees it.'

Kev slowed down in Whitley Bay, navigating the streets at indecent speed nonetheless, until, finally, he pulled over to the kerb just yards from the entrance to the Spanish City. They dismounted. He pulled the machine back on to its stand, and stood on the pavement removing his gauntlets. He pushed his visor up and nodded to the doorway of a nearby coffee bar. Mark followed him in and sat in the corner whilst his friend ordered two frothy Espressos, which he brought to the table, before plonking himself down and removing his helmet.

Mark had been to the Spanish City many times but never into this coffee bar. The place was really mod, he thought: it had glass-topped tables and chairs with plastic seats mounted on tubular frames. The floor was multi-coloured, and a huge glass-domed juke box occupied one corner. There were no other customers. The girl behind the counter was thin with a spotty, expressionless face. She clearly wished she was somewhere else. Anywhere else, probably, Mark thought. *Runaway* blared from speakers.

'Where do we meet them?' Mark enquired nervously, worried about Rita's reaction when she saw him.

'Here,' said Kev. He seemed to ooze confidence, Mark thought. Even so, he had resolved to say something about his friend's driving.

'How fast were we travelling on the Coast Road?' he enquired.

'No more than eighty,' Kev replied. 'I usually do the ton, but took it easy cos you were on board. I know your mam doesn't like you going fast.'

'Never mind my mam. I don't like it. We're dead ducks if anything happens, the speed you drive.'

'I live to speed and I speed to live,' Kev replied dismissively, taking a sip of his coffee. 'Relax,' he purred. 'We've got two lasses coming here any minute so let's enjoy the evening.'

Just then the door opened. They looked up, expecting to see Betty and Rita. Instead two other girls came into the café. They wore faded blue jeans and identical sky-blue tops with 'Too hot to handle' emblazoned across the chest. They stood together at the counter for a few minutes, before one of them turned to survey the room in a 'where to sit' gesture. She selected a table the next but one to where Mark and Kev were sitting. She looked at the back of her hands in turn, spreading her fingers backwards, checking her painted nails, then took a small mirror and stared into it meaningfully. Presently her friend arrived with two cups of coffee and they proceeded to talk in whispers, giggling now and then. Suddenly one of them spoke.

'Y'going to the Spanish City?' she enquired.

Kev answered. 'Aye.'

'We come most Sundays.'

Her friend cut in. '*She* doesn't hold the rail on the roller-coaster.'

'D'you go on the roller-coaster?' the other enquired.

'Too fast for me,' said Kev, winking at Mark.

Silence reigned for a few minutes before the first one spoke again. 'I'm Cynth,' she declared, 'and she's Dawn.'

'Dawn's promising thighs…' Kev sang quietly. Cynth tittered. Dawn was unmoved.

'I'm Kev,' said Kev.

The girls looked at Mark enquiringly. But Mark didn't answer. All he wanted was for Rita to appear. The suspense was killing.

There was an awkward silence.

'Tell you a joke,' ventured Kev to the girls.

'Not if it's rude,' said Cynth.

'Well, right. So, President Eisenhower was on a state visit to England and him and the Queen were riding on the royal coach down the Mall. Have you heard it? Anyway, just as they were near Buckingham Palace one of the horses, er, broke wind. It made a helluva noise. Know what I mean?'

Cynth was looking at Kev, the makings of a smile on her face.

Dawn stared vacantly ahead, blushing slightly.

'So the Queen, still waving to the crowds, spoke to Eisenhower, and still smiling graciously, said, "I'm terribly sorry about that, Mr President".'

'"That's okay, your majesty," said Eisenhower, "As a matter of fact I thought it was one of the horses".'

Cyth laughed; Dawn took a sip of her coffee.

At that moment Mark's attention was drawn to a flash of red hair outside. A moment later Betty and Rita came into the cafe. Betty raised a hand, said 'Hi there' and plonked herself down in the chair next to Kev. Mark didn't see where they went. He had eyes only for Rita.

'Hi Mark.' Rita was smiling, her hair looking redder and longer than ever. She wore a cream top with a sleeveless suede jacket over it, and jeans. Mark stood up, and gestured the empty chair next to him. Still smiling, she sat down with a 'Thank you.'

And here she was. The girl on the bus. The girl he'd looked out for, often in vain, so many times. The girl he took to bed with him, the girl he dreamed about, the girl he thought of explicitly during his noc-turnal bed-time activities. The girl he'd even given a name to: Connie. *That* girl. She was sitting next to him, smiling for him. He was looking at her beautiful, radiant face, admiring her lovely mouth, meeting her gaze. He'd not muck up this time for sure.

'Any chance of a coffee?' she asked.

For twenty minutes they sat: Kev and Betty facing one another at one side of the little glass-topped table, holding hands, stealing the odd kiss; Mark and Rita more reserved, like people just getting to know each other – which they were. No-one took the slightest notice of Cynth and Dawn.

'I used to look out for you on the bus every morning and every night,' said Mark to Rita. 'I usually didn't see you. I suppose our times must have been different.'

'I knew you were interested,' she replied. 'Why didn't you say something?'

'Too shy,' he admitted. She smiled. 'Anyway,' he went on, 'I thought you'd think I might be a nutter.'

She laughed. 'Well, aren't you? Calling me Connie? Who is Connie anyway?'

'Oh, Connie Francis.' The look on her face was asking why. 'Stupid Cupid,' he explained.

'Oh, I see. So you weren't calling me stupid when we met at the dance.' She laughed. 'I love Connie Francis. My favourite's *Lipstick on Your Collar*.' She sang softly: 'La-la-la-la-la-la… Lipstick on your collar told a tale on you…' He wanted to sing the next line but he felt too embarrassed. She knew it, and laughed again.

As they sat, Mark found himself struggling to think of something to say. He felt under some pressure; he'd wanted to meet her, but on a just-you-and-me situation. He wanted things to be spontaneous; instead, he felt he had to laugh and be gay instantaneously because they were with Kev and Betty.

After a while the two girls who'd come in – he'd forgotten their names already – stood up and with a noisy sliding of chairs they left the café. Mark saw them turn along the lane leading to the Spanish City.

Kev spoke up. 'Chatted us up, them two. Didn't they Mark?'

'Probably wanted you to pay for them on the rides all night,' said Betty.

'And buy them fish and chips,' said Rita.

They all left the café, and headed along the lane to the funfair. Loud music and the drone of machines could be heard dead ahead. Kev had an arm around Betty's shoulders, and there was still the odd kiss. Mark took tentative hold of Rita's hand. She laughed out loud at his obvious shyness. 'I don't bite. Honest,' she said.

At the funfair, the music was blaring, a mix of Billy Fury from one direction, the inevitable *Runaway* from the other. First ride they came to was the Carousel, expressionless horses moving up and down on the way to nowhere. Their saddles were mostly unoccupied. They were driven by a noisy engine, accompanied by whirlitzer music that drowned out, almost, Billy Fury and Del Shannon. They watched awhile before moving on to the Waltzer. The spinning cars had just come to a standstill.

'C'mon!' Kev bounded on to the boards and jumped into the first car. Betty followed. Mark turned to ask if Rita wanted a go but she was already following Betty. All aboard, Kev pulled the metal arm over. Gene Vincent saw them off. They went slowly at first, then sped up, the cars spinning violently, clattering up and down, threatening to jettison their occupants. In the mayhem, with everyone holding on for dear life, a young bloke, parading nonchalantly on the wooden platform, appeared with a 'Tickets please.' Kev paid. The young bloke gave their car a push, spinning it violently, and they hurtled on, Kev and Mark each with a protective arm around their partner's shoulders. People screamed. Onlookers came and went with amazing regularity. Finally, when it ended, Kev jumped onto the ground with an exaggerated stagger. Betty pretended to steady him. He turned and kissed her, holding her face in his hands. Mark wanted to do the same with Rita but his shyness held him back.

They moved on to the dodgems. Kev again led the way, leaping into an empty car. Betty followed. Mark and Rita took another. The car was small and cramped. Mark could feel his leg against Rita's. He slid an arm around her shoulder. She responded by seeming to get even closer. They waited for the power to come on. When he pressed the pedal they found themselves going backwards. As he spun the wheel, they were rammed broadside by a laughing Kev. Finally they moved forward, accompanied by the acrid smell of the electrics and the ear-splitting noise of music and laughter and crashing dodgems.

The roller-coaster was next. Mark hated it, and had always refused to go on it after his first and only time before when he was scared out of his wits. He could never understand how anyone could enjoy it. But Rita was obviously keen, so he followed. On the downward sections he thrust his arm around her shoulders, ostensibly for her security but in truth to secure a better hold than the safety bar provided. Up, down, this way then that until, at last, they rolled into the finish and got out. He saw Rita looking at him, and knew she knew what he'd gone through. She responded by taking a firm hold of his hand, threading her fingers between his and saying nothing.

They wandered over to the shooting gallery where Mark tried unsuccessfully to win a prize, missing all three metal targets. He knew the sights on the air rifles were crooked; that's what Bob always said, anyway. Kev stepped up and won a goldfish in a small polythene bag. He promptly handed it to small boy whose mother smiled appreciatively. The girls hooked ducks from water, threw darts and played hoop-la. Their funfair appetites sated, they sauntered out of the fairground and back along the lane.

'Fancy some chips, Reet?' Betty enquired of her friend.

'Reet?' echoed Mark. Rita laughed. 'It's what she calls me. Yes, I do,' she called out. They stood at the little chippy, each accepting a conical-shaped bag of hot, fat chips. Kev almost emptied the salt cellar on his. It was dusk, a fine and unusually warm October evening. Earlier, on the links, Mark had seen small boys kicking a ball around, watched by mams and dads and grandparents. Now the entire scene was almost deserted. Noise from the fairground drifted over, faintly. They sat on a wooden bench facing the sea, gentle breakers turning white almost apologetically. As darkness approached, they descended the steps leading down to the deserted beach, two young couples with their arms around each other.

'Isn't it romantic?' Rita's voice seemed low and husky now, as though designed to fit the occasion. Mark looked up at the dark sky, then ahead to where the heavy black cloud ended, showing an almost full moon beaming down on to a silver sea. 'It's like Blue Hawaii,' he said, 'only without the music.'

Kev suddenly ran off, whooping and shouting 'Yee-hahs'. Betty followed. Mark and Rita watched them go. At the water's edge Kev threw down his motorcycle gloves and helmet, removed his leather jacket and shoes and socks, then his jeans, throwing everything onto the sand, before running into the sea. Betty cast off her clothes too, dancing on one foot as she struggled with one leg of her jeans. The pair ran about in shallow water, dressed in their underwear, splashing each other and shouting. Rita ran after them, hastily removing her sandals and jeans, and joining them in the water. Mark walked slowly to the water's edge and watched them, three crazy fools silhouetted against the bright moonlight.

'C'mon Kidda!' Kev called out. But Mark ignored him. He hated cold water, like the times in the scouts when everyone swam in the freezing river. They threw him in once, fully clothed, in a sort of graduation ceremony. He'd hardly been able to breathe and he'd never forgotten the experience.

'Come on Mark,' cried Rita. But Mark stayed put and watched his friends kicking and splashing until, at last, Betty ran out followed by the others. 'Chicken!' said Kev, but Mark didn't care. Instead his focus was on Rita, now walking in her top and knickers, carrying her sandals and jeans. They walked across the beach and plonked themselves onto the sandy-grass, just below the links, two couples ten yards or so apart. Rita threw her clothing down carelessly and flopped on to the ground.

Mark and Rita sat motionless, looking towards the sea, until Rita lay back, looked up at Mark's face and closed her eyes, almost inviting him to kiss her. He lay on his side, looking at her, allowing his eyes to stray the length of her body: at the contours of her breasts, her naked belly and her legs, the latter speckled with sand and looking ghostly white in the semi-darkness. They had close eye contact for a moment before he lowered his head and kissed her mouth. It was a long, slow, lingering kiss. He was utterly lost to her: her physical beauty, her allure, the smell of her breath and perfume. He felt the natural reaction in his jeans – and the discomfort through lack of space and the God-forsaken wart.

He wanted to explore her, but hesitated, uncertain of himself, not wanting to offend her by touching her intimately so soon yet wondering if she wanted him to. They could hear the faint swish of the sea gently spilling onto the shore and, now and then, the sound of music and the motors of the Spanish City, carried on the breeze. And then, from closer at hand, the quiet moaning of Betty, and, occasionally, Kev's sexual grunting, which increased steadily until, with loud gasps, they climaxed together before becoming silent. Moments later Mark caught the distinctive smell of cigarette smoke as it drifted over the sand. He kissed Rita, and caressed her. She lay sexually aroused, sighing and writhing with desire. But still he held back in his uncertainty and the reason he could not disclose – the wretched wart. Finally she lifted her torso from the grass and in a movement pulled off her pants, then thrust a hand behind his head and pulled him towards her. She was gasping, her mouth open even as he was kissing her; and then she climaxed, and he felt her relax and go limp. He sensed she was finished, that she had accepted his reluctance to take her.

As they lay together in silence, he felt she would be disappointed because he had not made love to her, and silently cursed the wart. He wondered what she was thinking, and even if she would ever agree to see him again. 'Last bus in ten minutes, Reet.' He looked up to see Betty approaching, followed by Kev, who was struggling with his zipper. Rita sat up, reached for her handbag and fumbled for a cigarette. She lit up and blew smoke off to one side. Kev and Betty hurried for the steps to the links. Rita looked at Mark, an eye-to-eye contact that might have betrayed her feelings of frustration; but she had a cigarette and looked contented. Or so he thought. He knew about the wart; she didn't, and he couldn't tell her. If he had syphilis, he wondered, was this the way it would always be from now on?

'C'mon Rita!' Betty's voice rang out with a sense of urgency.

Rita stood up quickly, pulled on her jeans and quickly slipped her feet into her sandals. Without a word they hurried after Kev and Betty, crossing the links to a lonely bus shelter. Inside, she faced him and put her arms around his neck. 'That was lovely,' she said quietly. Mark thought so too, but felt anguish inside over the possibility that he might have a serious illness. The wretched old woman flashed through his mind, and he inwardly cursed himself for getting drunk that night.

They looked up as the double-decker approached. 'Will I see you again?' asked Mark, in a tone he would have admitted must have sounded doubtful.

'Yes, but don't call at the flat,' replied Rita, adding, 'Dad doesn't like visitors.'

The girls stepped on to the platform of the bus and the conductor dinged the bell. Betty blew Kev a kiss. 'Call me,' Rita called out. 'Cook's on Saville Row!'

'Well, did you?' said Kev, as the bus drove off. The look on Mark's face gave him his answer. 'That's twice she's been on this beach expecting a fuck and she's still waiting. We could've stayed there all night if you had a bloody bike.'

Kev plonked his crash helmet onto his head and walked off. It was only then Mark realised he'd left his helmet on the beach. He hurried down the steps, and located it in the semi-darkness. Picking it up, his fingers brushed against silky material that was entangled in the strap. Rita's knickers! He hesitated, uncertain about whether to discard them, or keep them and return them to her. Instinctively he thrust them into his pocket.

Back on the links, he stood awhile, looking seaward. The heavy black cloud had moved eastwards, restricting the moonlight to the distant horizon, where it shone as bright as ever on the sea. It was as though a giant, invisible hand had drawn the cloud across the sky. All was quiet, save for the gentle lapping below. Then he hurried after his friend, preparing himself mentally for the perilous journey home along the Coast Road.

14

Like anyone else, Carol didn't care much for Monday mornings. But on this occasion she was more upbeat, telling herself she liked her job and the people she worked with. The day had dawned sunny. It had brought with it a feeling of optimism: she hoped she would see Mark again, and had already made arrangements with Emma to go to Partners on Saturday; she felt sure Mam would see sense and come home, especially now Dad was off the drink and had decorated their bedroom and had even started on the kitchen. She was eighteen soon: it would be lovely, she thought, to enjoy her birthday with Mam at home and Mark round for tea.

She breezed through the revolving doors, strode across the lobby and pressed the button for the lift. Then, impulsively, instead of waiting for it she bounded up the two flights of stairs and walked directly to her desk. All was well in the world of Carol Kemp that morning.

At elevenses she decided to go up to the canteen, knowing one or two of the girls from Accounts would be there. She was always amused to hear about their weekend's activities. She pressed for the lift, and stood back half a pace, waiting patiently for its arrival.

'Good weekend?'

Carol turned to see Miss Carr. She was clutching the usual bundle of documents under one arm, and carrying an attaché case. 'Best I use the lift too,' Miss Carr was saying. 'I'd hate to drop this lot on the stairs. Be there the rest of the day picking it up if I did.'

Carol smiled, not sure what to say. She liked her boss, but still wasn't altogether comfortable with her. The lift arrived with a 'ping' and they stepped inside. 'Fifth floor for me,' said Miss Carr, positioning herself in a corner. Carol pressed the buttons for floors five and six. As the lift started up with a jerk, the documents Miss Carr carried slipped from underneath her arm, pieces of paper that fluttered this way and that before landing on the floor.

'Oh…bother!' Miss Carr exclaimed, bending her knees and gathering in the now-scattered documents. They picked up sheets of paper together. 'Don't worry about getting them in order,' said Miss Carr. 'I'll sort them out when I get to where I'm going.'

The lift doors were opening as they finished picking up the documents. Carol thought the bundle looked in a mess and didn't envy her boss having to sort it out. 'Thanks for your help,' Miss Carr said; but before walking away, as Carol had expected, she lingered. 'I was wondering how things were at home,' said Miss Carr. 'Has your mother been in touch?'

Carol nodded. 'She did call, yes. But…' She baulked, uncertain of what to say. Miss Carr raised her eyebrows slightly, inviting more information. 'She says she's met another man,' said Carol, 'and now she's not sure what to do.'

'How has your father taken it?'

'He doesn't know yet. But…'

Carol felt her boss's gaze on her, and felt she wanted to say something else, anything but head off to wherever she was going. When the lift doors started to close Miss Carr jammed her foot against them and spoke again, quietly this time.

'You know that little bar next to the Royal. Why don't we meet there after work and we can talk about it? I'm sure it'll do you good.' Carol nodded compliantly. 'Say 5.30?' Miss Carr strutted off with a 'See you then,' as the lift doors began closing again.

Carol nodded and went to the canteen, but stopped when she reached the door. For some reason she didn't feel like company now; she didn't want to hear about her friends' weekend exploits, only to tell them she had been stood up at the dance. She walked over to the window on the landing and stood awhile, looking across the city roof-tops towards the familiar green arch of the Tyne Bridge, and Gates-head beyond. Her mood had clouded. She no longer felt so certain about things. And now she was going to have to tell Miss Carr about it tonight.

Tommy and Mark hung about the workshop, the only ones left after their workmates had long gone to their respective jobs. Finally Smudg-er appeared at the hatch. 'No sign of Fred?' Tommy shook his head. 'Off you go, then,' said Smudger. 'If he turns up I'll get him to give Bert a hand here.'

Old Betsy was waiting nearby, on a meter. That's what Tommy called his Ford Popular: Old Betsy. 'Reminds me of a bird I knew in Aden,' he explained. 'Clapped out, on high mileage but still a goer.' They went for tea at the Haymarket, Tommy saying if Smudger came in they could always say they thought Fred might turn up. Smudger had known Fred for nigh-on thirty years, had a soft spot for the old boy. He wouldn't mind. After two teas and a bacon sandwich each they left and Tommy drove to the job in the wilds of Durham. They'd barely taken their coats off when the sound of a familiar voice was call-ing through the building.

'Tommy! *Tommeeee!*'

'Christ, it's Smudger,' declared Tommy. 'Quick, look busy before he sees us.'

Mark opened Tommy's toolbox, took out a hammer and started chasing the nearest wall.

Smudger appeared, looking flustered under his trilby, cigarette dangling from his lower lip. 'Been meaning to call and see how you were getting on,' he explained, before adding, 'Fred was taken to hos-pital at the weekend. Apparently a neighbour found him collapsed on the doorstep. Don't know any more than that but when I do I'll let you know.'

Tommy indicated teas all round. Mark nodded, asking if his foreman took milk and sugar. Smudger nodded, raising two fingers

Churchill-style. For the first time ever Mark fancied Smudger was displaying emotion, being upset over old Fred. He went off to make the tea. After they drank it Tommy and Smudger took a tour of the site. Smudger left after that, without comment or even ta-ta. By then it was time for lunch.

They ate their sarnies in silence, Tommy deep into his *Mirror* as usual. Mark chatted aimlessly with Max, the plasterers' labourer. When they'd finished Tommy stood up and screwed the top back onto his flask. 'Don't bother picking up your tools, Mark lad,' he declared. 'We're going.' He was packing his haversack. 'Smudger won't be back today, so we're having a flier. I want to work on Betsy's big end and you can go to the hospital to get yourself checked out.'

They packed up and left, Tommy driving in silence all the way back to town. He drove directly to the main entrance to the General Hospital. 'It's in there somewhere. You've probably only got the clap, so don't worry about it. A few pills and you'll be okay.'

Mark stepped on to the pavement. 'Where do I go exactly?' he asked.

'Dunno,' Tommy replied, glancing anxiously in his mirror. Mark could see traffic building up. 'Just ask for the VD clinic,' Tommy called out, as Mark closed the door. Tommy drove off to the sound of blaring horns and Old Betsy disappeared into a line of traffic.

Mark had been to the hospital complex before, through work. There were lots of buildings, some with strange names, like orthopaedic and neurology. There was nothing for it but to visit them one by one, until he came to 'VD Clinic' or similar. He set off slowly, walking up to doors that led to everywhere but one marked VD Clinic. He followed the road around until it emerged onto the main road again, but there was no sign of his goal. He retraced steps, again without success. After an hour of painstaking search he opted for a door marked Gynaecology and went inside, finding himself in a long corridor with a sign pointing to 'Enquiries'. The corridor led directly to a curved enquiry desk. Behind it sat a woman wearing headphones. Two nurses dressed in light blue uniforms and wearing upside-down watches were chatting on Mark's side of the counter. All three women looked at him as he approached. Seeing them he stopped, looked right and left and decided to turn back, but one of the nurses spoke.

'Are you lost?'

He felt his face redden as the women waited for an answer.

The receptionist spoke. 'Can I help you?' she enquired. Mark wished she had been sitting there alone, but the nurses were looking. He thought he could discern faint smiles on their faces. He stepped up to the desk and looked at the receptionist. He wanted to speak, but couldn't.

'Are you working here?' One of the nurses was looking him up and down. He shook his head. They waited. She turned to the receptionist. 'Call Security,' she said. 'You know the thefts we've been having, handbags and stuff. Best have him checked out.'

'I'm looking for the VD Clinic,' Mark blurted out.

The nurses looked at each other and smiled. The receptionist slipped her headphones off and stood up. 'Go back to the door where you came in,' she said calmly. 'Turn right along the road. Ward 34 is what you want. It's on the right. About a hundred yards I'd say.'

He thanked her and hurried off, detecting a titter from the nurses before thankfully leaving them behind and emerging into fresh air again. He followed the instructions, which led him to a single-storey brick building with a dilapidated sign in the long grass outside, with 'Ward 34' written on it in faded lettering. He walked up to a blank door and pushed it open, finding himself in a small reception area. There was a small, sliding window. There was no-one present behind the window, but he spotted a bell-push with a handwritten note on paper stuck on the counter alongside. 'Press for attention', it said. He pressed the button.

After a minute or so a man appeared. Mark decided there and then he was the fattest human being he'd ever seen. He had a huge moon-face and wore bottle-end glasses. It was all he could do to negotiate the narrow space between unoccupied desks to approach the window. He didn't speak; he just looked at Mark, gasping for breath.

'Is this the VD Clinic?' asked Mark.

The man didn't speak but reached to one side and picked up a card.

He slid it under the glass, along with a cheap biro. 'Fill this in then go through that door,' he said, indicating a door in the corner. He gave Mark a flat piece of wood with the number 53 engraved on it. Mark placed the card on the narrow ledge and filled it in: name and address (optional), name and address of G.P. (optional), religious denomination, the date you last had sexual intercourse. The last question he perused for a moment and left it blank. He slid the card back under the glass and went to the door in the corner. He opened it, and found himself in room occupied by half a dozen young men and a chap old enough to be his dad. All eyes looked up at him briefly, but returned to perusing the crumpled magazines most of them seemed to have picked up from a small table in the centre of the room.

He sat down and waited, noting the time. It was 3.30. Everyone sat in stony silence. One by one the men were called, and at twenty past four a door opened and a man's head looked into the room. 'Number 53,' the head called out. Mark stood up and followed its owner into a small room. There was a small wooden table and two chairs. 'Wait here,' he was told. Mark sat down and after ten minutes another man, wearing a white coat, came into the room and sat opposite Mark.

'What can I do for you today?' he asked.

'I think I might have syphilis, but it's probably the clap.'

'Really? And what makes you think that?'

'It was in the Daily Mirror.'

'What are your symptoms exactly?'

'I've got a nasty wart on my thingy.'

The man stood up and came to Mark's side of the desk. 'Let's have a look, then.'

Mark dropped his trousers. The man stooped and looked closely at his penis, lifted it a little and squeezed the wart gently. 'Hmm,' he said at last, before returning to his seat. 'Okay, pull your pants up.' He opened a small box then and took out a syringe. 'I require a blood sample,' he said, 'and then if you can go behind that curtain and pee into the receptacle. Then go back to the waiting room and we'll call you.'

It was over in minutes, after which Mark returned to the waiting room. After the last of the other men had been to see the doctor the man in the white coat appeared. 'The doctor will see you now,' he declared, holding the door open. 'Dr Arumagum. Along the corridor, second door on the right.'

Mark did as he was bid, encountering the fat guy from Enquiries in the corridor, now wearing a greatcoat and clearly off home, wheezing as he walked. He was hardly able to squeeze past him. He ended up at a door bearing the name 'Dr Arumagum'. He knocked gently and entered. The room was bigger than he had expected. It was almost devoid of furniture, save for a desk in the far corner, and a chair for him to sit on. The chair at the other side of the desk was occupied by a young Asian woman, late-20s at the most he thought. His other thought just then was that she was quite beautiful and he must have come to the wrong place.

'Hi,' the woman chirped. She was smiling, as though he was there to buy some liquorice allsorts. 'I'm Dr Arumagum. Do take a seat.' She gestured to the empty chair and remained seated herself. 'Number 53,' she said. 'Mr, um, Green?' He nodded, and sat and watched nervously as she perused the card he'd filled in.'

When she looked up he noticed her smile had vanished. Her voice was more formal when she spoke again.

'It's no use keeping secrets, you know. Not here. All information is accepted in confidence, and we need to be able to contact anyone else who may be affected.' She flashed the card at him. 'The date you last had sexual intercourse.' She laid the card on the desk, picked up a silver pen and said, 'Well?' He shuffled uncomfortably in his seat. 'You know what sexual intercourse is, I take it?' He nodded but said nothing. 'I really do need to know,' she said, 'and I also want to know the name of the person you had intercourse with. You do know who you had sexual intercourse with, I take it?"

He shook his head.

'Look,' she said, placing the pen down carefully in the centre of the card and clasping her hands in front of her. 'This is a hospital, and this is a clinic. I'm a doctor, and I need to have answers to my questions. Venereal disease is an infection that is spread through sexual intercourse. You may have got it off someone, you may have passed it on to someone. Do you understand?'

He nodded.

'Good. Let's start again. Have you had sexual intercourse?'

'I'm not sure.'

Her silence demanded an explanation. So he explained, as best he could: about getting drunk and the old woman.

'So,' she said at last, 'Why do you think you have…' She checked the card. 'Syphilis?' She waved a hand and stood up. 'Oh never mind.' She moved to his side of the desk. 'I understand you have a wart on your penis. Let me see.'

He looked up, mortified.

'Look. I've been here all day and I really do need you to co-operate. Now, drop your trousers and let me see this wart.'

He stood up slowly, undid his belt and lowered his trousers to the top of his thighs, whereupon she seized his underpants and pulled them and his trousers down to his knees. She motioned him to stand to one side and sat in his chair, her face now a matter of inches from his manhood. She held his limp penis between her fingers, pulled it about gently for a moment and touched the base of the wart. She lifted his penis up and peeked underneath. 'Any sweating been going on under here?' she asked, tilting her head for a clearer view. He shook his head. She squeezed the end gently. 'Any discharge?' 'I'm not sure,' he lied. She stood up then, saying, 'All right, you can pull your trousers up,' and returned to her side of the desk and sat down. When he had adjusted his clothing she motioned for him to sit too.

'Right. You haven't got syphilis,' she said. 'In fact, your blood sample indicates you haven't got any venereal disease. So that's good news, isn't it?' She was looking intensely at him, and at his haversack, which lay on the floor by his side. 'You do manual work, is that right?' She didn't wait for him to answer. 'Dirty work, anyway. You get your hands dirty. That's the problem. A speck of dirt has found its way into your skin, probably when you've handled yourself when you've been urinating. Blocked the pore, hence the wart.' She gave him a moment to take it in. 'You need to wash your hands before and after you pee,' she said. 'Cleanliness is Godliness, right?' She was smiling again.

She opened a drawer and wrote a prescription. 'This is for some cream to rub onto the wart, and some pills. Take as directed. Okay?' She slid her chair back slightly and stood up. 'You can go. And remember... What must you remember?'

'To wash my hands,' he replied, standing up.

'Yes, before and after. And not to get drunk and go with strange women.'

She saw him to the door, and was still smiling as he left. He was smiling too.

Once again Carol checked her watch. Miss Carr was late, which didn't surprise her, such was her workload. She felt anxious about their meeting, and would have been relieved if she had stood her up. She had Dad's tea to cook, after all. But even as she thought about going for her trolley, her boss appeared, smiling and with a 'Sorry I'm late.'

Before she could reply Miss Carr was leading her into the pub. She went to a table in the corner, took off her coat and laid it on a chair. Carol waited, uncertain about what to do.

'What'll it be?'

Carol had never been in a pub before. She looked at the bar, and around the room. 'I'd like a fruit juice, please,' she said, nervously.

'Nothing stronger?'

'No thank you. It's just I'm only seventeen...'

'Oh. Of course.' Miss Carr went to the bar. Carol sat down, regretting her decision to come. She had often wondered what pubs were like inside. She looked about her: lighting came from strategically-placed spotlights, and there were chairs with beige-coloured seats and fancy tables with ornate carvings on the legs. The entire room was covered with a crimson-coloured carpet and smelled of stale smoke. Modern-jazz music tinkled away softly. There were no other customers.

Miss Carr returned carrying two glasses, one containing pineapple juice which she placed in front of Carol. She picked the other up at once, said 'Bottoms up' and gulped half of the contents down her throat. Carol took a sip of her drink, and set the glass down.

'Now then,' said Miss Carr. 'I'm all ears. And by the way, before we go any further, it's Judith. So, your mum.'

Carol shrugged. 'She called to say she's met another man and she was going to the pictures with him. I haven't told Dad yet. I'm just hoping she'll come home.'

'Well, from what you say I think she probably will. A visit to the cinema is hardly the catalyst for a long relationship.'

'What's a catalyst?'

'I mean going to the pictures is one thing. A long term relationship quite another. For all you know she went and hated every minute of it. I expect she'll be in contact again soon. So, don't worry.' She took another sip of her drink. 'You're too young to be worrying about what your parents do anyway. You have your own life to live. So...' She emptied her glass. 'Live it.'

With that she stood up and gestured to Carol for another drink. 'Go on,' she said. 'Just one. You're nearly eighteen anyway, aren't you?' Carol shook her head. Miss Carr – Judith – went to the bar and returned with another drink for herself. 'It's gin and tonic if you change your mind. You can have a taste of mine first, if you like.' Carol shook her head again.

'So. You.' Judith was looking straight at her. 'What about your love life? Boyfriend?'

'Well, sort of.' Carol resented the question, but told her all about Mark: how they'd met, how she felt about him, how she'd told him to leave her house when he 'tried something', and how she now regretted it because although he'd sent her flowers he hadn't turned up at the dance.

'Sent flowers? A young boy like that? That's unusual, I must say. Was there a note? I mean, he might have been saying goodbye.'

'He said he was thinking of me.'

'And yet he stood you up.'

'Well, not so much stood me up. He just didn't come to the dance on Saturday night.'

'Are you seeing him again?'

'I hope so.'

Miss Carr took another drink. 'Typical. You don't give him what he wants, he leads you on with flowers then doesn't turn up.' She emptied her glass, and went for a refill. As she stood at the bar Carol sat and waited, wishing she could just go home. She thought about just walking to the door and leaving. But tomorrow Miss Carr would send for her, and want to know why she had left when she was trying to help her.

'Sorry to gallop through so many g and t's,' Miss Carr said, returning to the table. 'It's my escape after such a hectic day. And it's so nice to have someone to have a drink with, believe me.' Carol detected a slurring in her voice. 'Your dad,' Miss Carr was saying. 'You told me that time he used to knock your mum about. Gave her black eyes and so on. Did you see it happening?'

'Sometimes. But usually it was after I'd gone to bed. I'd see what he'd done the next morning.'

'What a bastard.'

'It was the drink,' Carol replied angrily. 'My dad would never do such things unless he was drunk.'

'Exactly. But apologies the next morning are no defence.' Miss Carr took a huge swig of her g and t. 'Men! They're all the same, mark my words.'

'He did it because he was drunk. Like you are now.'

Carol bit her lip and wondered what her boss's response would be to her words of rebuke. Miss Carr eyed her for a few seconds before placing her empty glass on the table, and fumbling in her handbag. She pulled out a packet of cigarettes and with trembling fingers lit up. She blew smoke sideways from her mouth. 'I'm so sorry,' she said at last. 'I shouldn't have said that about your dad. Like him, my poor conduct was through drink. Can you forgive me?'

Carol did not reply. Instead she looked hard at her boss, her face betraying her anger.

'Look,' said Miss Carr, 'I know you'll probably find it hard to understand, but after such long days in the office I just need to wind down. So I come here and let a few drinks unwind me. I live alone, you see, there's no-one to talk to when I get home.'

'You actually called my dad a...'

'I know, I know. But you must understand, I didn't mean it and I have said sorry. I get stressed up a bit.' She forced a conciliatory smile. 'Look, let me tell you something. D'you know how I relieve the stress at work? I go off on walks through the building. Those bundles of paper you see me carrying. They're all for show. They're my prop, so people think I'm busy. Well, I am busy, but I keep leaving the office to get away from the telephone and people. I'm a fraud. There! I've been honest with you. So can we be friends again?'

Carol nodded, but only slightly, and wondered when her ordeal might end.

'When you told me about the trouble at home,' Miss Carr went on, 'I thought there could be a way I might be able to help you. It's just I've a spare room, so if you need to get away you are quite welcome to use it. You only have to ask. Look...' She fumbled in her bag and pulled out a small notepad and pen. 'Here's my telephone number.' She wrote it out, gave it to Carol.

'Dad would never let me,' Carol replied.

'Of course.' Miss Carr was picking up her handbag. 'Not twenty-one yet, eh! But the offer's there anyway.' She stood up, and Carol did likewise.

Outside, Miss Carr seemed unsteady on her feet. Carol watched as she fumbled in her bag and pulled out her car keys. 'See you tomorrow,' said Miss Carr, 'and remember, my door is always open.' She hurried off then, leaving Carol to catch her bus. And to wonder what work would be like from now on.

When Mark got home that afternoon there was a black Ford Popular parked at the back gate. He knew the caller must be one of two, and he couldn't imagine Tommy calling to see him. He pushed the back door open to see Avril at the kitchen sink, washing cups and saucers. He nodded, she said 'Hi.'

He opened the door to the living room to be met with a wall of cigarette smoke. 'Hello pet, just finished work?' said Ettie, lipstick on her teeth as usual. He didn't answer, but passed through to the door to the stairs and went directly to his room. He wasn't surprised at the knock that followed a few minutes later. He opened the door to Avril. She was holding a mug of tea. He couldn't help notice the hole in her green cardy and the usual smell of fag-ash that permeated the air around her head. He took the tea with a gruff 'Thanks.'

'Your mam says you've got a lass,' she said. He shrugged.

'I'm going to that dance place,' she announced. 'Where you go. Partners.' She stood her ground, waiting for his response. Instead he merely looked at her, his feelings ranging somewhere between contempt and hate.

'I'm going with a friend,' she was saying. 'A boy I know. We're gonna learn to dance.'

She was looking at him, waiting. He took a sip of the tea, then closed the door in her face. He heard her footsteps on the stairs, and a few minutes later the sound of a car engine. It spluttered and coughed before kicking into life. He heard it being driven away, then went downstairs to find Bob had got in from work.

'Fixed up then, are yer?' Bob enquired.

'No, I've never fancied Ettie,' replied Mark.

'Ettie in the nettie,' said Bob.

'Eggshell and Ada in the nettie,' said Mark, glancing at the door in case Mam was about. As if on cue she appeared, after seeing Ettie and Avril off.

'You know, Avril's a nice lass, our Mark. Better than that floosie you were canoodling with outside the Club.'

Dad appeared through the front door from tending to his pigeons. 'Company gone then?' he enquired, tipping a wink at his sons. Before they could answer there was a loud knock at the back door.

'Sounds like the Gestapo,' Bob declared.

Charlie went to answer it. After a few seconds he returned. 'It's Jimmy Swinburne for you,' he said, looking at Bob.

'Eggshell? What does he want?'

'Best you ask him. Doesn't look very happy,' said Dad, taking a seat next to the fire. Bob and Mark looked at each other and went into the kitchen. Eggshell was waiting on the step.

'That your black jalopy outside?' Eggshell was looking at Bob, face a-thunder.

'It's my black Riley, yeah.'

'Aye. Well it's parked outside my gate. Shift it.'

Bob and Mark followed Eggshell to the back gate. 'There's no other car for miles,' said Bob. 'What's your problem?'

'It's obstructing the Queen's Highway. You've no business parking it outside my property. Shift it, or else I'll send for the polis.' Eggshell stood with his fists clenched, his face beetroot-red with anger. Mark noticed that apart from having no hair on his head he had no eyelashes either.

'I only parked it there because when I got home from work there was already a car parked outside our house.'

'Just shift it.'

With that Eggshell turned and walked off. Bob and Mark looked at each other, before Bob went for his car keys. 'How to make friends and influence people,' said Mark, as Bob stepped outside.

'I'll influence somebody, you can bet on it,' Bob replied. Mark glanced towards Ada's toilet door before going indoors for his tea.

15

Next day, Tuesday, Mark was late for work. It wasn't his fault; the bus had been held up in traffic. Not that that would wash with Smudger. Be late in your own time was his motto, along with a bollocking in front of whoever was standing within earshot.

Mark put a hand on the workshop door and pushed gently. Maybe he could creep in unnoticed. Instead the door caught the heels of Horlicks, standing just inside. In fact, everyone was there; no-one had as yet gone off to their respective jobs. 'We've been asked to hang on,' whispered Horlicks. 'It's probably another meaningful announcement from Smudger.'

So Robson's men and boys waited...and waited. It was turned eight before the door at the top of the steps opened suddenly, revealing Smudger, wearing his battered trilby and smoke from the inevitable cigarette curling slowly up his sleeve, and old Robson himself, the stub of a squat cigar sticking out of the corner of his mouth.

Hedley Martindale Robson's appearance at that time of the morning was unknown. Boss and foreman surveyed tradesmen and apprentices from the top of the steps for a few moments, before Smudger, coughing and wheezing, finally spoke. 'Mr Robson has something to say to you this morning,' he said simply, before descending the steps. Old Robson removed his cigar, took a moment to scan the faces looking up at him and spoke in the gravest possible tones.

'It is my sad duty to tell you all that Mr Outhwaite died last night in hospital. As you know he had been ill with cancer for some time. He was with this company for, ooh…' he and Smudger looked at each other, mutually sucking in air through puckered cheeks, 'over thirty years. In fact it was myself, Mr Smith and Mr Outhwaite who started the firm and it's been going ever since.'

'Who the hell's Mr Outhwaite?' whispered Horlicks.

'Old Fred, you duckegg,' hissed Bert, standing close by. 'The bloke you've known since you came to this company. The bloke who forgot more than you'll ever know.'

Mark felt sadness sweeping over him. Fred was dead. He knew it wasn't unexpected, but he'd never known anyone who had died before. Apart from his grandparents, but that was when he was a kid.

'He was sixty-two, so not a bad innings,' said Smudger.

'Yes,' said Robson, 'and the company supported him right to the end. We were a place for him to come to, a sort of refuge. Better than being on his own. He was one of us, after all.'

An awkward silence followed, before Smudger spoke again. 'Right lads. Off you go. We'll let you know when the funeral is.'

Bodies shuffled. Voices muttered. Tommy appeared from the throng and nodded at Mark.

'On his own?' said Mark. 'He used to blame his missus for making egg sandwiches.'

'Aye, he would,' said Tommy. 'But she five died years ago. He was alone but didn't want anybody to know it. He didn't want anybody feeling sorry for him. But I knew ever since day one, when his cancer was diagnosed.' They squeezed through the door to make their way to Tommy's car. Bert was already outside, smoking a roll-up. 'Robson and Smudger started the company with Fred right enough,' he said. 'But look at what happened. Robson got to be boss, Smudger was foreman and Fred was still on the tools right up till he pegged it. He was a good bloke. I fully expect we can go to his funeral in the firm's time.'

When Tommy unlocked the car Mark got into the front passenger seat. It occurred to him that it was usually Fred who'd sat there. He knew his eyes were moist. 'Life goes on, Mark lad,' said Tommy, turning on the engine. On the job Mark dumped his haversack on to the floor and spotted the old armchair Fred had sat in. Almost died in. It looked forlorn now, as though it was missing him. Fred was only a bloke he worked with, but he felt a sense of loss and sadness. Tommy saw him looking. 'Buck up, lad,' he said. 'Go make the tea.' Mark picked up their billycans, but he sensed that Tommy was sharing his sadness.

What the day held in store Carol couldn't imagine. Would Miss Carr ignore her? Send for her? She felt certain there would be an atmosphere if she did. She took her coat off, went to her desk and decided to get on with her job. She hadn't done anything wrong, after all.

At teatime she made her way to the stairs, passing her boss's office en route. Unusually the door was wide open, revealing an empty chair behind her desk. Carol hesitated, looked about as though was about to do something naughty and didn't want anyone to see, then stepped inside one pace. The coat rack was empty. It looked like Miss Carr wasn't at work today.

She was worried. Miss Carr was always at work. She had never known her to be off sick. Last night she had got tipsy and made a fool of herself over admitting she carried the bundles of paper for show; then she had offered to help her by offering her a spare room in her house. A spare room to a junior employee. Was that allowed? Carol wondered. Back at her desk she realised she was on edge, nervous. She felt guilty but she couldn't think why exactly. She would get through the day, but tomorrow would come: and sooner or later so would Miss Carr – Judith – who'd said her door was always open to her. But when tomorrow came there was still no sign of her. That lunchtime Carol couldn't resist another peek in her office. Patti from Sales happened to be passing. 'Looking for Miss Carr?' she asked. 'She's taken the rest of the week off. Just found out myself this morning.'

Carol's feelings ranged between relief and disappointment: relief that she wouldn't have to face her boss, disappointment that she couldn't get their inevitable next meeting over with. After all, as she reminded herself for the umpteenth time, they would have to meet

again, sooner or later. Still, she felt, even if was only temporary, the
pressure was off. So instead of worrying, when she went home that
evening her thoughts turned to Saturday evening – and Mark.

She opened the front door to find Dad sitting in the armchair by
the fire, reading his Chronicle. He nodded in the direction of the table.
'You're a popular girl,' he said, smiling. There, on the table, unwrapped
in cellophane, was a bunch of red roses. She snatched them up with
glee, and read the message on the card: 'Thinking of you'. Different
flowers, same message. Then she picked the card up and read it again.

It was signed, simply, 'J'.

***

By Thursday, thanks to antibiotics and cream, Mark's wart had all but
disappeared. He was fighting fit, and wanted to prove it. To anyone
he could, as a matter of fact. Any girl, that is. He was also looking
forward to Saturday – for the same reason as Carol. But he wanted to
ask Rita out too. He'd looked out for her on the bus without success,
and since she had told him not to call at the flat he would telephone.
Along Saville Row to Cook's, the adverts said. That's where Mam had
bought his clothes when he was a kid. Well, he was going to Cook's
again, or his voice was. When Tommy dropped him in town he went
to the nearest phone box and called. The telephonist put him through
straight away. When Rita answered he recognised her husky voice. He
tried a husky voice of his own. She sounded pleased to hear it.

'I wondered if you fancied the pictures,' he said.

'Oh, where? And when?' Before he could answer she spoke again,
this time lowering her voice.

'Boss is hovering,' she said. 'Where are you?'

'Outside C&As.'

'Could you meet me outside the store in ten minutes?' He could.
With pleasure.

He hurried to the store. She emerged with a smile, the same old
Connie, he thought: same coat, same red hair. They could go home on
the bus together.

'I only have a minute,' she said. 'Working late, and then going for a drink with the girls.' Her look said what did he have in mind?

'I wondered if you fancied the pictures Friday?'

'Sounds great. Where?'

'D'you fancy the Stoll?' he asked optimistically. He'd already calculated that a girl who was down to her knickers on the beach would be up for an 'X'.

'The Stoll? Yuk!'

For a moment he was lost for words, his heart sinking at the thought he'd upset her.

'When you said the pictures I hoped you would say the Haymarket.' Now she was smiling encouragingly. 'Blue Hawaii has been retained a second week. I fancy it. If you do.'

'Great!' He nodded, at the same time wondering if he'd be allowed in following the debacle with Marie.

She was all smiles. 'See you outside the Haymarket at seven then.' With that she leaned forward and kissed his cheek. Instinctively he raised his arms to her waist, to hold her close and kiss her. But she stepped back, laughing and held up a mocking, forbidding finger. She looked delighted as she hurried, still smiling, back into the store, leaving him to reflect on how utterly lovely she was and to bask in the satisfaction that the girl on the bus had just kissed him, and completely of her own choice.

He caught the bus home and walked up the Terrace, stomach rumbling. A stiff wind forced his head down into his dufflecoat, so he didn't notice the ambulance parked outside the Swinburnes' back gate until he was almost near enough to touch it. He was just in time to see Eggshell's back gate open and the man himself, wrapped in a heavy blanket, being carried in a wheelchair by the two ambulance crew. When Eggshell glanced his way Mark saw his right eye was swollen and blackened and there were spots of blood on his face.

He stopped to let them cross the footpath and watched as they lifted Eggshell into the back of the ambulance, where he sat sideways on, his injured eye closest to Mark. Mark had never seen such damage; the eye had closed completely, and his upper cheek had turned purple.

Seeing him looking, Eggshell snarled, raised his forearm and clenched his fist. Mark couldn't help notice his huge bicep and massive forearm. For a moment he thought he was going to climb out of the ambulance and lump him, so he turned away and opened his back gate, and entered the yard where he saw a familiar black bicycle leaning against the wall.

PC Moon was sitting in one of the easy chairs by the fire, holding one of Mam's rock buns in one hand and a mug of tea in the other. His helmet graced the floor by his side. Bob was sitting in the other chair. Their parents were sitting at dining the table, smoking and looking worried.

'Now then, Mark lad.' PC Moon was looking at Mark, his piggy eyes almost seeming to be trying to pierce his body. Mark looked at Bob.

Bob shrugged. 'I had to do it. And serves the blighter right if you ask me.'

Charlie Green picked up one of the dining room chairs and plonked it in front of the fire, between PC Moon and Bob. Mark promptly sat on it. Moon devoured a last mouthful of rock bun and gulped it down, before carefully placing his now empty mug onto the hearth. 'Now then, Mark. It's about Mr Swinburne next door. He's been assaulted. *Criminally* assaulted.'

'I saw him being put into the ambulance.'

'Aye, well. You couldn't fail to notice his eye, then. And it's nasty. Very nasty. And I gather you know why it happened.'

Mark looked at Bob, then back at PC Moon, and nodded.

'Mr Swinburne has indicated he wishes to make a formal complaint about this,' said PC Moon, 'an' it's my duty to get to the bottom of it and take statements.' He paused, as though allowing everything to sink in. 'Now then.' He harrumphed and cleared his throat. 'Can you tell me in your own words what you know. Why Mr Swinburne was assaulted, that is.'

'Him and Ada were doing it in Ada's lav.'

'And how would you know that? C'mon, you can't get into trouble for tellin' the truth.'

'I heard Ada say something that time I was outside the Club.'

A look of astonishment crossed the policeman's face. 'What? So you *were* the prowler outside the Club that night?'

Mark swallowed. PC Moon looked thoughtful for a moment before going on. 'Well, that's history now. But next time I ask you to tell me the truth you best tell it lad.' He paused again. 'Now then, let's concentrate on the matter in hand, eh? I gather you saw, or think you saw, Mr Swinburne the other night in next-door's back yard. Is that right? The truth mind.'

Mark nodded.

'Well, how did you know it was him? Did you see him?'

Mark nodded.

'Did you see anything else?'

'He came from their lav. I heard them.'

'What did you hear exactly?'

'They were making...' He hesitated, picturing the look on his mam's face as she sat behind, listening. '...Sex noises.'

'Aye, right.' PC Moon looked as embarrassed as Mark felt. 'Now, it would've been dark, so how can you be sure it was Mr Swinburne?'

'I saw the light reflecting off the top of his bald head. Then I heard next-door's gate, then Eggshell's gate.'

'Eggshell?'

'Mr Swinburne. Then I heard him open their back door. Then I heard Jane.'

'Jane? Who's Jane?'

'Jane Russell.'

'He means their Jack Russell,' said Charlie. 'Talk sense, son.'

PC Moon was undeterred. 'Did you see Ada? Mrs Cook, that is.'

'Sort of. But it was her voice I heard in the lav. I heard her back door open and close as well.'

'Right. Well your mam says you're eighteen so I'm gonna have to take a statement from you.'

Mark turned to face his father. 'I don't want to make a statement if it gets our Bob into trouble,' he said.

'Me in trouble?' said Bob. 'Why me? I didn't lump Eggshell.'

Mark was perplexed. 'But I thought…'

'It was Roger. I told him about what was going on with Eggshell and Ada because he insulted my car. I didn't think he'd go and pan him.'

'Huh, don't underestimate Roger,' said Charlie. 'Swinburne's a big man but Roger is an ex-boxer. Nowt to look at but he packs a punch. I saw him duff a bloke at the Club once for insulting Ada. Went out like a light he did.'

'What happens now, with Roger I mean?' asked Mark.

'I've already had a word with him,' said PC Moon. 'I'll pop in and see him again when I'm finished here. I expect I'll be reporting him for assault. Now then, can we sit at the table?' Charlie and Nancy made way and Mark made his statement, painstakingly written down by the policeman.

After PC Moon had gone Charlie said he thought a court appearance would be unlikely. 'Do you think Jimmy Swinburne will want this story appearing in the paper?' he asked. 'I expect he'll see sense and withdraw his complaint, mark my words.' Mark hoped so. The last thing he wanted was for his tryst with Beryl to appear in the *Evening Chronicle*.

For Carol, the week had dragged. From the start it had been difficult. Miss Carr's performance in the pub and then her flowers, still in their cellophane wrapping; nothing heard from Mam, and what was happening with that Ted chap. Now, leaving work on Thursday evening, there was just one more day till the weekend, and Emma had agreed to go to Partners with her on Saturday.

She hurried between homeward-bound commuters. She waited at the kerb, looking out for traffic. She was about to step off the pavement when, to her astonishment, she spotted Mark. He was standing outside Cook's store, wearing his work clothes and carrying a haversack. Her first instinct was to make a beeline for him; but then she saw he was talking to a tall, good-looking girl with striking red hair. The girl was smiling. She watched for a minute or two, expecting him to look in her direction and spot her. Instead he was in animated conversation with the girl. The girl could be anyone, she told herself. Someone who worked at the same place as him, perhaps. But then she saw her kiss him on the cheek, and step back, smiling, before disappearing into Cook's.

Carol hurried off and crossed the road, reaching the bus stop at the same time as her trolley. She joined the short queue, eager to disappear inside. She felt like a hunted animal, but she was sure Mark hadn't seen her and now the trolley was on its way. She just hoped no-one would notice her tears.

***

Mark checked his watch. Ten minutes to seven. Ten minutes before Rita was due. He had deliberately taken up a position away from the kiosk and from the view of anyone standing in the foyer. Less than a week since he and Marie had been ejected from the Haymarket, he thought the manager or the usherettes might recognise him. But there'd be no escaping running the gauntlet once Rita arrived.

He ran through the strategy again. No hanky-panky, or not much anyway. He couldn't afford to be caught doing sexy shenanigans again; they might call the police next time. So they'd watch the film. She liked Elvis; that's why they were going. Then he'd walk her to the bus stop – the bus to Blyth; Kev said Rita stayed at Betty's at weekends – and toddle off home like a good boy, job done. He looked forward to Whitley Bay's deserted beach on Sunday night: *then* they'd have sex.

She was on time, appearing from nowhere in the misly rain, her red hair spilling over her pure-white mac. Her lipstick matched her hair. She looked fantastic and he said so. 'Thank you,' she replied, slipping her hand under his arm. 'Shall we?' she asked, stepping forward. He paid for two tickets in the Upper Circle and they entered the foyer. He was so knocked out by her beauty, her presence, he almost forgot to look out for the manager and the two usherettes. Almost, but not quite. They negotiated the journey to the stairs and the woman who tore their tickets in two without any problem. But then, as they approached the door to the auditorium, his heart sank when he saw the usherette who was waiting was one of the dreaded two he'd encountered the previous week. He held his breath, but she opened the door with a smile and they passed through, locating their seats and settling in comfort. The lights were on, but it wouldn't be long until they were turned down. He began to relax.

He waited until *Blue Hawaii* was rolling before slipping his arm around her shoulders. She responded by moving a little closer. Having forced himself to watch the film, he found himself actually enjoying it. They were about half an hour in when she turned her face to his. The flickering lights illuminated her cheeks, and her eyes were wide and almost pleading: *kiss me*. He gently placed his mouth on hers and kissed her. Her eyes closed. After a while he began to pull his mouth away, but she wouldn't let him. He felt they could have stayed like that all night, their mouths locked together, with the wonderful smell that emanated from her lingering in his nostrils.

But he couldn't relax, worrying that at any moment he would feel a hand on his shoulder and a voice rebuking him. He opened his eyes and looked at the line of faces in the row behind: as far as he could tell all eyes were focused on the screen. He hoped to see at least one other couple similarly embraced, but there was no-one; everyone seemed to be engrossed in the movie. He looked at Rita's eyes again. They were tight shut. Finally, he eased his mouth away and gasped for air. He caressed her cheek, still worried about the dreaded hand on his shoulder.

They sat uncertainly for a few minutes. He wanted to pull apart for a while; she seemed to want more contact. She turned her head to him again, kissing him so firmly she was almost facing the back of the auditorium. He felt a growing erection, but still there was the fear of the dreaded hand on his shoulder, the rebuking voice. She placed a hand on his chest, a gesture that seemed to mean she wanted more. But he was too apprehensive to react.

Later, he turned to her again and kissed her cheek. There was no response, no turning of her head, no offering of her mouth. Later still, she turned to face him, looking into his eyes. He kissed her, but this time she pulled her head back slightly, so that their lips were touching, but only just. Then she licked his mouth briefly before sliding her tongue inside, at the same time sliding her hand across his thighs, groping for him. He opened his eyes to see if anyone was looking. No-one seemed to be. But he turned his head sharply away, and she withdrew her hand. He took his arm from around her shoulders then, and they watched the movie until *Hawaiian Wedding Song* played it out. When the lights came on she stood up without so much as a glance at him, and they left in silence, emerging onto the street almost as two strangers.

The rain had stopped. They splashed through puddles and across wet pavements to her bus stop. He felt relieved the evening was over, that he had successfully resisted her sexual advances and told himself things would be different at Whitley Bay on Sunday evening. At the bus stop they had ten minutes to kill. He slid his arms around her waist, but was surprised to find her rigid and unresponsive. It felt so awkward he withdrew his arms and simply stood facing her.

'I love your white mac,' he said at last, hoping she would allow him to kiss her. Instead she simply nestled her face against his chest. It was chilly; she was just trying to keep warm, he thought.

'Hope it's better weather Sunday,' he said, for the want of something to say.

She looked at him. 'Don't you know? Kev and Betty have fallen out again. So we won't be going to the Spanish City on Sunday.' She plonked her head back onto his chest and said, simply, 'Sorry,'

'We could still meet up,' he said, stroking her hair.

She lifted her head again, looking serious. 'No. I've decided to give it a miss this weekend.' She checked her watch, standing back from him looking out for her bus.

'Will I see you again?' he said at last.

She nodded faintly. 'Give me ring.'

They stood in silence then, until her bus rolled up and with a peck on his cheek she stepped on to the platform and disappeared inside. She never looked back.

He stood at the bus stop awhile thinking about her. Rita: the girl he'd called Connie, the girl he'd thought about so often. For weeks he'd had sexual thoughts about her, had sexual trysts with her in his dreams, yet in real life had spurned her sexual advances twice. But how could he tell her why? 'First time I had a wart on my willy, second time I was at the Haymarket with another bird and when we got to grips they threw us out'. It was just rotten luck, he told himself. Never mind, she had said to give her a call. Turning away, he was cheered by the thought that tomorrow he'd surely see Carol. Even though they'd only met twice, she was still his number one. She was the one that mattered.

16

As they alighted from the bus at Gallowgate, Robbie cast an anxious eye at his friend. Not the boozer again, surely. Not after last time, spewing up in the gutter on the shit-smelling Quayside. But no: Mark was already hot-foot for Partners. Amazing how lasses change things, Robbie thought. He'd changed too. Couldn't wait to see Emma. He didn't care about the dancing; didn't care about anything. Only Emma. That night on her doorstep. How they'd talked and talked. And how he'd wanted to kiss her but was too shy – so she did it for him. It was the first time he'd ever kissed a girl. *Please* be there tonight, he muttered to himself.

Mark loved walking through the door of Partners. It was entry to another world: a world of girls. Girls' perfume, girls' clothes, girls chatter, girls' laughter. Girls gathered at the entrance to the cloakroom, some going in, some coming out. They wore gaily-coloured dresses and necklaces. Some carried dancing shoes, to be put on only when they got to the dancefloor upstairs. The two pals lingered only long enough to see if the two girls they wanted to see were there. They weren't, so they bounded up the stairs to resume their quest to locate Carol and Emma.

The sound of *Wheels Cha-Cha* filled the room as two pairs of anxious eyes scanned the room. Bodies mingled, although only a few couples were on the floor dancing. Mark peered along the length of the wall, the one where girls stood waiting to be asked to dance, or others sat behind, waiting for friends or maybe too shy to get to their feet. There was no sign of Carol. There was nothing for it but to walk the length of the room. He turned to say so to Robbie, only to see his friend and Emma already reunited, facing one another, holding hands and mutually smiling. Mark felt touched by their obvious happiness.

So, where was Carol?

He stood discreetly by Robbie and Emma, waiting until he had their attention, casting glances right and left for a hoped-for glimpse of Carol. But their eyes were for each other, not an impatient bystander, until at last, Emma spotted him.

'Oh, hi Mark!' she exclaimed, smiling. 'Sorry. Didn't see you standing there. Can't take my eyes off *him*!' She looked so happy, Mark thought.

'Is Carol here?' Her answer, he thought, was a formality. Of course she's here. She's just powdering her nose. She'll be here in a jiff.

Emma's smile faded. 'I'm afraid she isn't. Sorry.' She was looking at him, as one might having just told someone bad news. Which, as far as mark was concerned, she had. 'She couldn't make it tonight,' she said simply, without offering any more information. Mark wanted more, so he waited.

They stood there, eyeing each other, as bodies brushed past them. An almost stand-off situation prevailed: he waiting for her to explain, she taciturn. Then Mark became aware of someone at his side. He turned to see a girl about his own age. She was short and dumpy and wore glasses with think lenses.

'Oh, Mark,' said Emma eagerly, 'this is Mavis. Mavis, this is Mark.' Mavis looked at Mark and smiled. Mark smiled back, or tried to, at the same time realising Emma's introduction – 'Oh *Mark*' – meant that he and Mavis should pair up.

'Hello,' said Mavis, looking at him, still smiling. 'This is my first time here.'

'Is it?' Mark looked at her with utter disinterest, then at Emma and Robbie in turn. He had to get away. Gather his thoughts. Decide what to do. 'Dying for the loo' was the best he could do as he turned and headed for the Gents. He reached the tearoom and sat down at a table, the only person there. He had to think, to deal with his disappointment.

When he'd spotted Emma he thought Carol must be here and then he'd discovered she wasn't: that's what was so disappointing. If neither had been that would've been OK. But Emma here, Carol not here. Why? He sat awhile, until, at last, his thoughts took on a more positive approach. He was here, he hadn't been drinking; he was in full control. Things seemed to look better when two pretty girls came into the tearoom and plonked themselves at a table right in front of him. There were lots of girls here. The evening was not a lost cause.

He returned to the dancefloor and stood in the shadow, looking at girls. He'd find someone to dance with, take it from there. There were girls now sitting out the foxtrot. Others in ones and twos stood at the side of the floor, all approachable he thought. When the foxtrot ended it was jive time. Cliff was singing *A Girl Like You*. It reminded him of Carol, but he was determined to cast her from his mind, for now at least. He spied two pretty girls in the corner, just as one of them accepted an invitation on to the dancefloor. The other remained where she was, forlorn-looking.

He went directly to her. 'Care to jive?' he asked, half turning and holding out a hand expectantly.

'No, thank you,' she replied, and looked away dismissively.

He wanted to say 'Why not?' But he knew it would do no good. She was staring straight ahead, as though looking at some interesting object in the middle distance. He stepped back, embarrassed. But positive thoughts returned. Trying to appear nonchalant, he drifted through the groups of waiting girls alongside the dancefloor. Cliff's song ended, Billy Fury came on. More approaches were being made to waiting females. And there, just a few feet away, he witnessed a young chap approach a girl, only for her to shake her head. The fellow ambled off, looking disconsolate. What was it that Horlicks had said about watching women say no to someone, then moving in himself?

He walked boldly up to her. 'Would you like to dance?' he asked, making sure he was smiling. That's what Bob said: always ask with a smile. She gave him the merest glance and shook her head. 'Why not?' he enquired. 'Why are you here if you don't want to dance?' Her response was to walk away and disappear into the crowd. Then he noticed a woman, thirty-ish, standing close by. He asked her too. She smiled, shook her head and as he lingered she added a 'No thank you' for good measure. He repaired to the tearoom, where he sat at the same table as before, feeling baffled and utterly deflated.

What was going on? Other blokes were getting lasses up. Why not him? He went to the Gents and looked in the mirror. He looked smart: nice suit, clean shirt, collar and tie, hair OK. He'd bloody-well try again. But even as he arrived on the edge of the dancefloor the jiving stopped and a voice boomed, 'Take your partners for the Bradford Barn.'

The Bradford Barn! There'd be no refusals for the Bradford Barn, where you went in a couple of steps, turned, came back again and moved on to another partner. It was just a matter of getting on to the floor. He asked the girl nearest to him. She nodded and followed him into the newly-formed line of people, a huge circle of humanity, all waiting for the music to start. When he looked, he realised the girl who had consented to his request to dance was the same one who had just declined his offer to jive. Before he could say anything Frank Sinatra's *High Hopes* started up. 'They're playing my song,' said Mark. She smiled, but didn't reply.

Men and women, boys and girls, came to grips, and off they went as one: two steps in, turn, two steps out, move on. Conversations were possible but brief. As Mark and his partner stepped inside, he thought he should say something, but she was looking away. No matter, he moved on to the next one, a young lass he'd noticed earlier. She was here with a group of girls, all having a good time. 'Great dance, this,' he ventured above the music. 'Love it,' she replied. And they all moved on again.

He loved the Bradford Barn. All those girls. Brief chat here and there. Some liked to be held close, others stood off. One record played, then another, then another. He'd moved around to the far side of the room when he came to a girl with short blonde hair. She was dressed all in black. Black top, black skirt. She was slim and she was smiling, holding her arms up ready to slide them around his neck. When he put his hands on her waist he was surprised at how slim she actually was. He was even more surprised when she pressed herself close to him and wrapped her arms around his neck, *right* around. She could almost have been hanging from him. Her cheek was right next to his. Two steps in and turn. On the way back she moved her face away slightly and spoke directly into his ear.

'How's Carol?'

He turned his head, thinking he must have mis-heard.

'Eh?'

'Carol. I just wondered how she was.'

He stopped moving and took his hands from her waist. Her arms fell to her sides as they faced each other. She was smiling, taunting him, having fun at his expense.

'You know Carol?'

She shook her head. 'I know *of* her. And I know you think about her.'

They moved to the side of the floor, allowing those dancing to pass them by. He waited for more information, but she said nothing more. She was still smiling when she was joined by another girl who looked at Mark, then her blonde friend, before they walked off together. As he watched them go there was a tug at his sleeve. He turned to see Robbie and Emma.

'Emma's told me why Carol didn't come tonight,' said Robbie. 'You wanna know?'

Mark was speechless.

'She saw you kissing some lass outside Cook's. Really upset, she is. Anyway, that's the reason.' With that he turned to Emma who took his hand. 'We're off,' said Robbie. 'Goin' for a hot dog then I'm taking Emma home. See ya.' They headed off towards the stairs, followed by Emma's friend. Mark couldn't remember her name. He decided to look for the mystery blonde, but there was no sign of her. He wondered where she could have got to – the tearoom maybe. When he turned to go there he found himself face to face with a girl who was eating crisps, her fingers delving deep into what was obviously an empty packet, before she tilted her head back and tipped the last of its contents into her mouth. Wiping her mouth on the back of her hand she smiled and spoke.

'Hi Mark. Thought I'd see you here.' Avril brushed more crisp fragments from the front of her jumper. 'I've been watching you. Who was that blonde girl you were with just now?'

He was lost for words.

'I'm here with a friend, Pauline. I think she's dancing with somebody. We came for the lessons. It's great here, isn't it?'

He looked at her, wondering how it could be that in a world of pretty girls, all wearing smart dresses, he should find himself talking to someone so unattractive who might have fitted herself out at one of Mam's jumble sales. Even in a world of sweet perfume he could smell fagash on her.

'So, who was the blonde?' she asked again.

He wanted the wretched evening to end. Right now.

He turned abruptly, walked directly to the top of the stairs and took them two at a time, passing through the entrance lobby and into the cold night air outside. He was angry at what he saw as his misfortune. He was jealous of Robbie, his quiet-spoken, shy friend who had fallen on his feet with Emma; he was frustrated, to think that Rita's peck on the cheek outside Cook's should have been seen by the girl he wanted most of all. He couldn't believe his luck could be so bad that Avril would turn up tonight. Nothing goes right for me, he told himself: I even thought I had VD. What did I do to deserve that?

Outside, he felt himself buck up in the night air. He'd go to the Oxford. He knew there'd be lots of girls there and tonight he wasn't drunk. To hell with Carol, Avril, Robbie. To hell with them all. He'd bloody-well meet someone tonight and start his life again.

He walked apace, head down, emotions in turmoil as he stormed full speed ahead for the Oxford. He didn't notice the three dark figures approaching on the pavement. And when he barged into one of them it was an unfortunate accident.

'Sorry!' Mark blurted out apologetically. He made to walk off. But the other guy barred his way. He tried to walk round him, but the fellow blocked him. Mark looked more closely at him. He was thirty-ish, powerfully built and wore no jacket, despite the chill in the night air. He had strong arms. Bare arms that protruded from his sleeveless tee-shirt. Tattooed arms. Mark had never seen so many tattoos.

'Sorry,' Mark repeated. He waited for the fellow to step aside. His two mates stood at either side of him, all of them blocking the way.

'Sorry – what?' The fellow in the tee-shirt had a snarl on his face. 'Sorry and what else?' he was asking.

'Sorry, my fault. Didn't see you.'

'He's got bad eyesight,' said the man. His friends laughed.

The man looked Mark up and down. 'Look at him,' he was saying. 'All poshed up in his fancy suit and black slip-ons. Goin' to a dance, are you?' Mark didn't reply. 'Y'look like a pufta,' said the man. 'What do you look like?' Mark stayed silent.

'What do you look like, I asked?' The man was clenching his fists. When Mark didn't reply the man spoke again, this time to his mates. 'Bet his name's Isaac, eh? Isaac Hunt.' He smiled sarcastically and spoke to Mark again.

'That's your name, isn't it? Isaac Hunt. What's your name?'

Mark looked about, but the men were standing so close he knew it was futile to try and run off. They were waiting for him to speak but he held his tongue.

'What's your name?' the man repeated angrily. 'Say it, I said.'

Mark looked him the eye but stayed silent.

'Isaac Hunt,' snarled the man.

'If you say so,' said Mark, fearing the worst.

The man sneered and looked him up and down. 'Tell you what,' he said. 'I like your snazzy tie. If you're sorry for assaulting me on the Queen's highway, let's have it. C'mon, or you'll get this.' He lifted his fist, threateningly. Mark looked beyond the three men, searching for possible help. But the street was deserted.

'Alright, Sunshine. You've got three seconds. Tie or this.' He waved his fist.

Mark never heard the footsteps approaching from behind. Nor

did the three men he faced pay any attention to whoever was making them. But the next thing that happened was Mark being knocked aside violently by an invisible arm. He staggered but kept to his feet, then braced himself for the blow that would surely come. Instead he would see an image he would remember for the rest of his life.

From behind a clenched fist connected point blank with his antagonist's face. The man was knocked backwards on to the pavement, both feet lifting spectacularly from the ground in the process. He sat there, stunned, his arms reaching backwards for support. Blood spurted from his nose, and poured freely down his tee-shirt onto the pavement. He put a hand to his face, but the blood simply oozed between his fingers and crept down his forearm.

Mark turned to see Tom Clark blowing softly onto his right fist. Beryl was standing behind him.

'Come on then, dickhead.' Tom, fists clenched, was offering the injured man the opportunity to respond. Instead, he crawled to the edge of the pavement, got to his feet and stepped on to the road, then staggered to the opposite pavement, blood dripping from his face. His companions stood, perplexed. Tom took another step forward. 'Want some?' he said, but the men backed away then ran across the road after their friend. Mark, Tom and Beryl watched them walk away, until they disappeared from view around the next corner.

'Never were a fighter, were you Greeny?' Tom was smiling, and gently rubbing the knuckles of the hand that had splattered the fellow's nose. 'Makes us even, eh. You saved me. I saved you.'

Mark nodded. He had wondered momentarily if Tom might punch him too.

'You OK?' asked Beryl. Mark nodded.

'Beryl's gonna have a baby,' announced Tom. 'That right Beryl?' She nodded, and smiled at Mark. 'See ya then,' said Tom, and he and Beryl hurried off, leaving Mark to wonder what the rest of the evening had in store.

Mark had been to the Oxford but once, the night he had been thrown out. But then he had been drunk. Tonight he was sober, cool and determined. He paid at the kiosk, went to the Gents – which he vaguely remembered – and then to the main dance hall where he bought a pint of bitter at the bar. And took stock.

There were women of all ages, from young lasses too young to drink to those whom Fred would have described as 'grab-a-grannies'. Mainly, though, they were late teens-early twenties, mostly in pairs or groups, a few alone. Some had already hitched up with male partners and now occupied one of the cosy booths around the perimeter of the dance-floor; others sat chatting in the bar where he now stood. Everywhere men drifted around, like hungry wolves. Some were obviously under the influence. How idiotic and pathetic he thought they looked; how obvious their intentions. It was just as he would have appeared on his last visit. Well, it wouldn't happen tonight. He leaned with deliberate casualness against a pillar, holding his pint. He would wait until he identified his prey. He liked that: his prey. Tom Clark's timely inter-vention just half an hour earlier had saved him from a bloody nose or worse, or losing his tie, which would have debarred entry to the dance. He felt relief now at his near miss with injury. Maybe his luck was turning. He thought Carol might show up. Ha! That would be a turn up for the books.

He was halfway through his pint when he spied Horlicks on the prowl. Horlicks, who said he'd wait until he saw a woman say 'no' to someone, then ask her to dance. He must think they wouldn't say 'no' twice, thought Mark. Or maybe it was a macho thing, to succeed where a rival had failed. He glided slowly away from the pillar, following him through the throng of women, but lost sight of him somewhere. Not wanting to be seen prowling himself, he sat at an unoccupied table and sipped his pint. When he drained the glass he thought it might be time to ask someone to dance; then he spied Horlicks again.

He followed him into the midst of a group of women waiting pa-tiently at the edge of the dancefloor. They were like objects in a shop, he thought. Or maybe at a marketplace: goods available for selection. A waltz was playing. He looked at the crowd on the floor. Nobody was actually waltzing. People just muddled through, holding one another this way and that, any-which-way they liked as long as they could chat or engage in close bodily contact. Horlicks prowled. Mark followed.

Then, like a panther spotting its prey, Horlicks was eyeing a girl with short blonde hair. She stood alone a few feet back from the dancefloor. Mark watched as a fellow approached her and asked her to dance. She seemed to frown, and shook her head in a 'no thank you' gesture. Just at that moment Mark fancied he'd seen her before. It was her frown, or non-smile. He watched now as Horlicks made his move, coming between Mark and the girl so that he could not see her response. It was soon obvious what her response was, for Horlicks, his mission having failed, walked off, leaving her standing alone.

At that moment Mark realised he was looking at the girl in black, the same one he had encountered only an hour or so before at Partners; the girl who had asked about Carol. But more than that: her unsmiling aspect gave her away. She was the unsmiling girl who'd served him in the florists. The other Carol. *Unsmiling* Carol. She must have changed her hairstyle, and would look different anyway, wearing a dress instead of an overall. But that face: it was definitely her. Where she had appeared unattractive in the florist's, tonight, dressed to kill and herself on the prowl, she looked stunning. Well, two men had failed to get her onto the dancefloor; but he reckoned to have an advantage. He could say, 'Would you like to dance, *Carol?*' The suspense! The intrigue!

He stood before her and smiled. 'Hi again – Carol,' he purred.

'Saw you over there,' she said, nodding towards the bar. 'I wondered when you'd appear.'

'Didn't recognise you before. But I do now.'

She smiled. 'I mustn't have made much of an impression if you forgot what I looked like.'

'You're making an impression now.'

They looked at each other for a few seconds.

'Well?' she said at last.

'Would you like to dance?'

'No,' she replied. 'But I would like a drink.'

As they walked towards the bar at the far end of the room one of the private booths became unoccupied. They dived in. A solitary electric lamp glowed on the table, giving a romantic atmosphere to the otherwise dimly-lit booth.

'What'll it be?' he enquired.

'Gin and tonic, please. No ice.' He returned with two.

She took a sip. 'So, what about Carol?'

He shrugged. 'She's just a girl I know.'

'A girl you buy flowers for.' She paused, looked at him in the eye. 'Are you going out with her?' He shook his head. She opened her handbag, took out a packet of cigarettes and lit up. 'Are you going to ask *me* out, then?'

'I'd like to take you out, yes.'

'Where?'

He shrugged, took a drink of the g and t. He recoiled at the taste.

She watched him, her face expressionless. 'Not to the pictures I hope.'

He tried the drink again. Gulping it down in a mouthful.

'You're supposed to sip it. Like this.' She demonstrated. The cigarette smouldered in the ashtray. 'Do you have a car?'

He shook his head.

'We could borrow my dad's. He'll do anything for his darling daughter. Do you drive?'

'Not yet. Taking lessons soon though.'

She seemed to be testing him, he thought. Had he a car? Did he drive? Why couldn't she just accept him for what he was? He began to wonder what he was doing with someone he didn't seem to care for. He felt the drink taking hold. He had to keep control. He looked across to the dancefloor. The band was playing a waltz. Bodies shuffled. Couples were clinging to each other. Some of the blokes had obviously had a few, yet attractive-looking girls still had their arms around their necks.

'Hey! You still here?' She was tapping her now-empty glass. 'Wouldn't mind another. If you don't mind, that is.'

He nodded compliantly, and headed for the bar. There was a queue, but a helpful barmaid called out to him. He ordered a gin and tonic for her and an orange juice for himself. As the barmaid reached for two empty glasses he turned to look at the dancefloor again. The lights were bright now, with everyone jiving to loud music. He wished he was. He paid for the drinks and returned to the booth, arriving at the same time as two couples.

'This one's free,' one of the men said, and four people with their drinks moved into the empty booth. Mark was certain this was where he'd been sitting with Carol. He checked the booths either side. There was no sign of her. He stood there, a glass in each hand, wondering where she was. The Ladies perhaps, but after five long minutes, when she hadn't appeared, he turned his attention to the dancefloor. She wouldn't have got up with someone else, surely.

So many moving bodies! He looked right and left, then straight ahead – and there was the now-familiar blonde hair as she danced happily, smiling, wriggling her slender hips, her hands raised above her head, doing her thing. He looked at her partner. It wasn't easy to see who it was, or even who was dancing with whom exactly. But when the music stopped and they stood together, smiling and in conversation, he had clear sight of her companion.

It was Horlicks.

***

Carol spent that evening lying on the settee, watching TV. Or rather she looked at it without paying the slightest attention. Emma had gone to Partners with Mavis. She had been on about Robbie all week. She hoped he was there for her. As for Mark…

The afternoon she'd seen him kiss that girl outside Cook's, she admitted to feeling jealous, but more than that she felt disgusted. He had sent her flowers, after all. What message was that supposed to convey? That he was thinking of her, as the message said, and that he wanted to see her again. He must have changed his mind. Or maybe he was simply a two-timing so-and-so. No wonder he was so forward with her that night. He must be used to being with girls. Playing the field. They're all the same, as Miss Carr had said.

'Not like you to be moping around on a Saturday night.' Dad, who was now decorating the hall and stairs, walked into the room, wiping his hands. 'What about that bloke who sent you the flowers? Hasn't he asked you out yet?'

She uncurled and stood up. 'No Dad,' she said, adding quickly, 'Would you like a cup of tea?'

He nodded. 'There were two blokes, weren't there? I read the cards. One called Mark, one signing himself 'J'. But no date on Saturday. What's up, girl?'

'Nothing, Dad.' It was bad enough she was stuck at home; she wasn't going to say the second delivery was from a woman. She put the kettle on and wondered what she might do tomorrow.

Housework, she supposed. As usual. Which brought Miss Carr to mind again. Miss Carr, who had a room to let. Wouldn't that be better than housework and cooking Dad's dinners and making Dad endless cups of tea and having to answer Dad's questions about her love-life, such as it was? Her own room; her own space. Her own life. Was it too much to ask?

17

Sunday morning. Mark never even got out of bed for his fry-up. Instead, he lay there, thinking, his mind going around in circles. Circles of girls' names. Carol. He'd given up. Rita. She'd given up, thanks to Kev and Betty giving up. Marie. He might as well give up; she played the field, that's how it seemed to him. Who else? Oh, the other Carol, *Unsmiling* Carol, the florist who wanted him to have a car before she'd go out with him; and Miss Raine, who was in her mid-twenties and was probably unattainable. That left Julian's mam, who seemed to have the hots for him, but, come on, she was a married woman in her forties. Avril? Forget it. And there was Robbie, quiet, shy, wouldn't say boo-to-a-goose Robbie. Fixed up in one and goodnight.

No spider's web in the corner. Where do spiders go when someone clears away their webs? he wondered. He got up, if only to speak to Bob. But when he went downstairs Bob was out. He peeped over the wall. Out in the Riley.

Roger was at his gate, looking up and down the Terrace.

'Aye-aye, Mark,' Roger glanced at him, then looked back down the street.

'Sorry about the assault business,' Mark replied, at the same time wondering how a spelk like Roj could banjo a hulk like Eggshell. Roger shrugged, kept his eyes on the Terrace, as though something might happen on a quiet Sunday morning in Weston.

Mam and Dad were out too, on their Sunday morning walk. So Mark had the house and his thoughts to himself. His stomach rumbled. He'd have some cornflakes and with luck Mam would cook him brekkie in about an hour. Tonight was the Spanish City, with Kev. He didn't really fancy it. He'd had enough of dodgem cars and Del bloody Shannon's distorted voice. Still, it was somewhere to go. That's if they got there in one piece, the speed Kev drove.

The knock at the door came *after he*'d poured the milk over his cornflakes. He opened it to find Joyce on the step. He noticed she'd had her hair dyed a sort of mauve colour.

'Hello Mark.' She smiled, sort of. 'Is he in?'

'He's out in...' Mark hesitated.

'The car. Can I come in?'

He stood aside. She entered, walked through to the living room and sat in one of the armchairs by the fire. Never even took her coat off. He loitered in the doorway, uncertain.

'Would you make me a cup of tea, Mark, please?' she said. He put the kettle on and wolfed down the now-soggy cornflakes, then brewed up and returned to the living room where he sat in silence while Joyce daintily sipped her tea.

Ten minutes later came the sound of a car engine, the click of the back gate and the sound of the back door slamming – then Bob's voice, calling out loudly, 'That fuckin' starter motor. Poxy thing's as much use as a one-legged man in an arse-kicking contest.'

Joyce greeted him with a simple 'Hello dear' and a wan smile.

Mark took his jacket from the hook behind the back door and went out. He wanted to gather his thoughts. Time for the rocking horse.

***

Kev arrived, on time, chucking his spare crash helmet onto the living room table where Nancy would see it. He was all smiles. So was Nancy, pleased to see her son would now be wearing a crash helmet on Kev's motorbike, and that Joyce had turned up that morning and that she and Bob had sorted out their differences and were back together.

They'd mentioned getting engaged, and that pleased her too.

Kev drove to Whitley Bay like a madman. 'Didn't do more than eighty, I swear,' he replied when Mark complained again. He turned into the car park just off the prom and pulled the bike onto its stand. He was going to ask Mark when he was getting one, but didn't bother. Mark had said he wanted a car 'like Bob's'. 'Each to his own,' Kev replied. And that was that.

They wandered into the little café. It was empty. The girl with the spotty face looked as bored as ever. She stood at the till, staring wistfully out of the window. Her face seemed spottier than last time, thought Mark. Kev ordered two coffees. As the girl went to the Espresso machine he saw Mark looking at her.

'Fancy her, do you?' he whispered.

'With my luck I don't think I could even pull her,' Mark replied.

They sat by the window. 'We might see those two lasses that came in here last week,' said Kev. 'They'll be around for sure.' After that they sat in silence, Kev impatiently tapping the table with his finger. Mark thought about mentioning Betty. After all, his friend's relationship with her had a bearing on Mark's with Rita. But, he thought: better to leave it and just get through the evening. When a couple with three noisy kids came into the cafe they left and headed for the fairground.

As they wandered around Mark wondered what he was doing here. It's just that now he was eighteen, he felt he was past dodgem cars and the Waltzer. Kids of fourteen and fifteen were abroad: gangling youths with spotty faces, lasses barely out of puberty flashing their wares. He thought of Bob and his posh Riley. That's what he wanted: a car, and to be able to drive. Carol would hate it here, he thought. Mature, sophisticated Carol. But they were here, and that was that. It was better than being at home, that's what it amounted to. They ended up sitting on the wooden steps of the Waltzer, two young blokes at a loose end, bored and, as the evening wore on, hungry.

'Let's get some chips,' said Kev. But even as he spoke the cavalry arrived in the form of Dawn and Cynth who appeared wearing tight jeans and short-sleeved jumpers, and eating candy floss. Mark couldn't remember which was which. Kev was at them in a shot, leaving Mark on his own next to the clattering Waltzer. After a minute's chat they were all walking together, Kev having already bagged Cynth, leaving Dawn, whatever Mark thought of her, as his exclusive company for the rest of the evening.

She was about seventeen, he supposed. And she was pretty. She was also taciturn. Kev had picked the chatty one, the giggly one. 'Aren't you chilly?' asked Mark for the want of something to say – although he was sincere in his enquiry. 'Not wearing a coat in October.'

'You sound like my mam,' said Dawn. 'I like to be cool and look cool. Boys are okay in jackets, girls have to show off.'

He engaged her as best he could. Where did she live? Was she working yet? Did she like Elvis or Cliff? Finally, having apparently abandoned his desire to buy some chips, Kev, walking with Cynth a few paces ahead, turned and declared they were going onto the links. Mark and Dawn followed. They walked on the grass for ten minutes or so until Kev and Cynth sat on a bench. Mark and Dawn did likewise. They all sat there, gazing out to a flat sea, as dusk closed in. Then they strolled down to the beach and walked on the hard sand by the water's edge, Kev and Cynth holding hands, Mark and Dawn walking apart.

After ten minutes or so Kev steered Cynth across the sand to the grassy area in the lee of the links. Mark knew he wouldn't want to be followed, so headed of in another direction, and simply flopped down on the sand. Dawn sat down next to him. They stared out to sea in silence. Mark wished he could be somewhere else, but he was stuck with the situation. He lay back, hoping she would lie next to him, but she remained sitting. He wanted to kiss her, to hold her to him, if only to keep warm. He ran a finger down her back, teasing her. 'Don't *do* that,' she said, glancing back at him reproachfully. They sat awhile in silence, before she spoke again.

'I'm cold,' she said.

He took his jacket off, gave it to her and she put it on. 'Very gallant,' she said, but he sensed she was chuffed. She sat in silence, possibly waiting for his next move. He leaned sideways and kissed her cheek. She responded by turning her face towards him. They lay back on the sand, kissing. He ventured a hand to her breast and squeezed lightly.

She sighed. She was willing, he knew. He slid his leg across her thighs, and slid his tongue into her mouth; she responded by licking it with hers. Was this going to be his first time, he wondered? With a stranger, a girl he didn't care about, a girl whom Kev had just passed over for another? If it was he didn't care. He was ready. She was willing. That was all that mattered.

And then she sneezed.

They lay for a few moments, before she started to giggle. 'Sorry,' she muttered. He backed off as she fumbled in his jacket pocket for something to wipe her nose. She sneezed again and they both laughed. But then, suddenly, she got to her feet, so quickly she almost fell over.

'Whose are these?' she hissed, at the same time throwing silky material into his face. He realised only too readily what it was. He'd meant to dispose of Rita's knickers, but had forgotten all about them, save whenever he thrust a hand into his jacket pocket when he felt pleased to discover them still there. Any explanation, he knew, would be pointless – either to Mam, if she'd discovered them, or to Dawn, who was now storming off towards the steps leading up to the links. He followed, wanting to apologise, but she wasn't waiting to hear. Up on the links she marched forward a few paces then stopped, looking dead ahead. He followed, wishing the evening, the whole wretched weekend, was at an end. They stood there, two strangers, each wanting to be somewhere else, with someone else.

'If you think I'm going to be one of your conquests,' she said angrily, 'you can fuck off.'

'I'm sorry, really I am,' he said calmly. 'I can explain, but I don't suppose you'll want me to. It's not what you think.'

She didn't reply, but started to shudder slightly. Mark realised she was crying. He didn't know what to say to her. He attempted to put an arm around her shoulders, but she shrugged him off and hung her head, and sobbed quietly.

As they stood in silence, Mark heard the deep-throated roar of motorcycle engines. He turned to see at least a dozen machines approaching on the main road, their riders to a man dressed in black. They pulled over, revving their engines. He noticed Dawn looking at them, paying more than casual interest. As they stood, he saw one of the motorcyclists push his visor up and start waving towards them. He was shouting above the noise, calling out. Mark caught the name: D-a-w-n!

Dawn seemed to come to life, and waved back. The mutual recognition ritual between Dawn and the motorcyclist lasted a few seconds until she suddenly ran towards him. Mark let her go. She obviously knew him, and he couldn't have cared less. He saw her in animated conversation with the figure in black, but then, to his consternation, he saw her cock a leg over the back of the machine and sit on the pillion. They roared off at once, followed by the other motorcycles.

'Hey, hey!' Mark called out and ran forward, but to no avail as the cavalcade sped off along the road. He ran after it, his efforts futile as Dawn, along with his jacket – and his wallet – disappeared into the distance. He stopped running, looked about him pointlessly and realised he needed to locate Kev as soon as possible. It was all but dark, and already he was feeling the cold of a late October evening.

He went to the far side of the links and tried to spot Kev and Cynth on the beach. But darkness had taken over. He headed towards the little café. He'd wait there; that's where Kev would look for him. It was all he could think of. When he got there the café was closed. He was hungry now, and there was a chippy close by. The smell of fish and chips taunted him, but all he had in his trouser pocket was a solitary threepenny piece. He hung about as youngsters drifted by, on their way home from the now-emptying Spanish City. He waited three-quarters of an hour. Where the hell was Kev? Were he and Cynth looking for him and Dawn? Sex on the beach, more like, he thought, and never mind the cold. But he'd stay where he was. This is where Kev would come, sooner or later. Sooner, he hoped.

It started to rain. Just a light drizzle, but the dampness made him colder than ever. The café doorway was deeply recessed and in darkness. He stepped inside and kept vigil, losing track of time and becoming so cold he sat down on his haunches and wrapped his arms about himself to try and keep warm. He shivered. He cursed the whole weekend, every minute of it. He thought of telephoning Mrs Soulsby down the Terrace to ask her to get Bob to come and pick him up. But there was the dicky starter motor, and anyway he was skint. He would just have to wait.

He must have fallen into a slumber, for he was startled by the sudden appearance of a bright light. It shone directly on to him, and seemed to illuminate the entire recess. He thought it might be the headlight of Kev's motorcycle, but realised someone was shining a torch. He stood up, lifted a hand to his eyes and tried to focus. Then he heard a voice. It was male and sounded authoritative. 'Aye aye,' it said. 'What's this, then?'

He felt a sudden pang of fear at the realisation that he was cornered in the dark doorway. But then he saw the glint of silver buttons, and a silver badge on a helmet. The policeman, standing close now, shone his torch on the door of the café and on the adjacent windows, before shining the light once again into Mark's face.

'C'mon, mister. Out here where I can see you.'

Mark followed the policeman to the pavement, and the officer switched his torch off.

'Weren't tryin' to break in were you, lad?'

Mark explained.

'Well, y'can't stay here son. Can't have the sergeant seeing you skulking in a doorway. He'll think I'm not doing my job.'

'But that girl. She's got my coat and my wallet. She *stole* my property.' Thoughts of a cup of tea in a nice warm police station, followed by a lift home, flashed through his mind.

'She hasn't exactly stolen anything, has she? Rode off on a motorbike, that's all. For all you know she's tryin' to find you to return it.' The policeman was silent for a moment. 'Look,' he said, 'over on the links there.' He was pointing. 'Y'see? There's a shelter. Go in there. You'll be out of the wind.'

Mark stepped out on to the pavement, and shuddered. The policeman walked off, slowly, glancing back to make sure he didn't return to his cosy doorway. He crossed the road and walked to the shelter. It was open on one side, the side facing the sea. The polis was right; he was out of the wind in here – but it was still cold. He sat on the long bench and peered out through the windows for any sign of Kev. But there was only darkness. Nothing was stirring in Whitley Bay at this hour. No people, no traffic. No motorbikes for sure.

He sat for ages, keeping vigil; but his eyes were closing and he was so tired he lay down on the hard wooden bench. He crooked an arm to make a pillow, and drew his knees up to his chest. Somehow it seemed to help against the cold...

Time passed. He became aware of a misty sea-fret, encroaching onto the links where it engulfed the shelter and clung to him, making his face and hair damp. The mist seemed to dance silently, as though to music that he couldn't hear. There was no sound, save the pitter-patter of rain on the roof of the shelter. Now and again he fancied he could hear the lapping waters of the sea, small breakers spilling onto the beach. The tide must have crept in, he thought.

He hated the mist. It clung to his shirt and seemed to creep up his trouser legs. Yet it fascinated him. Sometimes it seemed to be still, then it would swirl about in the breeze. Sometimes it seemed to lighten, then darken again. He felt sleep creeping up on him. Then, as he lay there alone in the darkness, he saw a distinctive form, a pink apparition emerging from the mist, directly in front of the shelter, as though coming from the beach or even the sea. The apparition approached slowly, and stopped a few yards away. Then, when the mist swirled again, he saw the apparition was a woman. She was facing him, looking at him. She knew him, he could tell by her face. And now he could hear music. Music he seemed to recognise. It was accompanied by the singing of a choir, just like in that film he saw about Bernadette who saw the Virgin Mary at Lourdes. The apparition, the mist, the music: he was spellbound, wide-eyed, enslaved.

For a moment the woman almost disappeared in the mist, but as the music became louder and the voices of the choir increased in volume he could see she was naked. And then he recognised her: it was Julian's mam. She was smiling, her mouth silently saying his name. She had found him here, in this lonely shelter, and she was coming to him. A woman has many needs, she had said. She must need him now.

She moved closer, until she was but a few feet away. He could see her clearly now. She was mute. She was smiling. She was compelling. Look at me. Look at *me*. That's what she meant. He was looking. She was beautiful, he thought. She was in her forties, yet she was beautiful. His mam was in her forties, and she wasn't beautiful. He loved his mam, but she wasn't beautiful. Kev's mam's in her forties and she wasn't beautiful either. All the kids he went to school with, their mams were in their forties and none of them was beautiful. But Julian's mam was beautiful. What was her name? He didn't know.

Wait! She was raising her hands slowly, palms upward, and curling her fingers in a kind of gesture. What does she mean? Does she want me to come to her? She's standing there, waiting. What should I do?

And then another figure appeared, moving forward slowly through the mist to stand beside Julian's mam. A tall, white female figure. Even in the uncertain light he could discern the redness of her hair. Connie. It was Connie. She was shaking her head slowly. No, no, no, her lips were silently saying. My name is Rita! Of course. Rita. And she was naked too. Tall and naked. And beautiful, her long, red hair falling over her breasts. Julian's mam was quite tall, but Rita was taller. Rita too was raising her hands. Both of them were smiling and beckoning. They must be cold, he thought. Yet still they stood there. They were standing there for him. Naked and smiling. Naked and smiling. And beckoning.

Then, another figure! He knew even before he saw her properly who it was. Marie was naked and smiling too. She stood beside Julian's mam, shorter, but looking beautiful. He had not realised until now how big Marie's breasts were. They were pure-white, and commanded his attention. And Marie was beckoning too.

Another figure appeared, next to Julian's mam but standing back a little. It was difficult at first to recognise her. Marie stood aside a little allowing the new figure to move forward. Miss Raine! She was naked too, except for her shoes. Her pretty shoes. She always wore pretty shoes. She was smiling, and running the tip of her tongue along her lips. She wants me, he thought. Miss Raine wants *me*. But he didn't move; he couldn't move. He wondered if she too would raise her hands and sure enough, even as he looked, she was beckoning him to come to her.

And look! There, pushing through: Beryl. Smiling and naked – and pregnant. Mark had never seen a naked pregnant woman before. Her tummy was round and smooth. Beryl too was beckoning. He saw her wink. Trust Beryl! The image of her running off that time at the club came to him, clattering past Walter's empties and disappearing into the night. And there she was now, pregnant and beckoning him to come to her.

Then Julian's mam and Miss Raine half turned, and from between them emerged another figure. It was Carol. Lovely, adorable Carol. She stood slightly forward of the others. She was naked; she was smiling. He looked at her hands and waited. Yes, she was raising her hands. She raised them until they were shoulder height, but her palms faced down in a forbidding gesture. Don't come, don't come! That's what she meant. She was forbidden fruit; she was out of bounds.

Then, as he looked, transfixed, they all lowered their hands and stood before him, naked. He'd seen naked women before, in Julian's *Health and Efficiency* magazines and in his parents' *Family Doctor* book. But they were made of paper. The women in his life, they were real and they all stood naked before him now. It was so sensual; so *sexual*. He could hardly believe it was happening. What should I do? he thought. If I stay here they will surely come into my shelter. If I go to them it will be cold and I might die. And Carol was saying no. Carol was the most important. He must abide by her rules.

The sound of the music and the choir reached a deafening crescendo, then faded rapidly. Now he could only hear the sound of the rising wind and the quiet *whoosh* of the little waves as they broke on the shore. Down on the hard sand, where he had walked with Dawn. Where was Dawn? She was nowhere. She didn't count. But now something else appeared, a huge, huge face, a smiling face, occupied the entire scene beyond the naked forms now standing before him. A face in the mist. A face that would have filled the sky had it been clear to see. A face that could never be touched. It was Fred. He was smiling. Fred knew about women, and now he was nodding his head slowly and knowingly. Had Fred sent naked women to him from his place in heaven? He'd have had 'em all by now, old Fred. Not pussyfooted about, dithering, as he had done. Fred, sitting in that old armchair that time. He was dying then. Mark realised it then, but it didn't seem real. How he wished he could have said goodbye.

And then, as Fred's kindly face faded, Bob's face appeared through the mist. Bob in his red and white striped jammies. The ones Mark kept ribbing him about. Bob was smiling his brotherly smile, his man-of-the-world smile. But more than that, he was speaking to him out of the mist, his voice booming out, like God in *The Ten Commandments*: 'Thou shalt not steal!' God's voice boomed out, as thunder clapped and lightning streaked across the sky. 'Thou shall not commit adultery!' More thunder and lightning. But it was Bob's voice he heard now, not God's. 'Look,' he was saying, his voice thundering from the mist, 'Look at them, standing there. As many women as you can, you said. Well, here they are, all naked, and beckoning. And how many have you had? None!' His voice tailed off in cruel laughter. A witch's laughter, Mark thought. Bob was a cackling witch.

'But the one I want says no,' Mark cried. 'Carol says no.'

Bob's voice boomed out again. 'There are plenty others. They are all beautiful and they are all beckoning and they are all naked. What more do you want. Wake up, Mark. Wake up, you fool. Wake up to reality. Wake up.' Bob was fading now, his face and the red and white stripes dissolving in the mist.

'Wake up. Wake *UP*.'

And now the images melted away into the mist: Carol, everyone. They disappeared. There was only greyness and the pitter-patter of the rain. He felt himself being shaken. And someone was shouting.

'Wake up, Kidda! Wake up, you fucking wombat!'

He opened his eyes to see Kev, his wet motorcycle leathers glistening in the darkness. 'It's me, Kidda. Get a grip and wake up. It's two o'clock in the morning, for Christ's sake.' Mark straightened his legs and swung them aside, so that his feet touched the ground. 'I've been looking everywhere for you,' Kev was saying. 'Even been halfway to fucking Blyth. Why didn't you wait at the café, you stupid sod.'

But Mark couldn't speak. He couldn't say or do anything because he was so cold. He shivered uncontrollably. 'Where's your coat?' asked Kev, but Mark couldn't tell him. Kev took his leather jacket off and wrapped it around his shoulders. 'Tell me another time,' he said. 'Right now we've got to get you out of here. Stand up. Stand *UP*!' Mark got to his feet, and Kev helped him put his leather jacket on. 'Sit here for a bit and try and get warm,' said Kev. 'It's gonna be a cold run home.'

But Mark couldn't stop shivering. He couldn't even speak. Kev told him to wave his arms about, to stand up and sit down. But still Mark shivered. 'Mebbe I should take you to a hospital,' said Kev, although he couldn't think of one in Whitley Bay. 'Where's the bloody crash helmet I gave you?' Kev wanted to know – but Mark was beyond answering. Kev pulled him to his feet. 'C'mon,' he said, and with his arm around his friend's shoulders he led him across the wet links to his motorcycle. The rain had stopped but the air was still damp. 'Best let me have my jacket back,' he said. 'Can't have the driver getting pneumonia, can we.'

Kev put the jacket on, straddled the bike and kick-started it. Mark climbed on behind. 'Put your arms round me, Kidda,' shouted Kev above the noise of the engine. 'Real tight, mind. Pretend I'm Brigitte Bardot. Right? We're off.' With that he opened the throttle and headed for home.

It was a journey Mark would never forget, although his lifelong memory of it would be a blur, always associated with the cold and damp as they drove home in the middle of the night. His shirt was soaking, and clung to him like a wet dishcloth; nor was there any warmth from Kev's leather jacket. But he closed his eyes and clung on tight, for every minute of every mile. He was conscious of Kev driving slower than usual, which was a relief. How long it took he didn't know, but after what seemed an eternity Kev pulled over to the side of the road, and Mark climbed off the pillion. When he took stock he found himself not outside his gate as he had expected, but at the top of the Terrace.

'I'll drop you here,' said Kev. 'Maybe you can sneak in without disturbing your folks.'

Shivering uncontrollably, Mark hurried to his back gate. He was relieved to see the house in darkness, but in that same moment his heart sank when he remembered his house key was in his jacket pocket. But a tell-tale light under the back door meant someone was up. He opened the door quietly but even as he closed it behind him his father appeared, and on sight of him turned and called out to his wife: 'He's home, Nancy. The wanderer has returned.'

Mark walked into the living room to find his tearful mother rising from her chair by the fire. She held a handkerchief to her face and looked distressed, her face a mixture of relief and anger at the sight of her son.

'Sorry Mam.' He stood in the doorway, shivering but glad at the sight of the fire.

'Where have you been till this hour, you little monkey?' she demanded. And before he could reply, 'I've walked this floor for hours, worrying about you on that motorbike.'

And before he could reply, his dad chipped in. 'You're soaked to the skin, lad. Where's your jacket? I didn't see you wearing it when you came in.'

He explained as best he could. He'd been with Kev in Whitley Bay. The bike had conked out and Kev had had to remove the spark plug and clean it. He'd had a problem that took ages to fix. He wasn't sure what he'd done with his jacket. And the crash helmet Kevin gave you? He'd lost it – and, yes, he'd come all the way home on the back of the bike without it. Sorry, Mam.

She told him to take his wet shirt off and sit by the fire. He did so gladly, peering into it, making out cats' faces in the flames. Dad stoked it up, then went upstairs for a blanket which he wrapped around his shoulders, then sat down on the settee. He asked Mark how it was exactly he'd lost his jacket. When Mark said he wasn't sure, his dad knew was lying. But no matter. He was home, safe and sound, if in a state, and now his wife could stop worrying he could go to bed. Shortly after Mam appeared, carrying a pint mug.

'Here's a nice Horlicks for you,' she announced, plonking it onto the hearth. Horlicks! The sight of his work colleague dancing with Carol – the *other* Carol – came to his mind, reminding him of the wretched weekend he'd had. Now, wrapped in the blanket, he sipped his drink eagerly, still gazing into the fire and hoping his parents wouldn't have many more questions. The obvious relief being felt by his mother seemed to satisfy her: he was home, he was safe. That was all that mattered to her. Bed awaited. His lovely, comfortable bed, where he would be warm and snug, where he could curl up and sleep – and dream. Dream, like before; a sexy dream. Only without Bob. It was enough that he could hear the usual noises emanating from the far end of the bedroom without his brother making a guest appearance among *les girls*, especially in his red and white bloody pyjamas.

But he didn't dream. Instead he lay in a coma-like sleep for hours and hours, dead to the world, oblivious to everything. Even naked crumpet.

18

Carol went to work on Monday with mixed feelings. She dreaded the inevitable meeting with her boss after their encounter in the Royal bar, yet the more she thought about it, the more determined she felt about moving away from home: from waiting on her dad, from being a skivvy during her mam's absence. So the room Miss Carr said was available was tempting, if it was still on offer and if her dad would consent. It was a big if.

At work she deliberately walked past Miss Carr's office. She wasn't there, but her coat was hanging by the door. She felt she would be sent for and the sooner the better; she wanted their inevitable meeting over with. As she headed to her own workspace she encountered her boss in the corridor. She was carrying the usual bundle of papers. Miss Carr greeted her with a smile and a 'good morning', and paused long enough to tell her to report to her office in ten minutes. When she did she was sitting at her desk. She looked up, and told her to 'come in and close the door please', and beckoned Carol to the chair opposite. Carol sat down, but Miss Carr kept her waiting, writing on some documents without looking up. Finally she put her pen down.

'Well, Miss Kemp.' Carol shuddered inwardly at the formality. 'There are one or two things that need to be said to clear the air between us.' She paused momentarily. Carol thought she looked nervous. 'First, I hope what I said to you at our meeting last week remains confidential. I mean, about me saying I carry a bundle of papers just to get out of the office. It's true enough, but I ought not to have said so. We all have our weaknesses. And I hope you haven't said anything to anyone about me having one drink too many. We're all human after all, are we not?'

Carol nodded. 'I haven't said anything to anybody about anything,' she said.

Miss Carr looked relieved. 'Good,' she said. She smiled and sat back in her chair. 'So, the situation is clear enough. I am your boss, and my door is always open if you have any problems you might want to discuss. Just like all my staff.' She stopped talking then. Carol wasn't sure whether she was finished. 'Right, then,' said Miss Carr with an air of finality. 'Unless there is anything else?'

Carol hesitated before replying. 'You said you had a spare room.'

Miss Carr looked surprised, but pleased. 'Yes, I did. It's still there if you would like to take it, and you are able to. Has your father given his permission?'

'I haven't asked him yet. But I will.'

'Let me know,' said Miss Carr, standing up. But Carol wasn't quite ready to go. Miss Carr looked puzzled and sat down again. For a moment there was silence between them, as they sat looking at each other. Finally Carol spoke.

'You sent me flowers.'

'Yes. I thought they would help.'

'Help?'

'Well, you told me about your parents, and you seemed particularly upset about your mum. Then there was that boy who…you know… made a pass at you. I'm your boss. It's my job to look after my staff…'

Carol left it at that. When she reached the door Miss Carr had the last word. 'Do let me know if you want to take the room.' Carol said thank you and left the office. All she had to do now was ask Dad if she could move out. Somehow she felt he'd be more likely to agree if Mam came home.

She would ask him tonight: my boss has a spare room and I'd like to move into it. But when she dished up dinner that evening she decided to leave it till tomorrow. Dad was back at work, he'd decorated almost every room in the house and he was off the drink. She didn't want to rock the boat. Even so, there were moments, Carol felt, when he seemed to be on a knife-edge over when, if ever, Mam would be coming home. She was afraid he'd be upset or angry if she said she wanted to leave home. Tomorrow might be better. But when tomorrow came she still couldn't broach the subject. Nor on Wednesday, when she realised there was another reason she couldn't say anything. Quite simply, she loved him; he was her dad and things were delicate right now. The thought of him coming home to an empty house, with no-one cooking his dinner, no-one doing the housework, no-one there for him; it was unbearable.

Carol, like her father, was waiting for Freda Kemp to come home.

That Monday Carol had been at work for nearly three hours before Mark opened his eyes. When he did, he became aware of two things: he knew without looking that it was well past his time to get up to go to work; and his entire body was soaked in sweat, so much so he was lying on a wet sheet. He fumbled for his watch and checked the time. 11.15. Why hadn't Mam called him? A minute later she came into the bedroom.

'Ah, you're awake.' She laid a hand on his forehead. 'Just as I thought. You're running a temperature. I've sent for the doctor. You might have pneumonia for all we know.'

He didn't say anything, just lay there hoping there would be no inquisition into last night's events. Mam sat on the side of the bed and gently ran a caring hand through his hair, then put her hand on his forehead again. He tried to sit up, but felt weak. 'Just lie there, bonny lad,' she said. 'I'll be back with the doc shortly.' So he lay there, as he was bid – still shivering from the effects of the damp and the cold. But relieved to be home.

The doc signed Mark off sick for a week, but after three days at home he went to work on Thursday. He didn't have pneumonia; he didn't have anything except a chill. He felt weak, but sitting about the house wasn't for him.

At work he was greeted by Horlicks, who had two pieces of news.

Firstly, Mark had missed Fred's funeral, which was on Wednesday; and second, 'that bird' they'd danced with at the Oxford – Carol, who worked at the florists – he'd seen her every night since and they were talking about having a weekend at Blackpool. They were going in Horlicks's dad's car. 'Bloody great Humber,' said Horlicks. 'She'll love it.'

Tommy was late in. Mark hung about waiting for him, finding himself alone in the workshop. As he waited the door at the top of the steps opened. Miss Raine appeared. She was smiling 'That girl who keeps ringing you,' she said. 'She's on the phone again.'

Marie was as bubbly as ever. Saturday: did he fancy going to Alnwick? 'I went there when I was little,' Marie explained. 'It's a great place. River. Castle. Nice shops. We can take the bus from the Haymarket. Have lunch when we get there, then have a walk by the river. It'll be great'

He hesitated, trying to think of the pros and cons. As he stood holding the telephone, he noticed Miss Raine, now seated at the desk, looking intently at him. She had a strange smile, and a face that was genuinely curious. He felt himself blushing under her gaze, and at the same time under some pressure to give Marie an immediate answer. 'Great,' he said. 'What time at the Haymarket?'

After the call, as he made to leave the office, Miss Raine spoke. 'She's really keen on you, isn't she? She's been on the phone every day this week.' Her gaze suggested to him that Marie wasn't the only one who was keen. Miss Raine had deep-green eyes that seemed to demand attention. 'Is she your girlfriend?' she ventured.

'Not really,' he replied, 'but we go out now and again.' As he looked at her he wondered what her first name was. She was known to everyone as Miss Raine. They were looking intently at one another, he standing halfway between her desk and the door, aware that Smudger might be loitering; she sitting with her elbows on her desk, her chin resting gently on her hands. Mark stole a furtive glance at the open doorway, then turned to her again.

'What's your first name?' he asked.

She smiled. 'Wouldn't you like to know?' She sat back in her chair. 'It's Lorna, actually.'

They held their mutual gaze a few moments more before his courage wavered; the thought of Smudger finding him there was too much. He nodded and left the room. He knew he wouldn't be able to get Miss Raine out of his mind all day, for several days in fact. He looked forward to Saturday, whatever it would bring. And he would nurture thoughts about Miss Raine – Lorna – in the meantime.

Tommy was waiting, car keys jangling in his hand. There were two more days at the club in Durham, he said. Two more treks into the badlands of the deep south, as Tommy put it. On Friday Mark took a last look at Fred's old chair, and they headed back to town early, job done. They were at a chemist's shop in Gateshead next week, Tommy said. It was being refitted and they were doing the electrics. As Mark got out of Tommy's car his mate had a piece of advice for him.

'Mind how you go with Miss Raine,' he said. 'She's got a fella. He's lean and he's mean, if you know what I mean.' He laughed at his own words. 'I'm a poet and I didn't know it. Seriously though, watch it. See you Monday.'

Being a Friday the odds were better than usual that Mark would see Rita on the bus, but there was no sign of her. He thought he might call her at work next week, but felt pessimistic about his chances. The thought of rejection didn't appeal. He called at Julian's on the way home, not to see his friend but his mam about a driving lesson, as promised. She was out. So was Julian. Mr Popham was in, looking pale and unwell. No problem, Mark lad, he declared. After lunch on Sunday, if that's okay. Mrs Popham will expect you at three o'clock.

Heading home, he felt good: good about his forthcoming day out with Marie; good about having his first driving lesson lined up and at no cost – driving schools were charging fifteen bob an hour; and good that the wretched wart had disappeared. Passing the Club he was reminded, as always, of Beryl and their fateful meeting that time. Now he could smile about it. But his spirit sank on sight of none other than Eggshell walking towards him. He was easily identifiable, with a white bandage around his skull, part of which covered his injured eye. He thought of running back the way he had come, but didn't see why he should. They met in the narrow confines of the path, where Eggshell's bulk blocked his way.

'You! You bastard.' Eggshell's fists were clenched, tattooed arms bare as usual. 'See what I've got through you? Tellin' Roger Cook I was knocking his missus off.'

'I never told him anything.'

'Oh aye. An' you expect me to believe that? How else would he know?' He stepped forward, an angry snarl on his face. 'Well, it didn't do Cookie any good, did it? I got the polis round.'

'I'm sure it'll all look good in the Evening Chronicle.'

Mark surprised himself at his own bravery. Maybe the fact that a skinny bloke like Roger could inflict physical damage on a hulk like Eggshell gave him the courage. He realised his own fists were clenched, and when Eggshell stepped forward again, his face so close that he was breathing in his face, he didn't flinch but stood his ground. Suddenly Eggshell pushed him. Mark staggered against the fence, but as Egg-shell threatened again he stood firm.

'Lay a hand on me again and you'll have another sore eye,' said Mark, at the same time dreading a thump from one of Eggshell's fists. They squared up to each other for a few seconds, whereupon Eggshell harrumphed, brushed past him and stormed off. As he made his way home Mark felt himself shaking, and he broke out in a cold sweat. He was pleased to have stood up to a bully, but when he got home he felt an urgent need to visit the toilet.

***

Saturday dawned fine: glorious autumn sunshine, a day to die for, as Bob would say. Mark stood by the parade of shops at the Haymarket, facing the stands where the buses to anywhere north of the city pulled in. The bus marked 'Alnwick' was ready and waiting; no driver yet, but Mark presumed Marie would show up in good time.

And there she was, appearing right in front of him, smiling and looking stunning in a sexy top and tight-fitting jeans. She carried a coat over the crook of her arm. She kissed him lightly on the cheek. Then he saw she wasn't alone.

A woman, fifty-ish, and a little lad stood close by, looking at Mark. 'This is my mam,' said Marie. 'Mam, Mark.'

Marie's mam nodded.

'And this is Ben. Say hello, Ben.'

Ben didn't say anything, just stared wide-eyed at Mark, sucking his thumb. He was about three or four, Mark thought. 'Mam gave me a lift in, and Ben came too. Didn't you, Ben?' Marie tweaked the little lad's cheek before turning to her mother. 'Right, thanks Mam,' she said. Her mother smiled and led Ben away. 'They're going shopping,' Marie explained.

The Alnwick bus now had its driver aboard. They sat near the back. Marie laid a forearm casually on his thigh. They sat in silence, looking out of the window. Morpeth came and went. Three-quarters of an hour later they were in Alnwick, where, Mark had to admit, he was relieved the journey was over. They'd walk around the shops awhile, said Marie. He followed compliantly, standing back as she explored bric-a-brac and various selections of shoes and women's clothing. On such a lovely day he became increasingly irritated at hanging around. It was only then that he began to ask himself what he was doing here with someone with whom he had so little in common. Had it been Carol, he thought, they would have chatted away every single minute. He was in the deep throes of boredom when Marie, emerging from a small boutique, declared they would have lunch.

For a moment he dreaded what her idea of lunch might be. Fancy foreign stuff with rabbit food wasn't to his taste. Happily they ended up in a basement café for fish and chips, which they ate mainly in silence punctuated by Marie's opinions on fashion and Marks and Spencer's, and her dislike of her boss at work. Throughout it all, Mark focused on what he regarded as the point of their meeting: physical contact somewhere. Shopping and wandering around aimlessly were simply something to be endured until he and Marie would get to grips – and getting to grips was something he knew she liked very much.

Outside again they killed more time before sauntering down to the river and taking to a path across open parkland. Now alone their situation was much more romantic. He was in thrall to her good looks, her sexuality. He felt good about walking with her. In town the furtive glances of other men at his partner had not gone unnoticed. They had already shared intimate moments, albeit surrounded by dozens of people in cinemas; and he knew she was turned on by sex and sexual images. Now, on a late afternoon by the Aln, with a faint autumn sun emerging from grey clouds, he wanted her and he was sure she wanted him. They weren't in love. But like the actors in the French films at the Stoll, they wanted to perform.

As they walked he put his arm around her shoulders; she responded by hooking her arm around his waist. Conversation was unnecessary. They walked on and on, until they seemed to be leaving Alnwick behind. Then they turned and walked slowly back the way they had come. Somewhere in town a distant clock struck six. Could he manoeuvre her into a situation where they could be alone, without fear of interruption? When the sun went behind grey clouds again he espied a lonely bench.

It was set well back from the path, by a small copse. Gently, he steered her towards it. They sat together, his arm around her shoulder, looking over the river to the distant castle. When he turned his head to kiss her she responded willingly. And when he slid his hand into her coat she seemed to relax, as though she had expected it.

They kissed, they groped, exploring each other, each lost in their own world of excitement. At some point they ended up on the ground, in the lee of the trees. He placed his coat carefully onto the grass; she lay on it and raised her arms, inviting him to lie on top of her. They kissed, and grappled with buttons and zips, struggled in their mutual desire to remove clothing. With a difficulty that caused her to laugh – she wriggling co-operatively – he managed to pull her tight jeans down and off completely. As he slid his fingers into the top of her knickers she spoke – quietly, but purposefully.

'Have you got something?'

He hesitated. Surely she hadn't heard about his visit to the hospital.

'Have you got something?' she repeated.

He raised his head up and looked into her face.

'Have you got some *protection*?' She had frozen, and lay still waiting for his answer. 'A Durex,' she hissed.

His face gave her the answer. She sighed, and lay back, deflated. He lay next to her, motionless and silent. After a moment she looked at him, and spoke. 'You don't want to make me pregnant, do you?'

She got to her feet, struggling to pull her jeans on. He wanted to speak but he couldn't think of what to say. He felt utterly deflated. The bus trip to Alnwick, wandering around shops, had all been a price to pay for what would happen at the end of the day. Yet they had been thwarted. The idea of buying a contraceptive hadn't for a moment crossed his mind; he wouldn't know where to buy any had it done so. They brushed the grass from their clothing, she picked up her handbag and they walked, apart, back towards town. They barely spoke until they reached the Haymarket, a journey that seemed to Mark to last for an eternity.

He walked her to her bus stop, where they stood side by side in silence, she checking her watch and looking intently in the direction of her expected bus. After five minutes or so it came into sight. She turned to him then, stood on tiptoe and kissed him on the cheek.

'Thank you so much for today,' she said. 'It's been great.'

'Yeah.'

'We can do it again you know. Next week, if you like.'

'What, go to Alnwick again?'

'No silly. Somewhere else. What about Durham. You'll like it there. Cathedral, shops. And it's lovely by the river.'

Her bus neared and she stepped forward. 'See you at the Haymarket next Saturday then. Same time?' she said, hesitating, her hand holding the rail. He nodded an okay. 'Night-night, then,' she called out as she stepped on to the platform, glancing back briefly before disappearing inside.

'Night-night,' he called back. It was all he could say, since she hadn't given him time to say anything else. He watched the bus go, regretting his missed opportunity, but reflecting that she had been right: he wouldn't want to make her pregnant. And what he'd missed out on by the Aln he could put right by the Wear.

Being a Saturday evening there remained the problem of Bob and Joyce – now they were lovebirds again. It was just before nine when he crossed the yard to the back door. He pushed the letterbox open, seeing only darkness within. Kev always said darkness would be the best time to have sex with Joyce. He knocked firmly and turned the knob – only to find the door locked. That wasn't surprising. He would hardly expect them to be at it with the door unlocked. He knocked again, but there was no answer.

And then he remembered: he still had no house key. There was nothing for it but to wait for his parents to return from the Club. An hour and a half at least. He thought he might go to the Club to ask Dad for his key but the thought of bumping into Walter put him off. So he sat on the doorstep in the darkness, his thoughts inevitably drifting to the girls he'd met, and more pointedly to Carol. He'd see her again, he had no doubt. At Partners. Or the Oxford. Or maybe he'd knock on her door. Hell, he hadn't done so wrong in trying his hand that time. Maybe he'd send her flowers again. That was another opportunity to renew acquaintance with her namesake at the florists. That's if she hadn't eloped with Horlicks in his dad's Humber.

Mrs and Mrs Green found their son asleep on the step, his back resting against the door. Charlie shook his head and said 'Never mind' to his dear wife. Once inside Mark scuttled off to bed and Nancy fetched the pig's trotters from the cold slab in the pantry. Charlie went to the radiogram and selected Bing Crosby's *Changing Partners*. Bing's crooning voice drifted up the stairs to Mark as was falling asleep. He was cold and tired but the title of the song wasn't wasted on him.

***

He was early, but she was ready. Standing in the porch, car keys in hand, a smile on her face. She wore a white blouse and flowery skirt, the former low cut and revealing a generous cleavage, the latter long and swishy. Once again he found it difficult to believe Julian's mam was about the same age as his mother. She opened the door on sight of him, waved the keys and closed the door behind her. No 'Goodbye darling,' to her husband – if he was in – but instead a purposeful stride to the gate.

'Come on then,' she called out, as though they were off on a day-trip somewhere. He hesitated, uncertain about which side of the car to go to. She went to the driver's door, laughing. 'You can't drive yet,' she said. 'Not till I've given you some basic instructions.' He opened the passenger door of the Austin Seven, noting the gleaming paintwork. Inside and out, the car was immaculate. She got in and slipped the key into the ignition.

'You can have a practise drive today,' she said, 'but not here. We'll go to some quiet roads where it's safer.' With that she started the engine and drove off.

He felt nervous, not only about driving for the first time but because she was Julian's mam. She was attractive; he knew she was flirtatious, but now they were alone he wondered if he was doing the right thing. Still, he reassured himself, it should be OK. She was teaching him to drive, that's all, and it wasn't going to cost anything. There were two L-plates by his feet. 'You can put them on when we stop,' she said.

They drove out of the village, leaving the main road and taking to country lanes, all familiar to Mark who had cycled them throughout his boyhood years. But even they fell behind as she drove on, until he no longer knew where they were exactly. Finally she turned into a nar-row lane with high hedgerows where she stopped just off the road by a farm gate. She reached forward, picked up the L-plates and handed them to Mark. 'They just stick on,' she said. He got out of the car and stuck the L-plates on front and rear, before returning to the front pas-senger seat feeling more nervous than ever.

'Right,' she said. 'Your first lesson starts now. The Highway Code. I take it you've been reading it?' He nodded, only just refraining from admitting he'd never opened the Highway Code since his Boy Scout days, and that was to learn about cyclists. He pictured in his mind the images the blank faces of policemen holding their arms out for drivers to stop, and level crossings with gates and without gates.

She produced a copy of the Code from somewhere and flicked through it. 'What is the sequence of traffic lights from green?' she asked. He could hardly believe it. Bob had gone through that with him only a couple of days before.

'Amber, red, red and amber, green.'

She looked surprised at his answer. 'Very good,' she said, closing the book. 'I don't think there's any doubt you know the Highway Code, giving such a confident answer as that.'

'Can I drive now?' he enquired.

'Not yet. I've to show you the controls and explain how the engine works.'

'I know all that.'

'Really? Tell me what the clutch is for then.'

He didn't know, and said so. When she didn't say anything he asked her.

'I'm not sure myself, to be honest,' she replied, and they both laughed. It seemed to lighten the atmosphere. 'What I can tell you is that when you want to change gear you have to depress the clutch which detaches the engine from the accelerator. Something like that.'

He realised she was as nervous as him. But all he wanted was to swop places with her and have a go at driving, so he waited in silence for her to speak again.

'Mark, do you remember that time I asked you if you found me attractive?'

He felt himself blushing, and even defenceless, in the presence of his friend's mam. She was staring at him, waiting for an answer. He nodded and looked away.

'Mark, we all have needs. I am a married woman but I have a husband who can't fulfil those needs. Do you understand?'

He shuffled in his seat, tried looking her in the eye but ended up looking away again.

'Mark, if you do find me attractive we could share something special.'

'But you're Julian's mam.'

She laughed. 'No-one will know.'

'Know what?'

'You know what I mean. Don't pretend you don't.' He was looking straight ahead now, as though focusing on some object on the empty road ahead. 'I'm an attractive woman, Mark. A woman going to waste. Look at me. Go on, *look at me.*'

He turned his head and looked at her. They held eye contact for a moment before she spoke again, slowly, in an almost commanding tone. 'Look at me here, Mark,' she said, and with that she pulled the top of her blouse down, revealing more cleavage. He looked, saw the top of her breasts. She was breathing deeply now, staring at his face, inviting him to act. He half turned and slowly slipped his hand under the top of her blouse until it was cupped around her naked breast. She sighed so loud it startled him.

She leaned forward and tried to kiss him, but was thwarted by the awkward shape of the seat and the gear stick.

'Let's sit in the back,' she whispered. 'There's more room...'

She didn't wait for an answer, but got out and sat on one of the back seats. He watched without moving; she sat there, waiting for him. 'Come on then,' she muttered, gently patting the empty seat at her side. 'Come to Doris.' Doris! It was the first time he had heard her name.

The initial feel of her naked flesh had turned him on. But now, clinically asked to get into the back of the car, he felt his sexual desire subside. Even so, he did as he was bid. When he'd settled they looked at each other for a few moments, then she slowly loosened the buttons on her blouse, one by one, all the time looking him in the eye. Finally she pulled it open completely, revealing a rose-coloured bra. To his surprise she unclipped the bra at the front and pulled the cups aside, exposing her bare breasts.

They sat there, two strangers occupying a moment frozen in time. She was looking at him, inviting him to make a move. Then she slid forward, lifted her bottom from the seat and thrust her feet over the driver's seat. He watched, transfixed, as she pulled frantically at her knickers. With a bending of knees and some writhing and twisting she finally dragged them over her feet and cast them onto the driver's seat. She lay back then, her skirt now pulled up to her waist.

'Come on to me,' she whispered. He found himself kneeling on the floor of the car between her legs. This was the moment he had dreamed of; the moment when he would, at last, enter a woman. Instead, the cold, detached way she had manoeuvred both of them into this position seemed to kill his sexual feelings. He felt like an object that was being used. He had no feelings for her, none at all. And then he found himself thinking about Julian.

Julian, his friend. Julian, whom he'd known since junior school when his mam collected him at the gate at hometime. The same Julian's mam who was spread-eagled under him now, undoing his belt, unfastening his jeans. With difficulty she managed to pull them down, partway. Then she was grasping him, stimulating him, urging a response that would not come. Instead of sexual feelings, he felt guilt; instead of desire he felt contempt. It was hopeless.

'Please, Mrs Popham. Stop.'

Her entire body seemed to freeze before she spoke angrily, her words emanating from between clenched teeth.

'Mrs Popham,' she hissed. 'Mrs bloody Popham. That's me, isn't it? Eh?' She sounded so angry she was scaring him. 'Get off me. Get *off*!' He tried to move away from her quickly, but it was impossible to manoeuvre easily in the back of the car. 'Get off. Get off!' she screamed. She was bending her legs, trying to slide from underneath him. He managed to slide backwards and sideways, finding himself kneeling on the other seat. He tried to pull his pants up to cover his deflated manhood. She laughed like a witch and sat glaring at him, watching him as he struggled with his jeans. She seemed to calm down before speaking again. 'Well, what a flop you turned out to be. You were bloody hopeless, sonny boy. I might as well have asked for a fuck with my useless husband.'

With difficulty she sat upright, fastened her bra and blouse, then got out of the car and put her shoes on before reaching into the front and retrieving her knickers. Glancing furtively along the quiet road she put them on, then straightened her dress before getting back into the driver's seat. He joined her in the front. They were silent awhile. He glanced at her face to find her staring straight ahead, as though deep in thought.

'Can I have a drive now?' he asked.

She drove to the bottom of the Terrace, on the way neither of them saying a word. He'd stolen a glance or two, and fancied he saw tears welling. He thought he should say something: 'Sorry,' or something appropriate. But he couldn't, and anyway he wasn't sorry. Instead, he felt he'd been used by a woman old enough to be his mother – and Julian's mother at that. There had been no more questions on the Highway Code, and no driving. When she finally spoke to him again her voice betrayed her anger. 'I suppose you think you're clever,' she said, 'leading me on then leaving me high and dry. Just so you can tell your friends, I suppose.'

'I wasn't leading you on. I wanted a driving lesson.'

'You knew perfectly well what would happen…' She broke off, choking on her words.

'I just want to learn to drive. I thought you were going to teach me.'

She turned and faced him, her eyes welling up with tears. 'I feel such a bloody fool. You'd better not tell anyone about this, I'm warning you.'

Now *he* was feeling angry, but before he could say anything else she spoke again.

'Look. Just go. Go on. Please. Get out of my car.'

He needed no second bidding. He opened the door and got out. She was pulling away even as he slammed it shut. He watched her go, his anger increasing. But as he headed up the Terrace his feelings turned to regret. How could he call on Julian now? They'd been mates for years. And there'd be no more driving lessons. Wouldn't Julian think that strange? Wouldn't he be curious about that? Wouldn't he wonder why Mark wasn't calling on him any more?

Standing at the back gate, Charlie Green watched his younger son approaching. He had his head down, and seemed preoccupied. When he reached the gate he looked up and seemed surprised to see his dad.

'Good driving lesson son?' Charlie opened the gate for him.

'Oh, aye Dad. Great. Thanks.'

Charlie thought Mark a troubled soul as he crossed the yard to the back door. Something was wrong; he didn't know what. He didn't ask, but followed him indoors. He might have expected him to plonk himself down by the fire; instead he went straight upstairs. Charlie went to the window and lit a cigarette. Something in the pit of his stomach told him all was not well with his boy. Come to think of it, he hadn't brought a lass back to the house yet. Eighteen now. Time he did, thought Charlie. Time he was sowing wild oats.

19

If Mark Green's mother was upset at the sight of her son reclining asleep on the doorstep on Saturday night, that was nothing to the condition he found her in at six-thirty on Monday morning after he got out of bed to go to work. 'What have I done now?' he wondered at the sight of her sitting on one of the armchairs by the newly-lit fire, holding a handkerchief to her face and weeping softly. She never even looked up as he entered the room.

When Charlie Green entered the living room he looked at his wife, then at Mark. 'Billy's dead,' he declared. 'Bob found him on the floor of his cage this morning.' Mark then noticed a small white bundle that lay on the table, a rolled-up handkerchief that obviously contained the deceased. 'I'll bury him in the garden by the shed after you've gone to work,' said Charlie. 'Come and get your breakfast.'

Billy had been a member of the family since Mark was a youngster. But unlike the time the Greens' cat, Smokey, had died some years before, Billy's passing had no emotional effect on anyone except Nancy. To Mark, Smokey had been a pet; Billy was never any more than a nuisance whose cage had to be cleaned and who'd got him into trouble when he escaped. All Billy's demise did was remind him of Smokey and how much he'd missed him when he died.

But any sadness he might have felt that morning was quickly dispelled when he remembered he'd be working at a chemist's shop this week. Bound to be lasses there. He'd met Marie through work, after all. Could be more productive than the Oxford. Even so, on the bus he was troubled when he recalled his so-called driving lesson the previous afternoon, when he recalled the sight of Mrs Popham – Doris – lying spread-eagled in the back of her car, and her angry face when he'd not done what she'd wanted. If he called on Julian again, how would his mam react when she found him at the door? He was sure she wouldn't tell anyone about what happened, least of all Julian or her husband, but the situation was anything but satisfactory and it wasn't his fault. She had accused him of leading her on, but such thoughts only started to make him angry again; so he looked out of the bus window and thought of the forthcoming visit to Durham on Saturday with Marie.

At the workshop Tommy said they wouldn't be starting at the chemist's shop till Wednesday. Instead they were off to a posh block of flats in Jesmond to service the lift. It was new work, said Smudger, with more to follow at other properties. 'Make a good job of it,' were his instructions to Tommy. As they turned to go the door at the top of the steps opened and Miss Raine appeared. She was holding a hand to her face, indicating a 'telephone call for you' to Smudger. Mark thought she looked stunning in a tight red dress. As she turned, she flashed him a brief smile. Then she disappeared into the office, leaving Mark decidedly turned on and feeling positive about approaching her and asking her for a date. Tommy noticed. 'I told you, mind,' he said, smiling. 'She's got a fella and he won't like you moving onto his patch.' She could make her own mind up, Mark thought, but said nothing as they headed off for Tommy's car.

Jesmond, to Mark, meant Carol. He wondered if he might bump into her, although he considered it doubtful since she would probably be at work too. Even so he felt excited when they located the block of flats, a six storey building just around the corner from Carol's house. Tommy parked his Ford Popular at the front between a Jag and a big Humber They went inside and took the lift to the top floor. The lift doors opened and closed with a shudder and the lift jerked alarmingly as it began its ascent. 'I hope this bloody thing doesn't break down with us in it,' said Tommy. Mark eyed a red button on the panel.

Underneath a small piece of paper was held in place by Sellotape. The wording, in biro, read, 'Alarm'. 'Bet that fuckin' thing don't work either,' said Tommy.

They reached the top floor with a jolt and stepped across the landing to a plain door. Tommy produced a key and they went inside. It was the room with the lift mechanism. Inside, they stood for a few moments, listening to the clicking of solenoids engaging as people below pressed for the lift.

'What do we do to service it? asked Mark.

'Fuck knows,' said Tommy, plonking his toolbag onto the floor. 'Go and make the tea.'

At the third door he knocked on Mark had an answer, an elderly lady who kindly put the kettle on. Back in the lifthouse Tommy was reading his *Mirror*. It was a full hour before he folded his newspaper and decreed how they would service the lift. He, Tommy, would check the solenoids and clean them up with wet-and-dry sandpaper; Mark would scrape out the dirt from the metal gutter where the bottom of the lift doors ran, the one in the lift itself, the others on separate floors. A screwdriver would do the job nicely. Working downwards, Mark had reached the second floor when someone tapped him on the shoulder. He looked up to see a woman he thought to be in her fifties. She was tall and slim, wearing a long skirt and a cream-coloured blouse. She had well-worn features and an air of authority about her. Her obviously long hair was piled up on top of her head in a bob.

'Are you an electrician?' she enquired. Without waiting for an answer she said, 'There's something wrong with my electric fire. Could you take a look?'

He followed her into her flat, where she indicated an old-fashioned 2-bar electric wall fire in the living room. 'It keeps turning itself off somehow,' she explained. Mark thought the fire looked decrepit. She left him to it, leaving the room and disappearing through a door leading to somewhere. It didn't take him long to identify the problem: a loose connection. He inserted the wire into the terminal and tightened the screw. Still kneeling on the floor he looked up and saw her standing in the doorway, leaning on the doorpost. He was surprised to see she was in her bare feet and wearing a dressing gown, and that her long hair now hung down her back.

'Any luck?' she enquired.

He nodded. 'I've fixed it but really you could with a new fire. I mean...' He felt some difficulty in coming to the point. She stood, waiting. 'It should be condemned.' She remained where she was, fingering the loose end of the cotton belt around her waist. Feeling uncomfortable he packed his toolbag and stood up to go.

'I suppose you'll want payment now,' she said almost in a whisper.

He moved to the door. 'It's okay,' he replied. 'It was nothing.'

She pushed herself dramatically from the doorpost and sauntered across the floor to where he stood. She stood close to him, the strong smell of her makeup permeating the air. It smelled like the stuff Aunt Ettie used – old woman's stuff.

'Come on, what do I owe you, dear boy?'

'Nothin'. Really...'

'It must be worth something, surely.'

He put his hand on the catch and turned the lock. She stood back then and changed her tone. 'Look, I must owe you something. Wait here.' She disappeared from the room and returned with her hand outstretched. 'Here you are, and thank you. Go on, take it.' She pressed something soft into his hand. He could hardly believe it, a ten shilling note or even a pound just for tightening a screw. She opened the door wide, and he left without further comment and in great relief. When he heard her close the door behind him he opened his fingers to see what was in his hand. He was holding five cigarettes.

Returning to the lifthouse, Mark told Tommy about his impromptu repair job and showed him his reward for mending the woman's fire. 'You might as well have them,' said Mark, handing the cigarettes over to his mate.

Tommy accepted them with indifference, an indifference that changed to interest when Mark told him about the woman changing into a dressing gown and the manner in which she had offered payment. 'Sounds a right goer if you ask me,' said Tommy, adding 'Was she attractive?' and 'How old would she be?' Mark answered his questions and that was that – at least until they'd had their sandwiches when Tommy, who had been looking particularly thoughtful, folded his Daily Mirror and started packing his tools away.

'Pack your bag, lad. We're having an early finish. Smudger won't be coming here today. Probably doesn't even know where the place is.'

In the lift, after Mark pressed the button for the ground floor, Tommy pressed the button for the second. 'Look, I'm gonna call on your woman. Check out her electrics, eh?'

The lift juddered to a stop and Tommy stepped outside. He turned to Mark. 'Straight home, mind. No hanging about town or you might bump into Smudger.' With that he turned and walked directly to the door of the woman's flat. Mark pressed for the ground floor again. What was it his dad kept saying from time to time? 'Takes all kinds to make a world'. Maybe he should introduce Tommy to Julian's mam, he thought – and he wasn't joking.

***

Carol's Monday was routine, the only thing worthy of note being the unusual amount of times Miss Carr appeared. Carrying her bundle of papers as usual, she popped up here and there, always within a short distance of Carol's desk. Carol wondered if her boss was hoping she would tell her she wanted the room, but she had decided to stay put, for now at least.

That afternoon something happened that convinced Carol she was right to stay at home, at least until her mother returned. Dad came home from work feeling ill, and by bed-time was lying on the settee doubled up in pain. Carol wanted to call the doctor but he would have none of it. But that night he was violently sick and unable to go to work the next day. 'It must be something I ate,' he explained. Carol agreed, but he looked dreadful so she called work and asked for time off. Her request was granted. She'd look after her dad.

Looking after her dad, in fact, meant no more than being downstairs whilst he lay upstairs in bed, asleep. Carol had never been off work for any reason; she wasn't used to be alone through the week when friends such as Emma were unavailable. But she was glad to be there for her dad anyway. She tuned into the Light Programme, made a cup of tea and did what she always seemed to be doing when at home these days: the housework.

At lunchtime she checked on Dad, finding him fast asleep. Dusting and hoovering over, she decided to take the living room curtains down and wash them. She plonked a chair in front of the window and was just about to stand on it when she noticed a young man on the opposite side of the street. He was standing there, looking in the general direction of her house. He looked like Mark, she thought. How silly she'd been in throwing him out. And hadn't he sent the flowers that time? If only she knew where he lived or worked, she'd call and ask after him. And then, as she looked, she realised it *was* him.

Her first thought was to rush out and say hello. But she hesitated; it was definitely him, she told herself, but what was he doing, just standing there? She watched him for a few minutes, uncertain about what to do. Then she heard Dad's voice calling from the top of the stairs. She moved away from the window and called out to him, asking what he wanted.

'Cup of tea, pet. I'll be down in a jiff.'

'Right, Dad.' She went into the kitchen, put the kettle on and returned to the window – to find Mark gone. She opened the front door and went into the street, and looked in both directions. But he had disappeared, leaving her perplexed and somewhat worried about whatever reason he had for hanging around the house.

Mark thought about knocking at her door, but decided there'd be no point. Like him, Carol would be at work. He thought about dropping a note through the letterbox, giving his work telephone number, but surely she would just tear it up. And if she was cross, as she might be, she might tell her dad and he might complain to Mr Robson or Smudger. No, it was best left. Yet he wanted to make contact again. She could only say no, after all. Maybe a weekend was best. Not Saturday though. Saturday he was with Marie; Saturday held the promise of sweet fruit.

Which reminded him: he had a rather delicate errand to make.

Tommy couldn't recall its name but the shop was just off the Bigg Market. 'It's dark inside so no-one will see you,' Tommy had said. Mark's early release from work on Tommy's say-so now found him outside the shop, and never mind his 'No hanging about town' instruction. At the shop he hesitated, then pushed the door open and entered, finding it so gloomy it took a minute or so for his eyes had to adjust to the darkness. A distant bell tinkled briefly somewhere at the back of the premises.

There was an old, gnarled wooden counter, cluttered with pieces of paper and piled high with small cardboard boxes. All around the shop floor were old books and huge, hard-backed ledgers, the latter looking years old. The window was covered by an old curtain that sagged in the middle. He felt dry in the mouth and even considered leaving; but Saturday's forthcoming tryst with Marie demanded that he would stay. He hoped no-one else would come into the shop, that's all.

After a few minutes an elderly woman appeared through a curtain of beads. She was dressed entirely in black, and stood on the other side of the counter looking at him, a smouldering ciggy hanging from her bottom lip. She reminded him vividly of the old woman he'd met outside the Oxford. She never spoke, just stood there, waiting. He swallowed and uttered the words Tommy had told him to say.

'Packet of three, please.'

For a moment she didn't say anything. Then she took the cigarette from her mouth and flicked ash onto the floor.

'What sort?'

'Er, just ordinary ones, thanks.'

The woman turned, took a small packet from the shelf immediately behind her and placed it onto the counter.

'That'll be one and nine.'

He gave her half a crown. Without comment, she handed him the packet and his change and he left. Outside, he was glad of the fresh air but felt himself shaking, as though he'd had a narrow escape in an accident. But he'd got what he needed. Best hide them till Saturday, he thought. Having his mother find a packet of Durex in his pocket was the last thing he needed.

***

It was big, as chemists' shops go. Lots of aisles with lots of shelves. They arrived just before ten o'clock. By noon Mark had made his considered assessments of the female staff, and Tommy had made his assessment of him. 'We're here to work lad. Keep your eyes at home.' Yet, as Mark noted, Tommy too had an eye for one of the staff, the manageress, a buxom woman called Wendy. At bait time Tommy declared, 'She's not wearing a ring. Bet she's a divorcee with two kids and up for it with a bloke like me. I wonder if she'd like a ride in my Ford Pop.'

'You're wearing a ring though.' Mark's pointed remark seemed to embarrass Tommy, who shrugged and opened his sandwich box. 'Make the bloody tea' was his only comment.

The three young shop assistants were Maureen, Clare and Sandra. That was all the girls in the shop, save for Wendy and an elderly woman called Florrie who never seemed to have anything to say to anyone. Mark spent the day eyeing the girls as he went about his work, threading new cables into newly-installed showcases. A new false ceiling was to be fitted later, so they would be on the job for some time. By the end of the day he had ascertained that Maureen was engaged to be married, and he didn't seem to have the chemistry with Clare, who ignored him entirely. He fancied Sandra and gave her the eye a couple of times, only to be met with indifference. But just before it was time to pack up tools he winked at her and was encouraged by her smiling response. Tomorrow, Thursday, was something to look forward to.

Walking up the Terrace he arrived at the back gate at the same time as Constable Moon. The polis always looked too big for his bike, Mark thought. PC Moon braked sharply and nodded. 'Good timin' lad. It's you I've come to see.' Mark waited, wondering what he wanted this time. He couldn't get into trouble for buying Durex, surely. 'Best we go indoors,' said Moon. 'What I have to say is best said in front of your parents.'

Moon dragged his bike through the narrow gateway, leaned it carefully against the wall and followed Mark into the kitchen. Mam was cooking tea. The look on her face told Mark she wasn't best pleased at the sight of the village bobby again and what on earth did he want now? Dad was in the living room, reading his Chronicle. On sight of PC Moon he stood up. Mam stood at the kitchen door, wiping her hands on her pinny and wearing a look of grave concern.

'Sorry to have to trouble you again.' PC Moon removed his helmet. 'All it is this time is to tell you that Mr Swinburne next door has withdrawn his complaint of assault against Mr...' He hesitated, then fumbled in his tunic pocket for his notebook.

'Cook,' said Mark.

'Aye. Mr Roger Cook. So...That means there'll be no further action and you won't be needed to testify in court.' He directed his next remark to Charlie. 'Nor will your older son, Mr Green, if you'd be good enough to tell him.'

'Thought that's what he'd do,' said Charlie. 'All the publicity there'd have been. Messing about with a neighbour's wife in their lav an' all.'

'Aye, well.' Moon turned to go. 'All's well that ends well, eh. Mind how you go then lad. You don't want me back here again I'm sure.'

As Charlie reached to open the door there was a knock. He opened it to two people on the doorstep, a man wearing a smart suit and a young woman who wore a skirt and coat. None of the Greens knew them, but it was clear PC Moon knew the man – and that he knew him.

'Cyril,' said the man to Moon. 'What are you doing here?'

'Just a routine enquiry, sir,' Moon replied. He turned to Charlie. 'This is Detective Inspector Williams.'

'And Detective Constable King,' said the woman.

Moon plonked his helmet on and stepped outside. He exchanged a few confidential words with Detective Inspector Williams before collecting his bicycle and leaving. The Greens and the newly-arrived detectives watched him go in silence.

'It's alright,' Charlie said to the detectives. 'Swinburne has withdrawn his complaint. Mark doesn't have to go to court now.'

'That's not why we're here,' Williams replied, eyeing Mark. 'Is this young lad Mark Green?' Being told he was Williams suggested they talk inside. They all went into the living room and sat around the table, except Mark, who stood at his father's side, and Detective Constable King, who stood by the door.

'What is it now?' asked Nancy nervously.

'I'll tell you,' said Williams, taking a small notebook from his inside pocket. He flicked it open. 'We've had a complaint of an indecent assault by a Mrs Doris Popham…'

Nancy gasped, and Charlie took hold of her hand.

Williams paused, then continued, his voice calm and assured. 'Mrs Popham's complaint is that when she was giving you, Mark Green, a driving lesson on Sunday last, you sexually assaulted her in the back of her car.'

Mark felt as if an invisible hand had grabbed his intestines and was twisting them. He noticed his mother's face had turned deathly white.

Williams flipped the book shut and looked at Mark. 'Now then lad, you don't have to say anything in reply to this, but I'll ask you anyway if you would like to.'

'What was her complaint exactly?' asked Charlie.

'Well, I don't want to go into specifics, but she says your lad, um…' He hesitated, glancing at Nancy.

'Go on,' said Charlie.

'She says he made suggestive remarks and fondled her breast.'

'Ee, our Mark!' Nancy exclaimed.

All eyes were on Mark. 'Well?' asked Williams. 'What have you to say?'

'She suggested getting into the back of the car so we did. It was all her idea.' When no-one spoke, he added, 'She wanted me to, you know… but I couldn't cos she's Julian's mam.'

With that he burst into tears, and Nancy fled into the kitchen followed by the woman detective.

'I'd better say at this stage,' said Williams, addressing Charlie, 'that Mrs Popham doesn't want any action taken or the matter to go any further. She just wants the lad warned about his conduct.' He looked at Mark. 'I'm sure you won't want to end up in court over this, so we'll just say I've warned you about your conduct and that'll be case closed. Alright lad?'

'No it's not alright,' snapped Charlie. He looked at Mark. 'Did you assault Mrs Popham, or doing anything to her against her wishes?'

'No Dad. I didn't.'

'Then we can't warn him about anything,' said Charlie to Williams.

'Well, I have to tell you that I have to report back to Mrs Popham who might then wish to make a formal complaint.'

'Aye, well, let her. But my lad's not accepting a warning for something he says he didn't do.' Charlie stood up dismissively. 'So go and tell Mrs wotsername to make her formal complaint and we'll see her in court.'

Williams went into the kitchen, where his colleague was standing by the distraught Nancy, now sitting at the kitchen table. The officers left without further ado, leaving Charlie to console his wife. 'Whatever you were up to lad,' said Charlie to Mark, 'you should know better than to sit in the back of a car with Julian's mam. And I'll tell you, I've had enough of polises coming here, so get to your room and have a think, and I hope you resolve to behave yourself in future.'

Just then there was another knock at the back door. Charlie opened it to Ettie and Avril. On sight of Nancy, Ettie showed great concern. 'What can be the matter Nancy?' she enquired, placing a caring arm around her old friend's shoulders.

Before a tearful Nancy could say anything Charlie spoke. 'It's our Billy,' he said softly. 'He's gone and died. It's a bit upsetting, that's all. But we'll get over it, won't we pet?'

Nancy looked at her husband, then at Ettie, then at Avril. She nodded slightly and sniffed, and wiped a tear from her eyes with her hanky. 'I'll put the kettle on, eh,' said Charlie. Mark left the house. It was time for a visit to the rocking horse.

A few minutes later Charlie left the house too, on his way to his little seat at the top of the garden. After a cursory look at his pigeons, he sat down and thought about his youngest son. He'd seen that detective off, and rightly so. Coming round here and talking about warning him about his boy's conduct without a shred of evidence. Even so, he wondered if it might be true. He'd seemed strange when he got home after the driving lesson. Then there'd been that business outside the ladies toilets at the back of the Club; Mark had denied that at first until Walter had found his union card and that brought the polis round. Then he'd come back home in the middle of the night, half dead through the cold. Just what had really happened then? Only last Saturday they'd found him asleep on the doorstep. He lit up a cigarette and took a long drag.

Behind him the pigeons cooed contentedly.

Friday morning. Mark took the bus to town in subdued mood. Mrs Popham's false accusation was hard to take. What would happen if she made the complaint official? Would he be arrested? It was her word against his. He knew the truth, but would anyone believe his word against hers? He had a mental picture of appearing in the dock, and the judge telling him to stand up before sending him to prison. At work his mood continued. He didn't chat Sandra up, as he had intended. Tommy noticed his silence but said nothing. Until, that is, it was time to pack their tools and head back to the workshop to order accessories from Bert, ready for Monday morning.

'What's been wrong with you today, bonny lad?' Tommy enquired. Mark told him. 'Christ,' said Tommy, 'what that woman was offering I've dreamed about for years. I mean, on a plate and you said no.' But Mark's worried face made him change tack. 'Look lad. If, as you say, she laid it out on a plate and you didn't take it you've nowt to worry about. Hell hath no fury like a woman rejected, especially a woman old enough to be your ma. That's why she's complained. My advice is to put it behind you and get on with your life. Chin up, and on Monday I expect to hear all about who you've shafted this weekend. Right?'

'Right,' said Mark, feeling much heartened. There was Marie tomorrow, after all. And things got better even as he left the workshop, when he espied Miss Raine emerging from the front of the building, stepping sprightly towards him. He stood his ground and waited for her. When she saw him she smiled.

'Off for the weekend, then?' he remarked, needlessly but it was something to say. Still smiling, she nodded.

'I was wondering…'

She tilted her head, and waited.

'D'you fancy going out sometime?'

The smile was still there. He thought she looked interested, if surprised.

'Where to?'

'The pictures?'

'Don't do pictures. Sorry.'

'A walk, then. By the sea.'

'Sounds interesting. Where did you have in mind?'

'Tynemouth?'

She pulled a face.

'Druridge Bay. It's lovely up there.'

She shook her head. 'When you said the sea I thought you meant maybe Greece, or Italy.'

'A friend of my brother went to Spain on honeymoon' was the best response he could muster.

She laughed and walked past him. 'Have a nice weekend,' she called out, strutting off. He wanted to follow, to press her for a date, but felt uncertain. The situation was resolved by the throaty roar of a sports car engine. He turned to see a bright red open top MG approaching, driven by a young bloke. It screeched to a halt by Miss Raine. The driver stepped out of the car without opening the door and smiled. He had a broad chest and bulging biceps. Mark thought he looked like the guy in the Charles Atlas adverts. Miss Raine flashed a smile at him as he went to the nearside door of the car and opened it for her in a gesture of gallantry. Then he jumped into the driver's side and the car roared off, leaving a puff of exhaust smoke in its wake.

Lennie Kemp was ill for three days. In the end, when Carol called the doctor in, he was diagnosed with food poisoning. 'It was that pork pie I bought, not your cooking, lass,' he explained to his worried daughter. She stayed with him and looked after his needs until, by Thursday evening, he was sitting up and feeling better. During the three days he was unwell she kept thinking about Mark and his unexpected appearance across the street. She thought she might go to Partners on Saturday, but Emma seemed to be tied up with Robbie these days and she wouldn't go alone.

She went to work Friday, and just after tea was summonsed to Miss Carr's office. Her boss looked up at her knock, bade her come in and closed the door after her. She asked kindly after her father before directing Carol's attention to Marlene Dietrich's picture. 'Lovely as ever, isn't she?' she asked, and without waiting for Carol to reply she picked up a framed picture from the floor nearby. She held it up for Carol's benefit. It was the same picture, only smaller.

'Thought I'd show you this. If you take the room as we discussed, this will be hanging on the wall right above your bed.'

Carol said a weak 'Thank you.'

'Have you made a decision yet?'

Carol shook her head. 'No. I'd like to stay with Dad, for now at least. I think he'll find it difficult on his own. Hopefully Mam will be home soon though.'

'Of course. Well, as I've said, my door is always open if you want a chat.' Miss Carr moved to the door. 'Don't forget,' she said as Carol left.

On the way home, Carol walked slowly past Cook's. She told herself that the chances of bumping into Mark were slim, and if she did he'd probably be with that girl again. So she went for her trolley, knowing her dad would be wanting his tea. Walking down her street she unexpectedly bumped into Emma, who was full of talk about Robbie. 'Can you ask Robbie to pass on a message?' asked Carol. 'It's just I saw Mark the other day opposite our house, so if he's interested could you ask Robbie to tell him to call? Any evening or weekend would be fine. Or he could call me at work. You can give him my number.'

'I'll pass the message on to Robbie tonight,' said Emma. 'Maybe we'll have a foursome one evening.' A great idea, Carol agreed.

First, though, she wanted a twosome. With Mark.

20

Marie and sunshine go together, thought Mark, as she walked towards him, smiling as always, looking sexy as always. As on the previous Saturday her mother and little Ben were in train.

'Hello you!' Marie bubbled.

'Hello to you. And hello Ben,' said Mark, smiling at the boy. Ben, who was wearing a coloured peaked cap, looked at him curiously. 'Like your hat,' said Mark, wondering if maybe this time he'd be traipsing around Durham talking aimlessly with Marie's mother and buying ice cream for Ben. But his worries were misplaced; Marie's mam and Ben were off shopping, leaving Marie and him to enjoy the delights of Durham on a lovely autumnal day: the river, the cathedral, and sex whenever and wherever it took place.

'Say thank you to Mark,' said Marie. But Ben wasn't saying anything.

Mark had been to Durham before, with Mam and Dad when he was little, and with Julian once when they'd spent the whole day in the city. He remembered the students on the river, practising, like in the Boat Race; there were young couples, like him and Marie now, strolling the riverbank, or lying in the grass, kissing; the cathedral he'd gazed upon in awe, although, as he recalled, they hadn't gone inside.

'See you later, then.' Marie's mam took Ben's hand. They walked off without further ado, leaving Mark and Marie to walk through the city to catch the bus for Durham. They walked in silence mainly, and sat on the bus in silence, all the way to Durham. It was strange, thought Mark, how they didn't seem to have much to say to each other. The sole factor that bound them was physical. But if sex was all they had that was fine by him. It seemed fine by Marie, too. She'd never once come on to him about a 'long term relationship', as Bob would call it. He didn't feel the same about her as he did for Carol; but Carol hadn't wanted sex and he did. Anyway, after last week's debacle at Alnwick he was ready: this time he 'had something', a packet of three. Well, two. He'd used one last night in a kind of experiment. Couldn't say he liked it, but if that's what it took...

In Durham they went for a coffee then headed for the river. It was wonderful, Mark thought: the stone bridges, the riverside footpath he walked now with this lovely girl. When they reached the weir they stopped and looked up at the cathedral, now towering majestically above. 'Isn't it lovely?' Marie whispered reverently, as though they were inside the building. She turned and faced him, her mouth so close he kissed her at once. They embraced then, caught up in a special moment. He felt himself stirring and pulled her close. She willingly responded. He'd thought they would make love in the late evening somewhere, yet now seemed perfect. But even as they stood there in their own world of youthful passion they were interrupted by the appearance of an elderly woman and her terrier dog. After running around them several times and barking the dog eventually won the attention of Marie, who patted it on the head. Mark stood there, a smile on his face masking his disappointment. They walked on.

They left the river and headed through the city centre, and climbed up the narrow cobbled streets to the cathedral. Inside they walked in silence, taking in the magnificent architecture and gazing in awe at St Cuthbert's shrine. Mark felt a close bond with Marie. He thought that maybe, after all, they could have much in common apart from their physical desire for each other. She looked lovelier than ever at this moment, and he was moved by her obvious reverence.

'Is St Cuthbert's body really in here?' she whispered, staring at the marble monument.

Mark could scarcely answer. This was a different Marie. She was fun-loving and sexy, yes; but he felt she was someone whose feelings ran deep, and moreso here, where they were staring history in the face. When they emerged from the cathedral, each had their own thoughts about what they had seen. At Marie's behest they went for a snack and a look around the shops before they found themselves by the river again on a glorious late afternoon. They walked hand in hand, arriving by the boat landings. Rowing boats, advertised for hire, bobbed up and down gently on the water. A few were out on the river, occupied mainly by young couples.

'How romantic!' Marie broke free and ran down the steps to the wooden landings, then turned, facing Mark with a smile. He could not doubt what she wanted. He liked rowing boats: been out on them with Bob and Mam often enough. He paid the money and rowed out into the middle of the river, upstream at first, then turned about and allowed the boat to drift with the current. Marie wore a permanent smile and kept looking around her, as though savouring this special occasion. Just like on the bus, no words passed between them: but where on the bus a lack of conversation meant indifferent silence, here words were unnecessary. They sailed the river in sunshine, a light breeze ruffling Marie's hair. Mark's attention was on her throughout, she sitting in the back of the boat, his natural line of vision directly on her face. Her smiling face. Her lovely face. Could he feel the same about her as he did for Carol? Could he feel love for Marie? He watched as she lazily trailed her fingers through the water and thought maybe he could.

They spent an hour on the river. Then they moved on, walking along the riverbank, away from town, holding hands again. Suddenly Marie broke free, laughing. She twirled a few times, then flopped down onto the grass. She drew her feet back and wrapped her arms around her legs. She looked so happy, so content. But Mark's ambition lay elsewhere along the riverbank.

'Let's walk further,' he said, standing by her side.

She looked up, still smiling. 'Can't tonight,' she declared. 'Got to be going soon, I'm afraid.'

'Going? Why have we to be going?'

'Mam's out tonight. I've got to babysit Ben.'

'But we're here. Surely you're not expected to look after your little brother on a Saturday evening.'

She stood up. 'My little brother? Ben is my son.'

'Your son?'

'Is that so strange?'

'But you never said.'

'You never asked. Anyway, what does it matter? It's not as though we're in a relationship or anything. And, let's face, we're not likely to be, are we?'

He wanted to tell her how he had been feeling about her, in the cathedral and then on the river, but he couldn't. He didn't think she would want to hear about his feelings. He didn't think she felt the same. He thought she only wanted the sex they shared, nothing more.

They walked off then, and made their way to the bus station. As usual their journey was made in silence. Back in town he walked with her to her bus stop, but he didn't linger. Instead he left her there, saying 'I'll give you a call.' It was only when he was walking away he began to think he felt more for her than he realised, and maybe she did feel something for him after all. Maybe she hadn't told him about Ben being her son because she'd been worried that he wouldn't want to see her again. Maybe she'd wanted more than sex but couldn't find the words to say so. Maybe she would find the words if she knew how he felt about her.

He decided to return to the bus stop and tell her he loved her. He hurried there, only to find the only occupant to be a forlorn-looking pigeon perched precariously on top of the bus stop pole. The pigeon glanced at him indifferently before spattering the pole in streaky white and flying off into the night air.

That afternoon, while Mark and Marie were exploring the delights of Durham, Carol was exploring the delights – to her – of Fenwick's. As she traipsed the floor at her favourite store, alternating thoughts of Mark and Miss Carr drifted in and out of her mind. She wondered if she'd done the right thing in asking Emma to ask Mark to call her at work. Did that make her seem cheap? She was missing Emma today. It's just the pair of them were regular Saturday afternoon visitors to town, and Fenwick's in particular, but that was before Emma met Robbie. A boyfriend changes everything, thought Carol.

As for Miss Carr, she couldn't make her out. Still, the thought of the room she had available was tempting. She would endeavour to keep close contact without the nonsense of going for a drink with her again. That was scary. Now, in Fenwick's, she went to the restaurant for a coffee, more out of habit than need. She noticed that everyone else there was in pairs: husbands and wives, boyfriends and girlfriends, mothers and daughters, the latter, Carol noted, nearly always the ones who'd bought the most clothes, now safely wrapped in *Fenwick's* shopping bags. The husband and wives, she noted, mainly sat in silence, as though in quiet reflection. Of their lives, perhaps. Everyone had someone – except her. She left her coffee and left the store, buying nothing.

She lingered in town, wandering in and out of shops. She didn't want to go home, to spend the rest of the afternoon sitting indoors listening to Dad snoring, a newspaper draped over his face, or simply being alone. Her time-killing was so effective she was surprised when the Goldsmith's clock chimed five. Best she got home to make tea, which reminded her: when, if ever, was Mam coming home? She'd been away so long now she was beginning to fade from her mind. They'd not met since that evening at Tynemouth. It seemed ages ago.

A dearth of trolleys meant it was nearly six when she closed the front door, calling out 'I'm home' before Dad could ask where had she been till this time and where was his tea? There was no reply. She called out again, but there was only silence. Entering the kitchen, she noticed the brown ale bottle was standing on the worktop next to the cupboard it had occupied for weeks.

It was empty.

***

Mark spent a restless night, thoughts of Marie filtering in and out of his mind. He overslept, opening his eyes to bright sunlight and a new cobweb above his head. At first his muddled brain told him he'd slept in for work; but it was Sunday and he relaxed, thinking more clearly now. He had reacted badly when Marie told him she had a son and she had to go home to look after him. He had expected so much and he'd been so disappointed. He wondered who Ben's father was, and if he was still in Marie's life? He doubted it. Did he, Mark Green, want to be in her life? Last night, after feeling so close to her in Durham, he thought maybe he did.

His thoughts strayed to the new addition to the household: Joey, a blue budgie, just like Billy. The only difference was Joey didn't talk yet.

The bedroom door opened and Bob's face appeared. 'You've a visitor. Gerrup.'

'Who is it?' Mark enquired lazily.

'You won't be pleased to know. It's Julian.'

Julian! Mark sat up sharply. Did he know about last Sunday? That his mam was sitting in the back of their Austin with her tits out and tearing her knickers off? That she'd told the police she'd been indecently assaulted? That she was a fucking liar? As he went downstairs the question seemed to bounce around Mark's brain. Does he know? Does he know? He opened the living room door to find his long-time friend standing by Joey's cage. Julian turned, smiled, looking like the naïve kid he was.

'I wondered if you fancied coming round tonight to see Sunday Night at the London Palladium,' said Julian, in such a way that an affirmative reply would be automatic.

'Can't,' Mark replied. 'I'm going out with Kev.'

Julian looked dismayed. 'We never seem to get together these days. What about next week?'

Mark nodded. 'Yeah, sure,' he said, so abruptly Julian left without further comment.

Dad emerged from the kitchen. 'He doesn't know about his mother I suppose. Well, he'll know soon enough if she makes the complaint official. The whole bloody world will.'

At that moment Kev arrived with a 'Watcha Kidda' for Mark and a more formal 'Mornin', Mr Green,' for Charlie. 'Just seen Nancy-boy Popham. He's got a face like thunder.' Mark made no comment. As he anticipated, the on-off situation between Kev and Betty was 'off'. 'Fancy the coast tonight?' asked Kev. As ever, Mark was first reserve. Still, it was better than staying home.

He nodded. 'Not the Spanish City, though. I'm sick of dodgem cars and schoolgirls.'

'Me too. What about Tynemouth? Slot machines at the Plaza? Fish and chips?' It was all agreed, with the pointless condition that Kev would 'take it easy this time' on the Coast Road. 'No more than seventy. Straight up.'

Ten minutes after Kev's departure Robbie turned up. 'You're a popular lad this mornin', our Mark,' remarked Charlie, adding, for Robbie's benefit, that they had a new budgie before leaving the room.

'Still courtin?' asked Mark, as Robbie plonked himself in one of the fireside chairs.

Robbie nodded. 'It's fantastic. We're at it all the time. What about you?'

'Playing the field.'

'Aye, right. Anyway…' Robbie checked the door, as though he was about to pass on confidential information. 'Got a message for you from Carol.' Mark's face betrayed his interest. Robbie smiled. 'Thought you'd be pleased. Anyway, she asked Emma to tell me to tell you to give her a call. She works for Northern Electricity. Here's her number.' He handed Mark a slip of paper.

Nancy appeared. 'H'llo Robbie. How's your mam?' Before Robbie could reply she was directing his attention to Joey. Mark carefully folded the piece of paper and slipped it into his pocket.

Carol's first thoughts when she woke that Sunday morning were of the Saturday evening she'd spent alone watching television, waiting in vain for Dad's return, hoping that maybe he'd succumbed to just one drink – the brown ale – and maybe had just popped out for some air afterwards. But he didn't return until after eleven, by which time she was in bed. She heard his key in the lock and the front door closing. Just like old times. The times when he abused Mam. How long, she wondered, before he abused her? It was the drink, he always said. So it was.

She'd wondered if he would ask her to make him some tea or a sandwich. She lay awake, hoping – praying – that he wouldn't call her name. He didn't. Instead, after half an hour or so she heard his foot on the stair and his bedroom door closing. She told herself she couldn't live like this; she really couldn't.

On the Sunday morning she got up and went out directly, closing the door softly behind her. She was going she knew not where. The morning was fresh after overnight drizzle. The air seemed to clear her head. The streets were empty, save for a passing policeman on his bicycle. She felt a sense of determination: to somehow grab the situation and turn it into her favour. She loved her father, had stayed with him during Mam's absence. He'd done so well, keeping off the booze, decorating the house, going to work, being the lovely man he was. But he'd failed. A solution had been offered. She would take it.

Miss Carr sounded surprised at her call. Yes, the room was still there for her. Yes, from tonight, if that was what she wanted. She lived in the Tyne valley. Take the Hexham train from Newcastle Central, she said, and she would pick her up at the station. Six o'clock, no later as she was going out to have dinner with a friend. Carol took a train now, to the coast. She would spend the day by the sea before taking trains again. She thought about Dad, felt guilty that when he came downstairs that morning she would not be there for him. But he had his life to live and had chosen the way he wished to live it. She would do the same.

At six Miss Carr was waiting. 'So glad to see you,' she said. 'But… have you no luggage?' Carol shook her head. She led Carol to her car and they drove off. 'Does your father know about you taking the room?' she enquired. The expression on Carol's face gave her the answer. 'Well, you'll have to let him know, and you'll have to call home for your things. Tomorrow, after work, I would suggest.'

They arrived at a delightful country cottage. There was a small garden, and roses all around the porch. It reminded Carol of the pictures in her Enid Blyton story books. Miss Carr led Carol into a hallway full of bric-a-brac and old pictures on the walls, then into a large well-furnished living room.

'Well, this is home,' she declared. 'Do you like it?'

'It's amazing. So different from our house in Jesmond.'

Miss Carr led her to a well-furnished bedroom with a double bed with iron bedstead, and dark-coloured furniture. The smaller picture of Marlene Dietrich hung above the bed. 'There she is,' Miss Carr declared, before showing Carol the rest of the house. When they got to the kitchen she put the kettle on. 'You'll have to clear things with your father, you know. But he's welcome to come and inspect the place if he wishes.'

'He'll probably want to stay here himself if he does,' laughed Carol. 'I've never seen such a lovely house.'

'Well, as I said, I'm out tonight. But there's the TV and lots of books. There's food in the pantry. Have a shower if you like. Just make yourself at home and I'll see you later or in the morning if you've turned in.' With that she left Carol to it, calling out 'cheerio' before driving off.

Carol spent the evening exploring the house. She loved it all: the bookshelves with lots of old books, the leaded windows, the way the furniture was arranged, the deep-pile carpets, the fireplace: she imagined what it must be like in winter, logs smouldering, throwing out a warm glow. There were mysterious plants everywhere, some big, some small, some with huge leaves. She couldn't find the television at first, but located it behind the doors of a wooden cabinet, secreted away until it was needed. Outside, the garden was awash with flowers, illuminated by the light from the kitchen window. It would be wonderful living in a house like this forever, she thought: out in the country, away from the noises and smells of the city. Maybe she would have one like this someday, which she could share with someone special. Like Mark...

She didn't watch TV. Instead she selected *Jane Eyre* from one of the bookcases and settled down on the sofa to read it. It was only as she sat in the silence of the cottage that she noticed the steady ticking of the mantel clock. The clock had an ornate face and chimed softly and almost apologetically on the hour. Later, she took a shower before crawling between the sheets of the double bed and settling down for the night with her book. She had no idea of the time when, at last, she reached out and turned off the bedside lamp. There'd be Dad to face tomorrow. She felt guilty that she hadn't waited for him to get up before telling him she was leaving, and why. He deserved to know. He would know tomorrow evening.

***

'No more than seventy you said. You're a bloody madman.'

Mark took his crash helmet off and waited for Kev to heave the motorbike onto its stand. Kev removed his helmet and undid the zip of his leather jacket. 'Chill out, Marky,' he said, smiling. 'We're here in one piece, aren't we?'

'Yeah. Somehow. Fat lot of use these crash helmets would be if we're bouncing off the road at 100 miles an hour.'

'I wasn't doing a hundred. Eighty more like.'

They were at Tynemouth, near the Priory.

'Fancy a swift one?' Kev was already heading to the nearest pub.

'One and one only,' Mark replied. And he meant it, no matter what. They entered the pub – Mark never noticed its name – where Kev went directly to the bar. Mark glanced into a corner and saw two girls sitting at a table, one with her back to him. The table next to them was empty. He went over without hesitation only to find, to his astonishment, that the girl who had had her back to him was none other than Avril. The other girl he didn't know. She was attractive, smartly dressed with dark hair. Mark couldn't comprehend why she would want Avril for company.

'Hi Mark,' said Avril, trying to sound as if they were best mates. Mark nodded curtly. An awkward silence prevailed until the other girl spoke to Avril.

'Who's your friend?'

'My cousin Mark. Well, we're not cousins really, but our mams used to say we were.'

Kev appeared, carrying two brimming glasses. He plonked them on to the table, and sat down next to the unknown girl.

'This is Thelma,' said Avril. 'And this is...?'

'I'm Kev. Would you ladies like a drink?' The girls shook their heads.

Kev took over. Mark sat in silence, as though in shock. All the way to Tynemouth at a hundred miles an hour and here he was, sitting next to Avril. He couldn't help but compare the girls. Thelma: attractive, smart; Avril, unattractive, smelling of fag-ash. He sipped his pint, declined another when Kev asked but bought one for himself, a half of lager for Avril and an orange juice for Thelma. Then Kev bought another pint and another half for Avril, but Mark resolutely stuck to the same pint he started with. After an hour Kev suggested a walk to the park and they left together.

'Avril's pissed,' whispered Kev.

'So are you,' Mark told him. 'And you're driving.'

It was dark now. Kev walked close to Thelma, Mark with Avril but keeping his distance. None of them spoke a word. Why are Kev and I always walking with girls? Mark wondered. Always at the coast, always with him and the good looking one in front. They reached the park and sauntered through the gates. The park was well illuminated by the street lights on the main road, but all was darkness behind the bushes and low hedges. Loud music drifted over from the Plaza opposite. The foursome stood at the side of the lake, surveying the scene.

'Fancy taking a boat out?' said Kev. His idea of a joke, Mark supposed, as the rowing boats were moored in the middle of the lake. A titter from Avril was the only response. Kev and Thelma walked on then, leaving Mark and Avril together in a silent world of their own. Mark saw Kev put an arm around Thelma's shoulder just before they disappeared into the darkness beyond some rhododendrons. He turned his gaze to the Plaza. There was a faint smell of fish and chips, which made him feel hungry.

'We used to come here when I was a kid,' said Mark. 'Mam and dad went to the pub. I used to take a boat out.' It occurred to him even as he spoke it was the first time he had ever offered any conversation to his 'cousin' apart from years before when they were little and their parents visited.

Avril struck a match and lit up, then threw the empty fag packet into the lake. They watched it bobbing aimlessly on the surface. Cigarette smoke wafted into Mark's face. He loathed her, not because she was unattractive; he could never hold anything against anyone who was unattractive. It was *her*: her greasy, unwashed hair, her tatty clothes, the food lurking between her teeth, the permanent stink of cigarette smoke that emanated from her hair, her clothes. He couldn't think of anything else to say to her. He thought of walking away and catching next bus to town.

'Where've they got to, then?' said Avril, peering into the darkness. 'I didn't see them further along the path.' She had a point; further on, the path was illuminated by a street light. Mark offered no reply. He pictured Kev and Thelma lying on the grass somewhere, he fumbling with her bra, she with her hands caressing his hair, moaning in expectation of what was to follow. But then, unexpectedly, Thelma appeared, emerging from the shadows, walking apace towards them. When she got close Mark could see she didn't look too pleased. A moment later Kev came into view. The little group reformed at the lake side. Kev looked at Mark and shrugged.

Thelma stood in an angry-looking silence, clearly wanting to go. Then she walked off abruptly towards the park gates. After just a few paces she stopped and looked back at Avril.

'I'm going,' said Thelma. 'You coming or what?'

Avril hesitated, then stepped forward, threw her arms around Kev's neck and kissed him on the mouth. Mark saw Kev's eyebrows rise up in surprise. Then it was his turn to be surprised when his friend raised his hands slowly and gently placed them on her waist. Mark and Thelma watched as they embraced for fully a minute before they disengaged and walked off into the darkness, Kev's arm around her shoulders.

'And they say romance is dead,' said Thelma, before turning away and walking towards the park gates. Mark followed. They walked together, back to the main street, two strangers thrust together through circumstance. Mark thought she was a few years older than him. Mid-twenties, he guessed.

'I'm surprised you're friends with Avril,' he ventured.

'We're not friends really. We happen to work for the same company.' She paused before continuing. 'I'm at the end of a long relationship. My boyfriend… he dumped me. I think he met someone else. Anyway, Avril suggested going out for a drink, so…'

Mark wondered if he should ask her out. But she seemed more worldly than other girls. Like Miss Raine. And look what happened there.

They walked on in silence, until Thelma stopped at a street corner. 'I live along here,' she said. She didn't walk off, but stood there, looking at him.

'D'you fancy a date?' He blurted the words out.

She smiled. 'I'm not much company right now.'

'Well, I think you are.'

'What did you have in mind?'

'What about the pictures?'

'That would be nice. Actually I'd like to see Blue Hawaii. It's on at the Haymarket. It's just I didn't want to go on my own. Have you seen it?'

He nodded.

'Somewhere else then?' she asked.

'What about the Stoll?'

She hesitated before replying. 'The Stoll? Isn't that where they show those X-films?'

Marie flashed though his mind. How she was responsive to sex onscreen. He wondered if Thelma would be the same.

'You know,' she said, 'you're all the same. Lads like you. All you want is sex. A quick grope, a cheap thrill. I would be looking for a meaningful relationship. I wouldn't want to sit among a lot of dirty old men watching pornography.' She laughed cynically. 'You and your friend, what's his name? Kev. You're two of a kind. Just immature boys. Look, it's been nice meeting you, but you'd have to grow up before I would go out with you.'

With that she turned and walked off. He watched her go, her steel-tipped stilettos clattering on the pavement as she disappeared from view. He wondered whether to run after her and start again, but thought better of it. It started to rain. He pulled his collar up and went for the bus for town. It was Carol he wanted anyway. It was Carol he loved.

***

A strange bed in a strange house. Carol slept soundly nevertheless, wearing the pretty nightie kindly left on the bed for her by Miss Carr. Judith. She must remember: it's Judith. Calling her boss Judith were her final thoughts as she drifted into sleep the night before. Now, on Monday morning, she stirred, happily content in the knowledge that she wouldn't have to make Dad his morning cuppa and toast or do any housework. She stretched out, yawned and turned over for a final few minutes before getting up for coffee and cornflakes – and even a lift to work.

Eyes still closed she imagined what the room would look like when she opened the curtains. Sun streaming through the window, lighting up the pretty pictures on the walls and heralding the promise of a new day. Stretching again, she opened her eyes and found herself looking at Miss Carr who was in bed with her, looking at her, smiling at her.

'Good morning. Did you sleep well?' Miss Carr's voice was soft and patronising.

'Miss Carr!'

'Judith, *please*! You don't call someone you're in bed with Miss anything.'

'What are you doing?' Carol lifted her head from the pillow.

'Looking at you, sweetness. And don't tell me you're surprised.' Miss Carr raised herself up on to one elbow and came closer, her face inches away from Carol's. 'Shall I tell you something?' She waited for Carol to speak, and when she didn't she went on anyway. ''I'm going to kiss your lovely mouth. Right now.'

She lowered her head slowly. But just before contact Carol turned her head away and moved sideways. 'What are you doing?' she repeated.

'Doing? I'm doing what comes naturally. I'm doing what you want me to do. You do want to kiss me, don't you?'

'I don't want to kiss a woman, thank you. It's not... right.'

Miss Carr sat up and held the bedclothes up to her chin. 'Don't you want me?' she asked.

Carol glared at her. 'Want you? What do you mean?'

Miss Carr lowered the bedclothes, revealing her naked breasts. 'Look at me,' she said quietly. 'Do you find me attractive? Do you want me now?' Carol shook her head. 'I'm so sorry,' Miss Carr said. 'I'm afraid I completely misunderstood the situation. We must get up and go to work, but you must go home afterwards.' When she slid out of bed Carol saw she was naked. For a moment they had eye contact before Miss Carr turned and walked from the bedroom. Carol lay still awhile, then got up and got dressed. She wore the same clothes as yesterday but they would have to do.

By the time she entered the kitchen Miss Carr was also dressed. 'I'll take you to work,' she said, 'but I do hope you won't tell anyone what has happened. I think you'll agree you can't stay here.'

Carol didn't want to stay. Not now. She kept her own counsel as they left the cottage and drove to town. As they parked, and Carol reached for the handle to open the door, Miss Carr spoke in what Carol regarded as her 'boss's' voice.

'Look,' she said, 'I want you to know that I totally misunderstood the situation about you and me. I thought we would, you know, hit it off. I find you attractive. I had the picture of Marlene Dietrich framed especially for you. I thought you got my meaning. Do you understand?'

'No. I don't understand how you can find me attractive. I don't understand how you think I might find you attractive.'

'Alright. You are young. But it takes all kinds to make a world. We are all different. We are who we are. You, me, everyone. What has happened is unfortunate, but I wish to make it clear to you that I do not consider I have done anything wrong. However, I must insist that this morning's events, this misunderstanding, remains confidential. Now we must get on with our lives and put this experience behind us. Okay?'

'Okay.'

'And you mustn't call me Judith.'

'I never did call you Judith.'

Miss Carr smiled. 'No, you didn't. But I thought that was just through shyness. Anyway, when we get to work I'm Miss Carr and you are Miss Kemp. Right?' Carol nodded.

Carol was shocked at what had happened, and disappointed that she would not, after all, be able to stay in her boss's lovely cottage. But already her thoughts were on other things. She would go home tonight and face Dad, and apologise for leaving without saying anything. But she would tell him that his drinking habits were unacceptable to her and she would be firm in her resolve to find somewhere else to live. Never mind she wasn't twenty-one yet. She would go and that was that. She would visit him, of course. He would always be her dad, after all. And after the experience with her boss she thought it might be best to find another job.

21

It was a typical Monday. Carol's phone never stopped ringing. She acknowledged quietly to herself that it was just as well; it ensured she didn't dwell on her life's current problems or the rights or wrongs of her boss's conduct. The call mid-morning might have been no different to any other, except that this time it was Maggie on the switchboard.

'I'm putting through a personal call for you,' said Maggie. 'It's a fella.'

During the short pause before the telephone rang Carol could only think of one personal call from a male. She waited, hand poised, ready to speak to the young man who had been in her thoughts for so long. The phone rang. She picked it up.

'Carol Kemp,' she said softly.

'Hello pet.'

Carol recognised her dad's voice at once. Calm, soft-spoken, caring.

'Sorry to call you at work. Just thought I'd check you're okay.'

'I'm fine,' she said calmly. 'Sorry I left without saying anything, but...'

'Aye, don't worry. I haven't called to tell you off. I just wanted to know you were okay and why you disappeared. Didn't you think I'd be worried? You've never done that before. First your mam, now you.'

'Dad, I didn't want to leave you, but...' She felt the tears welling up.

'The brown ale. You drank it. Then you went to the pub. I can't stand it any more. Mam won't come home if you're back on the booze either.'

'I drank the brown ale?'

'I found the empty bottle.'

'I poured it down the sink, that's why it was empty. And I was in the pub right enough. In fact I was in lots of pubs on Saturday night. The pubs in Shields. Looking for your mam. But I never had a single pint. Just stuck my nose in the door or walked through. And you know what? I was disgusted. To see people sitting there, drinking, wasting their lives. I'll never touch a drop again, whether your mam comes home or not.'

He was telling the truth; she knew he was.

'Anyway,' he was saying. 'Will you be coming home tonight?'

'Yes Dad. I'll be home tonight.' She was close to tears. 'Sausage and chips on a Monday, eh?'

'Aye, medium rare, like always.'

She laughed and cried at the same time, before replacing the receiver. She had barely gathered her thoughts when Maggie on the switchboard called again. 'Popular girl this morning,' she chirped. 'Another personal call for you. Putting you through.' Carol steeled herself. It must be Mark this time, she thought. It seemed to take ages, but the phone rang again.

'Hello. Carol Kemp.'

'Hello love.'

'Mam!'

Freda Kemp laughed. 'Don't sound so surprised. I *am* your mother.'

'But it's ages since you called. Are you okay?'

'I'm well enough. I was calling to see if you are okay. And to ask about your dad.'

'We're fine.' Carol wanted to ask if she was coming home, but she held her tongue.

'I was thinking of popping round to see you both at the weekend. Well, I was thinking about more than that. I was thinking of coming home.'

'What about that chap you mentioned? Tom, was it?'

286

'Ted.' Freda Kemp laughed softly. 'Turns out he's married. He was giving me a load of guff when all the time his wife was in hospital with cancer. The poor woman died and then he told me the truth. Can you believe that? Still, it was no bad thing. Made me realise what a lovely man your father is – and what I've been missing. There's just one thing, though...'

'He's never touched a drop for weeks,' announced Carol. 'He's decorated the house top to bottom. You should see it. He wants you back. He...' She was about to tell her about his endeavours to find her on Saturday night but she held her tongue. A moment later she heard the sound of her mother sobbing. It took a few moments before she could say anything else to her daughter.

'Tell your dad I'm thinking of him,' she whispered, and hung up.

Returning to her office, Judith Carr glanced in Carol's direction again, just in time to see her replace the telephone. She saw a smiling young woman, someone who had perhaps just received some good news. Back in her office, she sat at her desk and looked forlornly at Marlene Dietrich's picture and felt sad that she could only possess one of the two women she loved.

Two 'personal' telephone calls. Alas, by the time she finished work, the third Carol hoped would come did not. She felt buoyant nonetheless: she had been utterly mistaken about Dad's activities on Saturday but was certain all would be well. She loved her parents and desperately wanted then to be reconciled. All it would take now, she reasoned, was for Mam to come to the house. Maybe she would call at the weekend, as she said.

She couldn't get her head around what had happened with Miss Carr. It was clear to her now that all along her boss had been after something. That's why she'd taken her out for the drink that time. She held nothing against her. If someone felt as Miss Car did about someone then she was only acting in response to her feelings. Even so she felt uneasy now about working at Northern Electricity. She felt that Miss Carr would no longer treat her the same as any member of staff; nor could she, Carol, have the same relationship with her boss.

She felt good as she grabbed her coat and said a few 'goodnights' to her colleagues, before crossing the foyer and breezing through the front door of the building. It was raining, which she hadn't expected. Nor had she expected Mark to be standing outside, waiting.

But he was.

***

Sandra was tall and slim and attractive – and very aloof. So it seemed to Mark; but she had smiled when he winked at her last Wednesday so he'd thought he might have fun chatting her up, and to see if he could interest her a date. She'd not been at work on Thursday and Friday, but she was here now, on Monday morning.

Throughout all the shenanigans of the past weeks, he had not forgotten Carol: the way he'd felt about her, the way he still felt about her. That day he'd loitered outside her house: there seemed to be something about her street because *she* lived there. Now she wanted him to make contact. She may have wanted him to do so for weeks but hadn't wanted to ask. Now she had, Sandra didn't seem to matter any more.

He looked at Sandra now in the chemist's shop staff tea room. She was putting the kettle on for her work colleagues' elevenses. He saw her look up and smile. That was more than she would have done before he won her over with that wink.

'Did you have a nice weekend?' she asked, as he waited for the kettle. He did, he said, without saying any more. He watched as she poured boiling water into a huge teapot, stirred the contents a few times and plonked the lid on. She looked up at him then, the sort of look that seemed to be inviting what she expected: the chat. Instead he stayed silent, picked up the kettle, filled it and switched it on. He watched as she put the tea things on to a trolley, which she wheeled past him, looking perplexed.

The day passed without incident: Mark wiring new fittings in the display units, Tommy doing nothing much except thinking. He always said thinking now saved making mistakes and wasting time later. He was sussing out the room before the new false ceiling went up. That's what he said, anyway. Mark thought he was sussing out Wendy. Mark had no further contact with Sandra, whom he noticed looking his way a few times.

He wanted to meet Carol tonight, not call her on the phone. He calculated he'd have enough time to be outside Northern Electricity when she emerged. He worried that he was in his work clothes and carrying his haversack; she would be smart, all dolled-up for work in the office. It was five-fifteen when he arrived. He stood in front of the main doors and waited. He felt good; he felt excited. He'd thought of Carol for weeks, even when he was with other girls. He'd not forgotten how she seemed to be 'different', how he felt different just thinking about her.

He stood there, waiting, hoping there wasn't a separate doorway for staff. He looked in every direction to see if she might appear. Five minutes passed. Ten. Fifteen. He wondered: had he missed her, and should he have telephoned after all? There was something about catching her unawares that appealed. Drama, like in a Hollywood movie. Here's looking at you kid. He imaged music playing, rising to a crescendo when, at last, she would emerge from the building and see him standing there. Instead there was only the noise of traffic and the voices of passers-by. A noise across the street distracted him. He turned his head for a moment to see what it was. He couldn't tell. When he looked back at the entrance to the building she was standing right in front of him.

For a moment she seemed surprised to see him, then a smile appeared on her face as she stepped forward. Those eyes! Those green, green eyes. They were looking at him now, right through him almost. He felt a surge of emotion, love maybe, as she stood before him, looking up at him. After an awkward silence she spoke.

'What's a strange man like you doing loitering round here?' she asked.

'Waiting for a girl like you,' he replied.

Instinctively he kissed her cheek, then stood back, remembering his grubby work clothes. He had wondered what to say to get her to linger: go for a drink, but he didn't think she would; maybe a coffee, but he didn't know anywhere. He wondered what to say. 'I got your message,' was the best he could do. She laughed again. She looked so happy, he thought, and said so.

'I've had a brilliant day,' she replied. 'Just some good news about my parents, and now seeing you.'

It started to drizzle. They moved quickly up the street and took shelter beneath the canopy of the Odeon. They stood there, looking at each other, each waiting for the other to say something.

Mark broke the ice. 'I'm sorry I was so forward with you that night. I...'

'Never mind that,' she replied. 'We're here now. We should talk, but I really have to get home to cook my dad's tea.'

'Tomorrow?'

'Tomorrow. Would you like to come for tea?'

'I'll be in my work clothes.'

She laughed. 'Just come. You'll meet Dad. Then we can go out somewhere. Maybe for a walk. Anything. See you at six o'clock.' She kissed him briefly on the cheek, then hurried off for her trolley. He watched her go, then went for his bus. He felt so happy, and thought she felt the same. Passing the Balloon, he fancied he caught sight of some familiar red hair, but wasn't sure. He used to look out for Rita. Yet on that journey home she'd not featured in his thoughts, not for a moment. He felt dizzy with happiness and anticipation.

The rain had stopped by the time he hurried up the Terrace. On the way he found himself approaching a familiar figure. It was Tom Clark.

'Watcha Mark, 'said Tom, who stopped walking, apparently wanting a chat.

'He called me Mark', Mark thought. He'd never called him that before. Before it was always Greeny or something insulting. He couldn't think of what to say. Tom had helped him out that time, but he still felt uneasy in his presence. Even now he looked menacing, even though he was smiling.

'How's Beryl?' he asked weakly.

'Aye, she's fine. We're thinking of getting married. Babby's got to have a dad, eh?' Mark nodded assent. 'We'd like to emigrate to Australia on one of those assisted passages, but she's too young. How about you? Got yerself a woman yet?' Mark nodded again. 'Still scared of me, aren't you?' Tom was smiling. 'It's okay. Nowt to worry about, eh.' Mark stood there, as if waiting for Tom to discharge him. 'Well, see you.'

As Tom walked on he turned and called out, 'Sorry about Marshy. I know he was your mate.'

Mark's face indicated he didn't know what Tom was talking about.

'Kev Marsh,' said Tom, looking serious. 'Have you not heard?'

Mark shook his head.

'He's dead, mate. Killed on his motorbike last night. Coast Road, I think.'

For a moment Mark thought Tom might be having him on, but motorbike and Coast Road seemed to have elements of truth. Tom walked off then, leaving Mark to go home where the solemn faces of his parents confirmed the news. What was it Kev had said? 'I live to speed and I speed to live'. Something like that. Now he was dead. The fact was, he, Mark, would probably have been dead too if he hadn't taken the bus home last night. He went upstairs and lay on his bed. He'd known Kev since infant school. He couldn't believe he was gone.

That evening the Greens had a familiar visitor.

PC Moon sat back in the easy chair by the fire, out of puff through riding his bicycle the length of the Terrace. He plopped his helmet onto his lap, and took a moment to compose himself. He'd called about Kev's accident. There was no other vehicle involved, he said, at least as far as they could tell. 'Speed. That's what it was, pure and simple. Youngsters nowadays… Lads on motorbikes…'

Charlie and Nancy Green, and their two sons, stood in their living room as Moon, seated comfortably, went into the details. 'Must have been shifting. No chance the speed he was going.' He paused to survey the watching faces, as though to ensure they were paying full attention. They were. 'There was a lassie killed an' all,' he added, matter-of-factly.

A lassie? Mark waited for more; for the inevitable.

'Aye, riding pillion. No crash helmet neither.'

'Do you know her name?' Mark could hardly get the words out.

Moon looked up at him, then fumbled in his tunic pocket for his notebook. He flipped through the pages. 'Aye lad. Avril Bragg.'

Nancy gasped, instinctively covering her mouth with her hand. 'Avril!' She looked up at Charlie. 'What was she doing with Kevin Marsh on his motorbike? Ettie will be heartbroken.' Charlie pulled up a chair. Nancy sat on it, dumbstruck.

Moon said Kev's dad had told him his son was seeing Mark Sunday evening. Was that right? Mark told him it was: they'd gone to Tynemouth, walked about and, yes, Kev had had a couple of pints, no more. 'I only had one,' he said for Nancy's benefit. Why hadn't he come home with Kev? asked Moon. 'Because he met Avril,' said Mark. Moon made a few notes, and said he might have to return to take a formal statement later 'for the coroner'.

On Tuesday Mark made two telephone calls, one to work, telling Miss Raine his friend had been killed and would she ask Mr Smith if he could have some time off out of respect. She said she was sure it would be alright. Then he telephoned Carol, who understood he couldn't make tea that evening but would wait for his call to re-arrange things. He wanted to visit Kev's parents, but Dad said best leave it for now. Then he went to the rec and sat on the rocking horse. He used to sit on it with Kev when they were kids. That's what death does, he thought: it brings back events you'd almost forgotten about. Him and Kev on the rocking horse was one of his earliest memories. Kev, the first boy he knew to wear long trousers; Kev, who said he wanted to have a motorbike when he grew up.

He thought about Avril too. How they played together when they were toddlers. He remembered climbing into the old tin bath with her, splashing and laughing. Two innocents under the loving eyes of their mothers. Feelings of guilt crept in: how he'd blanked her every time she spoke to him. Well, now she was dead. She was in heaven now with Kev. He couldn't imagine Kev in heaven somehow.

He thought about the accident: what had happened exactly? He'd never know for sure. Kev probably lost it on the wet road doing a ton. He wondered what had gone through his friend's mind the moment the wheels went from under him. He wouldn't have suffered, not at that speed. It would only have taken a second or two. Avril wouldn't have known much, if anything. He felt tears welling and moved away from the rocking horse as some children appeared, their mothers pushing empty pushchairs, chatting, laughing. The children were laughing. Everyone was happy, except him. He sloped off, shoulders hunched, and went home.

He spent the day moping around the house, wondering what the point was of being off work 'out of respect' when he wasn't visiting Kev's folks. More and more, as the day wore on, his thoughts drifted to Carol. He could have gone to her house tonight, what difference would it have made? Kev was dead and gone now. But he knew Mam and Dad wouldn't have approved so he stayed home.

Carol was disappointed about Mark having to cancel his visit, but she understood. Dad had been fine when she got home from work the night before, saying he understood how she must have felt when she saw the brown ale bottle was empty. He looked forward to meeting this Mark chap. She'd said nothing about Mam's telephone call.

Arriving home Tuesday evening after work, Carol noticed a familiar coat hanging in the passage. She opened the door to the living room to find her parents sitting together on the settee. They were drinking tea and smiling.

'Hello pet,' said Mam, in such a way Carol knew she had come home – to stay.

When Mark went to work on Wednesday he was sent for at once by Smudger. Wondering what he might have done wrong he walked apprehensively to Smudger's door, knocked tentatively and entered. Inside he found his boss sitting behind his cluttered desk, wearing his battered trilby, cigarette smouldering in his hand. The office was thick with cigarette smoke. The only chair was stacked with small cardboard boxes. Just as Smudger was about to speak the phone rang. Smudger picked it up, and ran his hand through a few papers in his desk trying to find something. When he did he read something out to the caller, during which time Mark was able to remove some of the boxes and perch on the edge of the seat.

Replacing the telephone Smudger gave Mark a 'what do you want?' look before clicking back into gear. 'I'm told two of your friends were killed at the weekend. You took yesterday off, and quite right too, lad. I just thought I'd tell you, you have the sympathies of everybody here at Robsons. If there's anything you might need...' Mark shook his head. 'Now then, how do you feel about being at work today? You okay? Mind on your job?' Mark nodded. 'Right. Well, if you feel you need any more time off let me or Tommy know. We don't want you having an accident being distracted over your friends' deaths. Right-o lad?'

Right-o said Mark. He left the office, admitting to himself that the only distraction he was likely to have was Carol. He thought he should feel guilty about that, but he didn't. Tommy was waiting in the workshop. He offered his condolences as they walked to his car.

'Had a crack with Wendy yesterday,' said Tommy, as they drove to Gateshead. 'I reckon I could be in there.'

'Wendy?'

'The manageress at the chemists. She's a goer, I bet.'

'What about your missus?'

'Oh aye. She's a goer, an' all.' Tommy laughed at his own wit, but noticed Mark wasn't smiling. 'Look, you only live once. And what the mind doesn't know the heart won't care about. Tell you something, that Sandra's hot on you. Wendy told me.'

Hot on me? Mark thought. Such a pity they'd not met when he was footloose and fancy-free. 'I've got a girlfriend now,' he said dismissively. Tommy drove on without further comment.

In the chemist's shop kitchen Sandra was making the tea. She looked at Mark with a face of concern. 'I heard two of your friends were killed at the weekend.' Mark nodded, not wanting to discuss it. 'If you need a friend. You know...' She filled the huge teapot, placed it onto the trolley and left. Mark stood aside and let her go, his thoughts only of Carol. No-one could come between them, he thought. Not even a pretty girl who was giving him the nod.

He phoned Carol after lunch, expecting to be invited to her house that evening. Instead she had news of her mother's return. 'Could you make it Saturday,' she asked. 'I've told my parents about you and they'd love you to come for tea. They're dying to meet you.'

He wanted to see her as soon as possible, but accepted the situation and said he'd be at her house on Saturday. Being invited for tea and to meet her parents was a sure sign she wanted to be with him. So, it seemed, did Sandra. Having kept his distance from her, she closed in on him just before the shop closed for the day and he was packing tools away.

'Doing anything tonight?' Sandra, standing between Mark and the door, clearly wanted an answer. Mark gave a shrug as his reply. 'D'you know the Espresso coffee bar in the High Street?' she asked, pulling on her coat. She didn't wait for an answer before continuing. 'Me and my mates go there most nights after work. Great juke box and you can jive if you want. Sometimes we go to the park after. Run free, like.'

She was standing so close he could have kissed her. He felt certain she wouldn't have complained. She fastened her coat, waited for his reply, a faint smile on her face. Her piercing blue eyes stared unfailingly into his. She was very confident of herself, just like Miss Raine, he thought. 'We go starkers in the kiddies' paddling pool some nights,' she said. Her eyes were twinkling, teasing him, tempting him. He had resolved to keep his thoughts on Carol. But what was it that Tommy had said? "What the mind doesn't know the heart won't care about." 'Anyway,' Sandra was saying, 'we're going there tonight if you fancy it. It's just along from the town hall.' With that she turned, opened the door and strode purposefully away.

Tommy was waiting. 'Christ, when I was your age I'd have her panties off after an invitation like that. Starkers in the pool? I wouldn't mind a bit of that myself.'

'I told you,' said Mark. 'I'm courting. Name's Carol.'

He sat on the bus, pleased at his display of loyalty, yet frustrated about what had been on offer – 'On a plate, mate,' Kev would have said. He told himself he'd feel different once he and Carol were in a full relationship. He wouldn't want anyone else. He loved her, he was certain. He closed his eyes and imagined Carol's naked body lying on her bed, waiting for him to kiss her, to smell her, to make love to her then to fall asleep beside her. He was so distracted he never noticed the bus passing the Balloon, and almost missed his stop at the bottom of the Terrace.

***

He leapt from the platform at the back of the trolley before it had even stopped, crossed the road and turned into the street – *her* street. He felt good; he felt ready. Ready to meet his girlfriend, Carol Kemp, and her folks. It was surely no coincidence that it had been a lovely Saturday, and even now the sun, low in the autumn sky, seemed to be shining just for him.

He'd been into town earlier and bought new black brogues and, at Bob's suggestion, a snazzy new shirt, which he now wore open at the neck. The brogues would also be perfect for the two funerals he'd be attending next week, said Bob. His sports coat-tails flapped in the breeze as he walked, the brogues' steel-tipped heels clicking sharply on the pavement.

Carol's street, like his own, was long, with terraced houses. But there the resemblance ended. The houses on his street stood back to back, a rough roadway running between bordered by high brick walls and gates that led into secret back yards with privies and coalhouses. The houses on Carol's street had small, well-tended gardens at the front, accessed by small gates and bordered by small hedges or low brick walls or fences. In Carol's street you saw flowers and rose bushes. At home all was bare and uninviting.

He felt different when he was in Carol's street. *The Street Where You Live*. That was the song by David Whitfield. 'The towering feeling, just to know somehow you are near'. He was happy, carefree. Mark Green was in love. In love with Carol Kemp. He'd thought about bringing flowers, but decided it might seem corny. Bring some for her mam, Bob had suggested. No, he'd bring himself: no alcohol on board, not this time. This time he was in top gear. This time he'd knock Carol for six.

He came to the little gate, flicked it open and rang the bell. He didn't hear anything ring inside, but he waited patiently at the door. He was about to ring again when the door was opened and there she was. She wore a bright green dress that matched her eyes. He almost said so, but held his tongue. She was smiling a welcome and standing back slightly, inviting him to step inside.

He stepped forward, uncertain. She offered her cheek, which he kissed with uncertainty. Did he have a good journey? Yeah. Two Corporation buses and here I am! Go through, she said. He went into the living room and found himself looking at a man in his late forties, the same man, he thought, he'd seen a few weeks back when he was outside. He'd not cared for the look of him then, but now the man was smiling a welcome and stepping forward, hand outstretched.

'This is my dad,' said Carol. 'Dad, Mark.'

'Hello there young fella,' said Lennie, shaking Mark's hand with a firm grip. 'Pleased to meet you. Did you have good journey?' Mark nodded. 'Buses these days,' said Lennie, shaking his head. 'Not as reliable as they used to be, eh?'

They were standing there, the three of them, all wondering what to say next. 'Mam will be through in a minute,' said Carol. 'She's in the kitchen, sorting out tea.'

'Woman's place, eh?' Lennie winked at Mark.

The kitchen door opened and three pairs of eyes looked at the woman who emerged, smiling, the happy, welcoming host. Mark felt he'd seen her before, but he was uncertain. The woman was looking at him intently, as though she too might recognise him. In what seemed an age, but was a mere second or two, the smile disappeared from her face.

'You!' she hissed.

Lennie looked at Mark then back at his wife. 'This is Mark. D'you know him?'

'Know him!' She stepped forward, speaking through clenched teeth and maintaining her gaze on Mark's face. 'You might say I know him. I met him at the pictures. Isn't that right, young man?'

Mark's face said it was.

'The pictures?' Lennie asked, bemused.

Freda Kemp spoke calmly. 'We were at the pictures when this *young man* and the *young woman* he was with were almost…doing it. Right there on the seats. It was disgusting.' She paused, as though allowing Mark an opportunity to say something; but he couldn't say a word. 'We complained and they were thrown out. Isn't that right?' Mark felt her eyes almost burrowing into his head.

Lennie Kemp and his daughter now looked at Mark, who nodded almost imperceptibly. But it was a nod.

'And now he's in my house,' said Freda.

Lennie and Carol looked at her again. 'You mean they were having sex?' asked Lennie.

'Having sex?' Freda was almost snarling. 'I just wish I'd had a bucket of cold water with me, that's all. Really…!'

'Who were you with?' asked Carol.

'Just a girl,' said Mark.

'Yes, and she was very rude to me as I recall' said Freda. 'Disgusting, in fact.'

All four were silent until Lennie, fixing his gaze upon his angry wife, spoke calmly but firmly.

'Who's "we"?' he asked. 'You said "we" were at the pictures.'

Freda hesitated, but held his gaze. 'Just a friend I was at the pictures with.'

'A male friend?'

'Yes. Well, I did have a life when we were apart, you know.' She turned her gaze to Mark again. 'And you were at it on the seats. Isn't that right?'

'This male friend,' Lennie was saying. 'Do you still see him?'

'We don't see each other now, no.'

'Is that why you came home? Because you don't see *him* now?'

Mark felt a tug on his sleeve. He turned to see Carol nodding unmistakably towards the door. They left the room and went into the passage. 'You'd best go,' she said. 'I don't know what's going to happen now but my parents have a problem and you seem to be the cause of it.' She opened the front door and stood aside to allow him to pass.

'Look, I can explain…'

'Another time, maybe,' said Carol. He lingered. 'Look, just go. I've got to sort this out, or else Mam'll be off again.' She gently ushered him out.

'When will I see you?' he asked. She didn't reply, but closed the door gently, leaving him alone in the little patch of garden. He turned, opened the gate and retraced his steps to the main road and the trolley for town. Kev's face flashed through his mind. 'You messed up there, Kidda,' he was saying. Then David Whitfield's voice returned, ringing through his head as he walked, singing about the towering feeling.

He stood at the bus stop, alone, so no-one saw his tears.

22

The head was his favourite part of the horse. Made of metal and painted in a dull grey, it had weathered over the years, so that the ears and mane and even the nostrils were smooth. The rocking horse at the rec was a part of his childhood, and of his youth, as somewhere to sit and contemplate. He never could understand how, when he was little, the eight seats would usually be full, with other kids waiting impatiently for their turn, their mams happily gossiping and laughing, yet on this fine breezy Sunday the horse's seats, as usual these days, were unoccupied. Even the entire rec was devoid of humanity. Today's kids had other pastimes, it seemed.

So Mark had come here this morning for solitary contemplation. About the events of the previous evening, and the rotten luck he'd had that the woman who'd complained about his sexual jousting that night at the pictures was none other than Carol's mother. He was sure he loved Carol, and that she loved him. But what would she do now she knew he'd been at it with another girl, and that thanks to him her dad knew her mam had been at the pictures with another man? If her mother left home again Carol would blame him for certain.

Bob had said not to worry, that he was only eighteen and there'd be other girls whether or not he had a relationship with Carol. But everything seemed to have gone skew-whiff: his friend killed on his motorbike, numerous missed opportunities with girls for one reason another

– hell, he even thought he'd had VD – and now, it seemed, he'd lost Carol. So he'd gone to the rec, where a sense of proportion had returned. He could do nothing about Kev's death. But Carol: could he do something to get her – and her parents – back on board? Could he again feel as he had on Saturday evening when he walked down her street with David Whitfield's shrill voice ringing in his head? Maybe he could, but he decided to hold off for now, to allow time before he made contact again. By then, he felt the situation would be clearer: either there would be or there would not be a future for them. If she felt the same for him as he did for her, there would be. Nothing, not even her parents, could stand in the way of love.

This was the pragmatic view, he thought, as he walked home, head bowed in continuing contemplation – so bowed that he didn't notice the black Austin 7 approaching, and he was indoors by the time it stopped at the gate. He had just sat in one of the fireside chairs when Dad opened the kitchen door. 'Two people to see you,' said Dad. Mark looked up to see Mr and Mrs Popham entering the room, followed by Mam, wiping her hands on her pinny as usual and appearing gravely concerned at the arrival of their visitors.

Mark stood up at once, and looked with trepidation first at Doris Popham, then her husband. Mrs Popham stood uncertainly in the centre of the floor, eyes down, her face looking strained. Arthur Popham looked at Dad, then Mam, then Mark. An uneasy silence prevailed, during which Dad looked increasingly bewildered. When Mr Popham finally spoke, softly but firmly, it was clear he was addressing Charlie and Nancy. He spoke slowly and precisely, without discernable accent.

'You know who we are, I take it?'

Charlie nodded. Mark's reaction to their unexpected appearance had made identification obvious.

'Well, then, 'said Arthur, 'my wife has something to say. To you, Mark. But to your parents too.'

Mark and his parents' eyes fell on Doris Popham. She lifted her hands slightly and nervously picked at her fingernails. She uttered no sound. Mark thought she was close to tears or even collapse.

Charlie spoke, not unkindly. 'Won't you sit down?' He gestured to the table. Charlie and the Pophams sat down, but Nancy stayed on her feet at her husband's side, staring at Doris.

'Go on, my dear,' said Arthur Popham softly to his wife.

Doris looked up at Mark. He would never forget her face at that moment: strained and tortured, her eyes red through tears. She looked down at her hands again and spoke in a whisper. 'I want to say I am sorry for what happened,' she said, nervously but clearly. 'And for going to the police. I am so sorry.' With that she leaned forward, held her head in her hands and started sobbing.

Nancy Green spoke up. 'Are you saying our Mark never did anything wrong? That you made everything up?' Doris took her hands from her face, sat back and nodded slightly.

'Aye, I see you nodding,' said Nancy. 'But I want to hear you say it. We've had detectives round hear and there's been no end of worry. I want to hear you tell us the truth.'

Doris steeled herself and spoke firmly. 'Mark never did anything wrong. He's a good boy. I made the allegation up. I don't know why I went to the police. I just don't know...'

She broke down completely then, weeping uncontrollably. Arthur Popham leaned across to his wife and put a caring arm around her. 'She's not been well,' he explained. 'We've had problems in our marriage. It's as much my fault really. We're going to see a counsellor, aren't we dear?'

Charlie Green stood next to his wife. 'Aye, well, there's no need to say more,' he declared. 'Thank you for coming and we'll let the matter rest there.'

Mark glanced at his mam, thinking she didn't look too pleased to let the matter rest there at all. But Nancy held her tongue. He looked at Doris, who looked just as old as his mam now. He felt pity as she was helped to her feet by her husband. The parents of his long-time friend Julian then walked slowly from the room, followed by Charlie who saw them out. Nancy Green stepped forward and kissed her youngest son on the cheek, wiping away a tear with the back of her hand. 'Go and top up Joey's millet,' she said. 'And make sure he doesn't fly off over them rooftops.'

***

On Monday Mark went to work with a clear mind. Sandra asked if he'd had a good weekend and had he seen his girlfriend. He said yes to both questions without going into details. She seemed to sense his reluctance to say much, yet he felt she was suspicious about all being well with the 'girlfriend' part of her enquiry. Another of the girls made tea for the staff that morning, so he didn't have the problem of batting off any unwanted questions. He had a question of his own, though, when he'd made the tea: where was Tommy?

If his mate wasn't urging him to brew up he would normally appear sharpish as soon as he had. Today he was nowhere to be found. A nod from Sandra in the direction of the back door gave him his answer. He looked outside to see Tommy standing in the yard, leaning against the wall, in conversation with Wendy, the manageress. Mark saw her mutter something to Tommy, who turned and gave him a thumbs-up. When, over tea, Tommy asked Mark about his weekend, Mark freely told him about the Saturday evening debacle. Tommy's advice was much the same as Bob's: there'll be others. 'Look at me,' he explained. 'Been married twelve years. Me and the missus are still together but I'm in with *her*.' He rolled his eyes in the direction of where he imagined Wendy to be.

Mark didn't feel that way about Carol. Instead he felt love and loyalty and said so.

'You'll soon have that knocked out of you,' said Tommy, turning his attention to his *Daily Mirror*. But Mark's focus was on the forthcoming Tuesday and Wednesday. He had never been to a funeral before; this week he had two to go to.

The first, on Tuesday, was Kev's. He walked to the church with Robbie. Julian would – should – have come, but Mark had had no contact with his friend since a week past Sunday and he didn't feel he could knock on his door. On the way to church, when Robbie asked how things were going with Carol, Mark told him about the events of Saturday evening. But he decided to wait until after the funeral before asking him to pass on a message to Carol, through Emma.

Harrison, the vicar, conducted the service, speaking of the sad loss of one so young; 'a life tragically taken', he said. Tragically thrown away, thought Mark, reflecting again on what Kev's thoughts might have been when he knew he'd lost it on a wet road doing a ton. What was it he said again? Live to speed, speed to live. The congregation sang *Immortal, Invisible, God Only Wise*, which he remembered from school, and *Abide With Me*, which reminded him of the Cup Final. At the conclusion of the service they walked into the churchyard and Mark watched as his friend Kev was lowered slowly into the ground. Speed to live, Kev had said; but he'd be spending a long time where he was now without going anywhere, Mark thought.

Walking home, Mark's message to Robbie was to ask Emma to tell Carol that he still wanted to see her, no matter what her parents might think. He would wait a few days before making contact – but he would make contact.

The next day Mark, his parents and brother went in Bob's Riley to the crematorium. Again feelings of guilt came over him, over the way he had shunned Avril. Again he thought of when they were little: playing, sitting in the tin bath in front of the fire. They'd lost touch when they were older, then, when Avril reappeared in his life, she'd turned into a creature he loathed. In the crem he took his place just behind 'Aunt' Ettie. Never had Mark seen anyone so distraught, so emotionally broken. She had lost her husband some years before, now her only daughter. She couldn't cope, just sat there sobbing inconsolable at her loss.

Mark remembered Ettie's husband, Bernie. Big guy, always jovial, always the life and soul. He'd been to a pub over Jarrow way, come out and dropped dead on the pavement. Mam said he'd had something called angina. Ettie had come to the house shortly after. She was heartbroken, in despair over the loss of a man she had loved. But then she'd had something – someone – to lean on: her daughter. She would hold on to Avril's hand, like a drowning man clutching at a straw, Bob said. But she didn't have Avril now, thanks to Kev. Kev and his bloody motorbike. Kev doing the ton-up on the Coast Road. Hell, he used to do seventy coming up the Terrace. And now, even though Mark had grown to loathe Avril, he resented Kev for taking her life because of what he saw now: poor Ettie.

The message again was that a life had been 'tragically taken'. The congregation sang *O God Our Help in Ages Past*, then *All Things Bright and Beautiful*, by which time poor Ettie was in such a state she had to be supported by two men when they were leaving the crem, before being taken home to whatever was left of her life.

'I'll give her six months, no more,' said Charlie. Nancy, displeased at his remark, held her tongue.

You have one life, Bob had said. This isn't a rehearsal for another. So make the most of it. Having seen two young lives brought to premature endings, Mark was thinking that he should make the most of his; he loved Carol, but if she wasn't available for a few days, maybe Sandra was. But then, he thought, how could he be in love with Carol if he went with someone else? Tommy was philosophical. 'Look, I love my missus. But if Wendy's up for it, what's the harm? What the mind doesn't know...'

'The heart won't care about,' said Mark.

'Exactly.'

And today, Thursday, back at work in the chemist's shop, Sandra was making the tea. She glanced up as Mark entered the kitchen, said 'Hi' but nothing else. She was wearing her disinterested look again, the same one she had on when he first met her.

'Sorry if you think I was off with you,' he ventured. 'Just I had to go to two funerals in two days.'

'That's okay,' she replied. She smiled, picked up the tray with the mugs of tea and left the kitchen.

He filled the kettle, waited for it to boil. Sandra was attractive, and didn't seem to be the type who'd want to get serious. Carol would never know if he had a fling with her. One life, Bob said. He made the tea, but once again there was no sign of Tommy. He went to the back door, where he came across old Florrie. She had a serious look on her face. It was the first time he'd noticed her wearing an expression of any kind. He was so surprised he checked in his stride. Then she spoke. That was a first as well.

'S'pose you're lookin' for your mate?'

'I've made the tea,' he said. She nodded towards a door, just inside the passage where they were standing.

'He's in there,' she whispered, glancing sideways as though not wanting anyone to know she'd told him.

Sandra appeared. She stopped walking when she saw Mark and Florrie together in unexpected conversation. 'What's up?' she asked, looking at one then the other.

'His mate,' said Florrie. 'He's in there.' She nodded again to the door.

'In there? That's the broom cupboard.'

Florrie said nothing, just stared at the door. Sandra stepped forward and opened it a little. After peering inside for a moment she closed it again, put a hand to her mouth and giggled.

'I've just seen a bare arse,' she declared.

'You've found your mate,' said Florrie to Mark. She turned to Sandra. 'And we'll have less of that language from you, young lady.' With that she stormed off without another word. A short time later the cupboard door opened and Wendy emerged, straightening her uniform. Glancing neither right nor left she hurried off through the store, disappearing among the display shelves.

'Good here, innit?' said Sandra.

Mark lingered, wondering what to do next. Then he saw the tips of four fingers appear on the edge of the door, followed by the top of Tommy's head and a pair of furtive-looking eyes. Seeing Mark he pushed the door further open and spoke as casually as a man in his position possible could.

'Made the tea yet?'

The Espresso coffee bar she called it. Just along from the town hall she said. She went there most nights she said. He reckoned she would be there tonight. She was.

There were four of them. All girls. 'The fellas couldn't make it tonight,' Sandra explained. 'But don't worry, this is no hen party.' The girls giggled. She introduced her friends, but he forgot their names even as she told him. Mark bought four frothy coffees and a milkshake for one of the girls he later recalled as Esme. He liked female company. Even so, he sat in awkward silence, unable to join in a conversation about whatever or whoever they were talking about. After half an hour two of the girls left, smiling their goodnights. Sandra and Esme stood up. Walkabout in the park, he hoped. That was the reason he'd come, after all.

Esme was as attractive as Sandra, and he had to admit he would have been just as pleased if Sandra had said she had to go and Esme had offered her company instead. It was Carol he loved; Carol he wanted. Tonight was just for fun. Esme said it was nice to meet him, pecked him on the cheek and departed.

'Gets dark soon now, doesn't it?' Sandra stood facing him on the pavement, a flirtatious smile on her face.

'Happens every year,' he replied, along with his best smile. Kev – or maybe it was Bob – had said 'always smile' when you're with a girl. And make sure your eyes are smiling too.

'Are you okay?' she asked. 'I mean after the funerals an' all.'

He said he felt better now that the funerals were over. She said she was glad he'd come. 'Lovely evening,' she ventured. 'Too good to waste,' he replied. They walked off. When they passed through the park gateway their hands came together. They glanced at each other and smiled. Mark felt his spirits rise.

The path led between trees and rhododendrons, reminding him of the recent escapade with Kev, Avril and Thelma. Only here there was no smell of fish and chips, or music wafting through the trees, just the sound of distant traffic. They walked in silence, the path illuminated by the occasional lamp. They encountered two other couples and then a group of young lads, the latter walking abreast on the path. Mark felt a brief surge of apprehension when he saw them; they looked as though they might be no good. But they passed by with neither comment nor rancour.

As they walked he felt that he should be talking to her; but he couldn't think of anything to say except to mention the hit parade or Blue Hawaii. He held back on the latter, fearing she might ask to go.

Then it occurred to him that if he didn't take control of the situation they could be walking in the park for ages, getting nowhere. So he slid an arm around her waist. She responded by snuggling close to him. He could smell her perfume now, and her close presence was turning him on. He felt apprehensive about trying to kiss her, yet told himself she had invited him here, and her suggestion that on some nights she and her friends 'went starkers' seemed to mean that she wanted sex. But he could hardly ask her for it. What would Kev have done? he wondered.

At a turn of the path, close to a park bench, she stopped abruptly and stood facing him. The bench was in shadow and barely discernible. He kissed her, and slid his arms around her waist. He thought she might pull back, but she put her arms around his neck and they stood there as one, locked together. When he moved towards the bench, gently taking her with him, she responded. They sat down, still kissing. As he loosened her coat buttons she sighed and lay back on the bench. He lay beside her. It was uncomfortable but he didn't care. In the darkness he could just see her eyes. They were closed, which to him meant that she was content to let him take control. As they kissed he slid a hand down her thigh and tried to slide it up her skirt, but she jammed her knees tightly together.

'It's okay,' he whispered. 'I've got something.'

'You wha'?'

'I've got something.'

'What have you got?'

'I don't mean I've got something wrong with me. I mean... *I've got something.*'

'What have you got? Tell me.'

'A Durex.'

She sat up, and twisted around so that she was sitting upright.

'A Durex? What do you think I am?'

He froze, half on, half off the bench.

'I'm not some tart, you know,' she declared, standing up sharply. 'This is the first time we've been out together. I don't even know you. I don't know where you've been.'

He sat there, looking up at her face.

'I want to go now,' she said, and with that she stormed off.

He followed, and walked with her all the way through the park until they emerged on the main road. In her face, now illuminated by the sodium lighting, he expected to see anger; he expected her to walk away without so much as a goodnight. Instead she put her arms around his neck – just as she had in the park. She leaned forward slightly, put her cheek against his. Then she took it away again, so that her mouth was but inches away.

'Aren't you going to kiss me goodnight then?' She was so close he could smell her breath. When he hesitated she kissed him, a long, lingering kiss that left him turned on and perplexed at the same time. Finally she took her arms away and stood back. 'I expect I'll see you tomorrow at work?' she said. He nodded. 'Night-night then,' she said, before turning and strutting off, her footsteps echoing in the darkness as she disappeared from view.

He watched her go with feelings of bewilderment. He felt frustrated, hamstrung in his quest to make love to a girl. A girl who, minutes after she'd knocked him back, was pushing her tongue into his mouth.

Girls! He'd never understand them. Never never never.

***

'Pass me that screwdriver, Marky.'

Tommy, on top of the stepladders, lowered a hand. Mark obliged, at the same time observing Sandra's posterior as she passed along the shop floor. Moments later Tommy declared it was time for tea. Wendy was off sick, with flu apparently. So Mark could put the kettle on confident his mate wouldn't be in the broom cupboard when he brewed up.

Tommy bit into a sandwich and opened his *Mirror*. 'Told you that lass had the hots for you, didn't I? Wotsername. With the tight arse.'

Mark related the events of last night. It felt like a release, the sharing of a problem. Tommy looked up from his newspaper. 'You surely didn't expect her to do the business first night, did you? She will next time, or the time after that.'

'Or the time after that?'

'Patience is a virtue.'

Mark told him about the time with Marie at Alnwick. 'She asked me if I'd got something, and when I hadn't she said no. Last night with Sandra I had something and still it was no.'

'Because it was your first time together. Obvious.'

'Well, you and Wendy were doing okay in the broom cupboard. That was your *first time*, and you're both married.'

Tommy shrugged, said 'That's different' and went back to his *Mirror*.

Mark saw Sandra on and off throughout the morning as she flitted here and there throughout the shop. She smiled every time, but never said anything. He told himself he didn't care, that he had other plans. Like rekindling his relationship with Marie. Okay, she had a kid. So what. She'd have been be up for it in Durham if she didn't have to look after little Ben.

When it was time to pack up tools Sandra appeared. 'Have a good weekend,' she said, still smiling.

Mark nodded, and left the building with Tommy.

'Are you daft or what?' said Tommy as the door closed behind them. 'She wanted you to ask her out.'

'I'm playing hard to get,' said Mark. They both laughed. In town, Mark headed for the nearest telephone kiosk and dialled Marie's number. After what seemed an age a woman answered. He guessed it was her mother. He was right. Marie wasn't there, she said.

'What time will she be home?' he asked.

'Who's speaking?' her mother enquired. When Mark told her she remembered him.

'Marie won't be home tonight,' she said. 'Not this home anyway. She's got back with Simon, Ben's dad.'

'Well, I'd like to speak to her anyway,' said Mark, although even as he uttered the words he felt he was wasting his breath.

'She's in Manchester. That's where Simon works. I'll tell her you called though.' She put the telephone down, leaving Mark with nothing more than a steady burr in his ear and regretting not asking

Sandra out as Tommy had suggested.

He wondered what he'd so all weekend; no Kev, Robbie unavailable and Julian... Best leave Julian, he thought. He had to call at the workshop. When he walked through the back door Miss Raine appeared at the top of the steps.

'That girl who keeps ringing you,' she said. 'You'll never guess.'

A few of Mark's workmates, including Horlicks, were present, all smiling and just as eager to know about what to guess.

'What?' Mark enquired when no further information was forthcoming.

'She's here. In the front office. She called about half an hour ago and said she'd wait.'

'I've just been told she's in Manchester,' he replied.

Miss Raine shrugged and disappeared into the office part of the building. Mark looked at his grinning workmates, who were clearly waiting for him to follow. He did so, making sure the door was closed behind him. He walked directly to the front office and opened the door.

Carol stood up and smiled. 'There you are!' she declared.

What was it about her? Just a moment before he'd felt excited at the thought of seeing Marie again. And not long before that he'd been wishing he'd asked Sandra out on Saturday. Carol hadn't featured in his plans because he didn't think she was available, not after the ghastly scene with her mother. But here she was; and she was looking so happy. And she was making him feel so happy too.

'Third time lucky?' she ventured.

'What about your mam?'

She laughed. '*What about your mam?*' she mimicked. 'Well, my parents had a good old chat after you went. I heard most of it. Dad reminded her of one or two incidents when they were courting. Like the time my grandma found them in a compromising position in her bedroom long before they were married. Like the time Mam found out he'd been chatting one of the neighbours up *after* they were married.' She was staring at him. 'Mam's okay,' she said, as though reassuring a child.

'What about you? I mean, I was out with another girl.'

'Look, Can we go? We can chat outside.'

He went to the workshop to find his workmates had gone. He checked with Bert and returned to the front office. They went out the front of the building and stood on the pavement.

'It doesn't matter about another girl,' Carol said. 'Nothing matters, except us. New start. Clean slate. This is where we begin. Right here. Right now.'

He suggested a drink – 'just one' – and she agreed. She suggested the bar next to the Royal. They walked apart and in silence. Yet Mark felt a strong bond, that there was something unexplainable but special just about being in her presence. It had nothing to do with whatever they said to one another; it had nothing to do with his sexual feelings towards her, strong though they were. It was just *her.*

When they entered the bar Mark was immediately struck with its appearance. It was nothing like the other pubs he'd been in. This one was well furnished, with a plush carpet. Frank Sinatra's *Come Fly with Me* wafted from unseen speakers. The music was so quiet it was barely audible. The place was empty, except for a buxom woman behind the bar who smiled, patiently waiting for their order.

'Is this where you bring all your boyfriends?' asked Mark.

'I've been here once,' she replied, 'with my boss for a quick drink after work. We had something to discuss. My boss is a woman, incidentally.' She added the last sentence quickly. 'I'll have an orange juice, thank you,' she said, before walking off and sitting at a small table in the corner.

He bought a half of lager and an orange juice and sat opposite her. The barmaid disappeared. In the middle of a city centre bar they had the place to themselves.

'Third time lucky you said.' He sipped his lager.

'Yes. Once when you first took me home. Then the other night, when Mam recognised you as the sex maniac at the pictures. And now...' She picked up her glass. 'Well, now or never, eh.'

'Never say never.'

'Let's say forever.'

'Forever. With a girl like you.'

They sipped their drinks.

'Look, she said at last. Mam and Dad are getting along really well now, happy as can be. Mam is doing a special tea tonight, so I have to go in a few minutes, *but...*' she paused, took a sip of her orange juice, 'I want you to come to tea tomorrow evening.'

'I dunno. I'm not convinced your mam'll be too pleased to see me...'

'That's just it,' she cut in. 'Mam won't be there. Neither will Dad. They're off to Scarborough in the morning. A second honeymoon, they said. They're back Sunday evening sometime.' She smiled, sat back in her chair. 'There'll just be you and me. And I'm cooking tea. Pork chops and mushrooms, if that's okay.'

'I've never had mushrooms.'

'Never say never you said. I'm sure you'll love them.'

'I'll never love anything as much as I love you.'

'That's one never you can say. As often as you like.'

23

They'd agreed to meet under the Goldsmith's clock at two o'clock, have a coffee in Fenwick's then 'do some shopping', as Carol put it. Some shopping wasn't Mark's idea of the perfect Saturday afternoon – although he would have admitted, if asked, that he'd had enough of sitting on his bike watching Weston get slaughtered before arriving home perishing cold.

Carol remembered her last visit to Fenwick's: wandering aimlessly around before returning home to find Dad's empty bottle of brown ale and her mistaken interpretation of what it meant. Then, she had resolved to leave home; now she couldn't wait to see Mark and take him home.

It was a lovely autumnal day. He was early. So was she. They met with smiles and a kiss. They said little to one another, each content in their own world.

That morning he'd told Mam he was having tea at Carol's, bringing a whoop from Bob and a smile from his mam. 'Will you be home tonight?' asked Dad, a mischievous smile on his face, but a good question as he knew his wife would fret if their son didn't come home without telling her. Mark wasn't sure. 'Depends,' was the best he could offer. He said nothing about Carol's folks being in Scarborough.

'Well, you can invite the lassie here next week for tea if you like,' said Mam.

'He's lovely for his mother you know,' said Joey.

They sat in Fenwick's restaurant. She leant forward and placed her hands on the table. He did the same and took her hands in his. They looked into each other's eyes, then, as she leant forward a little more, he kissed her; not briefly, but a lingering eyes-closed kiss that might have lasted longer had he not opened his eyes briefly and noticed a stern-looking woman glaring at them. She looked like a member of staff, a supervisor perhaps. He sat back sharply. Carol, realising the reason, did the same. They let go of each other's hands and sat there smiling. She giggled. The stern-looking woman looked away, crisis over.

After coffee she led him into C&A's. Mam used to take him there when he was little. He hated being in the store, where women made frantic attempts to find a hat they liked from dozens piled up on display, and ashen-faced men followed their wives through lingerie and kitchenware. Today he couldn't have cared less. He was with Carol, and he was going to her house later, just the two of them. What else mattered?

They spent most of the afternoon wandering around town, and bumped into Horlicks as he emerged from Jackson the Tailor's. He was carrying a huge carrier bag. When he saw Mark he grinned. 'New suit,' said Horlicks. 'Gotta keep up the image.'

Mark saw him eyeing Carol. 'Carol, this is Bobby Hall from work. He's known as Horlicks. Bobby this is Carol. She's known as my girlfriend.' Horlicks offered a hand to Carol. When she took it he leaned forward and kissed her cheek. She stepped back, surprised, but smiling.

'Pleased to meet ya,' said Horlicks, before addressing them both. 'Not into girlfriends myself. No offence. Playing the field. That's me. Girl in every port. More the merrier. Hence the whistle.' He tapped the carrier.

Mark and Carol had blank faces.

'Whistle and flute. Suit. Cockney twang. Pigeon's wing. In thing. Get it?'

They all laughed, and Horlicks strode off, leaving Mark and Carol to stroll the city streets. They ended up in the cathedral churchyard.

The cathedral clock's Westminster chimes heralded the approaching hour when they would catch the trolley to Jesmond; but then, unexpectedly, she suggested walking. It was a beautiful afternoon, after all, and there was ample time. He concurred, and they set off: all the way back through town and along Jesmond Road. It was after six o'clock when they turned into her street. Before, when he had walked here, his emotions were on high at the prospect of going to her house and meeting her parents – only to come crashing down at the hand of wretched misfortune; today he had no such worries. He was with the girl he loved and there was nothing else to cloud already sunny skies.

He felt nervous as she slipped her key into the lock; just like he used to feel when taking an exam at school, like he still felt whenever he was going on a new job where there'd be people he knew would be watching him working. They took their coats off, hung them behind the front door and he followed her into the living room where he stood, uncertain. She told him to sit down. She went through to the kitchen, where he heard her taking pans and cooking utensils from cupboards.

'There's some books on the shelf,' she called out to the sound of her filling the kettle.

He went into the corner of the room where three shelves were stacked neatly with books: an entire *Encyclopaedia Britannica*, and some classics, including *Little Women*, *What Katy Did* and *Good Wives*. They contrasted with his own, he thought: *Coral Island*, *Robin Hood and his Merrie Men* and *The Adventures of Huckleberry Finn*. He scanned the titles of the rest, but without really seeing them. He was filled with excitement, anticipation and happiness at being with Carol. He loved her, he was certain. She was different from anyone else he'd met. Just like in love songs; just like in Hollywood movies; just like in real life, right now.

She appeared with a cup of tea and her usual smile. Yes, she was different; and she made him feel different.

'I can't explain what it's like, being with you,' he said.

'You don't have to explain,' she replied. 'Because I feel the same.'

Neither said anything more before she returned to the kitchen to cook tea. He switched on the TV. *Dixon of Dock Green*, starring a grainy Jack Warner, wasn't to his taste, so he switched it off again. He was restless; he wondered how to pass the time until she came back into the room. He was hungry, a little nervous. He returned to the bookshelf and browsed a random *Encyclopaedia Britannica* volume. Finally, she appeared, carrying two plates of food. Pork chops with mashed potatoes, mushrooms and veg. They ate in silence, as though it was a ritual to be endured before they engaged in the main course of the evening.

She was impressed when he offered to help with the washing up. Bob does, he explained. She laughed. She washed, he dried. When they returned to the living room she switched on the TV. Somebody was singing, he didn't know who. He didn't care. She sat next to him on the settee, and nestled up close when he put an arm around her shoulder. They stole an occasional kiss. He was unsure of his ground. He didn't want to be too forward, nor too hesitant. The telly was on. They were together, alone. Nothing else mattered. Except, as the evening wore on, he had a problem.

'I'm not sure what time the last trolley is,' he said, as nonchalantly as he could.

She looked at him, a faint smile on her lips.

'Why would you want to know that?'

'To time it for the last bus to Weston. Mam doesn't like me on the all-night service cos of the drunks.'

'Oh doesn't she?' She laughed. 'Well, you don't need to worry about catching buses tonight. You can stay here. That's if you want to.'

Neither spoke until the news came on, when she got up and switched the TV off. She turned, and yawned. 'I'm feeling sleepy,' she said. 'How about you?'

He nodded.

'Bedtime then,' she declared.

'Is this a bed settee?' he asked.

'No, it isn't. You're sleeping upstairs. I've got a three-quarter size bed.'

'Three-quarter size?'

She laughed. 'Room for two, silly.' She kissed him on the mouth.

'Follow me,' she whispered.

He followed.

Sunday morning. Mark opened his eyes and listened to the sound.

The sound of silence.

At home, on a Sunday morning, there was *relative* silence: a silence interrupted by the clanking of milk bottles on Dixon's lorry, the occasional barking of dogs, the chatter of Mam and Ada next door – although that was no longer commonplace. Here, he could hear nothing: no traffic, no dogs, no voices.

He turned his head sharply. Carol wasn't there. Instead the blankets that had covered her were turned back, leaving a ruffled sheet and indented pillow. He looked about the bedroom, *her* bedroom, now dappled in sunlight. And then he remembered last night.

She had led him upstairs, told him to sit on the bed and slowly taken off her clothes, her every move illuminated by the streetlight outside that penetrated the thin curtains. He watched her with feelings of sexual excitement and concern: should he or should he not tell her he *had something*? The Durex, two of them, were in his coat pocket – downstairs, but in his coat pocket nevertheless. Would she be angry, as Sandra had been, at his apparent presumption that he expected to make love to her tonight? Or would she expect him to have them, as Marie had done, only to turn him away if he said he didn't?

He needn't have worried about such things. Not with Carol. Not with the girl he loved and who loved him. Naked, she stood before him and slowly undid the buttons of his shirt. He had never felt so turned on, so alive, so *wanted*. There were no words; none were necessary. Only touch and smell mattered. They made love. Then they made love again so many times he lost count, until they fell apart, she pulling the bedclothes over them and the pair of them falling asleep in each other's arms.

He could hear a sound now; the sound of a kettle being filled and crockery being taken from the cupboard. Minutes later she appeared in the doorway, wearing a long dressing gown and carrying two cups of tea. She placed them on to the bedside table, and took off her dressing gown, revealing a short, pink nightie. She was smiling. She got into bed next to him and made a 'sit up' gesture.

'Tea for two cha-cha,' she said, handing him a cup. 'Then we can do what we do best again. That's if you want to.'

He wanted to.

The breakfast she cooked was as good as Mam's. Well, almost. She did burst the fried egg. Then they took the bus to Tynemouth.

Being on a bus with her reminded him of the visits to Alnwick and Durham with Marie. Now, as then, there was almost no conversation. But there was a difference. With Marie he had been with a girl he liked; with Carol he was with a girl he loved.

At Tynemouth they wandered around the priory ruins, before strolling off hand in hand above King Edward's Bay. The morning was sunny with a brisk but warm autumn breeze. They said little. Their eyes were for the sea or each other. They passed the road end where he had parted with Thelma. He had been keen on her then. She didn't matter now.

Approaching the Plaza she suggested a detour into the park. The rowing boats were moored. A Sunday, but no trip on the lake. She was disappointed. His thoughts drifted elsewhere: to Kev and Avril. He saw them now in his mind's eye, as they disappeared behind the rhododendrons. He imagined he could see the very place where they would have lay on the damp grass, Kev tugging at her clothes, Avril a willing helper. This was the last place he had seen his friend and his 'cousin'. Now they were dead. He said nothing to Carol. They moved on to the sound of a train rattling along the railway close by, and returned to the pavement above Long Sands. The beach was all but deserted, just a few walkers, a dog or two plunging into the sea to re-trieve a piece of wood again and again. The shuggies were tied up, the shutters on the candy floss hut firmly in place.

'Isn't that your friend?' Carol was looking in the direction of the Plaza.

Mark saw a young man chatting to two girls. 'Horlicks again,' he exclaimed.

'I'm popping to the ladies,' said Carol, walking off.

Mark walked towards Horlicks and the two girls.

'Watcha Mark.' Horlicks was all smiles. 'Meet my new friends.'

The girls tittered. It seemed obvious to Mark they had just become acquainted with his work colleague.

'Told you I was playing the field.' Horlicks put his arms around the girls' shoulders. 'Hey, where's your girlfriend?'

'She'll be back in a mo,' said Mark. 'We're just out for a walk.'

Horlicks steered the girls towards the Plaza entrance. 'We're gonna play the slot machines,' he declared. 'See ya.'

With that they walked off, and Mark turned to see Carol approaching.

'Where's he gone?' she enquired.

'He's playing the field,' said Mark, and they walked on.

At Whitley Bay they sat on a bench on the links and ate fish and chips. Again his recent past came to haunt him. That girl – he couldn't even remember her name now – the girl who had gone off with those lads on the motorbikes, along with his wallet. And the policeman who found him shivering in the doorway of the café. The café was open now but looked deserted. They walked on, past the shelter where he'd had the dream, where Kev had found him close to hypothermia. Kev again. You don't know someone so long and lose them without missing them. His emotions plunged from contented happiness to melancholy. Carol was looking at his face. 'Kev and me used to come here a lot,' he explained. They walked on, caring nought for the time or anything else. They crossed the causeway to St Mary's Island and sat near the lighthouse.

'Better watch out for the tide or we'll be cut off,' said Carol, casting an anxious eye seawards.

'Who cares?' he replied, sliding an arm around her.

They sat there for ages. Time was an irrelevance. Silence was golden. Then she spoke.

'I've decided to look for another job.'

To Mark the words were unexpected, out of context with the occasion. His face was asking why.

'It's just I want a change. A new challenge.'

He felt there was more to what she was saying than 'new job'. But she didn't say what and he didn't know what it could be, so he said nothing. After sitting a while longer they sauntered back to Whitley Bay. It was getting late, and with her parents due back from their second honeymoon they returned to Carol's house.

'Are you looking forward to meeting my parents again?' Carol enquired, mischievously.

'I can hardly wait,' he replied, making light of his worry about meeting her mother again.

Her parents were supposed to be home by seven o'clock. When they failed to appear by eight Carol made cheese on toast. As they ate the food, with the plates on their laps, Mark had a vision of Carol's mother appearing and telling him to get out. She must still be angry, he thought, still seething at their encounter at the pictures when she had seen the lad who was now dating her daughter having his hand away with that trollop of a girl who had sworn at her. When the mantel clock struck nine Mark could bear the strain no longer.

'I think I'd better go,' he said, standing up. 'Maybe your mam doesn't want to meet me again after all.'

He had barely spoken when they heard a noise at the front door.

'They're here,' said Carol. 'They'll be fine, you'll see.'

They stood together, waiting for the appearance of Mr and Mrs Leonard Kemp. Mark was resolute: he loved Carol, and nothing anyone could say or do could change that. He wanted her parents to welcome him into the fold, but if they didn't he would tell them he loved their daughter however they felt about him.

The door from the hallway opened and Lennie appeared. Carol stepped forward and kissed her dad on the cheek. Lennie looked directly at Mark and smiled.

'Now then, young fella,' he said, stepping forward and offering his hand. 'Seems you and me've had good weekends, eh?' He tipped a wink. 'Good to see you lad,' he added, before half turning to look at the doorway he had just come through. As if on cue Freda appeared. She stood in the centre of the room, facing Mark.

'We meet again,' she said.

Mark could only nod an uncertain response.

'Come to tea Wednesday,' she said, an unexpected invitation Mark felt was clearly intended to make him welcome, whether or not she had laid her demons about their encounter at the pictures.

'Thank you, Mrs Kemp,' he replied.

'Oh none of that Mr and Mrs stuff,' Lennie interjected. 'It's Lennie and Freda. That right, love?'

'Of course it is,' said Freda, now heading for the kitchen. 'Who's for a cuppa?'

They all were.

***

On Wednesday Mark went to Carol's house again, still uncertain about her mam. Lennie had seemed okay on the Saturday, so that was something. After work he'd gone home, had a bath and changed first, only just arriving in time for tea. Freda watched Coronation Street before washing the dishes, while Lennie dozed off in front of the fire. Mark and Carol sat next to each other on the settee, flicking though the pages of a few volumes of *Encyclopaedia Britannica*. Later, Carol told her parents that she intended to look for another job, bringing on their mutual disapproval and causing them to ask why. Because she felt like a change, she said, and anyway the money wasn't that good at Northern Electricity. At ten-thirty Mark took his leave, and Carol accompanied him into the hall to say goodnight. They kissed and embraced before she whispered something into his ear, clearly not wanting her parents to overhear.

'I've got a problem,' she said, her voice so low it was barely discernible. 'They don't know yet, but I've a small lump on one of my boobs.' She paused to let what she had said sink in. 'The doctor has referred me to the General a week Friday and I'd like you to come with me.'

Her statement was so unexpected he couldn't think of what to say. Nor did he wholly understand what she meant.

'Will you come with me to the hospital?' she enquired. 'The appointment is at three o'clock.'

'I'll have to ask Tommy,' he replied. 'But it should be okay.'

They embraced again, tightly. He felt himself going hard. She felt it too.

'Behave,' she whispered, kissing him one last time before standing back and reaching for the catch on the door. 'See you Saturday at Fenwick's. Two o'clock. Night-night.'

She pushed him gently out and closed the door behind him. He headed for his trolley, head down, feeling uncomfortable, not understanding what she had said. He thought he'd ask Mam about it when he got home, but she was in bed and the next morning at breakfast hardly seemed an appropriate time to raise the subject of Carol's breasts. Instead, he waited until teabreak at work next morning and asked Tommy.

'What's it mean when a girl has a lump on her breast?'

Tommy, just into his *Mirror*, didn't look up but shrugged, saying, 'Could be cancer.'

Tommy turned the page of his newspaper. They sat in silence until he swallowed the last mouthful of his sandwich.

'Strange question to ask me on a Monday morning, Mark lad.' He took a pen from his pocket and turned to the page with the crossword, then looked up at his young apprentice. 'So, go on, why did you ask me that?'

'My girlfriend says she has a lump on one of her boobs. But it can't be cancer. She's not even twenty yet.'

Tommy lowered his newspaper. 'Anyone can get cancer. Nowt to do with age. What did she say exactly?'

'Just she has a lump.'

'Best she gets it checked then. Just to be on the safe side.'

'She is. She has an appointment at the General a week Friday and wants me to go with her. If that's okay.'

Tommy went back to his *Mirror*. 'Aye, no problem. I told Smudger we'd finish here that Friday but we'll have cracked it by Thursday I reckon. We'll just make an appearance on the Friday morning and have a flier.'

Mark accepted there was nothing he could do in the meantime, and saw no reason to mention the problem to Mam. Instead he would carry on as normal and looked forward to meeting Carol again on Saturday. After traipsing around the shops with him she was coming to tea.

Mam liked her from the minute she crossed the threshold. Mark knew she would. Wearing her pinny, her tea-towel over her forearm, she greeted Carol like the long-lost daughter she'd never had. It occurred to Mark she'd never regarded Joyce in that way, not in his opinion anyway. As Carol smiled and said hello Charlie Green stood back and beamed. Mark was a good lad. Bringing home a lass like that.

Bob and Joyce were there especially for the occasion. Tea for six it would be. Salad, of course. Did Carol like salad? asked Mam. Oh yes, Mrs Green, I love it. Salad cream too.

The occasion marked a diversion from the Greens' usual Saturday evening visit to the Club for Bingo and the Go-as-you-please. They would still go, but just for a drink, and Bob and Joyce were welcome too. To Mark's amazement they accepted. Joyce in a workingmen's club: that was a first. The Club was ten minutes' walk, but Mark and Carol were naked on the floor before they reached it. An hour later, spent but happy, they got dressed. 'They might be home any time,' said Carol. She was right; Bob and Joyce left early and after a tactful knock entered the living room, Bob winking at Mark. They left soon after in the Riley, leaving Mark and Carol alone again. He would accompany her to town for the last trolley.

They spent Sunday in Durham. It was Mark's idea. Shops, cathedral and riverside walk, he said. Carol asked him when he'd last been there. He said he couldn't recall. Inevitably he thought about Marie, how happy he had been with her that day, and how disappointed he had been when the anticipated sex by the river had been thwarted. But his love was for Carol. And Durham – all of it – on the day of their visit, was so wonderful even the worry of the 'lump' faded from their minds.

The following Wednesday he went to Carol's for tea again, this time ticking along nicely with her mam, who seemed particularly pleased at his offer – accepted – to dry the dishes when she washed up. She asked him about his family, his childhood, his work. He was in the scouts? Well, she'd been in the guides. He liked the countryside? So did she. When he left that evening she was all smiles. So was her husband. So was Carol. He hurried for the trolley to town, a young man drenched in happiness.

Except there was the lump. The day after tomorrow they'd know what it was – and what it meant for their future.

***

As Tommy had predicted, they finished the job at the chemist's shop on Thursday afternoon. Friday morning they returned to tinker, kill time, anything but go back to the workshop – then have an early finish. At ten o'clock, having made the staff teas, and before carrying them out of the kitchen on a tray, Sandra had something to say to Mark, who was waiting patiently for the kettle.

'Fancy Espresso's tonight?' The question took him by surprise. He thought she'd given up, accepting he had a girlfriend or had simply lost interest. 'There's a few of us going. Weather should be nice for the park after, if you fancy it.'

He shook his head.

She put the tray down. 'Why not be sociable and see a few people tonight for coffee and a bit of fun?'

'Because I'm seeing my girlfriend.'

"I'm seeing my girlfriend" she mimicked. 'You weren't seeing your girlfriend the other night when you fancied a quick leg over with me, though, were you?'

'Sorry, I was out of order,' he said. 'I just thought you wanted a good time that night. Please, let's leave it at that.'

'And if you had had your wicked way the other night with me, I suppose you'd still be seeing your girlfriend. You just think I'm some kind of tart, don't you.' She picked up the tray and stormed off.

He left by the back door. Sandra was history.

They met in town and took the bus to the General. They said little, but sat patiently among others: young, middle-aged, old, people from all walks of life with one thing in common: a problem with their health.

Faces were blank, ashen; no-one spoke. A few flicked through the crumpled magazines that lay untidily on a little table. Mark imagined they were tidied up first thing every morning, only to end up scattered by people who weren't really interested in them anyway. Carol picked up *People's Friend* and trawled the pages. His mam had it delivered every week. He used to read Will and Wag when he was a kid. He watched as Carol flicked through to the back of the magazine. Will and Wag were still there.

At five to four a nurse called Carol's name. Almost an hour later than the appointment time; a lingering hour of torture. She stood up and without a word followed the nurse along a corridor and out of sight. He sat in silence, finally picking up magazines at random from the little table. People who had been waiting disappeared one by one, until he was sitting alone. As he reached forward to pick up yet another magazine Carol appeared, waiting for him to accompany her out of the building. She said nothing as she led the way to the door, nor along the corridor beyond. Finally, when they were outside, she stopped walking.

'It's not malignant,' she said. 'Just a cyst. They're going to take it out in a week or so.'

He wasn't sure what malignant meant but he smiled, because she was smiling and he knew it must be good news. Just as words had been unnecessary on their way in, so it was on their way out. Until, that is, they chanced upon a small, isolated building with a dilapidated sign: Ward 34. Mark's visit came flooding back: the fat guy in reception; the interminable wait in the belief he had VD; Dr Aruma-thingy, whatever her name was and her intimate examination of him.

'Isn't that that workmate of yours?' Carol enquired. 'The lad we saw in town, then outside the Plaza?'

Mark noticed someone loitering in the doorway of the building, someone who had stepped back obviously not wanting to be seen at a VD clinic.

'It's Horlicks!'

'He seems to pop up everywhere,' said Carol.

Mark stood at the end of the narrow path and called out.

'Hey! Horlicks!'

Horlicks, looking sheepish, stepped forward, his frame occupying the open doorway.

'Watcha Mark.'

'Still playing the field, then?'

Horlicks smiled ruefully. 'I'm in the clear,' he said, giving a double thumbs-up.

'What's he on about?' asked Carol.

'He's saying he's in the clear,' said Mark. 'C'mon. Let's go for a coffee. I want to tell you what it's like to love a girl like you.'

She's on the bus.

He'd spotted her at her usual stop in the queue. A quick glance back and there was the unmistakeable red hair. After what, two years, Rita was there in the flesh, going home after work.

He always thought of her when the bus stopped here. He'd assumed she'd moved on, got married maybe, had a kid maybe. After all, he had. He and Carol were married not that long after her all-clear at the hospital. She was pregnant, of course. No matter: they loved each other and would have married anyway. She didn't have to change jobs after all, just stayed where she was until little Jonathan came along. They had a council house near the rec. He could see the rocking horse from the bedroom window. Jonathan sat on it these days, his little hands grasping the horse's head.

She was pregnant again. Oh well, maybe Mam would get a granddaughter this time. Bob and Joyce were married too, but no kids yet. As for the two Durex, he still had them. Kept them in the dressing table drawer. The 'something' he bought but had never used. Keep 'em for a rainy day, Tommy had said, whatever that meant.

He thought about things that had changed since he last saw Rita. Kev and Avril were dead. Robbie and Emma were still an item, courting, steady, spending nights at the pictures and having tea at each other's houses at weekends. The Pophams had disappeared, gone to no-one knew where. Beryl had had her baby; he saw her now and then with her kiddie in its pushchair. She always said hello and smiled. She and Tom never made Australia. They never made anywhere. Tom wasn't good enough for a doctor's daughter. He was a pisshead now, drunk as a skunk every weekend. Been arrested for fighting in the Bigg Market, so he'd heard.

When the woman sitting next to Mark stood up to get off the bus, Rita sat beside him. She looked lovely: all smiles and looking smart, that familiar red hair still falling sexily over her shoulder.

'So! How's Mark?'

'So! How's Connie?'

She laughed. 'Stupid Cupid. I remember.'

He said he was married. He had a son. Still lived at Weston.

She said she'd been living with a chap at Blyth, but when they'd split recently she'd moved home to the flat behind the Balloon. With her parents? Oh no, on her own. Her father had got into trouble and was in prison. Her mother, what with the shame and everything, had moved to her sister's at Cramlington. When she, Rita, had split with her boyfriend, the flat was the perfect solution.

They were approaching her stop.

She stood up and shouldered her handbag. 'Pop in for a coffee one evening if you like,' she said. Then she was gone. He saw her cross the road.

Pop in for a coffee, she said. On a rainy day maybe?